A Mermaid's Kiss

"I am in awe of this book . . . *A Mermaid's Kiss* remains with me, and I imagine it will for a long time to come."　　　　—*Wild on Books*

"The sheer magnitude of magic in this story weaves a spell around [readers] and draws them in. A beautifully written novel that's reminiscent of an adult fairy tale . . . Extremely thought-provoking. An outstanding book from an outstanding author."

—*The Romance Studio*

PRAISE FOR THE NOVELS OF JOEY W. HILL

"Sweet yet erotic . . . Will linger in your heart long after the story is over."　　　　—*Sensual Romance Reviews*

"One of the finest, most erotic love stories I've ever read. Reading this book was a physical experience because it pushes through every other plane until you feel it in your marrow."

—Shelby Reed, author of *Love a Younger Man*

"The perfect blend of suspense and romance."

—*The Road to Romance*

"A beautifully told story of true love, magic, and strength . . . A wondrous tale . . . A must-read."　　　　—*Romance Junkies*

"A passionate, poignant tale . . . The sex was emotional and charged with meaning . . . Yet another must-read story from the ever-talented Joey Hill."　　　　—*Just Erotic Romance Reviews*

"This is not only a keeper but one you will want to run out and tell your friends about."　　　　—*Fallen Angel Reviews*

"All the right touches of emotion, sex, and a wonderful plot that you would usually find in a much longer tale." —*Romance Reviews Today*

A Mermaid's Ransom

Joey W. Hill

BERKLEY SENSATION, NEW YORK

THE BERKLEY PUBLISHING GROUP
Published by the Penguin Group
Penguin Group (USA) Inc.
375 Hudson Street, New York, New York 10014, USA
Penguin Group (Canada), 90 Eglinton Avenue East, Suite 700, Toronto, Ontario M4P 2Y3, Canada
(a division of Pearson Penguin Canada Inc.)
Penguin Books Ltd., 80 Strand, London WC2R 0RL, England
Penguin Group Ireland, 25 St. Stephen's Green, Dublin 2, Ireland (a division of Penguin Books Ltd.)
Penguin Group (Australia), 250 Camberwell Road, Camberwell, Victoria 3124, Australia
(a division of Pearson Australia Group Pty. Ltd.)
Penguin Books India Pvt. Ltd., 11 Community Centre, Panchsheel Park, New Delhi—110 017, India
Penguin Group (NZ), 67 Apollo Drive, Rosedale, North Shore 0632, New Zealand
(a division of Pearson New Zealand Ltd.)
Penguin Books (South Africa) (Pty.) Ltd., 24 Sturdee Avenue, Rosebank, Johannesburg 2196,
South Africa

Penguin Books Ltd., Registered Offices: 80 Strand, London WC2R 0RL, England

This book is an original publication of The Berkley Publishing Group.

PRINTING HISTORY
Berkley Sensation trade paperback edition / December 2009

Library of Congress Cataloging-in-Publication Data

Hill, Joey W.
   A mermaid's ransom / Joey W. Hill.—Berkley Sensation trade paperback ed.
      p. cm.
   ISBN 978-0-425-23068-8
1. Angels—Fiction.   2. Mermaids—Fiction.   3. Vampires—Fiction.   I. Title.
   PS3608. I4343M48 2009   2009032626
   813'.6—dc22

PRINTED IN THE UNITED STATES OF AMERICA

10   9   8   7   6   5   4   3   2   1

One

BRIMSTONE. How on earth did she know what brimstone smelled like?

Maybe she remembered it from that time she'd ended up in the outer catacombs of Hell, looking for the caverns where her parents had first met. She'd been twelve, and fascinated by the story of how Anna had hidden Jonah there when he was hurt and being pursued by Dark Ones. Of course, Lex hadn't been thrilled to run smack into Lucifer while on her romantic quest. She'd been told in no uncertain terms she would *not* be swimming down into his realm again, not if she knew what was good for her. She was twenty-one now, but the memory still made her shudder.

God, she loved her parents, but they had such scary friends. The Lord of the Underworld was her father's best friend, while Anna's was the seawitch Mina, a creature whose name no merperson would speak above a whisper.

But whether or not Alexis was smelling brimstone, this had to be a dream. Mainly because that part of the mind that kept things from being too frightening in dreams said so, even though there was a tenuous note that made it more hopeful suggestion than sure fact.

She was floating in fire. While she felt its heat, she wasn't burned. It was licking at the fronds of her tail, another curiosity. Usually, she appeared in dreams in her human form, not her birth form, which was merangel—half-mermaid, half-angel, with tail, fins *and* wings.

As she started to turn to see what was behind her, a hand touched her wings. Strong, male fingers penetrated the thick layers of feathers, curling to grip, knuckles stroking the fragile network of bones beneath.

Ah, it was going to be *that* kind of dream. This might be worth the nasty brimstone smell, though a funny, fluttery feeling in the pit of her belly recommended she run, even as her body refused to move. The hand teased the feathers where they were attached to flesh, the most sensitive area, and she drew in a breath. Tipping her head back, she found a broad shoulder waiting to support it. It was attached to a very male body pressing against her back, his bare thigh against her hip. The intriguing, muscular plane of a stomach brushed her wings. Another hand parted them as if opening a garment and slid down her spine, making her shiver.

As his breath caressed the side of her throat, because it was a dream, her hair conveniently tumbled over her right shoulder to give him access. His mouth closed over her skin. It wasn't a kiss. It was as if she was about to be eaten, her flesh savored. The fire was advancing up her body, making her wonder if it came from him, a creature of fire and hunger.

A fang scraped her, and she yelped as he punctured her beneath her delicate gill slit, bringing pain but pleasure as well. Because of that, she remained still, willing to give him blood. His hands made their torturous way to her hip bones, stimulating the tight overlapping scales below them. One hand drifted to the silver and diamond piercing through the thin skin of her navel. *Oh, Goddess.* She was so responsive there, almost as much as her neck. His lips moved on her, suckling, and she could hear the rush of her blood, eager to nourish him.

Her father had frowned when she got the navel piercing, but Alexis was enchanted by the way it sparkled. If she touched it with light fingers as she lay in bed at night, it sent frissons of sensual energy rippling out like tropical waves, making her imagine a lover's hands.

She'd never had a lover. It was hard enough to be an empath, but then to have an angel's energy on top of that? Men were attracted to her like insects to a bug light, but they didn't come close enough to be zapped. When Lex was in her teens, Anna, her mother, had pointed out that this trait saved lives. Jonah would have had little patience for the hormonal missteps of young males when it came to his only child.

Would have pinched their heads off like ticks on a hound.

Not her mother's words, of course. Alexis had a human friend, Clara, who'd been born in Georgia and who described her own daddy's attitude about boys that way. Since it seemed to apply to Jonah, Alexis couldn't help thinking of it when the issue came up.

But she wasn't a child anymore. And this was definitely a *very* grown-up dream. A little more than she'd ever experienced, actually. It was the last coherent thought she had as both of his hands slid up her abdomen, teasing the piercing again before they kept going. She arched back into his body, holding her breath, wanting him to go exactly where he was going, her flesh aching.

There. She gasped, dream or not, as calloused palms closed over her bare breasts, for apparently that was the way her dream wanted them to be, and who was she to argue? She'd gone to sleep in an oversized nightshirt printed with a sardonic pink bunny over the caption *It's All About Me.* It certainly wouldn't have fit with this dream.

Raising her hands, she closed them on his forearms. He stilled, as if he hadn't expected her to touch him. He was still drinking deep, making her dizzy, increasing the roar of her heartbeat. As she rocked with the motion of the fire, she brushed her backside against his groin. The hard evidence of his desire sent a thrill of apprehension and excitement through her. It was a little too real, a little intimidating.

"You will take the fear. Reach behind you and hold me in your hands."

The voice was rough, as if scarred by searing clouds of smoke. It rumbled through her body like thunder, the kind that preceded heat lightning, not cooling draughts of rain. Perspiration gleamed on her skin now, heat increasing, and she looked down at his hands. The nails were long, almost like claws, the tips leaving thin red rivulets over her flesh, but the strength in his grip, the erotic kneading, balanced her apprehension. Plus, she couldn't tear her eyes away from the sight of those hands on her breasts, the way they cupped and held her, so sure and powerful, the glide of thumb and forefinger together to capture the nipples, squeeze and roll them in a way that had her swallowing, hard.

"Grip me, now. I command it."

Reaching behind herself pushed her breasts further into his palms, and gave her the quaking sense of being bound, her arms pulled behind her back. Her fingertips slid along a muscular thigh, then over, grazing shyly over a heavy testicle sac to find the base of his shaft. His tongue flicked against her neck, and she gasped, her hand closing over him in spasmodic reaction.

Oh, great Goddess. This might be a dream, but it was difficult to believe it wasn't something more, because she'd never had her hand on a man's cock before. How could she register in such detail not just the thickness and velvet length, but the hard heat, the remarkable smoothness of the skin stretched over it, the crease and flare over the head? Viscous fluid made her fingers slippery, instinct motivating her to rub them down his length.

He growled and pushed himself into her hands more urgently. It was so marvelous, so breathtaking, she had to smile at the joy of it, press her temple into his jaw, a thanks for giving her the gift of his passion, his need.

All those hard muscles tensed as if he'd become a marble statue behind her. Her dream was ending. Reality was pulling her away from the fire, from him. Panicked, she twisted around to look up into his face, see who or what he was. What had she done wrong? Could she get him to change his mind, let her stay?

Dark hair tangled over his forehead and around insanely beautiful features. Since she was the daughter of an angel, the most breathtaking species in existence, that was saying something. Then she met his eyes.

Red, gold, orange. The pupils were a tunnel of darkness in the midst of fire. She fell into them, his loneliness and despair, rage and violence closing around her as if he'd clamped a fist around her body to hold her in this stasis of yearning agony.

She'd learned early to stay away from hospitals, slaughterhouses, prisons—wherever suffering of such magnitude existed that she couldn't adhere to the lesson she'd finally learned and let the Goddess's cycles take their natural course for those inflicting or suffering pain. She had to fix it or go mad with the agony.

His pain was all those places and more. A suicide's dead despair, a killer's rage, a victim's uncomprehending pain. His sensual lips were curved in a permanent cruel sneer, her blood on his mouth. If he could, he'd drink all of her blood, tear the flesh away and gnaw on her bones, trying to get to the very soul of her. That was what he had to have, what he wanted.

The flame began to burn her flesh. An urgent force pulled at her, trying to take her away from him. Instead, she lifted her hand and laid it on his mouth. Fire exploded through her, igniting all her nerve endings, contorting her mouth with an involuntary scream, but before it all swirled away, she registered the shock in his eyes at her willing touch. Then she was alone, burning alive, screaming for help in a world where everything had disappeared, sucked into that pitiless void in his eyes.

———

ALEXIS erupted from her bed, sending T into a squalling leap for safety. The cat knocked over her Victorian hurricane lamp, though the glass bulb shade fortunately tumbled into the mountainous pile of stuffed animals that overflowed from the corner. She spun around.

"Whoa, *whoa*." Clara danced back, holding up both hands. "Easy there, Lex. It's me. You left your door unlocked again, you trusting idiot. I've been trying to wake you for five minutes. Goddess, you're strobing like a disco ball."

Clara was a clairvoyant. While Clara didn't know that Alexis was a merangel, Lex was happy to have the closest thing possible to a normal friendship with her, because Clara could get past the vibrating light of Alexis's aura to the girl beneath.

As she swayed, getting her bearings, Clara proved it by rubbing her hands along Lex's arms, grounding her further. "Easy now. You're here. You're with us. That must have been one hell of a dream."

Alexis choked on a wild chuckle. At Clara's alarmed look, she panicked, thinking she might have shifted some portion of her anatomy. A glance toward the dresser mirror told her she looked like any human woman, with her curling brown hair to her waist, blue eyes—though right now they were giant marbles bugging out of her head—and completely human body. No wings materializing, no fins or tail dropping her like a clumsy trout on the carpet.

"I'm okay." She sank down as Clara shoved her desk chair beneath her. "Just talk to me while I get it together."

"Okay, hon, okay." Clara pressed against the back of the chair, her hand in Lex's hair, stroking. "I had about an hour before classes, and thought I'd stop in to see if you want to audit Greek Mythology with me. It's being taught by a visiting Greek professor, and holy *gawd*, is he hot. Talks with the accent and everything."

"You want me to bait him for you." Alexis tilted her head into Clara's abdomen, gazing up the valley between two high, rounded breasts, probably sculpted by the latest in underwear engineering to show them off to best advantage. Her friend's humor brought her feet back down to earth. Only she wasn't sure if "up" wasn't more accurate. The dream had seemed deep inside some strange planet, far from sky or water, or anything she'd ever known.

"Well, you are my friend, and what are friends for?" Clara curled a lock of Lex's hair around her ring-bedecked fingers and tugged, though her eyes still showed worry. "We can do our usual thing. You spin the web that catches him and I'll nail his cute, tight ass. Unless you want the honors for once?"

You will not *let him touch you.*

Alexis yelped, bolting out of the chair. She tripped, tumbling on her backside into the cushiony paws of an oversized teddy bear, nothing like the embrace of her dreams. Clara was still standing at the chair, staring at her. "What the hell was that?"

"I'm sorry, I guess I'm still spooked. I just—"

"No, not that." Clara knelt by her side, tentatively reached out and closed a hand on her forearm. "Okay, I'm losing my mind, but for a second there your skin got so hot I *had* to let you go. You okay?"

Alexis tried a nod and pulled off a circular motion that didn't reassure Clara or herself. Clara sat down beside her, squashing an Eeyore and Pooh pairing, but clasped the Tigger that fell in her lap as she drew up her knees.

"If you drank, I'd say you'd had one too many last night at that Mexican place we tried. But other than your usual high-on-the-nectar-of-life great time, you didn't drink."

"Yeah. Great time. Every man in the place noticed me, but not one wanted to do anything more than dance. They even did that *way* outside my personal space perimeter."

During adolescence, before she'd fully understood her powers—such that they were—she'd suspected Jonah had cast a magical chastity aura over his daughter at birth. In time, she'd realized all daughters of Arianne were born with special gifts, and this was hers. An exceptional intuition for emotional pain, combined with the tranquil angel power that emanated from her.

Initially, she'd followed her heart instead of her head, wanting to ease pain wherever it happened. She'd resisted her father's warnings, and made some terrible mistakes. As was often the case, her mother's words provided the gentle balm to accept Jonah's painful wisdom.

Suffering is one of the important ways we grow, Lex. You must allow others to suffer. Use your understanding wisely, when it is truly needed, or when it will not derail someone from the path they need to walk. If you do not have that wisdom, it is best not to interfere.

Sometimes, she wondered why the Goddess had given her the gift at all, because the only way it seemed useful was to make people feel happy-fuzzy being around her. In short, she could give a moment's breather to a girlfriend experiencing the blinding agony of being jilted by a guy, or stop someone from jumping off a building. Everything in between needed to be hands-off. Since she couldn't switch off either ability, they drew people to her.

She didn't really mind that. What was frustrating was that the same light that sent out a "come hither" feeling also had a "too good to touch" vibe when it came to males. Unconsciously, they remained at arm's length, keeping *their* hands off.

Alexis scrubbed her face. "At least the guy in my dream was different, even if he was sort of a hellspawn, scary demon-vampire type."

Clara slid an arm around her, a reassurance Alexis gratefully accepted, along with her friend's cautious but teasing smile. "Tell all, girlfriend. Was he hung like a moose?"

"Oh, Goddess." Alexis rolled her eyes. "Is that all a guy needs?"

"No, of course not. I expect intelligence, a sense of humor, an enormous bank account and a great body coupled with a decent but manly fashion sense. The well-hung component only becomes requisite if we get that far. But in dreams you can assume those things are given and jump ahead to the good parts. Literally."

Alexis tried to laugh and instead drew a deep, shuddering breath, thinking of the man in her dream again. While she could feel his emotions, for the first time in her life, they'd been so overwhelming they were mostly incomprehensible. Maybe because it was a dream. *Just a dream.* When she pressed her face against Clara's shoulder to stop the spinning, the girl closed both arms around her, rocking her.

"Take it easy, now," she murmured. "I got you. You're such a strange friend, Lex. I don't think I've ever loved anyone more, because you love back like it's the easiest thing in the world, and you have enough for everyone. But you also worry me. Sometimes you're way too alone, even though everyone adores you. It's as if you're pulling away, toward a destiny that's kind of scary. I don't want to lose you."

Okay, here was one of the reasons having a clairvoyant friend was *not* fun. Clara's observations always held truth. Since Alexis had the same lingering feeling, her anxiety swelled, tempting her to tell Clara everything. But that was one of the rules that couldn't be broken.

Over twenty years ago, a huge apocalyptic battle had happened. Humans had briefly seen angels in the sky, even fought beside some of them to push back the tide of Dark Ones unleashed through a rift. After that, for reasons known only to the Goddess, the angels had been commanded to disappear from human sight again, leaving humans to wonder whether they'd experienced a spiritual revelation, a visit from outer space or some mass hallucinatory trip brought on by sunspots. Budgets to investigate extraterrestrial life had tripled in all developed nations. As accounts varied, life returned to normal again, angels and other paranormal creatures remaining speculative fantasy to all but the select few humans ready to handle the truth.

So Alexis hugged her, straightened and pushed Clara's straight red hair away from her forehead, touching the delicate diamond and gold ring she wore in the right nostril. "I already told you, you're *going* to lose me one day. I'm going to run away with the circus. I'll free all the lions, tigers and elephants, and take them back to Africa on a raft I make out of wishes."

The shadows cleared from Clara's gaze. "There you are. Doing that thing you do."

"What?"

"Talking like a kindergarten teacher, while all of us eat it up like five-year-olds."

Alexis made a face. "By the way, he *was* well-hung. I didn't see it. I *felt* it."

"Yuck." Clara giggled and shoved her away, throwing the Tigger so it bounced off Alexis's shoulder. "I never imagined my kindergarten teacher wrapping her fingers around anything except a piece of chalk. Was he someone we know?"

"No." Alexis sobered, picking up the stuffed animal and considering the foolish face, the broad nose, while her fingers flexed in the soft fur. "I don't think so. It was kind of a crazy dream. Lots of fire, darkness."

She raised her gaze to Clara. "He needed me, more than I think anyone has ever needed another. So strong, he'd shatter the universe to get me."

"God, that's romantic."

Actually, it was pretty frightening. Because Alexis knew just how fragile the universe was.

Two

D ANTE'S chest worked like a bellows, his fingers digging into the blood-soaked stone beneath him. Curling back his lip, he let his fangs stab flesh as he pulled in more air. The pain had become so intense, he'd feared he would have to shatter the spell. Right before he'd retreated back through the dream portal, his internal organs had been cooking. Even now, they were uneasily simmering, reminding him what it would have been like to be incinerated from the inside out.

That didn't matter. Vicious triumph surged through him. Though he would be dangerously weak for several hours, he'd done it. Damn the seawitch, and all the angels, he had defied them, created a way to touch the world outside of his prison. The single-minded focus of twenty years had at last paid off.

Blood trickled down his sweat-drenched flesh to the growing pool of it around his bare knees, pressed into the stone. He'd used the blood to paint the proper symbols on himself, and heat had dissolved them to streaks. But they'd held long enough, seared into her dream soul. He'd connect with her far more easily next time.

His attention shifted to the body lying several feet away, the staring silver eyes and tangled brown hair of his female sacrifice. Now that he'd figured out the proper order of symbols, incantations and timing for the release of blood, he could use the same vessel several times to open the portal. But it wouldn't be necessary. The next time the girl gave herself to dreams, she would be here, and his.

A surge of hunger went through him as he thought of her silken skin, the vivid feel of it even through the illusory world of dreams. He'd be willing to sacrifice ten times as much blood if he could burn the marks into her physical flesh now.

Despite the solitary fierce pleasure that gave him, he reined it back. The powerful rages and needs of his dark soul had to be harnessed if he wished to achieve his objective. He'd learned that long ago.

Perhaps he had the devil-cursed seawitch to thank for that understanding. If he had the opportunity, he'd thank her personally. By ripping off her head, drinking her blood and casting her body into the deepest pit of vile waste he could find.

Focusing on the dead humanoid female next to him again, he imagined it was her. Satisfaction intensified, like the grim pleasure of stealing a meal *and* having the time to savor it, the closest thing to a miracle in the Dark One world. Well, until now.

Twenty years ago, the seawitch had destroyed all the rifts that allowed exit from the Dark One world. Piecing together the magic to re-create even one had been painstaking. He'd discovered a way to do it underground, under this tower, knowing her eye could turn upon his world whenever she chose. His early attempts created a limited, weak conduit that allowed him access to barren worlds. But at last he found one which included a humanoid species.

They were a primitive, nomadic people with only rudimentary defenses. Despite their pronounced brows, broad faces and incomprehensible babble of language, their blood was a rich food source for him, after having been nourished on the weak poison of Dark One blood these two decades. Their strong, sweet fear of the unknown enriched and strengthened him as much as their blood.

He couldn't go into their world, because his physical body couldn't cross any rift, even one he'd created. Which was why the dream portal was his victory, his way of circumventing the curse that had locked him here.

While Dark Ones couldn't survive long away from this hated world, they could hunt anywhere for limited time periods. He controlled exit and entry through that rift, and they knew if they displeased him he would leave them there to weaken and die. Because they were as eager for the fresh blood as he, they went. And because knowledge was a power of its own, the Dark Ones brought him choice pickings for his blood needs and rituals like this. So far, only one Dark One had not returned. Dante let it be known that the Dark One had displeased him and was cut off from this world, a death sentence. In reality, he assumed the creature had fallen upon some mishap, but additional fear of his power was always useful.

His place here had certainly changed over these twenty years. When the seawitch had come, he was a skulking scavenger, probably no more advanced or articulated in his desires or goals than this dumb creature he'd just killed.

Then came the apocalyptic battle between the angels and the Dark Ones for possession of the human world, and the seawitch's decision. Dante didn't like to think back on that terrible day. This world had always been a prison for him, but it had windows, a way for him to gaze out into other worlds. When she chose to destroy them, she'd bricked up his cell door, sealing out everything, condemning him to relentless fire and darkness. A coffin with no death, nothing but screaming and terror, pain and anger.

She had said, "Prove to me you deserve to be set free. And perhaps I will come back and do just that."

He hadn't believed her of course. Words meant nothing. But she had affected him. Because of her, he accepted two absolutes. Power was the only avenue to change. And hatred was the fuel that would allow him to obtain it, if he honed it to accomplish his ultimate objective. Within a month of the rift closings, mad with bloodlust, he'd brought down his first Dark One and forced the creature to submit to his feeding upon him.

She'd taken away his fear and left rage. Rage combined with cunning was a formidable weapon. All the stronger Dark Ones were gone. What was left were a few thousand lower and middle echelon Dark Ones who had been rudderless.

Straightening, he swayed, but forced himself to walk across the now broken ritual circle, stepping over the woman's body. He took a seat on the throne he'd created for himself out of the hard, shiny black wood that came from the only type of tree in the Dark One world. Appearances were important, so he ensured his posture was one of casual indolence instead of physical exhaustion before he sent a mental compulsion to the Dark One he knew was waiting outside the chamber. He released the spell cast on the chamber door to allow him entry.

When the skeletal creature slid in, talons scraping against stone, red eyes quickly darting over the area and then hungrily latching onto the fallen corpse, Dante inclined his head and spoke in the rasping language the creature understood. "You may take her for your own food now. However, you will go through the rift and find me another as soon as you are done, or I will remove her from your belly before you digest her."

There was no night or day in the Dark One world, only unrelenting gray earth and fire in the sky. Time had no meaning, existence measured by breaths and meals, pain and survival. Either you were alive to eat the next meal, or you weren't.

"Yes, my lord." The creature's voice rasped, as grating as its talons on stone. Another reason Dante liked having his private chamber. He could shut them all out, not hear the grunts and hissing, the interminable roar of fire, the pops and snaps of flame. The whistle of icy winds over a landscape devoid of anything but the skeletal black trees and the creatures that pulled themselves through the ice and mud, serving as food for the Dark Ones when nothing fresh from the outside was handy.

As the creature departed, dragging the body by a stiff arm, Dante's eyes followed the tangle of brown hair that was long enough to trail down the female's back. Snarled and bloodsoaked though it was, it made him think of the girl's brown silken curls under his hands. When she turned toward him at the end, he'd wanted to tilt up her chin so he could see her blue eyes, bring her mouth closer to his.

He didn't want to think about the softness of her flesh, the catch in the back of her throat as he'd touched her. Those had been unexpected things, a different, disquieting form of pleasure. Something inside him stilled when he touched her, was close to her, and he'd never felt still. Everything about his world was movement, change, agitation.

The surge of hunger returned, but it had a different quality to it. Perhaps it was a yearning for what he'd never known, what that despicably innocent girl represented. He'd been passive during the first forays into her dreams, drifting there as a silent witness before he ever entered onto their stage, because interacting with her physically took far greater amounts of power, as his abraded internal organs knew. But this time he'd experienced her emotions, things that seemed as if they should be familiar, but were disconsolately not. It angered him past the point of frustrated fury, but he was still too weak to rise. He settled for a low growl, his fingers gripping the chair.

He would prove to the seawitch he deserved to be set free, all right. She'd have no choice, unless she wanted her goddaughter to suffer torment beyond anything she'd ever known. He almost hoped that Mina would take her time in deciding. He wouldn't mind making her goddaughter suffer as the witch had made him suffer.

———

"THAT'S a great big rock."

Alexis crouched next to the young girl peering dubiously through the glass of the viewing tank. "No, that's Buick. Manatees are very still when they sleep, and the darker ones can look like great big stones. Here." She lifted the child, and let her reach down over the rail into the water to touch the placid creature's back.

"He feels all prickly."

"Yes, they have tiny, coarse hairs all over them. See right there? That's where a propeller hit him. Once he's all healed up, they'll take him back to a cove in Florida where a lot of other manatees live, and he'll be free again."

"So he's in the hospital?" The child's brow furrowed.

"Exactly. You're one of his visitors. And visiting hours unfortunately are up. We're about to close."

As Alexis set the little girl back on her feet, the child held on to her neck. She gave her a squeeze, noting with amusement the girl's shoes had mermaid laces. Her mother approached with a boy in tow, obviously looking for their errant family member. "Be sure and come back again, so you can learn more about him," Lex mentioned, and was gratified by the girl's enthusiastic nod.

"She's usually shy with strangers," the mother marveled, giving Alexis an assessing look. "You must have a way with children."

"She has a way with everyone." Branson, the aquarium manager, spoke from his perch on the deck at the deeper end of the pool. He had his bare feet in the water as he untangled diving gear. Leroy, the other manatee in the tank, nuzzled his toes each time he passed on his circular patrol. Sometimes he would float there, letting Branson use his callused soles to give him a good back scratch. "Anytime we have anyone come in with an attitude problem, she straightens them out with just a smile. Even crying babies," he added with a wink. "She can tame anyone down."

On a normal day, Alexis would have teased him, suggesting that was just an excuse so he didn't have to leave the tank, his favorite place. But thinking of surly or unpleasant Conservancy visitors turned her mind back to the angry man of her dreams. While she was glad' for the distraction her job at the Florida Conservancy gave her, it hadn't completely worked. The dream lingered as if burned on her brain, the reality around her fuzzy.

Absently, she watched the family drift out of the main marine viewing area, the girl chattering about her encounter with the manatee. Branson gave her a curious look, but Gwen called from the lab area, saving Lex from questions as he got to his feet to check on her. Alexis glanced into the tank as Leroy butted Buick in the side. "Leroy, he's sleeping. Give him a break."

A *whuff*, and the manatee rose again, this time to secure a floating piece of lettuce. Alexis leaned on the rail and rubbed her brow with her fingers. Classes had been a total waste. She'd dutifully gone with Clara to snag the Greek professor's attention. If there wasn't a true attraction between the two, Lex's gift wouldn't have any lingering effects after her departure, so helping "bait" Clara's trap never bothered her. Of course, Clara was pretty much irresistible. Lex likely wasn't needed for such romantic efforts. In this case, that was a good thing, because she could barely focus on his lecture. Normally, Lex was so eager to learn something new Clara likened her to a sponge. Her friend often teased her, claiming she'd be a hopeless geek if it wasn't for her peace-and-love mojo.

Maybe that was true, but it wasn't a façade. Whether or not it was truly useful, the aura and her empathy were a part of herself, no different in Lex's mind than her blue eyes or brown hair. Sometimes it was a little lonely, since only Clara could wade through it all to see the real Alexis was even more than that. But being among humans was nowhere near as isolating as growing up among mermaids and angels who expected the range of her quietly subtle power to alter the course of the universe, because her parents had done so with theirs.

Right now, she felt that isolation keenly, as if viewing everyone else through a long lens. She didn't like it. She should meditate tonight. Or maybe she should take some type of over-the-counter sleep aid to keep her deep in sleep, not quite as aware of her dreams. The thought startled her, brought her up short. She never used any kind of drug, because while she could shift to human form, her blood was not human.

Definite meditation night. After she checked with Branson and confirmed he didn't need her help with anything else for the afternoon, she bid the manatees a good night in their own language, admonished the younger Leroy again to let the convalescing Buick have his space, and left the center. It was only a short walk down to the marina, and from there she picked up a short, sandy path to an isolated strip of beach along the waterway, little used since it wasn't really wide enough for walking or sunning. It was nearing high tide.

Leaning against the retaining wall, she let the water rush over her bare feet. As always, the touch of seawater, the smell of the ocean, sent a reassuring shiver through her. But an unfamiliar prickling of heat came with it. Not entirely pleasant, it made her skin ultrasensitive, as it might feel after a brief encounter with a hot stove.

She'd wanted to see his face for more than that brief glimpse. Did he fear what she would see? *Beauty and the Beast* was one of her favorite fairy tales, because an empath could see it all. The monster beneath the flesh, no matter how beautiful the mask. The beauty of the soul, no matter the disfigurement. But she hadn't wanted to assess the balance within him. She'd needed to look into his eyes for a reason she couldn't define, but it had been all-consuming. If she'd seen the darkness in him outweighing the light, would she have clung to him anyway, because he needed her? It was a desperation that went deeper into the soul than even she'd ever delved. Down to the dark, frightening places where children screamed but no mother came, pain and fear were the air one breathed, and the earth had no magic beneath the soles of the feet.

"Alexis?"

A warm light had spread over her skin. She raised her gaze to her father's dark eyes. Apparently when she hadn't responded right away, he'd intensified his energy field, a polite way of drawing her attention rather than jarring her. They were not outside of human view here, but the distant boats wouldn't matter. As Prime Legion Commander for the Goddess, Jonah wielded enough power to keep humans from seeing anything he didn't want them to see.

"Seabird." When he put his hands on her shoulders, she shivered. For a single, shocking moment, she didn't want him to touch her. That snapped her out of the fog in a way that sleepwalking to the shore and having an angel land right before her hadn't.

"Pyel," she said, using the mermaid word for *father*, a reassurance to herself as well as a greeting. "I'm sorry. I haven't been feeling well today. Not illness. Just . . . a dream I can't shake."

She'd been about to say "bad dream," but had it really been bad? Or just disturbing? The thoughts she'd had most of the day were frightening only insofar as she wasn't sure she'd ever reacted that strongly to a male before.

Jonah cupped her face in one large hand. Angels were immortal, so his breathtaking handsomeness never faded, but he was well over a thousand years old. His hair was black with a few stray streaks of copper from sunlight, his eyes solid almonds of liquid onyx fire, no whites. To most, the eyes of angels were unfathomable, but even without her gift she knew their nuances, how to read emotion from them as well as minute changes of his face. The things she saw there, could feel from him, told her he was truly ancient. He'd seen and done both terrible and awe-inspiring things. Yet he was her father. Anna had told her the day Alexis was born, Jonah had shed half the weight off of his heart to match the airlike joy of his daughter's.

He ran his thumb over her cheek. While she could see his concern, far more penetrating and shrewd than she could handle right now, he seemed to read her mind. His lips slowly curved. "Care to be dropped from a great height, if I promise to catch you?"

"Not if I catch you first."

Three

SHE stripped off her clothes, bundling and putting them in a safe spot under a shrub planted along the top of the retaining wall. Modesty was not a trait most shapeshifters could afford, and she was no exception.

That said, she was surprised at a ripple of self-consciousness under Jonah's quick, appraising gaze. It was a father's check for her physical well-being, something he'd been doing since she was an infant. But after her sensual dream, her body felt . . . awake, in a very non-daughterlike way.

As always, he scowled at the navel piercing, but she knew he did it just to win a sassy grin out of her. That helped her shake off the odd feeling. Returning to him, she lifted onto her toes and looped her arms around his neck. Easy as that, they were aloft. She had human friends that feared heights, but she'd been in the sky as much as the ocean all her life, and had no fear of either. What was there to fear?

Jonah took her up over the cloud cover, so an overcast day became one filled with sunshine, driving back the shadows. Hooking her legs on his calves, she indulged the pleasure she and her mother shared, burying her fingers behind his shoulders into the soft layers of long feathers, far thicker than her own. He had a magnificent pair of silver white wings, and the hard body under the clasp of legs and arms made her feel safe.

Had the dark stranger ever felt safe? It was an unexpected thought, considering how intimidating he'd been.

The cloud banks were tight rolls, forming a deep mattress she knew an angel could make corporeal, sustaining weight. She'd spent wonderful days of her childhood reclining on them, reading books while her father did the same nearby, her mother weaving cloud wisps into a temporary crown for her daughter's head, or creating animal shapes to amuse her. Sometimes Jonah practiced arms with the other angels, holding her awestruck with the display of flashing steel, quick acrobatics, and best of all, the banter that all men-at-arms shared, even though they'd kept it very clean for her young ears and her mother's, only hinting at the ribald insults they might normally exchange.

Now, though, he took her above even that, until the air was thinner and she could sense the stars waiting above, the Earth far, far below. Then he slanted a look at her. "Ready?"

For answer, she pushed off his thigh with an impish smile and took a swan dive back into open blue sky. As she twirled, managing the air currents, she let the wings emerge from between her shoulder blades. Scales lapped out onto her hips, her legs and feet coming together in a tight point to allow for the fusion transformation that culminated in her tail, the gold and red scales glittering in the sunlight, delicate fins unfurling to fan the air.

He was near as she recovered and swooped upward, maneuvering around and under him, evading the playful grab. When she was young, the game had a serious undercurrent, teaching her flying skills. She'd learned her lessons well, so while he could catch her, he had to expend effort to do so. She'd learned to be satisfied with that, for his speed and agility far superseded hers. He could circumvent the globe in the time it took her to have a thought.

Eventually tiring, she hovered and enjoyed the wide expanse of sky, the reach of the sunlight, the dots of birds in the distance. Far below, the clouds had shifted so she had a glimpse of green and blue terrain. The troubles of its inhabitants were not part of her mind right now, giving her a quiet breathing space.

"Are your filters still working, Seabird?"

He was at her shoulder, but she didn't turn, preferring to gaze at the Earth. "I never have any trouble with them, Pyel. I can feel what people feel, but it doesn't drain me, thanks to my angel half. I just like the quiet sometimes. You know?"

"I do." He gave her time to relax into it, let the meditation ease her mind further, then teased her into another game of cat and mouse. By the time she was breathless again, they were reclining on a cloud bank. Propping himself on his elbows, he glanced at her. "Want to go see your mother now?"

"I know you do." Slanting him a grin, she lay flat on her back, her arms drifting up and down in the mist like a butterfly's slowly moving wings, her own curved beneath her. "You've been away from her for what, an hour?"

"Has it been that long? She'll think I've run off with a water nymph."

"I'm going to tell her exactly that." Alexis levitated and shot off through the sky, her father hot on her heels. Or tail, in this case. The flash of sunlight on her scales attracted the attention of a flock of birds, who deviated off course to follow her. She and Jonah twisted and turned in the sky among them, laughing, then she let him take the lead, leaving the birds behind.

But as she closed her eyes, feeling the wind currents from his wing movements tease her lips, she spoke again. "Was it always like that for you two, Pyel?"

"Always. Time is short, Seabird." He glanced over his shoulder. "When you love someone, there's never enough time to spend with them."

As an angel, Jonah would live indefinitely, until something struck him from the sky. Thousands more years were possible. Anna had a life span of three hundred years. Because of that, Alexis understood why Jonah felt as he did, but part of it was just how they felt for one another. As strong as his energy was, when he was with Anna, it was brighter, even more intense. Alexis had been bathed in their love for each other all her life, enough to make her hope for the same one day. Perhaps she'd been longing for it more lately, explaining her fanciful dreams.

Her father was intimidating to many. Even now, he wore a weapons harness, which sheathed a wicked short sword. Because angels of the Legion only wore a red half-tunic, the layers of rippling muscle on his upper body and thighs were obvious, and daunting. But she'd never feared him. Instead, he'd always been there for her, so that she was certain he could stand between her and the worst the universe could devise.

An incomprehensible shiver went through her at the thought, but then they were spiraling down through the clouds. They headed toward the small sand spit where Anna was sunning, her water-sensitive tail half submerged against the lazy heat.

Forty-one now, Anna looked no older than Alexis. Long golden brown hair, burnished from the water, clung to her pale shoulders. A gold choker with a ruby pendant glittered at her throat, embellished with pearls, a gift from Mina when Alexis was born. She also wore a thin gauze wrap across her breasts long enough to wrap the ends around her lower torso. If she shapeshifted to human, the trait Lex had inherited, it provided a covering to keep from attracting too much attention. Though of course her extraordinary beauty likely made that a moot point. Her eyes, opening to gaze up into the sky, were the same violet blue as Alexis's.

Lex landed in the shallows, easing her tail into the water, her upper body to one hip to recline next to her mother. As she adjusted her wings, the tips scattered droplets against her mother's bare abdomen, rolling down her hip bone to the first layers of midnight blue and purple silver-tinged scales. Just like Jonah's feathers, Alexis twined her fingers through her mother's hair for the pure pleasure of doing so, a sheet of wet silk.

Jonah settled on his heels on the other side of his mate, gazing fondly at them both. "Your daughter wanted to know if you were always completely besotted with me."

Anna tilted her head toward Alexis, acknowledging the caress while looking at Jonah, a smile curving her mouth. "Besotted? I tolerated him, Lex. Large, grumpy bird. I took pity on him and agreed to be his mate until I had something better to do. I had you so you could help me. He's a great deal of work."

Lex chuckled. "No arguments there."

Anna, despite her words, reached up and ran her fingers over his strong features. His eyes softened and fired at once, a response of love and desire Lex had seen countless times between them. Beneath Anna's words was a poignant truth. Because she would die long before he did, Anna had wanted to be sure he had family left to care for him. Lex would be that, along with all the sons and daughters that came after. She loved children, but she knew she would have had them no matter what, because neither she nor her mother could bear the thought of her father's loneliness. Angels only mated once in their entire life span. Their first love was their last love.

The thought made her lonely for that intimacy, a bond that would last through the generations. That wasn't like her, either. Yes, she'd been frustrated with her inability to win more than platonic adoration from any male as she matured into a woman, but she received so much love and warmth from the people around her, it had balanced. This was the first time she'd ever felt the sharp knife edge of envy, a needy yearning that shot her right back into the grip of the dream, and made her wish for its return.

Jonah brushed a kiss on Anna's willing mouth. "I'll be right back."

As he went aloft again, Lex cocked a brow. "You know, it's really obvious when you two do that. The unspoken strategy of, 'If I make myself scarce, I think she'll tell you what's bothering her, then you can rat her out to me later.'"

"Well, he is a warrior, not a spy. Subtlety is not his strongest suit, trust me." Anna leaned back on her elbows and studied Alexis's face. "So what's happening? Why did you ask him about our feelings for one another?"

Lex shrugged. "I just wanted to know. Did it take everything over, make you feel as if everything was about to change? Like maybe the world was about to upend itself and you weren't sure which way to fall, or if you were even going to fall?"

"Have you met someone?" Curiosity sharpened Anna's expression.

"Does it sound like I have?"

"It does," Anna said. "You've mentioned young men at your college you wished felt more for you. Is it one of them?"

"No. I actually haven't met someone. Or maybe I have. It was a dream, but it felt like not a dream, you know?"

Anna straightened to a sitting position. "Lex, I know you live in a human world. Sometimes that can make you quick to dismiss the unusual as they do, thinking it's coincidence or indigestion."

"Shades of *A Christmas Carol*," Alexis noted, trying to smile.

"But you are not human," her mother persisted. "It's best not to assume a disturbing dream is just a dream."

Oh, hell. She should have known better. This was leading right into whether she was spending too much time in the human world, a concern Anna and Jonah both shared, for different reasons. Anna knew that Lex, because of her differences, could never truly belong in that world, and feared the hurt of being an outsider would eventually cut too deep if she attached herself to human society. For Jonah, it was much simpler. He didn't trust humans. Or merpeople. Or anyone, really, except his own Legion. He'd be happiest if she stayed in the Citadel, the seven-level fortress in the Heavens used as the angels' base of operations.

But she loved her life. She'd understood early on she would always be an outsider, no matter in which world she made her home. She wasn't pure mermaid or pure angel, but she could shift to human form. So she'd created a world for herself there and, as an empath, she felt she was given as much as she gave back. She was loved for her differences, not shunned.

"I'm fine." Since her mother's emotions were worrisome storm clouds, Alexis used the singsong lilting notes of the mermaid language. "Don't worry, Myel."

"Can you tell me about it? Your dream?"

Alexis shrugged, feeling color rise in her cheeks under Anna's interested regard. "It was a private dream, of sorts. I wouldn't want you to have to tell Pyel about it. He'd think of ways to invade my dreams and drive off illusion men."

"It was a dream about a man."

Lex nodded. "An incredible, amazing man. Full of fire, but also so full of pain. I've felt terrible things from a soul before, but this . . . Myel, he's surrounded by evil and death, and he's part of it, but not. Like a soul that's drawn evil around him as camouflage to blend, but he's pulled it inside himself, so he can't take off the mask. Maybe he doesn't even know he's wearing one anymore."

"Are your filters working?"

Lex bit back impatience. "Yes, I told Pyel they were. Why do you both always ask that?"

"Because we remember when you didn't have them."

Her mother's reminder, a gentle rebuke, helped curb her irritation. The natural filters with which she'd been born kept outside emotions from drowning her soul, but they didn't make her deaf, mute or blind to those feelings from others. They simply provided her with emotional distance. If she used the filters, the emotions backed off a bit, gave her time to absorb them at her own pace.

As her mother had pointed out, she hadn't had control of her filters at first. Mina had used her powers to lock them down until Lex was old enough to start handling their manipulation on her own. It had nearly driven her mad before they figured out what was wrong. A child's mind couldn't comprehend the suffering that every being carried in some measure. Thanks to Mina's lock, until she came of age, people's emotions had been distant images and impressions, like the background murmur of television.

"Some babies cried from colic." Anna twined a lock of Lex's hair around her fingers. "I didn't know if mine was crying from her own distress or that of the whole world."

Her parents had to keep her isolated until she was ten. Even after that, they'd been obsessively protective. Lex knew it had been necessary. She also knew the history of her mother's ancestors. Before Anna, every daughter of Arianne had been born with a curse that made it practically impossible to exist without causing harm to herself or others. Anna had been the first exception, thanks to Mina's magic. No matter that Mina had assured Anna the curse appeared to be broken when Anna passed the age of twenty-one, something no other daughter of Arianne had done, her mother had suffered more than one agonizing period in those early years, thinking it had simply skipped a generation and struck Lex.

Lex knew that, because her mother's pain and fear had been the sharpest of the many emotions that had speared her as a child.

She took her mother's hand now, irritation gone. "But just like colic, we got past it. Myel, this is who I am, and I wouldn't change it. I have an amazing, beautiful life. If the Goddess gave me the gift to see into hearts and give them ease and comfort, then I know it was intended. I don't shirk from it because I see awful things. I know I can't fix everything."

Her mother managed to push back her emotions, because they receded. Anna gave her a smile. "All right then. So tell me more about this intriguing dream man."

"I've never felt anything like his pain. Most of the time, no matter how terrible their lives have been, or the pain they're carrying around now, there's some balance. There's some part of their life that gave them joy or ease. He had none of that. Not a single moment of happiness or rest. No sense of safety. Nothing, Myel. It's like his whole life is death and terror. Pain. A savage need to survive." Taking a breath, she laid her head on her mother's shoulder as Anna lay back.

"I was overwhelmed by his determination to survive, because who would want to survive if they had *nothing* good to remember? I've experienced suicides. He has their despair, but instead of resignation, he has a rage, a determination to survive despite his circumstances, almost as if his goal is to thumb his nose at Fate. But even that's more camouflage." Caught in her analysis, she was only vaguely aware of her mother's close scrutiny. "It was the first time in my life I didn't immediately understand what was going on inside someone. I thought it was because it was a dream, but . . . What's your goal, if all is darkness?"

"An end to darkness."

She tilted her head. "Okay, but what if you've never experienced anything else? How do you know an end to darkness will be any better?"

"You don't. But it's different, and when your life is unrelenting torment, anything different, any change, has got to provide something." Anna frowned, thinking. "Or perhaps he hasn't experienced it, but he's seen it somehow. He's seen the light others have found, and desires that for his own self."

"Do you think he's real?"

"I'm not sure. Would it please you if he was?"

Lex pressed her lips together. "I don't know. He frightens me. Not like ax murderer fear."

"I'm relieved to hear it," her mother said dryly. "But how does he frighten you?"

"As if I'm somehow powerless with him, and he could take me over in a way I've never experienced. Like being at the top of a really big roller coaster, not sure how the ride's going to be, but knowing it's going to take everything I've got to prove myself brave enough for it."

"Have you dreamed of him before?"

"Nothing like last night's dream, but yes. Brief snippets, impressions, a shadow passing me. I can sense him." Those times, she'd woken in the darkness of her room, heart pounding and hands gripped in her sheets.

"I want you to talk to Mina."

"What?" Lex blanched and sat up. "Oh no, Myel. It's nothing like that."

"You don't know what it is." Anna lifted her upper body as well, tempering her words with a hand on Lex's. "You have an extraordinary gift. During your youth, we've encouraged you to treat it gently, but we've always known it could have a depth you've yet to tap or any of us to understand. It would be wise to let her know about the dream."

Lex grimaced. "She's so sarcastic. Her tongue could be used to slice through metal. And her darkness . . . even with the filters, it's hard for me to keep things straight when I'm around her. She's scary, Myel." Startled, she realized what she felt from Mina wasn't very different from what she felt from her dream man.

Anna chuckled. "She scares all of us, except perhaps David. But we love her, too, and as your godmother, she would do anything to protect you. Think about it?"

Lex nodded reluctantly, then bit her lip. "May I also speak to Lord Lucifer?"

Anna's shock made Lex wince. "You're reluctant to talk to Mina, but you'll *ask* to meet with the Lord of the Underworld? What on earth would you—"

"I think this man may be there," Lex cut in hastily. "There's so much fire and pain where he is. If he's real, could he be someone in Hell that's somehow tapped into my dreams? Lord Lucifer might know."

"He might." Anna pursed her lips. "I'll ask Jonah to approach Lucifer about it. If Luc is willing, he'll grant you an audience. But Mina first. As soon as possible."

"All right. Hopefully David will be there. It's easier. Less creepy." Relieved, Lex sensed her mother's worries receding again, a manageable tide. "This won't make Pyel worry, will it? I don't want either of you concerned. Even if it is real, it's just some lonely guy reaching out to me. Not much different from all those sea animals and unhappy merpeople who used to follow me home when I was a teenager, feeding off my proximity to make them feel better."

"He will always worry about you, because he loves you more than anything, dearest. So do I." When Anna opened her arms, Lex settled into them again, laying her cheek against her bosom. She traced the lovely jeweled line of blue and purple scales that formed a diagonal line over Anna's hip bone. The slim arm pressed against her body had a swirling silver tattoo marking.

The whisper of the ocean, the blissful heat of the sun and her mother's heartbeat gave her peace, as it always did. They sat that way for some time, two sea creatures in sync with the rhythm of their world, no need to say or do anything. The unique tranquility of it was the main reason Lex knew her parents didn't have to fear the human world's hold on her. When she told her mother that, Anna's arms tightened around her, stroking the downy feathers inside the curve of her wings.

"You understand so many things well, Lex. But sometimes you're blind to what is closest to you. Though he can be very protective, your father listens better than you expect. You could have no better ally. He would hold off the universe to protect you."

As the creature in her dreams would destroy it to have her. She shivered again, not sure where that thought had come from. Anna was right. She did need to talk to Mina, much as she hated to admit it. Tomorrow. Tonight she wanted to think. And perhaps to dream one more time, before her decisions took him away from her.

When Jonah dropped from the sky, landing lightly on the sand, Lex allowed humor to push away her worries, for now. "You two are so well synchronized it's scary," she pronounced.

Over Anna's chuckle, Jonah gave them both an indulgent look and produced two mangoes, as well as a pair of exotic tropical flowers. He tucked the latter behind the delicate ears of each of his women, his large hands lingering on their faces, then indicated the mangoes.

"How about a snack before I take Lex back home?"

Four

THE flower was in a cup beside her bed, the fragrance of mango still lingering on her tongue. Lex had turned on some soothing music and heated chamomile tea, but still she couldn't bring herself to lie down and let sleep have her. As she paced, she almost regretted not seeing Mina tonight. How could she want and fear something at the same time? Normally, something like this would make her err on the side of caution. She knew the margin of error between compassion and instinct. Even so, she'd never had such a strong urge to throw caution to the wind and yet run away from the dream at the same time.

She'd tried meditating, but that had been too difficult. Those hands in her dream kept sliding along her arms, touching her wings, stroking her skin. She'd thought about pleasuring herself as a form of relief, a way to focus, but in the end she stretched out on her bed, tired of struggling. *To hell with it. Bring it on.*

Gripping Tigger hard in both hands, she focused on his silly face. "Only way to resolve this is to catch the Tigger by the tail. And hope he doesn't bite my face off. Here, kitty, kitty . . ." As drowsiness closed in, she began to murmur it. "Here, kitty, kitty . . ."

It will be okay. Even if he's real, it's just a dream. We're just meeting in a dream. I will help him. It will be okay.

FIRE. He was always surrounded by fire, but tonight the heat was un-comfortably hot and suffocating. Flames shot up in a wall all around her. Panic invaded her mind. But then he was there, several feet away, in the only circle where fire didn't exist. He was naked, all lean male muscle and arousal. His flesh had been cut, marks on his arms and stomach streaming blood. Since she was in her human form this time, she moved to him on burning bare feet. "What happened? You've hurt yourself."

He watched her come with a peculiar still look, like an animal used to capturing its food and waiting patiently for it, no matter how harshly hunger gnawed away at his insides. Though the heat pressed in on all sides, he seemed unaffected. Even his silken black hair, rippling loose over his shoulders with the wind created by the flames, defied the flickers of sparks. She'd like to touch those long strands, weave beads and feathers into it as if he were a Native American. She imagined he came from a tribe of that race because of his broad brow and sculpted proud cheekbones, the firm, cruel lips.

His hands closed over her upper arms. There was a different quality to his touch this time. Not slow and seductive, mixed with a thrilling tease of forcefulness. This was pure dominance as he brought her to him, taking her mouth. Alexis made a keening noise, caught between anxiety and pleasure as he delved deep, his tongue lashing at hers, his lips caressing and demanding at once. His hands moved, following the curve of her spine to her buttocks where they spread out and gripped, enough to lift her onto her toes. Her sensitive sex pressed against the hard bar of iron that was his engorged cock. She gasped. "Please . . . I'm . . . frightened."

"You're mine," he responded ruthlessly, raising his head to stare down at her. Alexis tried to focus past the wave of demanding heat pulsing from his body, to feel what was going on behind the fiery eyes. Did he *want* to frighten her? Before she could delve further, he'd lifted her, forcing her to open her thighs and wrap her legs around his hips, her calves resting on his taut buttocks, crossed heels brushing his thighs. She had to hold on to his shoulders for balance, and that put her fingers in his hair as she'd wished. It was like her father's feathers, so soft and pleasurable, an odd contrast to their surroundings. It was the one reassurance she had, such that she gripped it with both fists. Then malevolent intent exploded in her mind. Anger, rage . . . revenge.

"Don't—wait—"

He shifted her body and with one powerful thrust, penetrated her.

His kiss had moistened her enough that he'd been able to get his broad head in her gateway, but she'd never been taken before. The pain was immediate and excruciating, such that she cried out, but he wouldn't let her free. He held her on him, seated to the hilt in her body, his arms banded about her.

"It hurts . . . please stop. Please."

His breath rasped in her ear, a beast in mindless rut, and she struggled to get past the pain and panic of a pinned butterfly. She had to reach him, to understand why he was doing this. Gripping her buttocks again, he began to work her up and down his shaft. She whimpered at the abrasion of raw tissue, at his battering assault on her virginity. While it didn't feel exactly . . . wrong, it was far from right. He was supposed to care about her, protect her. Even if he didn't know it, that was the way it was supposed to be. He wasn't just betraying her . . . he was betraying both of them.

She knew simple ways to defend herself, but against his irresistible power, there was only one way. Though he was strong, the power of a shift was as unstoppable as the force of water. Her wings erupted from her back. The tail transformation swept her lower body, dislodging him. If the quick hitch of his breath and his curse meant anything, the scales had sliced him. She fell from his grasp, but he stumbled to one knee beside her, clamping onto her upper arm. She sucked in a breath, for this time his touch burned. No, not his touch. She'd landed in a bed of flames, and it was licking over her. She was helpless in this form, her wings catching fire, her tail flopping uselessly.

When he lifted her free of the fire, dousing the flames, she saw burn marks on her flesh and smelled singed feathers. "Your fear is different," he said at last. "Not like the others. Their fear stinks, like something rotting. Yours . . . it's sweet and sad at once."

Like a dying flower, she thought, and wondered if he knew what that was.

"I liked your cunt," he added baldly, still holding her with his intense stare. "I want to be inside it again. Change back." His voice was the growl of the mythical monster under the bed, but with a mesmerizing quality that would coax her out from under her protective covers, bring her to her knees to look beneath and meet the eyes of the beast.

Beauty and the Beast. "I can't," she whispered. "I'm afraid."

"You will, because I command it."

It's a dream, a dream, a dream. Hold on to your sanity, Lex. If it's a dream, you can control it. "No." She lifted her chin, forced herself to hold that blazing look. "You hurt me. You weren't gentle. You're supposed to be gentle. And make it pleasurable."

He blinked. She thought she felt surprise. What else did she feel swirling from him? Lust for certain, and while it now scared her, it sent another shiver through her as she remembered his more seductive ways of touching her.

"Show me, then," he said. "What do you mean by *gentle*?" He stumbled over the word, as if it was part of a foreign language.

"How you were kissing me before, in the earlier dream. It was . . . passionate, but gentle at the same time. Like this." Still trembling, she put her hand to his jaw. It was smooth, no facial hair. Swallowing, she stretched up, aware of his arms banding around her back and her tail below the roundest part of her hips.

She met his lips with a tentative caress, trying to dissipate the cold fear his violent assault had triggered. She *had* desired him. The edge of it was still there, waiting to be stoked to life by his touch. *It's a dream, Alexis. You weren't raped in real life. It was just a dream . . . And it wasn't rape. You wanted him, he wanted you. He just . . . maybe he had no clue what he was doing. Or he thought you did.*

But he'd acted with animal determination. No, that wasn't true. Even animals had ways of saying "not interested." He'd acted as if he was conquering her, subduing her like an enemy. She couldn't deny that wave of rage, the lust for vengeance, even as he stayed immobile now. While she nibbled shyly at his lips, he watched her, eyes of fire so close to her face. Grasping courage in both hands, she teased his lips open, licked his fangs, then flirted with his tongue, easing forward so her arms closed around his shoulders. She pushed herself against his chest, trying to reclaim balance in this odd and terrifying dream.

His powerful arm constricted on her back, his lower fingers curving in to stroke the scales low on her hip, a sensitive area that made her fearful shiver become something different. "If I woke, would I have burns from your fingers on my skin?" she whispered against his mouth.

"You would. Your thighs would be sticky with your virgin blood. Shift back for me. Let me lick it off."

She swallowed. "I'm afraid you'll hurt me again."

"You are mine to do with as I will."

"No," she responded softly. "I'm not yours to harm."

"Then shift back, and let me prove to you that I won't."

She held his gaze, her attention distracted by the sensual lips, held hard and tight. He was all hard and tight, not a relaxed muscle on him. But she allowed her body to shift, wings dissolving, her tail giving way to human legs again.

Lowering her to her feet on that patch of nonburning ground, he eased her down to her back. Her fear returned with him looming over her. But then he knelt, placing a hand on her thigh, widening her. His gaze studied her sex, the smears of blood on her thighs. The muscles in his biceps bunched as he leaned over her. His tongue traced the inside of her thigh, taking the blood away as he'd promised. She was tense, she couldn't help that. Her trust could only go so far, because she couldn't read his intentions clearly, a problem she'd never experienced. It was a confused jumble, perhaps clouded by her own distressed state. But she had felt his vulnerability, his pain so sharp and clear. All the things that drew her to a person . . .

Oh, Goddess, had it all been a trap?

His tongue was making it difficult for her to decide. Working his way over both thighs, then up to the center, he tasted flesh that had never experienced a man's mouth. She arched with an unexpected cry as his tongue eased the pain of her sex and replaced it with waves of pleasure. She *was* his, all his . . . Oh, Goddess, this was a mad magic . . .

When she could bear it no more, she reached down, gripped his hair in hard hands, wanting more, somehow. Lifting his head, he looked up her body, his eyes wandering in a decidedly possessive way. "You no longer wish me to be . . . gentle?"

Startled, she had to stifle an uneasy laugh. Goddess, here she was, a virgin trying to explain the unpredictable and minute nuances of a woman's arousal to a creature who apparently had no basis to understand it. Of course, through Clara, she knew how hard it was to explain it to *any* male with reasonable brain function.

"It's . . . as I get more . . . aroused, you can be less gentle. Can you tell when I'm more aroused?"

He seemed to think that through, then nodded.

"But if it hurts, I'll ask you to stop. You have to stop then. Okay?"

A glint of fire went through his gaze before he bent to her thighs again.

Her trepidation quickly disappeared. Perhaps he had more than reasonable brain function, because he didn't need to be told something twice. He started off easy once again, but as she bowed up to his mouth, mewling, he growled against her flesh, penetrated her more deeply with his tongue. Holding her wrists to her sides, he gave her an anchor against which to pull and strain. She dug her heels into the charred ground as he pushed her legs further apart with the movements of his head, the imposition of his body between her legs. When she began to buck, she rubbed herself against his lips, the hardness of his jaw. His sharp fangs pricked her, her erratic movements raking one across tender flesh. It made her moan even harder, because his mouth sealed over it, suckling tender flesh.

Then, just as she was trembling on the pinnacle, he slid up her body. This time, when he came into her, the passage was slick and wet, and he moved slowly. She didn't know if that was for her benefit or his, because there was a studied concentration to his face as he braced his arms on either side and thrust with slow deliberation into her still sore sex. She didn't protest, except for soft cries of pain and pleasure at once as she kept her eyes locked on his face. Her whole body, inside and out, trembled for him, taken over by his strength and fire, the intensity of that extraordinary gaze.

When he was in to the hilt, she felt as if she couldn't move, except for her legs locking on his hips by pure instinct. Taking her hands again, he held them above her head, bringing his chest down against hers, softness meeting hard muscle, the bloody symbols painted on his body now pressed to hers. Glancing down, she saw her flesh begin to glow to match those symbols, a mirror image. A wild warmth swept over her at the evidence that they belonged together.

"I want you to surrender to me. Open yourself fully when I take you over. Say yes."

"Yes," she whispered, caught up in the urgent need behind the words. It was a command, but more than that, it was a plea. He was so lonely, it swamped her as much as his desire. How could she deny him this moment to feel completely connected to another, even it was only in their shared dreams?

"I'm here," she said, and then he began to move. A thrust and retreat that built, creating a rocking motion between their two bodies like ocean waves. As the waves became a storm, slamming against one another, she left the metaphor of cool water far behind, nose-diving straight for the flames. Something was about to shatter. She feared the dream would end.

"What . . . is . . . your . . . name?" she gasped.

Darkness coated his gaze for an instant before it was swallowed by the red and orange again. His body tensed everywhere it touched her, but in reaction she strained upward against his hold, toward his lips. While he drew back, denying her, his gaze settled on her bare breasts, the hungry upward tilt of the nipples. Dropping his head, he nuzzled her there, his mouth covering one and suckling hard, causing another cry to rip from her throat as he kept moving in her body. He licked and teased her so thoroughly, though his pace inside her body kept stopping just short of completion, taking her up higher and higher. She was on fire, dying, trembling, gasping tiny pleas to a man whose name she didn't know.

"Dante," he answered her at last, lifting his head to lock gazes with her once more. Then he surged over her, clamping down on her mouth, seizing possession of her mind, and thrust hard, deep. The tissues he'd abused earlier complained, but the rest of her body absorbed it, scrabbling for that peak his friction, inside and out, now brought into reach. "Say my name," he muttered into her lips. "Tell me you surrender to me."

"Dante," she managed, and repeated it, a caress, a reassurance, because she sensed he needed both. Her empathic gift was wide-open to him, no more restrained than her body's need. His expression did not change, though, and while he became even more intent on her response, he seemed more distant at the same time. The fire was closing in, bringing their time to an end. She didn't want it to, even though something felt wrong. She couldn't determine what, because there was too much swirling around her. Magic, dreams, emotions and her own physical response were too tangled together.

"Say my name, too," she pleaded. "Please."

Something shifted in his gaze, but his mouth remained hard, implacable. "Give me your surrender, Alexis."

"I surrender to you, Dante. I'm yours."

The blood marked on both their bodies burst into flame, matching the leap in his own eyes. Startled, she inhaled blood and heat, but it didn't burn her flesh. His body and the fire surrounded her, a cocoon shutting out everything except Dante's weight upon her, his demand between her legs. They were turning, spinning now, and the pinnacle was reached. The climax ripped a scream from her throat, the first of her life she'd had while a man was inside of her.

The spinning lost symmetry, became a flailing, like an uncontrolled fall from far up in the sky. She had no wings. The climax stuttered, leaving her body vibrating and needy, wailing for its loss, but something was so wrong her alarmed brain cut off the sensual response, far too late.

Dante was gone. She was alone in the fire, and it clamped down like the lid of a flame coffin, burning her flesh again. Screaming, she thrust outward, seeking him. Instead, her fingers disappeared into the leaping orange flames. Ice touched them somewhere on the other side, a cold that invaded her hands, seizing her arms and freezing them in place, even as the fire continued to burn her flesh.

"Help! Dante, *please* help me."

She'd never had a childhood friend who was cruel to her. Never been lost where she hadn't been found by a kind stranger and returned. Even the times she'd brushed too close to those too lost for her to ease, help had been there to draw her from harm. The fear of what might happen to her had always been her parents' fear, never her own.

Surrounded and nurtured by love and the best in peoples' hearts all her life, it was hard for her to wrap her mind around what this was. A betrayal. And not a minor one. This was major league, oh-god-what-have-I-gotten-myself-into betrayal.

Breath for screaming was snatched from her. The fire roared over her like a blanket covering a corpse. She smelled her own flesh burning, saw the ends of her hair catch fire as her fingers and arms turned whitish blue from cold.

"Dante, don't do this. Help me." *I'm so afraid . . .*

———

HUMANS were often oblivious to the delicate balance on which their world rested, but angels and other creatures were wired to it, such that a minor shift could be felt in the blood. The feeling that shuddered through the firmament now, shaking Heaven, Hell and the Earth caught in between, brought every angel to a full stop. Particularly one Legion Commander, his hand automatically gripping his sword, fury and fear twisting in his gut.

At the bottom of the ocean, a mermaid seeking shells to make a necklace for her daughter froze, her heart thudding up in her throat.

And deep in the Nevada desert, a seawitch who rarely visited the sea anymore erupted out of her porch swing, her gaze narrowed on something no one else could see.

"Oh, bloody, fucking hell," she snarled.

Five

DANTE squatted in his locked chamber at the top of the tower. Hidden behind a screen of tattered cloth pieced together, he studied the merangel lying in an unconscious, crumpled heap in the circle of blood. The edges were marked with symbols that would keep her inside of it, but it was the symbols now burned on her flesh from throat to pubis that would keep her invisible and beyond the reach of those attempting to retrieve her.

By releasing a serum in his back fang during his first blood taking, he'd made it impossible for her to escape him. He could find her, no matter where she was. This time he'd used the second serum, which opened her mind so he could read anything there. He'd heard her voice in his head. *I'm afraid. Help me . . .*

He possessed a third serum as well. It had an ethereal blue color to it. Before his mother could teach him more about that one, she'd descended into madness. She'd mumbled that the other two serums had to be administered first, and there'd been something about the third being used to bind someone's soul, but even her memories hadn't been able to offer much more than that.

As an experiment, he'd tried injecting it into one of his Dark One feedings, when he'd been strong enough to force his meal to await his pleasure, but nothing different really happened, though he'd had a tingling sense something was supposed to. Of course, his mother was long dead, so vampire peculiarities weren't something he could explore, except in the sketchy memories she'd left implanted in his mind. Those, along with the windows provided by the rifts before the seawitch had closed them, had helped him understand many things about the blue and green world that should have been his home.

It was this world he'd had to survive, however. His Dark One half had helped with that, but the cunning, speed and strength of his vampire blood had brought him to this point. He hadn't needed whatever that third mark did. And until now, he'd had no interest in binding someone's soul to him. He wasn't even certain if Dark Ones had souls, which might explain why it hadn't worked.

As Alexis moaned and turned over, her bloodstreaked face damp with sweat and tears, his thoughts returned to her. Perhaps he could have stretched it out to one more dream, taken it slower, but the ritual was draining, and he couldn't afford to be weak too frequently in his world, even behind closed doors.

His lips curled as he recognized that as a lie. He should despise what he'd done because it was a loss of control. He hadn't wanted to wait, and could have missed his chance irreparably by rushing himself. He'd certainly felt bloodlust before, and knew how to manage that. But when he put his mouth on her flesh, his cock had become a monster with a mind of its own, demanding he rut on her like he was a lower echelon Dark One with no control at all over his urges. Once he was inside her, it had gotten worse. He'd wanted to take her again and again, in all sorts of twisted ways, mark every part of her with his claim.

It had nothing to do with her, of course. He'd snapped because he was so close to his goal, after planning and waiting for so long. Inside her body, it was bliss, sheer bliss, cool and heat at once, but not like the ice and fire of his world. Different, like her world.

"My lord?" Epherius, possibly the most advanced of the remaining Dark Ones, spoke through the closed doors. "May we see your victory?"

We. More than one of them, always a situation to be approached with caution. But this would confirm he was supreme over all of them, and the ongoing possibility of challenge might lessen. Not that he intended to be here for much longer.

"Enter," he said brusquely, going to his throne.

Epherius was accompanied by eight of the others, the nearest to him in intelligence and strength, obvious because of their similar height and upright stance. The lower echelon was often commanded by these when they went on scouting expeditions in the primitive worlds Dante had been able to access. They all had the deceptively skeletal arms and legs, leathery wings that slapped against the stone as they pushed into the room. All were naked, their genitals hanging between their legs in grotesque bobbing display. Dark Ones had unrelenting carnal urges, which they relieved upon any weaker Dark One who could not repel them. At one time, they had relieved them on him.

Sometimes, just the sight of those naked organs incited a cauldron of simmering rage in him. He'd unleashed it before, incinerated a few with the powers he'd cultivated in the Dark One texts none of them knew how to read. It had gone a long way toward making them wary of him. No one touched him now. If they did, it was an attempt to kill, not subdue or sodomize.

They hissed excitedly at the sight of the female in the circle. She'd asked him to call her by name, and he'd done it that one time, but it disturbed him, almost as much as having her say his name had wrenched something inside of him. Names meant nothing and everything. He didn't want to think of her name.

She had roused at their knock on the door, as he suspected she might, with so much evil gathered close to her sensitive mental receptors. With them crowded around her, he knew she would see all of their hideous faces first. It would disorient and terrify her further. She might try to get out of the circle, but without him releasing the wards, she would simply burn herself further. He heard her startled scream as she caught her first glimpse of their world. Should he revel in that? If so, he was as dead and empty as he often felt. It didn't matter. He needed to get out of here, and she was the way to that. That was all. Nothing else was required of him but that objective.

One of the Dark Ones surged forward, apparently intending to enter the circle, and was flung back, light strobing over his thin flesh, illuminating the skeletal contents within it.

"Do not touch the circle's edge," Dante said, dark satisfaction in his voice.

"But we want to touch her. Play with her."

"No. You may look, and then you will go. I will need more blood to hold her here as long as I want her to be."

"What if we insist? She is the first like her we've ever had here. We should touch. Taste. Feeellll." The words drew out as the creature's fangs were exposed, and his eyes turned with malevolence on Dante. His claws cupped his sizeable genitalia. "Many of us. One of you. Why you want her? What you be doing? You have toy and we do not. We take her and give her back when we're done. You always let us do that before."

As Alexis woke, she became aware she was in some kind of shallow basin filled with cold, slimy liquid. The metallic, sickening smell drove the first nail of fear into her heart, for she knew it was blood. Opening her eyes, she had a brief impression of gray stone all around before she tried to scramble out of it. She yelped as she hit a shielding that knocked her to her back with a wet splat that soaked her feathers. The basin was a ritual circle. She couldn't shift. She tried, with mounting terror, but she was stuck in her merangel form. On land.

Her stomach and chest hurt. Looking down, she swallowed another terrified noise as she realized the symbols she'd seen on Dante, and glowing on herself, were now burned into her flesh, explaining the raw pain throbbing there. Her clothes had been shredded during whatever had happened, so she pulled their remnants away from her, so tattered they were only a hindrance to her movements. Where was she? This was no dream. But then, she'd known Dante was real all along, hadn't she? That's why she'd been unable to deny him, deny his pain. He'd used it to trap her, take her wherever this was.

The air was stifling, heavy. It was difficult to draw air into her lungs, and for a frightening moment, she thought she was somewhere there was no oxygen, no way to breathe with gills or lungs. But realizing she had oxygen was a short-lived relief. There was something wrong here, something draining the energy from her like a punctured gas can. It buzzed in her head like a continuous headache, made her organs strain to do their work. Her heart rate was accelerated, and she didn't think it was only terror. As an empath, she could sense the rightness or wrongness of her surroundings, and this place was extremely wrong. She wasn't meant to be here. No one was supposed to be here.

Trying to orient herself, she saw she was in a chamber at the top of a round stone tower. The flat and mostly barren landscape outside an open arched window suggested they were high up, perhaps fifty feet or so. Naked black trees were scattered over ground that appeared to be oddly symmetrical areas of fire and dull gray ice. The smell in the air was death, pain . . . suffering. Winged creatures, far distant in the sky, still made her shudder.

Then her head snapped around at the sibilant voice behind the door. Dante answered from behind a black-draped panel she hadn't yet examined, thinking she was alone. She sloshed around in her macabre bath to face it, but then he was striding from behind the ragged cloth, taking a seat on a large black wooden chair. He ignored her as he called out a command to enter. The door swung open.

A blast of desolation, hopelessness, fear and torment hit her directly between the eyes. She scrambled for her filters, but it was like using a paper napkin to stop a bullet. Her palms slipped, and she was writhing in that shallow pool of blood again. *No, no, no . . .*

She heard their words, saw what they wanted, felt it, but even more terrifying than the threat of violation was being sucked into the abyss of what these things were. There was no escape from it. Once there, she would wander forever, lost, just as she'd remembered from the last dream. A place where babies screamed, but no mother came. She grasped for Anna's image in her mind desperately. *Oh, Goddess, help me.* Did the Goddess even have sway over this place? How could She? The Goddess, Mother of Earth and connected to life in all ways . . . no. There was no way She had a part of this.

Holy Mother, she was in the Dark One world. How could she not have recognized it? He'd even reminded her of Mina, and Mina was the only living Dark Spawn in her world, half Dark One, half mermaid. But in Lex's dreams, she'd only seen the trappings of fire and darkness, and Dante. Even from him she hadn't felt this utter lack of hope or light. It was incomprehensible, beyond any understanding she had in her world. The darkest soul she'd ever met there didn't come close to this.

She struggled to hold herself back up on her arms. Though she knew she had nowhere to go, a wild animal's mindless panic closed in, seeing all those leering faces around her, that terrible energy. She flung herself at the circle's edge, toward the creatures, hoping to break through them. The boundary blasted her again, hard enough to knock her into the opposite side. She would have ricocheted back to the floor, writhing with pain, except one of the creatures dared to shoot a claw through that boundary. Talons dug into her breast as he howled, for the circle's binding was an electric current, locking them together in the brutal grip of its barbed protection. Alexis screamed thinly, no air to give voice to the pain and horror of feeling as that dark poison invaded her. *Help me, help me . . .*

She was dropped, and now the cool wetness of the stone was welcome, though her muscles jittered in the aftermath of the voltage. A snarl, a thudding of bodies, another howl. She saw a flash of something that might have been steel, then magic surged through the chamber. Like gunpowder, it tickled her nose. More shrieks, sharp talons scraping stone as the creatures beat a hasty retreat. But when they hit the door, it was obvious from their panicked shrill grunts they were not able to get it to open.

The one who'd grabbed her was lying on the ground, trying weakly to make its way to its other companions. Dante stood over it, his lips peeled back from lethal fangs. The others froze as his gaze pinned them. Still watching them, he dropped to his knees, wrenched the creature up from the floor and sank his fangs into its neck. The Dark One hissed and gurgled as Dante ripped into flesh as well as blood. Alexis was frozen in horror, unable to look away as blood trickled down its throat, splattered the narrow chest. Dante's powerful back muscles rippled as he took a long, deep draught, then rose.

Before she could hide her eyes, he tore the creature's head free of his body and hurled it at the cowering group at the door.

"Get this out of here, and get out of my sight. I will have whatever I wish to have. You have what I give you. Be satisfied with that or become like him. Go get me more blood. *Now*."

They scrambled forward, staying as far from Dante as possible as they caught their dead comrade by a loose arm. Hauling him out the now open door, they closed it on his leg in their haste, so they had to reopen it, jerk the leg through and then slam it. The reverberation was loud in the silence.

Alexis could hear her own laboring breath. At least with their departure, that suffocating desolation eased from unbearable to intolerable. But she was covered in blood. It was in her wings, her hair, the crevices of her scales. She wondered that her mind had not shut down at the ghastliness of it, but there was no mercy in this place, such that ruthlessness permeated even brain function.

Dante stood exactly where he'd killed the creature, his eyes pinned on the door. She realized his lips were moving, and that terrible feeling was lessening even further. It had come in with those creatures, and left with them, so he had this room warded from whatever it was they emanated, at least enough to make it manageable.

While she'd never been so frightened in her life, she had to think. Though she'd never anticipated needing such a thing, she'd taken a self-defense course with Clara. Grasping for anything to calm herself, she remembered the most important thing the instructor had emphasized. *You may not know how to get out of a situation, but if you keep your wits about you, something may present itself. It's probably the hardest thing, but you have to stay calm. Above all else, protect your ability to think.*

That community college course was hell and gone from where she was now. But she supposed a woman pursued by a mugger into a dark alley felt the same way. Her father, who'd fought Dark Ones for centuries, said the same thing about being in battle. She'd heard him instructing new recruits. "You *always* stay levelheaded. That's the most important thing."

Easier said than done. Her body was still twitching from that latest encounter with the charged sides of her prison. She pushed herself up on her arms again. At least the blood was helping keep her scales somewhat lubricated, but that wouldn't last long. Dante stopped his chant then. He picked up a tattered cloth from the arm of his chair, wiped his face and chest with his back toward her. As he turned, a smear of it remained on his throat and jaw, like a warrior's face paint. Her heart leaping into her throat, she took her first look at her captor, her dream, in the terrible flesh.

The dream had been a bridge between their two realities, not a distorted view. At least not physically. Still tall and beautiful in an unsettling, unearthly way, still sculpted with lean muscle. He wore a pair of ragged trousers only, and she wondered where he'd obtained them in this strange place. Then she remembered his words. *Bring me more blood.* She recoiled. *Whose* blood was she in? Whose blood had provided the tracings for those brands on her flesh? He'd put his mouth on her, his hands, his . . . Oh, Goddess.

"Why?" she rasped, when he didn't seem disposed to speak first.

He crouched on the outside of her circle. Unlike his fellows, apparently the caster could cross the edge. But when he did, reaching toward her face, she scrambled back, careful not to hit the opposite side, but making it clear she was not willingly going to allow him to touch her again. "It was all a trap. A lie."

His face remained dispassionate. "Yes. A trap."

"Why? What do you want from me?"

"Nothing." He cocked his head, a sparse motion. "A witch made a vow to me. I'm holding her to it, and you are the way I will do it."

"Mina?"

He nodded. "She promised if I proved myself capable of leaving this world, she would free me. I have taken her goddaughter, and you will die, slowly, painfully, if she does not release me. That shows I am capable of doing what is necessary to leave this world. I have sent her that message. It was even more difficult magic than what was necessary to come into your dreams, so the message is short. But if she heard it, she will respond to me."

"Please . . ." Lex tried to drag in another breath. "Stop scaring me."

Dante's brow creased. "I am simply telling you what is."

"I can't breathe."

"You are in your merangel form, so your lung capacity is diminished. The air here is not suitable for your life-form. Any of them," he added, his attention pausing on the wings, then coming back to dwell on her face.

Her father and mother spoke little of the Dark One world, but she knew that something that wasn't a Dark One couldn't survive long here, no more than a Dark One could survive long away from it. Which meant the being before her was at least a sorcerer, for she was being protected by his spell. Since her breath was still labored and the crush of all those despondent energies upon her felt like she was in a box that would soon cave inward, either the spell was weak or the outside energies were that strong. Studying his crimson eyes, she was betting on the latter.

"What are you?" Though she wasn't sure she wanted to know. His ability to tear the head off a creature that looked strong as an ox confirmed he wasn't just a sorcerer.

"Dark Spawn. Half vampire, half Dark One."

"Vampire?" Of course he was a vampire. He'd drunk her blood in the dream.

Think, Lex. What are your strengths here? What can you do? Now that the other creatures were gone, her skills as an empath were more accessible. She could detect his feelings and emotions. He hadn't been an easy read in her dreams, but what about here? It was possible her own feelings had distracted her there, not any shields he had.

He'd circled around to the other side, and was trying to touch her again. Lex scooted away and winced as several of her scales rubbed the wrong way. "Stop it."

"Why? I wish to touch you."

"You've kidnapped me, thrown me in a pool of blood, threatened me with gang rape by a group of monsters and told me that if you don't get what you want I'm going to be the pawn you kill—painfully and slowly."

"I did not say I would kill you. I said you would die. You liked it when I touched you before. Why would you not take pleasure from that now, particularly if there may be no pleasure later?"

Alexis stared at him. "You must be joking."

Dante's lips firmed. "There is no laughter here. At least, not the kind you suggest. I've seen that," he added. "When the rifts to your world could be opened, I saw it as if through this window here." He nodded toward the archway. "Sometimes the rift opening gave me little except for the colors of the terrain, but sometimes it would open into a smaller place, like a building, and I could see humans.

"I did not know then what I saw was laughter, but the Dark Ones called it that. What causes laughter? I saw you do it when I followed you in your dreams, before I ever touched you. You laughed a great deal." He stretched out his hand again. "I want to touch your face. Come closer. Or I will come into the circle."

Alexis held his gaze, her mind whirling. "No. I don't want you to touch me."

There was a quaver to her voice she could tell he registered, but she held her ground. He could come after her, yes, but she would not move.

After a long, charged moment, when she wondered if he'd throw her against that electrified barrier himself, he spoke. "If you were not frightened or hurt, would you want me to touch you?"

When she swallowed, she realized her jaw hurt from holding it so rigid. In fact, her whole body hurt for that reason. She'd never realized how being terrified could turn the body into stone, all the muscles stretched to the point the fibers would break, the stomach in permanent knots.

"I don't know. You really can't do anything about that, can you? I mean, you just said you'll do terrible things to me if Mina doesn't let you go."

"That is later. What matters is now. What can I do now that will make you less frightened?" There was a touch of impatience in his tone.

"Of course later matters." Lex struggled to stay calm. "How can I just forget what might happen later?"

Dante sat back on his heels, propping his elbows on his thighs. There was frank puzzlement in his expression. "Because here, only now matters. Nothing is hurting you right now. Nothing is happening to frighten you. In five minutes that might change, so you should not waste this moment thinking about what will happen in five minutes."

It was Zen, but Zen applied in a way she'd never considered. No, that wasn't correct. Something about the words was familiar. Forcing back her anxiety with her circumstances, she searched her mind. Yes, that was it. A book she'd read in a sociology course she'd audited, written by a survivor of the Holocaust. He'd spoken about the need to savor the maximum in every relatively peaceful moment in the concentration camp, because that moment was all you were assured. When you lived in daily horror, there was nothing else to do.

She took deep breaths, a meditation exercise much easier in the tranquility of her back porch with the sun rising and a day of pleasures stretching ahead of her. "Dante, how long have you been here?"

"I was born here."

"Your parents, then. They—"

"My mother was brought here. I was spawned by the Dark Ones who raped her."

She knew little of vampires, but natural offspring were very rare and usually hybrids. Dark Spawn, as he'd said. "Is your mother—"

"I killed her."

While his expression didn't change, Lex felt something from him, her senses grasping through her fear to find it. It wasn't regret, but it was loss. Muted, dulled, but there. The truth was more than a cold-blooded life taking. She just wasn't brave enough to pursue it further at this second.

Plus, she was picking up a strong yearning. He did want to touch her. It wasn't a sexual need, though there was a component of that there. It was more like he craved something he'd had for far too short a time, and he wanted more of it.

"All right," she said quietly. "I'm going to try to live in the moment, but you're going to have to help me, because we don't do that in my world. And I am very frightened, Dante. You scare me, and those creatures, they scare me even worse."

"They will not touch you." The change in his expression and voice was instant. Strong, deadly, and his hand closed into a fist on his thigh. "They should not have tried. They will not do so again."

She nodded, digesting that. Knowing her pulse was leaping in her throat like a bird about to keel over dead from stress, she flexed her hands on the wet stone. She winced at the slimy texture, the stronger waft of odor making her stomach turn over again. "Do I have to stay in this circle?"

"It was to keep you from running away, and them from getting to you. I have warded the door, but you would be able to leave."

"I won't leave," she said, and meant it. She knew what was out-side that door and no way in hell was she going out of it. "But it would really help if I could get out of this blood and clean up. Is there water? My tail needs to stay moist. It won't fall off or anything, but the scales get brittle if they dry out, and it's painful."

He held her gaze again, that penetrating stare. It was astounding, how handsome he truly was. Knowing she might be dealing with a sociopath of a magnitude even humankind didn't have the circum-stances to produce was beyond unsettling. "You want to touch me, too," he observed.

"It's a biological reaction, not an emotional one," she snapped. His brow raised and she pressed her hands to her face, trying to calm herself. It smeared more blood on her cheeks. "Please, let me out of this. I can't bear it."

He leaned forward in his kneeling position, one foot entering the pool. She flinched as he slid his hands under her body. "I don't want you touching me."

"Yes. But you can't walk, and you are too weak to fly or pull yourself across the chamber."

Gazing over his shoulder as he strode across the room, she saw his bare foot leaving a trail of bloody prints. As he moved into a separate, smaller area, she tried to wrap her mind around what she was seeing before her.

It looked like a miniature replica of an aboveground small pond, complete with tall grasses clustered around it, colorful, sparkling flowers peeking through their strands, rocks piled around the base to hold them. There was a butterfly in a sphere of light, floating over the water like a bubble.

"The water comes from our ice. I cut it into chunks and put it here, and it melts. It is not very clean, but I was making one of your ponds."

"That's what it looks like," she said. His surge of satisfaction was instant, though it was guarded, bound up tightly in other emotions she couldn't read.

As they moved closer, she saw the reality of what he'd created. The vat was a large piece of metal roughly molded into something capable of holding water. The edges were sharp, unfinished. What appeared to be grass were tendrils of hair, waxed and textured to emulate the wheaten blades. The flowers were precious jewels bound with pieces of the hair to slender black twigs so they bent like flowers. The butterfly in the sphere was real but dead, its wings forever spread.

It was macabre, but an undeniable artistic accomplishment. She tried to focus on the latter as he lowered her into the water. It had a terrible sulfur smell, but at least it wasn't blood. She reached out with trembling fingers to touch the lighted sphere. She couldn't bring herself to ask the question, but he answered anyway.

"It came here before the Earth rifts were sealed. It fell off the body of a human and the other Dark Ones didn't notice. Preserving it was the first magic I learned."

"Did someone teach you?" Alexis pushed on it, watched it circle back to her, float around her head.

"Before the Mountain Battle, our strongest Dark Ones were mages. I was taught to read their texts to help them with their spells, but I wasn't able to try any of them until after they were gone. This tower was destroyed by the witch, but I dug out the books and rebuilt it. There were many things to learn here. I learned all of them. And more."

There was no boast to it, only simple acknowledgment. Digesting that, Lex rubbed the blood off her body, working carefully around the throbbing symbols burned on her sternum, below her breasts, and on her lower abdomen. She wanted to douse her wings as well, but when she tried to bring them into the "pond," they caught on the unfinished edges of the tub.

As she struggled to free herself, Dante bent forward. Grasping the curve, he stretched out the closest wing and lifted it free, then guided it into the water, following the contour so she could fold it to her back. He repeated the same process with the other. He stroked her feathers before letting her pull them in. The way he studied them brought to mind how the Dark Ones had leathery wings, no softness or feathers to them.

When she'd removed the blood, she stretched both wings out, lifting them high enough to clear the tub this time, and gave a vigorous flap to dislodge the water. Water sprayed everywhere, including over the immovable Dante. *What causes laughter?*

"If circumstances were different," she ventured cautiously, "*that* would have made me laugh." *Very different.* Laughing was the last thing she wanted to do right now.

His brow furrowed, the droplets sliding down his cheek. His crimson gaze moved from her wings to her throat and face. Leaning forward, he kissed her.

Six

N O. A part of her immediately rebelled, but as if anticipating her, he put his hand on the back of her head, holding her in place.

Live in the moment, Alexis.

Now that she knew she wasn't in a dream, his voice in her head stunned her, such that she remained frozen. He should have been rank with blood, and she did smell it on his breath, but perhaps because he was a vampire, it was integrated into whatever he was and didn't repel her as she expected it to do. But her own body's response confused her even more.

Her betraying lips softened under his, parting as he slid his tongue between them, played with her mouth in a way that reinforced again how quickly he adapted to direction. Gentle but passionate at once, and it muddled her head in a way it shouldn't have. No, it should. Because she was getting myriad signals from him. The simple ignorance of a cruel child, a man's passionate, overwhelming desire for her and something deeper, the thing that perhaps was most confusing and compelling of all. She couldn't say what it was, but somewhere beneath the layers, it drew her. It was related to need, his need for her specifically. Her certainty that this need wasn't related to her role as a bargaining chip was what kept her from drawing away. This was something indefinable, maybe something even he didn't recognize.

"Why did you do that?" she asked when he raised his head.

"You relaxed when you kissed me, before, so I thought it would help you be less frightened. And I wanted to kiss you." His eyes heated. "I want to be inside you again."

It was possible to do that, of course, even in her merform, but she wasn't going to tell him that. However, when his gaze flickered, she stilled in shock. "You can hear my thoughts."

"Yes. The second mark is one of the ways I was able to pull you through to my world. That, and many sacrifices."

"Sacrifices? As in living beings?" Lex's gaze went back to the circle. *Of course, living beings, you idiot. Did that kiss scramble your mind? The blood didn't come from him.* Despite her attempt not to go there in her mind, she remembered the blood streaked on his body, along with the barely leashed savagery she'd welcomed as a titillating part of her dream. But as an impassioned lover, not as a creature who'd come to her by ripping away the life of another. What was the matter with her?

"That's hideous. Stop touching me." She drew as far away from him in the tub as possible, the trapped feeling of her weakened and transformed state returning. "Oh, Goddess, you don't get it, do you? Please tell me you don't, because I don't want you to be this hideous. I don't want to know that I enjoy kissing a complete monster."

Dante frowned. "It needed to be done. It was the only way to become free of this place. The seawitch said—"

"That's not what Mina meant," she shot back. "She meant you had to prove yourself *worthy* to leave this place. A good person. Good works."

He gave her that look as if she were speaking a foreign language again. "I've fought to be the leader of all that are left here. I hold complete control, if I am ever vigilant. I have mastered what magical energies exist in this world and myself to bring you here. What else can I do?"

He stared at her, a hopelessly beautiful man in ragged piecemeal trousers, his broad chest still stained with blood, black hair lying on his shoulders like a silken prince's mantle. Crimson eyes intelligent, piercing, but so uncomprehending. Despairing, so close to giving in to her own hysteria, Lex glanced toward the window, and saw the barren landscape again. Chilling images of fire and ice, those horrible, soulless creatures circling like flies searching out carrion, though flies had a nobler purpose, a part of Nature.

She recalled again the Dark Ones who'd been allowed into the chamber, the overwhelming flood of desolation and death from them. She'd felt no compulsion to ease their suffering, because there was nothing to them but death and evil. It was the first time in her life she'd felt that way. So if they were the only species in this world, all he'd ever known, what could he have done to prove he was capable of living in that other world?

"Why didn't you just ask for help?" she asked.

When she turned her attention back to him, she could tell she'd surprised him. He was still squatting on his heels by his makeshift pond, his fingers curled on the lip, unaffected by the sharp metal edge. Swallowing her fears and following instinct, she made herself move back across the tub and laid her hand over his. Focusing hard on their hands and not the blood staining his body, she pressed her fingers into the spaces between his, moving his attention there so she wasn't pinned under the weight of that unsettling gaze. "When you were in my dreams, why didn't you just ask for my help?" she repeated. "I'm her goddaughter, after all."

"Why would you help me? You have no reason to do that, nothing to gain." He raised a shoulder. "Once she'd known I was in your dreams, she would have sealed that avenue to me. It has taken me a very long time to build it. Ever since she came here."

Over twenty years. Alexis couldn't wrap her mind around the idea of dedicating twenty years to anything, but then, what else was there to do here? Starbucks obviously hadn't set up a franchise in this place. Mentally she thanked Clara for helping her develop an involuntary sense of humor, to carry her through times completely devoid of it. Until now, she'd never realized how useful it might be in a crisis situation.

Dante had risen, moving to a rack constructed of more black wood. It held assorted cloths of dubious cleanliness and textures, everything from wool to denim. He brought one back as a makeshift towel. "I am going to take you over there." He nodded to a bundle of rags in a wood frame, something between a nest and a bed. "Unless you'd prefer to stay where your tail stays wet."

"No, that's fine. I just have to wash it down every so often. It doesn't have to be immersed." The somewhat slimy liquid was far from the fresh rush of water of her ocean, so with the blood removed, she was more than ready to get out. But then she thought of what he might want if he laid her in the bed. The traitorous tightening of her body alarmed her even more than his intentions. "Why are you taking me over there?"

"You said you did not want to be in the circle, and you do not want to stay in the pond. Unless you wish me to lay you on stone, it is the best place."

She glanced at the large wooden chair. While it was imposing and somewhat sinister, she saw the same skill in the interweaving of the thicket of black shiny wood as she saw in the construction of his "pond." "There's that. I can sit up."

"Only I sit in that chair." Lifting her, he took her toward the bed. Curving her hand around his neck, beneath the strands of his hair, was the most obvious place to hold on. His hair truly was like silk, the cords of muscle beneath his smooth skin tempting touch. *Goddess help me. His sorcery isn't just for magic spells.*

"I might sit in it later, and hold you on my lap, if you wish." He seemed to roll that around in his mind. "I think I would like that."

Lex swallowed. "What . . . how long will you wait for Mina's answer?"

"*Ssshh.* There is only now."

Though the child of extraordinary parents, Alexis realized she wasn't immune to the coping mechanisms of any kidnap victim. Trying to identify with her kidnapper in psychologically hazardous ways, feeling an empathy for him she shouldn't. But unlike other kidnap victims, empathy was her extraordinary ability. She didn't know if that would make her more vulnerable to the pitfalls of those coping mechanisms, or if it gave her strengths and defenses that would prove useful. Of course, as Dante had said, she only had this moment, and since she had nothing better to do . . .

Since he could hear her thoughts, there was no dissembling, no hiding of her strategy. But she also couldn't hide her confusing array of reactions to him, and so far he didn't seem concerned with her thoughts, at least not enough to retaliate to them. He was dispassionate about many horrible things, but when it came to her, he was far from dispassionate. That had to be useful also, right?

When he knelt to lay her down, she noted he had no more trouble with that than if he'd been carrying a small doll. Vampires had great strength, or so the lore went. From the little she knew, they were considered dangerous and unpredictable and, like all creatures that humans considered supernatural, didn't go out of their way to be noticed.

"If you were born here, how old were you when your mother . . . died?"

"When I killed her, I was about one half of the size I am now."

So he'd been an adolescent, perhaps about twelve or thirteen. She gathered her courage. "Why did you kill her, Dante?"

Settling her on the blanket, he considerately adjusted her hips so her tail was straightened. As he eased her back, there was time for her to fold her wings beneath her. The ragged blankets were musty, with lingering traces of blood, but she suspected they were as clean as any place she'd be offered here. The wooden support wasn't uncomfortable. Just her surroundings.

As he looked down, it was hard not to look away. The pros and cons of empathy she understood, but this was incomprehensible. When he did that, his face so close, she couldn't help but think of his kiss.

You want me to kiss you again.

Ignoring his thought, she tried to understand it in herself. Was it shock, her mind's way of blocking her from the true horror of what he'd done to her and to others? Did it make any sense to even dwell on that right now, when survival was paramount? She could have moral dilemmas later. Of course, wasn't that pretty much what he'd said to her earlier, about living in the moment? Did she have to *become* him to survive this?

He touched her chin so her gaze lifted from where it had fallen to his bare chest, coming back to his perfect, soulless face. No, he had a soul. That was the problem. That was where an empath connected. Only if she let what she felt there make her oblivious to everything else would she be guilty of the destructive coping syndromes so many captives used. If she used it as the tool it was, as finely tuned as an artist's brush, then that would be all right.

The logical grounding point steadied her. Unfortunately, that touch didn't. And it was only the knuckle of his crooked forefinger, slowly following the line of her jaw. Up, up toward her ear, the other fingers alighting on her throat, the leaping pulse. When his index finger stroked along the sensitive gill slit just beneath her ear, her fingers dug into the bundle of rags.

"Dante," she managed, "you didn't answer my question."

"What question?" Leaning down, he settled his lips on the path his fingers had traced. She drew her breath in through her clenched teeth as his arm around her back tightened, bringing her upper body against his bare chest. Her breasts rubbed against the hard muscle. Lex scrambled for focus.

"You know what. You're just trying to distract me."

"I have no need to do that. Whatever your question is, I will answer it when I wish. Until then, just feel, Alexis."

It was the first time he'd said her name aloud, outside of dreams, and she desperately thought it possessed all the power that magic claimed came from giving someone your true name. Alexis was the name she gave others, but she had a birth name as well. It was only known by her parents and Mina and David, as her godparents. It had been used to spin protective magics around her at birth, only they hadn't been enough, had they? Of course, if it was her own actions that had brought her here, perhaps she herself was to blame for overriding those protections.

"You liked me in your dreams. You looked forward to coming to me. So why do you not want to be here now?"

"I didn't know you were hurting others. I didn't think you'd hurt me."

Despite the fact her body was sizzling at his touch, her own words brought her up short. She didn't *think* that someone would hurt her.

She knew it. She even knew the distinction between malevolent intent, and someone who, because of the dark madness of his mind, might do harm without intention. At this point, Dante could fall into either category.

She'd had a lifetime of training, and she had to believe in it. He was right. Not only had she wanted to be with him, she'd been sure that was where she was meant to be. She still felt it. Why would her intuition draw her to a being of darkness, unless he was more than that, possessing a hidden light only she could find?

Bringing her attention back to him, she saw his eyes following every expression of her face. "You won't hurt me."

"Yes, I will. I will do what I must to leave here."

"Would you be sorry?" At his look of incomprehension, she almost despaired, then she seized on another thought. "Would you regret, Dante? Do you regret killing your mother? Did it make you feel sad?"

He drew back from her, and the loss of his touch was staggering, particularly in these desolate surroundings. While the change in his expression made him more feral looking, he also looked younger, suggesting he was looking back into that earlier version of himself.

"No. I didn't regret it. But it did make me sad. Because I was alone then. They always had her chained, because she was strong. I didn't realize that I had her strength, not for a long time. They often denied me blood, kept me weak to hide my strengths, make me always afraid." He lifted a brow, his crimson eyes glowing. "I do not fear anything anymore."

He lifted a shoulder. "They knew just enough about a vampire to keep her alive, year after year. Before she died, my mother gave me her memories, through her blood. She also spoke of your world, when I was old enough to understand her words. She told me that was my home, not this place." A hint of fang, a vicious anger like volcanic lava roughened his voice, then was gone. "A place of green grass, blue skies."

He settled then, one knee bent, the other folded beneath him. Since the ragged trousers were thin, and touching her had aroused him, his organ was clearly outlined. Remembering its punishing invasion, a part of her flinched, but another part contracted, moistened, as if she sought him again.

"What do you wish first?" He moved his hand down to give himself a functional stroke. "This, or my words?"

"Your words," she retorted. "I don't want that. And yes, I know you'll say it's a lie, but like I said before, it's biology. Anatomy."

"No, it is not only that. It's curious. I didn't expect to want you this much, either." After that enigmatic statement, he continued. "When her mind broke, she lost her will to live. She stopped speaking to me. She was my only food source at that point, but . . ."

He paused, and Alexis watched his expression shutter further, though she sensed him delving even deeper, perhaps for feelings he hadn't examined in some time. "There was a moment her importance to my survival didn't matter. I didn't like seeing her that way. I killed her, because she begged me to do it. She told me to kill myself, too. Told me how to do it. It was the last thing she said to me."

His gaze narrowed on her then. "I can hear your thoughts. This makes you feel sad, for me."

"Yes," she said honestly. "It was truly terrible. She must have loved you very much, to have held out as long as she did. What happened when they found her dead?"

He shrugged. "They hurt me worse than usual, for a time. But I am the only child that has been born here. No captive ever survives the Dark One world more than a few days. Humans die within hours. For a time, Dark Ones thought they'd found a way to procreate, and they sought to bring more vampires here, but the few they found did not conceive and they gave up. My mother told me vampire children are extremely rare."

"So you've never had females here, except your mother."

"No." He shook his head. "The witch came here, with her mate. She injected him with Dark One blood so he could bear it. I didn't get to touch her, though. But when the Dark Ones took her to the top of the west tower, a lock of her hair caught on their claws and it drifted on the wind. To me. It twined about my hand." Lifting his fingers, he studied them as if remembering the way it had looked. "It was the foundation to the dream portal. I had to be so careful, for she is very clever, the witch. I could see her reality, but had to be a shadow, never noticed. I saw her at your birth. Saw her later, involved in your teaching. Saw she was fond of you, and you were the weakest thing that mattered to her."

"I am not weak," she protested.

Circling her slender wrist, he held her arm up. When she tried to pull away from the hard grip, she was unable to move. His touch wasn't bruising, just overpowering. She felt his arousal increase at her resistance, and her stomach fluttered. The impressive array of lean muscle across his chest tightened as well. "You cannot prevail against me."

"Not with physical strength. But I could completely whip your ass with my mind."

"No, you couldn't." He went to one elbow next to her, stretching out on his hip in a disconcertingly casual pose she'd seen students on the campus lawn assume when studying on a pretty day. Though this was as far from those surroundings as she could imagine. "You use your mind to live," he pointed out. "Mine has been used to survive, to plan and destroy. To conquer and invade."

She set her teeth. It was a good thing she'd dealt with angels all her life. Jonah and his all-male Legion defined arrogance with a capital *A*. Vampire males seemed to have a similar attitude, though she had to admit, both had cause. Dante didn't seem prone to exaggeration. Jonah wasn't, either. Tears pricked her eyes at the thought of her father, so far away. As a little girl's fear rose in her breast, she pushed it away, because she couldn't afford that here.

Dante shifted closer. In a swift movement she didn't anticipate, he'd turned her to her side, bringing his body flush against the back of hers, his chest pressed into her wings, his arms coming around her to take possession of her breasts like in her dream. Hard male hands closed on soft female flesh, fingers stroking the nipples in a way that had her arching and pushing her hips back against him in involuntary response.

Her caudal fin was a feathery gold, as satiny as hair under water. With no water here to let it float, it was folded against her. It concealed the dampening channel to her sex that could be reached through the layering of scales that were softer there, allowing for penetration.

"Dante," she said in quiet desperation. "You were talking about your mother. And how you . . . brought me here." *Ah, Goddess, that felt too damn good.* What was the matter with her?

"Yes, but I will not permit you to be afraid. This distracts you from your fear."

"Won't permit, or can't bear? Does my fear bother you, Dante?" The word came out on another gasp. While he'd left a hand tormenting her breast, the other slipped behind her, trailing down her back, through the folding line of her wings, down the layered scales on her hips and buttocks. As if her mind was a treasure map he read as easily as a pirate could read his own charts, he moved the limp caudal fin and found those soft scales, stroking and causing her to quiver, then cry out softly as his fingers pushed into the slick heat waiting for him.

"Not just biology," he whispered against her ear, a fang grazing her cheek. "Biology would be my touch making you wet. But you were wet before my fingers pushed into you. That is your mind. You want me. Take me now, and let go of your fear."

The denial rose to her lips, but his command was extraneous. He would do as he wanted, for to his way of thinking, she was his. And his possession meant more to him than her status as his prisoner, because it was that to which her body was responding.

She'd automatically tensed, remembering his earlier invasion, but this time, after a brief adjustment of the thin trousers, he seated himself in the opening of her sex, a sensual taunt that undulated her against him. He moved with her, as if they were two sea creatures in truth, twisting in the current of the ocean. She didn't know what current they were dancing in now, but it did exist, even in this terrible place that offered nothing but this brief pleasure.

He crossed his arms in front of her again, one palm holding each breast, creating a unique dance there as well. Exploring and squeezing, stroking, pinching, a thorough self-indulgent use of her body for his pleasure that had her even more slippery. When he slid in another inch, she moaned, spasming against his length. One hand dropped, a palm flattening against her belly, and he found the navel piercing, today a tiny silver dolphin with a sapphire stone. Teasing it, twisting it, dipping his finger into that indentation, his other fingers fanned out low on her pelvis. She should have anticipated him, but she was lost in the sensation, so that when he used that hand to push her all the way down on him, taking him deep, it was a spear of pleasure that ripped another cry from her throat, not pain.

This is new. I have not known this before. The way you respond to me . . . it's as if nothing else exists, but in a way different from living in just one moment. This moment is all that is, ever was, or will be.

Because of the fluid, poetic wonder of his words, she wasn't sure if he was speaking directly to her or had opened his mind, allowing her to tap into the flow of his subconscious thoughts. Because of that, she didn't question her own actions. Alexis reached back to find his face, threaded her fingers in his hair and mewled when he laid a hot, open-mouthed kiss on her wrist. She clutched him, working her hips harder.

Yes, I like that. Slide yourself up and down my cock.

Now that was a direct thought, for the note of command in it spurred her own reaction. She obeyed, but as she tired, his strength took over, helping her to keep climbing. While stress and fear had drained her, she knew her physical strength had been sapped by the poison of this place. It had robbed her of breath and energy to reach the pinnacle her body desperately wanted.

His own urgency was a fire that swept through her blood. When he bent his head, set his teeth to her neck, she let her head fall back to his shoulder, overwhelmed. *You won't hurt me, you won't hurt me . . .*

Her tail thrashed with her movements. Usually it would have been a powerful muscle to aid their rhythm, but now it floundered along his calf, her tail fins unfurling on his feet, over the strong, callused arches. He was buried in her wings, his shoulders likely teased by the layers of pale feathers. A couple of them floated past, dislodged by the intensity of their coupling. Damn it, the lack of oxygen was making things gray around the edges, and yet she was so close.

Then he bit her. Something released in her blood that sparkled and tingled like the surprise pleasure of champagne, with an afterburn that intensified the experience. A drop rolled down her throat, but when it reached the curve of her breast, it was her blood mixed with an ethereal blue color, almost reminding her of the color of angel blood. Whatever it was, it was an aphrodisiac with all the emotional intimacy such a physical drug lacked. All of a sudden, she was bonded so closely to him, the sensation of his orgasm took her over the edge. She moaned, moving with him as if they were the same body. Clara had told her finding such a rhythm was supposed to be both fun and frustrating for two lovers. In contrast, with this melding, she knew everything he wanted at the same blink in time he did, a dance where she was already in his head, learning the steps, so they twirled amid terrible fire and pain. But the heat merely fanned the intensity of the orgasm. When she saw it yawning below her, she realized the chasm of violence and rage she was staring into was the deepest level of Dante's mind. Then all was black and shuddering pleasure, as the climax stole her breath and whirled her into oblivion.

Seven

"JONAH," Mina warned, "Do not make me knock you unconscious."

In her human form, the witch's head barely reached the middle of Jonah's chest. But David didn't feel like laughing, nor did anyone in the seawitch's underwater cave. As Prime Legion Commander, Jonah was the second most powerful angel in the Goddess's army, capable of destroying worlds with barely a thought. As powerful as he was, Mina could outmatch him, her dark powers capable of consuming a galaxy.

"This is not helping," David said. Since he was normally the quiet one, they glanced toward him. David met Jonah's gaze, nodded to the ledge behind him, hoping the reminder would help him hold on to his self-control. Anna sat there, her tail immersed in the water Mina had pushed back with an airbell so the assembled angels could stand on the wide platforms of stone. Anna's hands were clasped on her lap, her head down as if in deep thought. The golden tresses were so long the shining curls pooled in her lap, covering her fingers.

She'd always been a creature of joy and light; in fact it was her very nature that had turned Jonah away from darkness and the potential of world destruction nearly twenty-one years ago. But now she had a look of anguish so profound, David could understand why Jonah was willing to tear anything apart to get his daughter back. That, plus the commander loved his daughter deeply. Alexis was the precious symbol of their love, grown into a remarkable young woman they would willingly die to keep safe. As would everyone here, even his irascible witch.

On that thought, David turned his gaze back to her. "Mina," he said. "Tell them what happened, as you explained it to me."

She gave him a querulous look with her unusual bicolored eyes, one jewel blue, one crimson red. Whereas Jonah used clean, hot rage that could shake the firmament like an earthquake, his witch would choose bitter, deep-seated anger that would skin it alive. They each had unique methods of dealing with stress. Both were effective when properly channeled, but scary when rubbing rough edges against one another. It was a delicate situation. David could handle Mina, but handling both was an unsettling business. He wished Lucifer was here. The Lord of the Underworld was strong enough to remind the usually levelheaded Jonah that he needed to think like a commander, not a father.

"All right," Mina spoke at last. "Somehow, Dante pulled Alexis's physical body into the Dark One world through dream magic."

"You should have killed him when you saw he was gaining power in his world," Jonah said tightly.

Mina arched a brow. "You were just as aware of him, because I have been giving you the reports when I view that world through my visions and the doorway." She glanced behind her, toward a darkened tunnel.

At one time, Mina had lived in these underwater caverns, and this had been her library. She returned here now only to practice spellwork that required stronger wardings, because this was one of the most heavily warded places on Earth, containing the one remaining physical portal to the dangerous Dark One world. For over two decades, she'd used it only as a one-way window, as she'd referenced now.

"He obviously concealed much, because he is aware of my scrutiny. That ability was as impressive as the dream portal. He has become far more powerful in the past twenty years than either of us gave him credit to become. So do not lash out too much with your blame, Commander, until you flog yourself with it first."

Jonah made a noise that echoed through the caverns with the

deadly malevolence of a Kraken come to life. Mina hissed back, baring the sharp canines that revealed her Dark One origins. Her one blue eye and one crimson glittered with warning from beneath the strands of thick dark hair scattered across her fair brow. David tensed.

"Please, stop it. Both of you." Anna, now shifted to human form to move across the rock, slipped past Jonah and gripped Mina's arm. Her face was pale but determined. "Mina, tell us what to do. I can't bear this . . . please."

When Mina glanced toward Anna, relief swept David. The person for whom the two shared a deep love might be as effective as Lucifer. Temporarily.

The seawitch sighed. "To be honest, I'm not sure yet. He sent me a message. It was faint. I think he depleted a great deal of his reservoir bringing her across. He's lucky it reached me," she grumbled, as if she wanted to chide him like a reckless student. "But it says"—she hesitated under Anna's strained glance—"'I want out, as you promised me. This proves my worth. Release me, or she will die in forty-eight of your hours.'"

David noted she didn't give them the full message, as she'd given it to him. The part detailing how Alexis would die, painfully and slowly. His witch had come far in twenty years. It would serve no purpose to share that with the agitated parents.

"Let him out," Jonah growled. "He will not have time to draw one breath here."

"A magic user capable of this may be capable of much more. You once underestimated me," Mina reminded him, the derision in her tone making David wince. "If we open a rift to him, he may bring the rest of the Dark Ones with him. Though it will be a much smaller force, he may have augmented them with more powers than they once had, and they were formidable then. Can you risk many in this world for one life?"

Jonah snarled. "I will risk whatever is necessary to bring her home."

"Which is why you are *not* the one who should be making the decision," Mina said ruthlessly.

Jonah spat out a stream of invective in the angels' ancient language that was creative and frightening. Mina stood impassively, waiting him out, and his fists clenched. "You are as cold and heartless as ever, witch," he snapped. "Perhaps our mistake wasn't only leaving *him* alive."

David stepped forward then. "That's enough, my lord. She's right. Listen to yourself."

Jonah's gaze shot to him. A cool rush of air, tinged with sulfur, heralded another arrival. Lucifer materialized from the water, wielding his scythe. The dark angel's face was cold, mouth set. Jonah didn't turn, holding his attention on his lieutenant.

"She's in that world, David. You told me what that world is. Have you forgotten that I *saw* what they did to you? She's never known . . . from the minute she was born, I . . . Damn you all, she's our child."

The powerful angel broke off abruptly, turning away from them. Jonah had known loss for far too many years as a battle commander, the oldest of the non–Full Submission angels. He'd dealt with the fallout from that, but no one in the room needed to be told that his mate's love was what had brought him back to them. It was a fine line they all walked, fighting for the Legion.

David swallowed and looked away, as did the four other angels in the cavern. Marcellus was one of them, Jonah's right-hand captain until he'd been nearly killed in the Mountain Battle. He bore scars that hampered his flying, at least for full battle, but his loyalty to Jonah had brought him here today. David knew the whole Legion would be in this cavern if they would fit.

While they waited uncomfortably for their commander to get a grip on his emotions, Anna had no such reservations. She met his turn with open arms, holding him as she was subsumed in his own embrace, her body quivering in his arms. But she shed no tears, not now. The look on her face, the strained determination, reminded David that sometimes a mother showed a strength that could surpass the father's. It didn't mean her suppressed pain wouldn't shatter her if they lost Alexis. And if they lost Anna to that kind of grief, they lost Jonah. In Lucifer's face, he saw the same knowledge.

Mina moved in then. In one of her unexpected acts of compassion, she touched Anna, bringing the parents' attention back to her, though her expression remained as flat as ever. "We'll get her back. She's my goddaughter, and I'm sworn to protect her. If you do not believe in me, believe in my resolve, which as you know is quite formidable." A cynical smile twisted her lips then. "I didn't say we were without options. I can bring them through but separate them, contain him, with a magic similar to what he used. But it will take a great deal of preparation."

In Mina's gaze was a wealth of things David understood that no one else did, including the fact that Jonah wasn't the only one who'd seen what the Dark Ones had done to David. Mina had had a front-row seat. He knew the witch's heart was his, as much as every part of him was hers. As a result, when she looked at him now, he let that knowledge fill his gaze. The tension across her brow lessened.

"I'll give you a list of stores I'll need from our home." She glanced back to Anna and Jonah. "I'll need blood from both of you, as well as my own. It's going to be a lot," she added, attention going to David again, "so cookies and juice for Anna might not be amiss, and manna to replenish Jonah when I'm done. I also need to work very fast without taking time to reassure or explain to anyone what I'm doing, because it will take hours to prepare. In forty-eight hours she'll be dead, no matter what he does to her."

"Why is that?" Anna gripped the seawitch's arm. Rather than drawing away with the disdain she normally demonstrated at unwelcome touching, Mina covered the mermaid's hand with her own, met her blue eyes without flinching.

"Because nothing other than a Dark One, and Dante, can live in the Dark One world longer than that. It drains life energy. You know that," she added softly. "She is weakening even now. She might have longer if he's shielding her somehow, but knowing Dante, I wouldn't count on that."

Anna's lips quivered, but she firmed them. "Will she be okay, once she's back?"

"We make sure she gets back here, and then worry about that," Mina said in her usual brusque way. "There's nothing we can do until we have her here."

"All right, then." The pragmatic strategy seemed to rally Jonah.

He kept his arm around Anna, however, as he turned to Lucifer. "I know your answer, but I will ask anyway."

Lucifer shook his head. "The Lady sends Her grief and comfort, but you know She cannot touch the Dark One domain. Mina is your gateway." The Lord of the Underworld was the only angel with crimson lights in his dark eyes, and he shifted them now to the seawitch. "Though She said if you need additional energy to shore up your own, you need only call. Like all of us, She loves the merangel."

A strangled sob escaped Anna, and Jonah laid a hand on her hair. "Is there somewhere she could rest, Mina, until this—"

"No." Anna caught an edge of Jonah's wing, mopping her eyes in the feathers before tears could fall. "I'm fine. Alexis needs me to be fine. I'm not crying." She set her jaw and locked gazes with Mina. "Do what you need to do to get my daughter away from this bastard, so my mate can end him once and for all."

The harsh mother's anger that rolled through the cave was so unlike Anna's gentle voice, a shiver rippled up David's spine. But Mina simply nodded. "Let's get to work, then."

———

WHEN Alexis roused from her postcoital doze, her limbs felt heavy. It was strange to feel unwell and sexually sated at once. The buzzing roar was louder in her head, and she had a hard time lifting her upper body. But she pushed herself up, wrinkling her nose at the stench of blood, which seemed more pronounced than it had been when she was distracted by Dante's seduction, or perhaps—

"*Stop*," she cried out, but it was too late.

The humanoid, who reminded Alexis of the early Neanderthals she'd seen in pictures, was female. It was obvious because she was naked, and she'd been raped, her sensitive flesh torn, thighs and buttocks stained with blood too plentiful to be otherwise. Her breasts had been bitten, torn open. Where she lay on her stomach next to the ritual circle, her head was over the shallow basin. As a result, she was struggling, trying to keep her face out of the blood.

Dante had a knee on her back. When Alexis cried out, he'd seized a hank of the female's hair, pulling up her head at a hard angle. The knife made his intent clear. Lex was already off the bed and moving, pulling herself by her arms, flapping her wings despite her weakness.

He was far quicker. The efficient slash cut the female's throat open. Blood spurted into the circle, replenishing the pool. Alexis stopped, frozen, as life died out of the woman's eyes. She held Alexis's horrified gaze to the end though, as if she knew that was the only source of mercy in the room.

Even as her body jerked, the soul struggling to free itself, Dante shoved a cloth in the wound, soaking it. When he dropped the head with a liquid *thunk*, the face landing in the blood, Alexis flinched. Moving to the door without further attention to either female, he began to refresh the broad slashing marks there, muttering another chant.

Alexis scrambled to the female's side and lifted her head in both hands. With difficulty, she held her in one arm and used the fingers of the other to wipe the blood from the eyelids so the woman could see her. Alexis placed a trembling hand on the smelly, bloodsoaked hair, feeling the woman's terror and pain slowly ebb away with her life. She must have been brutalized out in the Dark One world, during the hours while Alexis slept. *Bring me more blood*, Dante had said. He hadn't specified how it was to be treated. That didn't matter to him at all.

"I'm sorry. Go in peace." As she murmured the prayer of passage taught to her by King Neptune himself, the heart made its final beat, the woman's eyes now empty glass.

Dante knelt on the other side of her, dipping the cloth in the fresh blood again. With a snarl, Alexis launched herself at him, using the wings to take her up and over the body. Weak as she was, she didn't get the clearance she needed, so she rolled the body like a log against him. But that added to his surprise as she plowed into him.

She'd never been a violent creature. She'd dutifully learned to pro-tect herself through Jonah's teachings and that self-defense course she'd taken with Clara, but she had no killer instinct. No plan propelled her, no thought of escape, just fury at what she'd seen. Self-revulsion gal-vanized her attack. Goddess, she'd felt bonded to him, connected. She hated this place, she wanted to go home, she never wanted to dream again. She wanted to bathe for days. She wanted to close her eyes, curl in a ball in her bed, surrounded by her stuffed animals, and not think until all the terrible memories of this place went away. And she never, *ever* wanted to smell blood again in her life.

While Dante was much faster and stronger, she had the satisfaction of knocking him on his ass and getting in several swift, if ineffectual, punches in his face, one of which caused his fang to stab his lip and created a flow of blood.

"Why did you kill her?" she wailed at him. "She didn't do anything to you."

In a flash of movement he shoved her off him, lifted and slammed her against the stone wall. Several of the slender bones in her right wing broke, crushed beneath her. She snarled in pain, but the adrenaline carried her through it with barely a blink. She bared her teeth. "You're a monster. Mina shouldn't free you. You should be locked in a cage."

"I am in a cage." He dropped her, so she fell to the stone at his feet, her wings limp around her shoulders like a blanket. Her scales scraped the rough stone. When he stepped back, his crimson eyes were orange and yellow flame, his mouth a hard slash. He pointed at the door. "Those symbols protect you from what's out there. That, and me, are the only things that protect you from what happened to her, and from you dying sooner here than you would otherwise."

"I'm *not* going to thank you when you're the one who pulled me over here in the first place," she retorted, blinking back tears. "I would never want you to kill someone."

"Even to preserve your own life?"

"I don't have that right. No one has that right."

A muscle flexed in his jaw. "That's incorrect, Alexis. In your world, lives are taken every day as a choice. Animals, because they cannot fight you. People, in wars, or in self-defense."

"That's different."

"Yes, it is." He pinned her with that hard glance. "Here you only live if you kill. You only survive if you kill. You only gain something of your own *if you kill*. I won't allow them to harm you."

"What about her?" She looked back at the woman. Because she didn't want to be near him, she dragged herself back across the ground. The woman had blue eyes, like Anna. Like Alexis. "What about her family, where she comes from? Why did you let the Dark Ones hurt her first?"

"Because there is a balance here," he said flatly. "You were awake to see it. I give them as much as necessary in order to maintain control over them. I may be more powerful than they are, more clever, but if they all turn against me at once, there is little I might do against them. Now be still and let me finish this."

He resumed his gruesome task, turning his back on her as if she mattered as little as the cooling corpse. A tool for him. Alexis stroked the woman numbly, studying her hard so she didn't have to look at anything else. *This will be me soon. Painfully and slowly . . .* She didn't know what was more difficult for her mind to process, what he'd just done, or what he knew they'd been doing to her while he'd been caressing and arousing Alexis's flesh.

"Did you think of her at all? Feel any remorse?"

He stopped, his arm poised over his head. The cloth was so wet blood dripped down his forearm, but he didn't appear to notice it. "Remorse, regret, sadness. Mercy and compassion. You want me to feel all these things. Have you ever raped someone to prove you could hold power over them? Killed them in cold blood because they stood between you and survival?"

She swallowed. "No. I can't even imagine such a thing."

He turned then, pinned her with his gaze. "Then you have the answer to your question. You cannot feel what you've never known. Nor can you pass judgment on it."

He returned to the door. Alexis drew a trembling breath, her fingers digging into cold rock as she tried to breathe through her mouth so she wouldn't inhale the blood smell anymore. She should go curl up on those rags, shut down and wait for the resolution of this without speaking to him further. Jonah and Mina, the whole heavenly host, would rescue her, or she'd die, and it would be over.

But she didn't sit around and wait for people to take care of her. Her parents had wanted her to stay in the safety of the Heavens or sea for at least another decade, but she'd chosen to go out on her own, take a human form and live a human life.

Holy Goddess, it was ridiculous to compare that kind of bravery to this. One moment she was deep inside his soul, touching something indefinable but worth understanding, an elusive knowledge that called to her. The next moment he was a brutal monster she couldn't fathom.

But she'd always trusted her gift. Anna was right. It was far more than a quirky personality trait. It was a blessing of the Goddess, to be used for good. *We don't know the full extent of your abilities . . .*

The Goddess might not have an influence in this world, but it didn't mean that this wasn't part of the destiny Alexis was supposed to fulfill. What if *this* was the type of situation in which she was supposed to stretch her abilities to their fullest? What did she have to lose?

The idea of concentrating her light force here the way she did back home was a herculean effort. She was already weak. But hell, if she was going to be dead in a few hours, shorting out her brain from overexertion was a minor issue. She spun the tendrils with painstaking care. When she sent them out, they wove along the ground like the concentrated passage of centipedes, for she couldn't achieve the normal lift for them.

The magic further bogged down in the blood splattered outside the circle. Lex faltered, remembering the frightened eyes of the dying woman, but then gave it another, harder push. When it finally reached Dante's heels, she closed her eyes, shutting out the chamber, every terrible thing she'd experienced here, even the weakness of her own body.

The passive side of her gift and angel light were what drew life unconsciously to her, as Branson had cheerfully observed. Only hours in the past, the memory seemed like a decade gone. She also could offer comfort to a sick soul, light to guide them to a better path. Mina had told her that, in addition to her gift and angel light, Lex had the innate goodness her mother carried. The witch had likened it to a virus that infected all it touched. Since her mother had merely looked amused, Lex assumed it was what passed for a compliment from Mina.

She didn't have to see the light to know where it was. Her subconscious felt it twining around his roped calves, the lean thighs and hard upper body. Did he never relax? How could he? How had a child survived here?

It was a reminder that her empathy not only opened up her target; it also opened up her own heart to a deeper understanding of the soul. The power was in the synergy between the two. Still vibrating with the horror of his crime, she knew she'd never needed the healing touch of that knowledge more, for herself even more than him.

Goddess, give me the courage to open myself to him, when everything in me wants to run.

Eight

Dante went back to marking the symbols, determined not to look at her. He hadn't intended to hurt her. He knew he'd broken her wing. While she'd attacked him, she wasn't strong enough to do him any harm. His reaction had been too emotional, out of control. The way she looked at him, when he was doing his best to protect her, displeased him. He wanted her to return safely to her world. He didn't want her to die. He'd had no wish to kill the female humanoid. It was simply necessary. That was all there was here.

Alexis's feelings weren't incomprehensible to him. Through his knowledge of her world, he knew what life could be there. While it seemed like a distant dream, so opposite from his existence here, it was her reality. She was not capable of understanding his, though, and that made him feel . . . empty.

No, he hadn't given a thought to the humanoid being brutalized before being brought to him. He'd suffered such brutality for decades before gaining an upper hand. How could he spare sympathy for this creature who'd had to experience it for barely one of Alexis's hours before they delivered her and he quickly and efficiently ended her life? A small exchange for keeping the balance of power in his world.

Alexis's horror, the tears in her eyes, the revulsion when she looked at him . . . What bothered him the most was not knowing why it bothered him. He liked it better when she looked at him with wary interest, or asked him questions. He wanted her to go back to that.

His need for cunning, his mother's memories and the higher echelon Dark Ones had honed his intellect, but there was no one to engage in conversation. For years he'd practiced talking with himself, so he could sound intelligent and precise, like his mother before her mind broke.

But Alexis was real, here, so he could speak with her. He would soon be in a world where he'd have many conversations, but he wanted to talk to her. That disturbing impatience returned, a lack of restraint he knew was dangerous. When it came to her, it was unwilling to be curbed, no matter how he tried. She made him feel connected to another in a way he'd never experienced.

He also liked how she acted when he touched her, aroused her. His hunger to do it over and over was unsettling. But it was not the physical part of the act that held the fascination, though that alone was enough to distract him. The rush of physical sensation became something else as it escalated. Or rather intertwined with something inside of him, a tangle of emotions he didn't understand. As much as he wanted free of this world, he found himself wishing he could spell them permanently in such a moment. Then her world and his world, none of it would matter, because there would be nothing else of importance, nothing to concern himself with ever again. Just as he'd told her in his mind. He hadn't expected to share that with her, either.

It was dangerous madness. Everything about his world was control, focus, vigilance. Drifting in a confusing, lust-saturated cloud was a sure way to disaster.

Then he felt her touch.

———

NOT her physical touch. Given her last attack, he was well aware of her proximity to him in the chamber, but he'd stayed out of her head, not wanting to hear further deprecations against him. But this was her gift, her empath's touch. He stiffened, intending to slam a protection over himself, but instead he waited, hovering on indecision, as the warmth of it slid over his skin. It burrowed deep, reaching into cold, dark areas, questing, like her gentle fingertips had sought his face, discovering him.

When he pivoted away from the door to face her, she'd moved back to the bed and was sitting up, the broken wing held at a careful angle, the other folded tight against her body. Her tail was a curve of red and gold, embellished with the gold fins. Her beauty was intensified by the contrast of her filthy surroundings. Something twisted in his chest. He should have done more to prepare the chamber for her.

"I'm trying to understand," she said. He heard the thickness in her voice, saw the effort in her strained face of exercising her magic here, in a place that rejected angels, humans . . . anything, really, except Dark Ones, and one particular vampire Dark Spawn. "I want to understand. Will you take me outside?"

He paused, not sure at first he'd heard her correctly. "No. It's not safe for you out there. There are no protections. You will weaken even faster."

Comprehension dawned in her gaze. Knowing how frightened and fragile she was, he grudgingly admired her ability to hold on to her courage, keep her wits and think. "That's what you meant, wasn't it? I'll die slowly and painfully because I can't live here, not because you're going to torture me, or kill me yourself."

"Of course." He cocked his head. "I have no intention of torturing you."

"Of course," she murmured, and a grim smile tugged at her mouth. "I'll take the risk. I need to see your world. Can you take me out for a while?"

He considered it. "There is a place near this tower I could take you. The path in between is not shielded from the Dark One energy, as this place is, but once we get there, it is. The Dark Ones will be able to see you, however, and you will be able to see them."

She bit her lip. "They won't be able to come near me, will they?"

"I will not allow it." Aggression surged through him at the idea, remembering the one who touched her in the circle. He saw her flinch at his reaction and he uncurled his fingers. "But they may still get close enough to unsettle you."

"Well, that'll be a change. Everything about this roller-coaster ride has been so calming." A strangled chuckle came from her tight throat.

"Roller coaster?"

"It's an amusement park ride." She appeared to seek the right explanation, but he saw the image in her head and straightened, his eyes widening.

"Why do people ride this?"

"An amusement park is a place people go to have fun, play games. Wow, you took that right out of my head." As she made a feeble attempt at another smile, he noted she was fighting not to let her eyes be drawn back toward the circle. He should have gotten rid of the sacrifice. He would send a message to Epherius to do so while they were gone.

"Did you ever have a time, maybe when you were young and your mother was alive, that you created some kind of game?" At his blank look, she pressed on. "A way to pass the time, or to forget for a little while how horrible things were here? I mean, you do think it's horrible here, else you wouldn't be trying so hard to leave, right?"

"Yes, Alexis." He preferred her mind occupied like this, not dwelling on how monstrous she thought he was. "Everything I have done for the past twenty years, *everything*, has been toward that end. There is no game to make one forget he is here."

But he wanted that revolted look in her eyes to go away, so he struggled to think back to those years he'd forgotten. "I think . . . yes, there was something like you describe. I would take sticks and stones and create small shelters from them. They were no bigger than my hand then, because anything the Dark Ones noticed they would destroy. I imagined how I would make those shelters stronger, if I could make them bigger, so no one could reach me. I put marsmas inside the finished ones. They seemed to like them."

"Marsmas?" Her brow rose and he set aside the cloth. Pausing after a moment's thought, he rinsed his hands in the water of his makeshift pond before coming to her, squatting at her side. Reaching out, he touched her scales, felt the odd dominolike give of the layered covering over her hip. She quivered, but her mind was a confused tangle. Her body wanted him to touch her, but her mind rebelled. He decided to focus on the former and figure out how to drive the latter feelings away. She seemed calmer when he talked about things like this, so he continued.

"They are small creatures, so small they can sit in your hand. Their skin is poisonous and they will bite. Teeth almost longer than mine, proportionate to their bodies. But if you do not frighten them, sometimes they won't. They prefer to leap away rather than fight. They have long, powerful bent legs and can jump great distances."

"Frogs," she said abruptly, that odd, strained smile returning, making something stir in his chest, such that he wanted her to keep doing it. "You have frogs. Or froglike creatures. Ours don't have fangs, though I think some do secrete poisons in their skin. You were building frog houses. We do that, too, because frogs are good to have in gardens. They eat bugs."

"Garden? I know what that is." He paused, a confused, lighter feeling leaping through his chest like one of the marsmas. "I have one."

———

WHEN she'd said the word *garden*, he'd flattened his hand, tightening it over her hip. Fortunately, he was so close, he blocked the dead female behind him, so it was easier to focus. Pushing aside guilt at her body's reaction to his touch, knowing survival was most important here, she reminded herself once again the one weapon she had was her mind. Her angelic light was still playing around them like mist, which also helped.

"You have a garden, here?"

"Nothing really grows here, but I made something like it. Like the pond." His face closed down. "But you won't like it."

His disappointment, anticipation of her rejection, swallowed the startling leap of excitement she'd felt from him. It was the widest range of emotions he'd displayed so far.

"Why do you think I wouldn't like it?"

"I created it out of what I had. Out of . . . what the others brought here."

She thought then of his "pond," and the hair he'd shaped into the grass surrounding it. He was right. She didn't want to see it. But she needed to.

"Take me to it. Please."

He met her gaze. "You know I can hear your thoughts. You don't want to see it. You're trying to figure out how to save yourself. Do you think you can trick or trap me? Even if you succeeded, you'd end up dying much more horribly here, without my protection."

"You can hear my thoughts, but my feelings confuse you." She forced her voice to stay steady in reaction to the cruelly impassive accusation. The resulting flicker in his gaze confirmed it: her emotions were a foreign landscape to him. While she couldn't block the thought that his lack of comprehension reassured her, there was more to it than seeking an escape. She could tell he was smart enough to sense that as well. "I'm trying to understand you."

"Why? What advantage does it give you?"

She'd already seen his cunning side. While his bald honesty could be just as unsettling, right now she found it useful. "Understanding you makes me feel more in control of an uncontrollable situation, and that keeps me from going crazy. But I . . . my gift is empathy, Dante. I feel what people feel, I know their moods, their darkness and light. And you have a strange combination. Very little light," she admitted, "but what's there, when it comes forth, it's a flame that burns so hard and strong . . ." *I can't resist it*, she almost said. Then she cursed as she realized she didn't have to, for the look in his eyes changed as soon as she had the thought. "It confuses me, and what confuses me, I want to understand."

"I feel that way about you as well," he said slowly. "You are here because I need you to be free of this place. But in the dreams, and here now . . . The way you make me feel . . . I do not understand it."

Why that should make her breath catch and her heart hurt, she didn't know. Perhaps more of the same confusion. She forced herself to push that aside, knowing they were on a roll, hopefully in a positive direction. Clara would be laughing her ass off right now—Lex, the eternal optimist, even in the bowels of the Dark One planet. "You must think I'm not a threat, if you're telling me that."

"Anyone has the potential to be a threat, Alexis." His answer surprised her. "The one who appears the weakest may be the most dangerous of all. The Dark Ones here learned that about me. I do not underestimate you, but I am in your head, and I sense no duplicity to you. Not yet."

His expression hardened, reflecting how quickly the darkness could swallow that burning point of light inside him again. It was like a beacon on a storm-tossed sea, only visible when the raging of the waves allowed a glimpse of it. The *Beauty and the Beast* fairy tale crossed her mind again. How simple Disney had made it, resolving the Beast's dysfunctions in just over ninety minutes.

"*Beauty and the Beast?*" His brow furrowed, which had the despairing effect of making him look even more handsome. He had to be a vampire, to live in a world of such violence and cruelty and not have a mark on him. *Only on the outside*, her mind whispered to her. *You can see the inside.* The inside was battered and torn, crippled and savage. Yet she was as drawn to it as the beauty on his outside.

"It's a fairy tale." There were books in the chamber, heavy tomes that appeared to be the magical grimoires he'd referenced earlier, belonging to the long dead Dark Ones Mina had destroyed. Did the Dark Ones create the books, or were these all stolen, scavenged?

"Stolen," he answered her thought. "The Dark Ones rarely create. They travel into other worlds and take. That is, until the witch made that very difficult for them."

"But wasn't that a good thing? They kill and destroy when they go to other worlds."

"It wasn't a good thing, because I could no longer see anything but this world. Do you know what it is like to be shut into a coffin, Alexis?"

"This world is much larger than a coffin."

"No." He shook his head. "It's not."

"How did you learn to talk like that?" She winced as her wing slid across the stone. Because of the break, it was painful to move it without help, and she couldn't reach behind her to do it. Goddess, she wished she could shift. First the tub, now this.

"Here, be still." Reaching over her, he brought his upper body close to her face. "Lean against me." When she hesitated, he slid a hand under her arm to her back, eased her forward so her forehead was touching his broad, bare shoulder. He didn't smell clean, not by a long shot, but it didn't seem to matter. His nearness affected her, and she had to suppress the urge to press her face into his shoulder, seek comfort from the very one causing her distress. The craziness of it was going to . . . well, drive her crazy.

"Why do you deny yourself?" That velvet tone emerged, stroking her nerves further. "As I've said—"

"Yes, I know. Rather than indulging myself in mind-numbing fear about what may happen, I should go into carpe diem hypersonic mode," she snapped. "But I have to make sense of this. You, the way you act, is contrary to everything I know is right and good. Being attracted to you despite that is just a tad unsettling to me."

"Life is random chaos. Trying to make sense of it, by its nature, makes no sense." He slid his fingers through her feathers, below the broken area, and she tensed.

"I won't hurt you," he said. "Tell me what you need."

"Please help me ease it to a half-folded position."

Proving exactly why he unsettled her, the being who'd ripped the head off a powerful Dark One and just cut the throat of a female handled her with remarkable gentleness, causing minimal discomfort.

"You still haven't told me about *Beauty and the Beast*."

"Tell me why you talk like a Harvard graduate . . . like you're well educated."

"My mother was well educated." He sat back on his heels again. She'd noticed he didn't necessarily always meet her eyes when he spoke, preferring to gaze at her wings, her tail, all the area in between, with a rapt attention that would have been flattering if it didn't spread disturbing warmth over her skin and make her nerve endings tingle.

Goddess, Alexis. Dead woman, right behind him. Cap-tor, two syllables.

She wanted to smack him for the sparks in his eyes, revealing her wayward hormonal thoughts had caught his male interest. But he answered her question. "If they use up the energy of their soul, a vampire may transfer all their knowledge into another right before they die. It took some assimilating. I was quite mad for a while." He lifted a brow, reading her thoughts. "Even more than you perceive me to be now. As you have said, everything here is different from what you've ever known. For me it was the same, understanding the images of her life, the thoughts she had. Some parts of it are still unclear, particularly things that were more intuitive to who she was than conscious knowledge, things about being a vampire." His gaze swept the chamber. "There was a time I cursed what she gave me. My desire to escape became that much greater."

"And that desire drove you to do whatever was necessary," she murmured. She realized she was still leaning forward into his body, her hands gripping his biceps. His palms were under her elbows. Their bodies formed a quiet, still tent there, and she was reluctant to pull back despite her next words. "Including harm me."

"Take you," he corrected. "I have no desire to hurt you. *Beauty and the Beast*?" he prompted.

"In a minute. She used up her soul energy? You mean she destroyed her soul to give you that knowledge?"

"Yes. It was a reasonable thing to do. She had no more use for it after death."

Alexis gazed at him. "But what about an afterlife?"

At his puzzled reaction, Alexis realized she wasn't up for a theology discussion, at least not here. She herself had wondered if the Goddess had influence in this desolate place. "*Beauty and the Beast* is a story, a fairy tale," she repeated. "Did your mother tell you any?"

He shook his head. His expectant look reminded her of the manatees, the way they swam up in the morning when the staff arrived, their bright eyes vividly curious about every small new thing that would be presented to them that day. In their far-too-limited environment, anything different was of value.

"Fairy tales are considered children's stories now," she said, pausing as he moved the hand resting on her hip to her abdomen, idly stroking bare flesh and toying with the navel jewelry. "They were intended to teach people moral lessons. But time has made them more fanciful, more appealing to children. Anyhow, here's the shortened version."

"I want the longer one."

"It's difficult to talk for too long," she said, not without regret. "Hard to breathe."

"Oh. Short is fine, then."

However, because she saw disappointment in his gaze, Alexis spent more time with it than she'd intended. She set up the tale and painted the scenes, even when she had to stop a couple times to get her breath, pressing her forehead to his shoulder again to rest her spinning head. During that time his hands never stopped moving, exploring her. Stroking her hair, learning the shape of her skull. Teasing the curve of her spine, the small of her back. Fingering the scales. It was arousing, but she didn't sense that was his intention. He needed to touch her, which unsettled her further.

"In one version, as the Beast spent time with Beauty, he kept entreating her to marry him, but she couldn't get past his appearance. Not until she realized he was going to die of a broken heart because of her withheld love. Then she realized how much he needed her, and that changed her feelings. She agreed, and when she agreed, his enchantment was broken. She found the Beast was really the Prince who had been speaking to her in her dreams all along, entreating her not to be deceived by appearances." She hesitated at that, then pressed on. "There's another version, where the Beast is a terrible, cranky thing who spares her father's life if she agrees to stay with him. Through her love and kindness, he learns to be a better soul, so that he releases her, rather than hold her captive."

"He gives her up, even though she is what he wants most?"

She nodded. "It's when he releases her that he truly captures her heart."

Dante frowned. "This woman sounds hard to understand."

"The Beast realized, in order to forever keep Beauty, he had to prove her happiness was more important to him than his own. That allowed her to love him back."

"Hmm. Perhaps when the witch releases me, you'll read me the complete versions of the story."

If they brought him back through to rescue her, did he really think they'd just let him go, give him a welcome-to-Earth packet and send him on his way?

Alexis shrank back at the change in his expression, from intrigued listener to forbidding captor. "I wish you'd stop doing that," she said desperately.

He stood up, towering over her. "If they let me out of this world, I will do as I wish. They will regret it if they stand in my way."

"No." If he fought them, Mina and her father might kill him. Or they could end up killing each other. Dante had already proven more resourceful than she was sure Mina had anticipated. Thanks to his mother's willingness to sacrifice her soul to give her son her schooled intelligence, he was no mindless Dark One driven by bloodlust.

She cursed her inability to stand on human legs, hated being trapped in her merform without the propulsion of water. And now, with her wing injured, her ability to fly was hampered. In the face of his anger, it made her feel that much more helpless.

"Take me out of this room," she mumbled, fighting it back. "Please. Show me the garden."

He muttered something vile and sharp, making her flinch when he moved. Turning on the ball of his foot, he strode to the other side of the room. He sat down on the edge of his chair, his body tense, expression dark. "Why would they stop me? They have a whole world. Why would they not let me be?"

"They'll be concerned about what you want to do. Dark Ones are violent killers. You . . ." Knowing she was risking his wrath, she flicked her gaze meaningfully to the circle and the dead female there. "They don't know your intentions. What you want. What do you want to do there, Dante?"

He held that stone-faced posture, except for a quivering through his limbs she recognized as an attempt to restrain his reaction. Her fingers curled into the bedding. Despite his stated desire not to hurt her, she suspected she might be moments away from being torn limb from limb. The danger and fury emanating from him were equal to the task and far more. Her fear for Mina and her father went up several more notches. Maybe Mina was right to think he should be locked in this world.

Alexis drew in a dismayed breath, but she'd won a break. It appeared Dante was not listening to her thoughts while he brooded. Maybe he didn't have a Rewind button on her brain.

Apparently he was doing more than thinking. The door opened, bringing a surge of fear with it, but the Dark One that skulked in kept his head down, scuttling to the middle of the room without lifting it.

"As you wish, my lord," he rasped. Grasping the dead female, he hefted her onto his back while Alexis closed her eyes, said another prayer. Then the door closed and the Dark One and Dante's victim were gone.

As the short waft of air from the outside overpowered her senses for a suffocating minute, Lex felt something from Dante to balance it. Even though his emotions continued to fight like rabid dogs over what she'd told him, he was hoping the woman's removal made her feel better. While she wanted him to regret the act itself, not its effect on her, she had to pick her battles.

"Dante. You promised to show me your garden. Will you please show it to me?" She was just going to have to accept the quavering in her voice as something outside of her control. She was lucky the nervous spasms of her whole body had settled down to an every-few-minutes cycle, rather than a continuous knocking that made her teeth chatter.

Several long seconds passed. While she wasn't sure he'd heard her, she lacked the courage to ask the question again. Instead, she listened to the muted but constant roaring noise coming from outside the tower. Perhaps it was the combination of fire and wind, occasionally punctuated by a keening shriek or terrible snarl, the day-to-day of the hate- and rage-filled creatures here.

He wasn't all hatred and rage. He was exuding a terrifying level of it right now, yes, but there was that *other* quality to him. So far, it had helped her stay calm and maintain a thread of hope, while the rest of her feelings were a monotonous circle, the pacing of a trapped animal, anxiety continuing to spiral.

She firmed her chin, straightened her spine. "Dante?"

Slowly, his focus returned to her.

"Please. Your garden? Show it to me?"

Nine

WHEN at last he moved, his expression did not change, but as he knelt beside her, the hands sliding beneath her body were not rough. She winced a little, though, because her scales were drying out. "Before we go, can we immerse my tail again?"

He dipped her back in his pond. While she undulated the red- and gold-scaled portion of her lower body in a rhythmic motion to distribute the moisture into all the crevices, he continued to hold her. Her hand clasped his neck and shoulder as he held her up, and his long black hair brushed her cheek. Her movements slowed, uncertain, as his head dipped. He only rested his jaw against her temple so she couldn't see his face, but it was what she felt from him that gave her pause. Wearied by his frustration and rage, he was giving himself a respite, some of the tension leaving his body and mind.

She didn't want to know what had gotten him past this bout of anger, since she might not like what he'd resolved about her eventual rescue. His hair was a curtain in front of her face, and though it smelled like sulfur and blood, she made herself touch it. Once she did, it was easier to run her fingers through it, wonder if he'd ever braided it or tied it back, or if it had always been like this, as wild a creature as he was.

"You are done?" he asked.

When she nodded, he lifted her again. Thank goodness her hair was long enough to mostly cover her breasts. If he looked at her body, it reacted. Though the female sacrifice was gone, the memory was too raw in her mind to handle the betrayal of her own flesh.

Without comment, he moved toward the circle. "If I'm going to take you out there, you will need additional protection."

Every cell was repulsed at the idea, but Alexis made herself bear it when he dropped to a squat there, balancing her on his knees with one steadying hand around her back. As he dipped his hand in the blood and painted symbols on her upper arms and then her forehead, he muttered the protection chant to supplement the ones burned on her upper body. Those brands tingled at this additional enhancement.

I am the daughter of the Prime Legion Commander and a direct descendant of the Princess Arianne. My godmother is a seawitch with uncharted powers.

It was an old-fashioned thought for a very modern girl, but she grasped her heritage with both hands, thinking of great battles and sacrifices of honor and nobility, the power of the sea and the sky come together in her blood. No matter the enemies he'd faced, Jonah didn't even acknowledge fear. Anna did, but she'd willingly faced down a Dark One army to save him from becoming one of them. Their blood ran in her veins, so Alexis *would* get through this. Though the Goddess might have no sway in this world, she was connected to the elements enough to know patterns were always there, even if their cycles were unexpected. She had to figure out the pattern that was Dante.

He lifted her again. The part of her that had writhed under his commanding touch and climaxed in response to his desires, responded to the strength that had him squatting on his heels, holding her on his knees and then rising with the same ease. She held on to that purely female reaction, letting the mindless power of lust steady her more discriminating intellect.

"Remember, it will be far worse out here until we reach the garden. The additional protections I gave you should hold and make it bearable."

She had a feeling his idea of *bearable* and hers were very different, so she tightened her grip on his neck. Dante's arms flexed under her back and the bend of her tail, squeezing her in a gesture she might have taken as reassurance. He opened the door with one spoken command.

———————

SHE vividly recalled the brief but overwhelming moment when the Dark Ones had flooded their chamber, the terrible sense of despair that had suffused her to the point she couldn't think, only thrash and try to escape like a frightened rabbit, every attempt at bravery or even thought far beyond her reach or understanding.

He'd said it would be more bearable, and it was, but only insofar as she had the scrap of rationality to realize how insane she'd been to insist on going out here. Abandoning anything else, she was desperately glad for his protection.

The door wasn't really a door, but a double shuttered window, with a flat ledge protruding over a twenty-foot drop. The tower was built out of rough-cut stone held with gray green mortar and ice. She had a brief impression of that, and then her wings unwisely but automatically tried to snap open as he stepped over that ledge.

Because he held her firmly, those wings were pinned under his forearm, so the distress to her injury was minimal. He landed on his feet as if he'd stepped off a porch stoop. Apparently blood drinking, excessive strength and the ability to scale or drop from great heights without difficulty were all true parts of the vampire lore.

He landed among a huddle of Dark Ones keeping grim, tense vigil around his tower. When they scattered back, Dante increased that distance by baring his fangs and emitting a long, menacing hiss that made her tremble in his arms even though it wasn't directed at her.

She couldn't look at them, the skeletal yet powerful bodies, the leathery flap of wings, fangs as long as her fingers and every one of them pulsing with the need to kill, rape, destroy, obliterate—

Alexis, stay with me. Stay in my mind. Close your eyes.

She did more than that. She buried her face in his throat, holding on to the beat of his heart. Thank the Goddess it *was* a vampire myth that they didn't have one. She found that reassuring on a couple of levels. Digging her fingers harder into his hair and the muscle joining neck to shoulder, she tried to think of anything else. Oh, Goddess, she couldn't. She knew what they were feeling, what they wanted. They didn't want to merely hurt her. They wanted to destroy any thought she had except hopelessness and bowel-loosening terror. The weight of it would tear her out of his arms, and they would devour her, but leave her soul to wander this terrible place forever, because she was trapped. A coffin, like he'd said. He—

Why are your eyes blue, Alexis? Tell me.

His voice cut through the miasma of fear, drove it back the determined way he'd driven back the Dark Ones, only using firm insistence instead of fearful threat this time. Steady, sure.

My . . . mother's eyes are blue. Violet blue.

So why didn't you get your father's eyes, instead? What color are they?

They're . . . black. All angels' eyes, those that are born angels, are black. Solid black, no whites . . . like yours, with the red fire. I don't know. I didn't pay enough attention in genetics, about dominant and recessive genes, and I'm not sure if that even applies to nonhumans.

What are genetics?

She stumbled around an explanation of that as he continued to poke and prod at her, irritating her, because she needed to react to the horror of her surroundings. It was going to claw away her sanity and make her struggle out of his arms to get away, no matter that she couldn't fly, or swim, or walk . . .

Abruptly, it eased off, as if someone had rolled a giant stone off her chest and pounding head. Gasping, she opened her eyes and found she couldn't see any Dark Ones, not close at least. The tower was about a hundred yards away. As she turned her head, she saw the desolate landscape at eye level, its impact even more dramatic. Dull gray green patches of ice and sucking mud that shot out fire. Oozing and crawling things gave the ground a sinister look that made her glad she couldn't walk. The smell of sulfur and death was unrelenting. Since the sky was fire and gray as well, it was like being locked inside something in truth. The four elements were here, but in forms devoid of magic and life. No bursting vitality like what she felt from all living things at home, whether blade of grass, beams of sunlight or wind flirting across her face, droplets of salt water a tang against her lips.

Not too far distant, she saw groves of the trees that had formed his chair. Black, leafless, the bark smooth as seal skin, giving the twists and convolutions an eerie comparison to traumatized skeletons, reaching to the Heavens for salvation that would never come. Since there was light in this world, but no source of sun she could see through the constant cloud cover, she wondered how they grew so tall. Everything she felt was the antithesis of life, yet it existed. She shivered, thinking of the deity who might have created it for his or her diabolical amusement and then abandoned it when bored.

Dante shifted her, drawing her attention to the left. They stood inside a stone archway that brought them into a circular garden area ringed by rock, branches and other items to form an unexpectedly attractive fence to mark the magical boundary she could sense around it. A deer fence, so to speak. He already possessed a marketable job skill for his immigration to Earth. She pushed down a hysterical giggle, the residuals of the Dark Ones' oppressive presence crackling along her nerve endings.

He had a small grove of the same trees in the garden, only they had leaves and flowers on their branches and in clusters around their base. There were rocks in artful formations, creating an almost pleasing landscape. Or one that was desperate to be pleasing. As he moved her closer, she dreaded what medium he'd used to create the leaves and flowers, but it appeared to be mostly scavenged items. Tinfoil, jewelry, scraps of clothing, all of which had been twisted, cut or folded to make the shapes of flat, pointed leaves or tightly coiled flowers. He'd done credible semblances of tulips, geraniums, even flat-petaled flowers like daisies.

On one of the trees, hair had been intertwined with the jewelry and scraps to form intriguing but macabre vines in the tree branches. Roses, so like what she knew from home, though a more muted color, were affixed to the branches. Flat stones formed a curving path through the garden, with carvings upon each one. Animal shapes as well as magical ones. Renderings of dragons, fairies, griffons. Larger rocks had been chipped and sculpted into animals. A small bear, a dog. A rabbit with long ears, one broken off but smoothed, so he appeared to have one ear far shorter than the other.

"Did you do this?"

He nodded, and though he was looking at the rabbit, Alexis had the feeling he was intently attuned to her reaction. "Can we get closer? I'd like to look at the tree with the roses on it. Did you see all these things in your mother's mind, or in the rift windows?"

"Yes. But the Dark Ones, before the rifts closed, also brought back many things. They never last long. They're either destroyed when they're fighting over them, or they throw them on the ground and the ground eats them. But I'd steal what I could, hoard them away, study them until the hiding places were discovered. I learned about roses that way. It was dropped during a fight over food, and I took it. I felt its softness"—his fingers moved across her upper arm—"and had a brief sense of its scent before they took it away. I remember it still."

His hold on her tightened, and his nose and mouth touched the crown of her head, nuzzled her hair. "Like you. You smell so different. Not of death and fire, decay and hatred. I don't even know what scents cling to you, but I could . . . I want . . ."

He stopped, lifted his head. "I did my best to re-create it, physically. The rose."

For lack of anything else to say, unnerved by his mercurial moods, Alexis turned her attention to the roses. She couldn't imagine how many hours it took him to fashion the layers of petals, figure out how to put the material together. She reached out toward a branch and touched the edge of one, amazed at the soft texture. Then she swallowed and closed her fingers, drawing her fist back to her chest.

"They're human."

"Human skin. I tried it with scraps of paper, and cloth, but they'd all rot away. Metal worked for some things." He nodded to the flat-petaled flowers that gleamed in the dull light. "But I wanted the softness I remembered. I figured out how to preserve it, make it hold its shape."

Leather. He'd figured out how to make leather. And spent hours re-creating a flower he'd held once, until he could perfectly duplicate it out of the remains of the terrified victims Dark Ones had brought here. Nausea gripped her.

"You don't like it."

"It's not that." She tensed as darkness roiled through him at what she couldn't conceal. "Dante, I *feel* their deaths. Do you understand that? Their pain and terror."

Alexis made herself look up into his face, and something twisted in her, hard, at the flash of pain in his eyes. He'd brought her here because he thought she'd like it. He wanted to offer her something beautiful, something like her world, show her that he was different.

It was such a quick, staggering flood of emotion, she reeled from it. Instinctively, she reached toward the hideous flower again, intending to take it in her hand, make up for her reaction. Instead, he stepped back, taking her out of reach.

"I can read your mind, Alexis," he reminded her in a dull monotone. "Do not pretend what you do not feel." He set her down on a bench created of the black tree branches, blissfully without any embellishments using body parts, or remains of clothing. He returned to the tree, and stood with his back to her, looking at it.

Whether he could read her mind or not, Alexis had never been one to hold back her feelings about any situation. Sadness, laughter, anger, whatever the moment required, feelings were a natural flowing river through her heart, because she received them so clearly from others. She was horrified by this, but it was tempered by him. He'd tried to be more than what his environment demanded of him, and used the materials at hand. He'd thought this garden a way to connect to her, which meant he wanted something more from her than ransom leverage.

From the very first, she'd felt his loneliness, and it swamped her again now, so strongly it clogged her throat, leaving her anguished and confused, uncertain how to proceed.

"May I have a part of you?" he asked at length.

He didn't move, still staring at the macabre blossom he'd created and grown out of death and despair. For some reason she recalled a piece of artwork depicting a flower growing out of a tiny crack in the concrete. In this instance, Dante was that flower, wasn't he? Her mind struggled to solve the mystery of it. "I don't understand," she said.

Turbulence hovered around him as thickly as an impending storm. "If somehow I am unsuccessful, I would like to have something of you here, to remember you."

It was unwise to agree, not that she could really refuse him. He'd said he'd used Mina's hair to reach the dream world. But he'd asked Alexis, not demanded. When he looked around at her then, she made her decision.

"What . . . would you like?"

Watching the grace and power in his walk, the way his hair fluttered back over his bare shoulders, the firm set of his mouth, she recalled the Christian idea that Satan was the most beautiful of all the angels. Reaching her, he knelt again, and put out a hand. She made herself lay her own in his palm without hesitation, despite the trepidation fluttering in her belly.

"Not going to take one of my fingers, are you? I'm pretty partial to having ten."

"No." He shook his head. He stared down at her fingers, lying so tentatively in his grasp. His thumb moved, banding over them, sliding over her knuckles.

"Why did you ask me all those questions, on the way out here? About my eyes, and genetics?"

He didn't lift his gaze. "My mother made me do that—it was a way to keep me from giving in to my childhood fears. When they didn't drive me off, I'd sit by her leg, which of course was chained, and she'd ask me questions. Teach me to reason, until she lost the ability herself. I don't know why it was important to me, for you to like this."

Alexis couldn't help it. She turned her hand over, slid her fingers in the spaces between his, drawing his eyes back up to her. "Because when you create something, you want to share it with someone. No one is solitary, Dante. Everyone needs someone."

"I don't care about any of them. I've never felt anything for those they brought here to die." Though she flinched at his words, Alexis made herself stay still as his gaze sharpened on her. "So why do you matter?" he mused.

"You might have cared, if caring and compassion had a place here. They don't. There's nowhere for it to exist."

"They do, inside of you. And you are here."

"Yes. But that's because I've known caring and compassion." Drawing a deep breath, she swept the garden with a thoughtful look, knowing her mind and heart were open to him. "I think you've created a place where your hopes had a place to hide. I think you brought me here, because some part of you knows that. You're allowing yourself to care, maybe for the first time."

"Is that what you know, or are you simply hoping?"

Because her father had the same solid-colored eyes he had, she could tell the conflict within the crimson depths of Dante's, with or without her gift. So instead of answering, she looked down. In his other hand, he held one of the roses he must have drawn off the tree when he had his back to her. Right now he was clenching it in his hand as if he wished he could crush it. He'd wanted to offer it to her. She felt his quenched desire. But then he'd realized it had no smell, no beauty, nothing of the world she'd left, and that its material revolted her.

His anger and violence, his desire to tear it to pieces, to tear everything around him to pieces, was spiraling outward like a slick black oil spill. Just as his muscles tightened, she reached down, and cupped both her hands around his, around the rose.

Empathy was her gift, but she was not unskilled in other arts. She just had to pull deep for it from a body already weakened by the suffocating despair of this alien environment, so far from the magical energies of the Earth and the Goddess. But she dove into what reserves she had, though a sickly tremor swept her limbs, her neck cording with the effort as she murmured the enchantment. As she did, she punctured her finger on the thorn he'd created on the flower's stem, a rusty metal tip that allowed her to touch the flower with her blood.

"Alexis, what are you—"

"Look," she gasped. "Smell. Quickly."

Letting her hands drop, she pushed his up, pulling at his fingers so he opened in reflex. The rose had transformed, shimmering with the temporary nature of the magic, a soft pink that stunned him enough she had to push further, carry his palm to his nose. His nostrils flared, and she caught the scent herself, that sweet, haunting fragrance that could never be inhaled too deeply, but intoxicated the senses. It made her want to weep for home. For lazy meadows and afternoons on the beach, for the freedom of sky and water, and all the earth in between, as different from this place as the difference between Heaven and Hell.

IT was a heady combination. The wafting, brief fragrance of a sun-drenched flower and the temptation of her blood, so close. Her quick frown at the puncture, the pain making her tired face look more haggard, bothered him. The track of her tear as she recalled her home, the quivering of her body that said her time was growing shorter, bothered him. As did the constant turbulence of her emotions and thoughts, which told him her fear was held back by a thread as thin as the knife blade. It all bothered him.

She herself was like the rose, her life and scent clinging to her, making her fragile and breathtaking at once, an immutable force that reined in his savagery just by her proximity. That very delicacy, which his brutality could destroy in an instant, rending the petals away and leaving him nothing to experience but what he'd always had, kept him in check and left him confused about his own feelings.

She cried out, the muscles in her stomach knotting, and her hands fell away, her body doubling over and then toppling her onto her side on the bench. Her temple would have hit the wooden arm, but he dropped the rose to catch her head in his palm, his arm curling around her waist, holding her.

"Used too much magic," she gasped. "It will pass."

She was gazing down at the ground, and he followed her look, so they both watched the rose fade back into cured skin.

"You're right," he said roughly. "That's a mockery of the real thing."

"No." She shook her head. "What you made . . . it's beautiful,

Dante, in a terrible and strange way. Because of why you made it, not the substance itself. It's hard to get past . . . substance, sometimes. Oh, Goddess, this hurts."

"The Goddess doesn't come here. No one comes here who isn't forced to." He lifted her, and then sat on the bench, cradling her in his lap and holding her with one arm as he cut open his wrist with a fang. "Open your mouth," he ordered.

When he brought the heat of his pulse against it, the smell of blood, she tried to wrench her head away. He was much stronger, though, and held her still, made her take his life energy.

Alexis's mind rebelled, but her stomach didn't. For some reason, where the blood in his chamber had sickened her, the smell of his blood now provoked an inexplicable hunger to taste him. Her lips pressed on the wound, throat muscles working as she swallowed. Tentatively, her tongue began to lick at the wound.

As his body shuddered beneath her, she heard his growl of approval. The tips of her breasts tingled, and the tender flesh of her sex reacted, wanting him. But that was not the most unexpected change that occurred.

As she ingested his blood, the low level buzzing that had occurred when he first started speaking inside her head came back to life. Only now it expanded like the rush of the ocean, taking up the horizon of her mind so that he was all that was there, his presence, his need . . . him. Her body jerked as if it were transforming, just like it had when she'd first learned how to manage her transitions. He held her, and she wanted him to always hold her. He was part of her, as near and vital as blood and bone, breath and feeling. It was frightening, all consuming, as if she'd just given him her soul and therefore could not be without him. But her hands clutched him, one latched on his biceps, the other behind his back, pressing into powerful muscle and ribs, sensing the flow of blood beneath.

The rolling feeling, as if she were on wave after wave of surf headed toward a far distant shore, went on for some time, even after she stopped drinking. She could do little but lie there, letting the blood energy he'd given her help her recuperate. It was hard to reclaim her senses though, as he was busy arousing all of them, moving to her mouth to tease away the remains of any blood, nipping at her throat as her head fell back in surrender to him, working his way down until he reached her breast and closed over a nipple, suckling her deep. He was oh-so-careful with those fangs, so she only trembled in fear a little, and maybe not because of that. Something elemental had changed, something she didn't understand, but it had taken the connection she'd felt for him in that very first dream and made it permanent. Made Beauty the willing slave of the Beast before she even made the decision herself.

She clutched at him now, another, softer cry coming from her throat at his provocative pull on her breast, his other hand sliding beneath her hips to find the soft entranceway to her sex. The scales were brittle, but he eased in carefully, and found wetness waiting. He didn't pause, taking two then three fingers in deep, almost matching his own thickness, teasing her with the thought of that as she pressed down on him, his cock rising hard and heavy beneath her weight.

That was what she wanted. She was too weak for it, despite the fact his blood had given her this new surge of energy, but she had to have him inside her now. It was this overwhelming feeling, and more than that, it was the one thing that felt right, a defiant scream against a place that should never exist.

Please . . .

She couldn't give voice to it, but she didn't have to. He could read her every thought and desire. Sliding himself free of the ragged but blessedly accessible clothing he wore, he kicked it away, no modesty to him, and then reseated her on his lap, replacing his fingers with himself. He was more gentle than he'd been before, but still just as inexorable in his progression, taking her down inch by inch on that thick staff.

I like it when you beg. It makes me harder.

The rough lust in his thought made her wetter in response, but she vaguely caught another undercurrent. Was he as unsettled by what had just happened as she was, as baffled? She was not ignorant of energy use, and something powerfully magical had just occurred.

Now was not the time for questions, though. He seated her against his thighs, his cock thrust deep in her, and she writhed, wanting more friction. Instead, he slid an arm around her waist and the other diagonally across her chest, settling his palm around her throat like a collar, coming in under the joint of her wing. He held her back against his body, her tail trembling and flexing its muscle between his spread knees, her tail fins unfurled over his bare feet. The ridges of his abdomen were a wall against her lower back, his chest buried in her wings and pressed against her shoulder blades. She could turn her head, put her mouth below his ear, her face into his hair if he'd allow it, and he did, though he kept his hold on her throat and waist, forcing her to stillness. She shuddered.

"You can come, even if I hold you motionless like this," he whispered against her ear, a tempting demon. "It takes longer, and makes the buildup more powerful. I can feel it in you, see so deep into your mind. Your every desire and need, your every dark fear. I will protect you from all of them, but you must give me everything you are."

Frantically, she took a nip of his jaw as spasms rocked through her lower body. Goddess, she could feel the pulse of blood in his cock, pounding against her walls. She wanted to pump herself hard, as she would in a strong current, send herself spiraling forward in the warm waters of her own desire. But, anticipating her, he lifted his legs and locked them over her tail, strong thighs flexing against her sleek, tight scales, ankles crossed and planted between the vee of her tail fins. She pleaded in a wordless moan, and he answered by increasing his grip on her throat.

"You are mine," he reminded her. "I want all of your soul, not just a piece." He stopped, and through the haze of her desire, she sensed an odd hesitation in him, a brief flash of confusion. "Though I believe I may have already taken it."

Her outer body he could control, but she had other muscles. She tightened on him inside, the ancient ways of the female body surpassing her limited experience, knowing how to tease and seduce what she wanted from him, even if he tried to control all else. She rippled along his length, and heard his breath suck in, a rattling growl.

Stop that.

No. She did it again, and again. She started to jerk again, because his own grip was easing as he began to move instinctively against her, thrusting into her body with the coaxing movements of her slick muscles. She'd kept her face turned into the side of his, but now, obeying some compulsion or instinct of her own, she turned her attention outward, stared at this garden he'd made.

It had taken years to scavenge and hide for it, until his power was enough to create and then protect it from the others. He'd shared it with her, an offering Hades might have given to Persephone, hoping a creature of light and life would see something worth staying in darkness and death with him, give him what he longed to have but was forever outside of his reach. He would keep her there against her will, too desperately alone to do otherwise, always hoping she would at last stay willingly, learn to love the Beast.

The mythology and fairy tale whirling together in her head, becoming her own unique story, Alexis turned her face back to his jaw, to the pulse pounding high in his throat. As a sensuous groan broke from his lips, heralding his own unwilling release, the surge of triumph in her own female power roared over her, taking her with it. She climaxed with him, biting into his throat again, swallowing beneath the too-tight grip of his hand. She didn't understand the truth, but she could feel it, and it was too frightening to face. She chose oblivion instead.

Ten

COMING back was even more difficult this time. She drifted in a hazy world, her heart pumping slow, erratic. She felt him there, in her mind, in her soul perhaps. He was worried. He was stroking her hair, her lips with his clever fingers.

She was on the bundle of rags again, back in his protected chamber, because her nose recognized the blood stench. Goddess, she wished she was home. What would it be like to turn over in her own bed, run her fingers over his chest, down to his groin and find the thick length of him? Maybe even take her mouth down, down, while he slept. Close over him, suck deep and feel him wake in her mouth as he woke above, tangling his fingers in her hair.

Were these her thoughts or his? She'd never been wantonly sexual or adventurous, even in her imaginings, probably because she'd barely held out hope for a decently passionate kiss. Tingles of sexual awareness had been pushed away, locked down in some part of herself. Behind that closed door, her mind had obviously been quite busy, because now her fantasies were in full bloom in the midst of a nightmare. Leave it to her to embrace sexual consciousness in the midst of a hostage crisis.

Shame swept her. What must be going on in the world she'd left? Her mother and father. Oh, Goddess, Jonah. His wrath would be terrible. She hoped Lucifer was with him, and Mina. *Please, Goddess, if you hear me, if there's any way to let them know, please tell them I'm okay.*

But Dante said the Goddess was not in this world. Did that mean She was deaf to prayers from it? She said them anyway.

"It would be a lie, telling them you are okay."

She cracked open eyes that flinched from any light, the pounding in her head increasing. Fortunately, the chamber was dim. No sunlight in the Dark One world, and he'd put out all his torches, so the only light came from the window, that surreal block of flame and gray wasteland. Shadows hid most of his features from her, but the magnetism of his presence was strong enough. He squatted next to the bed.

As she met his gaze, embers in that darkness, she knew. "I'm dying, aren't I?"

He nodded. "But you will be . . . okay. You will regain your strength in your own world. The witch sent me word they are preparing to open the rift. We will go through soon."

There was no triumph in his flat tone, no indication of his thoughts. His feelings were once again too tangled for her to unravel. She groped across the blanket, but he'd withdrawn his touch, moved out of reach. "I thought that was what you wanted."

"It is. But it will not be so easy. The doorway she has allows one through at a time. It has not been used in a long time, and even it suffered some damage during the Mountain Battle."

"So you'll go first, to be sure they let you through, and then I'll come behind you." She shied from the idea of being left alone in this world, even for a second. What if the portal didn't hold? As terrible as this place was, without Dante . . . of course, if that happened, she wouldn't live much longer, would she? But if the Goddess wasn't here, how could her soul find its way home? Would she be trapped here anyway?

He spoke, cutting across her panic. "There will be some trickery. They want you back, but they do not want me there. Her communication left me time for a response. I told them I would be putting a binding on you here that only I can release, and I will do so only after I am safely outside of their influence. Then you will come through."

"Did they promise you safe passage?"

"What is a promise?"

Alexis put effort into the reach this time. She needed to touch him. A lump grew in her throat when he deliberately moved beyond her grasp. Something cold and frightening was inside him, waiting. The predator in him knew he was facing death or battle, and he would not be distracted.

She'd already seen he was far more powerful than Mina likely suspected. The people she loved would be on the other side of that portal, waiting. Her mother. Oh, Goddess, please let Jonah have forbidden her mother to be there. Gentle Anna, almost as defenseless against power like this as Alexis, and her father couldn't survive both of their losses. Everyone knew it.

Dante's fiery gaze flickered like wicked candlelight, telling her he heard her thoughts, but he offered no comfort. The male who'd been inside her body was gone. Instead she was facing the creature who'd survived here for Goddess knew how many decades. Perhaps even centuries, though she suspected it was decades. Something about him seemed younger than the angels she knew who'd reached their first century mark.

She was going to die. This was it, she knew it. So the question was, how would she spend those last minutes? In fear and cowardice, or embracing the destiny the Goddess had given her? She could hate him right now for being willing to sacrifice her for his own freedom, but she'd seen too much here, felt too much from him, even now. While she'd had so much, so many wonderful things, love as vast and deep as the oceans nurturing her, Dante had had none of that.

The male that had been inside her body wasn't gone. He might not be physically within her reach, but his emotions, his desires, they were all still there, only gone dormant behind the formidable weapons he'd use to gain what he wanted, what he'd sought to have all these years. And these might be his last moments as well.

Though tears gathered in her eyes, she swallowed, made her voice steady. "Dante, I do want you to have your freedom. If I die . . . I want you to know that."

"You will not die."

She continued, though she was certain her heart was going to crack open. She struggled between what she needed to say, and the jumble of thoughts rolling through her head. *Clara. I wanted to see Clara meet someone and get married. To watch her truly fall in love for the first time. I would have loved to put Pyel's first grandchild in his arms, let him know he'd never be without us, even to the end of time.*

"The first thing you should do is go to The Butchart Gardens, near the Todd Inlet, in Canada. You'll see things there you never imagined. In fact"—that ache grew jagged teeth as she thought of how many more times *she* would have liked to go there—"you'll need to sit down on one of the benches, because it will be overwhelming. It's all going to be overwhelming."

She stopped, wheezing for breath, and the crimson glow disappeared, as if he'd closed his eyes in the dim light, though his voice came through the darkness strongly enough. "Stop talking. Think in your head if you must, but don't use your breath."

She ignored him, because speaking was the only way to keep her thoughts for herself separate from the words she meant for him. "We have lots of sun. I don't know if it's true or not, but supposedly vampires can't be out in the sunlight. So don't go out in full sunlight until you're sure whether it will burn you or not. Maybe the Dark One blood will protect you. If so, you should go to a beach, watch people play volleyball, or just watch the water. Sometimes you'll see dolphins. With your eyesight, you'll probably see merpeople playing under the waves."

A wave of coughing took her then, and a new terror gripped her as her vision grayed, threatening her with unconsciousness. Gritting her teeth, she dragged herself upright. Despite the ringing in her head, her nausea, the fatal weakness she could feel claiming her, she pulled herself across the covers, the rough fabric snagging her scales painfully. She'd follow him across the chamber if she had to.

"Stop this," he ordered. "You weaken yourself unnecessarily."

"No, you do. I want your hand. Stop avoiding my touch."

She wasn't the commanding sort, not by a long shot, and definitely not with him. But she had to have this one thing. He might be heartless enough to withhold it from her, but she was determined to have enough heart for both of them.

Muttering a curse, he erupted into motion, scooping her up and taking her to her back on the bedding. He lay half over her, pressing his bare chest down upon her breasts, his hair falling forward over his shoulder and brushing her lips, her cheek. "There. I am touching you. What is it you want?"

She lifted a hand, spread her fingers out like a starfish. "Your hand," she repeated.

He stared at her, then lifted his hand from beside her head, met her palm to palm. Linking her fingers with his, she noted the slimness of hers next to his callused, strong ones. While he watched, his mouth a hard slash, she felt a tremor in his body.

"You are *not* going to die," he said. "I will not allow it."

She could feel it in her bones, a creeping tide that couldn't be held back. She didn't know how long she'd been here, but perhaps the things they'd done had weakened her. Perhaps because of her unique mixing of angel and mermaid blood, she had a more fragile constitution than he'd expected. But death was close. She wished she could send one more message to her parents, because if she gave it to Dante, they would never hear it. They wouldn't listen to the male they'd rightly see as her murderer. But with all her many gifts, she knew one thing for certain. He was more than that.

"What is a promise?" he said, and now his other hand was cradling her cheek, the lines of his perfect, handsome face tense, strained.

"It's an oath. When you tell someone you're going to do something, and it's a point of personal honor that you do it. If you don't, it takes something away from yourself." She'd never realized how difficult it was to explain something that didn't exist in the environment of the person asking the question. "Like why you've done all this. You made a promise to yourself, to do everything necessary to win your freedom. You are honoring that promise to yourself."

As he remained silent, she sensed he was examining her thoughts inside, even as he listened to her words outside. "No," he said at length. "A promise is more than that. As is honor. I sense it. Otherwise it wouldn't be so important. Tell me more. In your thoughts."

Shaking her head, she swallowed, realizing how dry she'd become, scales, throat and skin. But it didn't seem to matter. Staying conscious long enough to speak to him was most important. And to nurture the last thoughts of her life and friends instead of her fear of what would happen to her soul in this place.

"To my father, a promise and honor are things you offer to protect others. You make the world a better place when you honor a promise, not just your own circumstances."

"You seek to talk me out of my goal."

She found she had moisture after all, because tears were leaking out of her eyes again. "What you're doing is wrong, but I don't know if I would have done it differently, if I'd experienced what you've been through. So no matter what happens, Dante, I understand. I also believe that once you're free, you'll understand honor and promises much better. I feel your heart." Freeing her hand, she laid it on his chest. "While there's so much darkness in you, probably more than I've ever felt in anyone, there's a light in there so strong, just waiting. Embrace it, and I promise I won't . . ." A sob caught in her throat, her fingertips spasming on his skin, "I will miss my life, but I won't hate you. I *promise*." Goddess, even her lips were tired, but they still managed to twist in a wistful smile. "And thanks for my first time. It wasn't exactly how I'd planned, but it was as earth shattering as I heard it could be."

His expression darkened, his fingers curling into her hair, hard enough that the strands tugged painfully at her scalp. "Alexis, I forbid you to die. Do you understand me? Look at me."

The sharpness of his command had her returning her focus to his face, despite the hammer of pain building in her temples. He locked her into his gaze. Oddly, something there did make her entire body, deep down into her bones, respond to the command in his voice, hold on to that tenuous thread connecting her to life. To him.

"You will obey me. You will not die."

"I don't want to die," she managed. "I really, really don't."

He caught her tears on his thumbs, dampening the soft hair at her temples as he stroked her there.

An energy shift made her cry out, for it was like an electric shock snapping through the chamber. Her fingers clung to his arms, an anchor against the pain. He stiffened, his head lifting as if he were listening to something else. "She is calling. The portal is ready."

In a swift movement that had Alexis gasping in pain, he had her up off the bed and was carrying her back to the hated pool of blood. New things had been laid out there. A sharp knife, a spellbook and a second circle next to the original blood basin. This one was marked with a pungent concoction looking like tangled entrails. It made her feel a need to retch, though she was glad it came from the insides of something she'd mercifully not had to see.

"Please don't put me in the blood again," she said. She didn't want to die there.

"I must." He put her down into it, despite the sob that escaped her, the shameful clutch of her hands he had to loosen, though he was not unkind about it. She cringed as the blood seeped into her scales again. "It will only be a moment. I will stand there"—he indicated the other circle—"and I will go through first."

Alexis yelped as something large landed against the tower door, followed by a shriek of rage. Many shrieks of rage. She gasped as two Dark Ones flew past the open window, their burning gaze landing on her, fangs bared.

"They sense a rift opening," Dante said. "I haven't summoned one of them to go through at the lower level of the tower, where I have an opening just for them, so they know something is amiss. The window and that door are shielded, for now. The circle will protect you for a time from their attack if they burst through. As soon as I am clear, I will release the hold of the circle, and the rift will pull you through after me."

If everything went as it should. But she remembered that feeling of horrible despair as they'd poured in before, the way it had drained her, even inside the circle. She didn't have enough strength left. It would finish her. She would die in this terrible world, in the blood of a terrified woman and who knew how many other sacrifices, surrounded by those soulless creatures.

"Dante," she cried out, terrified anew.

But he was already standing in his circle, and when she tried to move toward him, the circle's shielding had returned, keeping her where she was. As he turned his back on her, energy began to shimmer throughout the room again. He was chanting, setting up his passage and perhaps hers, words she didn't know but she was sure Mina would. She'd wanted to learn more about magic, but there'd been many things she'd wanted to do.

Dante's magic had an innate energy to it. She felt it wrapped amid his emotions, an inextricable part of him. The Dark Ones may have taught him rudimentary preparations to save them gruntwork, and Dante may have read all the grimoires they left behind, but a great deal of the magical energy pressing in on this room was his own, a natural sorcerer's. Did he know it?

Dante, don't leave me here. I'm so afraid. Dizziness closed in, her arms barely holding her up. *No. Please let me lose consciousness before my face falls into the blood.*

He was tracing symbols that shimmered in flame and then seared themselves into the air so she could see their outline. Power sizzled, burning her lungs, her eyes. Flame shot up around them, and still she yearned toward him, hoping, even though hope didn't exist here. Mercy didn't exist here. She felt nothing from him now, just a pure, focused intent to get the hell out of this place.

But Jonah would sacrifice all he was to hunt him down and claim vengeance for his daughter. Her mother's heart would break, her spirit shattered. It all rolled into the pain of loss, an end Lex had never imagined for any of them. She couldn't bear it.

Please, Dante . . . If he did it this way, he wouldn't find what he sought. He couldn't. She knew it. And that was as heartbreaking as all the rest.

It was too late. The flames shot higher, and now she saw the rift outline, a spiral of starlight, flame and darkness within its boundaries that would take him into her world. Into destruction, of far more than just himself.

While she would be alone and terrified. It was demeaning for that to leap to the forefront now, ahead of everything else. His back flexed, that beautiful body moving forward. Would he even look back at her, or had he already forgotten her existence? Her soul cringed at that final betrayal, so irrationally deep she wobbled, afraid the breath she rasped before he stepped through would be her last.

His form shimmered, and she drew in a cry, a painful denial. It was all the strength she had left. As if her arm muscles had turned to water, she fell forward, so hard her face hit the stone at the bottom of the shallow basin. Blood, its wetness and smell, invaded her nose and mouth, forcing her eyes shut. She always kept her eyes open underwater, but this was cold, slimy and brought none of the reassurance the sea did.

Terror spiked through her sluggish body as the banging on the door became thunder, wood splintering and stone crumbling. She was going to die, chained forever to their hopelessness.

She screamed as she was grabbed. Adrenaline kicked in enough for her to strike out feebly. Her Dark One attacker pulled her out of the bloody circle, turning her over so fast in its grasp, it was as if the world tilted, upending her onto the cool stone so he and his fellows could rape her flesh, strip it from her bones while there was life left in it.

"No," she wailed, wishing she could be brave, wishing she was anywhere else, wanting her father or mother . . . or Dante.

Hands cradled her face, the thumbs swiping over her eyes, taking away the blood. She let her gaze spring open, and saw Dante's hard face above her.

"You will go first," he said. "You will not die."

She felt the terrible knowledge in him, what he held at bay like a finger in the dike of his emotions. The larger part of himself was howling, demanding that he sacrifice anything he must to get free, to do what he'd dedicated his life to doing. It was like watching one lone man battle all the forces of hell erupting from his soul, and it was a terrible energy, pouring over her, telling her how close he was to changing his mind. But he thrust her down in his circle, straightened and shouted out the proper words, defiant, angry, his shoulders back. His crimson eyes were as fierce as the flames rising around them, stifling her with their heat.

She was so weak, she could only watch. She wanted to tell him they would help him get back through, they would honor their agreement . . .

Only they hadn't really had one, had they? They'd agreed to open the portal for him under duress, in exchange for her life. If they had her, they would close it. Nothing he'd done would merit their consideration, because they were not seeing him right now. Only she understood the cost, and even she couldn't completely comprehend it, because she'd only experienced two days of it.

Her arms started to shimmer as the portal transfer took a grip on her body, a hard, painful suctionlike pull.

Emitting a piercing snarl that her mother would have recognized in the echo of her father's battle cry, Alexis used a reserve of strength she didn't really have. By force of will alone, her wings and tail muscles shoved her upright, toppling her toward him. In automatic reaction, he grabbed her, because, bless the Goddess, he hadn't shielded this circle to hold her inside it as he had hers.

Wrapping her arms around his waist, Lex pressed her cheek against his abdomen and flipped over, making him stumble the necessary couple of steps into the circle. Holding on as if the universe was at stake, she closed her eyes. With an ominous scream of wind and energy, or perhaps those were the shrieking voices of those being left behind, the portal pulled them both in.

Eleven

H^{E'D} said the portal could only take one at a time. She knew enough about magic to know it was idiotic to go against its rules. While it had been pure impulse, she realized she might have killed them both, because she felt like she'd been shut up in a dryer, blasted with searing heat as she was pummeled, turning and spinning.

Though she shrieked from the pain of it, she kept holding on to him. She'd made a fist and locked her other hand on that wrist, even knowing if the energy grew strong enough, there would be nothing she could do. As a mercreature who knew she could be knocked off course by a few cubits of water, she knew the force of the elements far exceeded mortal abilities, or her feeble grasp.

She could only try, though. Digging deep, she dredged up the life energy she knew she had left, and poured it into her grip, even as her reserve ebbed like an hourglass. If it went on too long, it wouldn't matter. She'd be a dead merangel, spinning through a vortex between worlds. Like the oblivious bodies of the crabs washed up on the beach, but at least that would be better than a soul adrift in the Dark One world.

Oh, hell, it wasn't going to work. She was slipping, and if she let go, one or both of them would be lost.

One of his arms wrapped around her back, then another. As strong as he was, she hadn't realized he had the power to fight through that tornadolike compression. *Thank the Goddess*. His heat was under her cheek, the thundering of his heart. His curses rumbled in her mind, threatening her with all sorts of bodily harm for going against his wishes, though she knew she hadn't. He wanted this more than anything, and it was what was right.

Fire, wind, stars spiraling, and then, as abruptly as they'd been seized, the tornado let them go. Her battered body hit something solid as a concrete wall. Pain overwhelmed her, but it didn't matter. She could smell salt-laden air. The ocean. *Oh, Goddess*.

Something was wrong. The energy was still there, pulling at what was in her arms. It would tear her into pieces if she didn't let go, if he didn't let her go, but they were both too frozen to do anything, still caught in the grip of the portal magic.

"Let go, Alexis. *Let go*." She'd never thought her godmother's acerbic voice would be so welcome, or that the feel of humid air against her flesh, in her nostrils, would be Heaven. But she couldn't loosen her arms. The pain and energy storm made it impossible to think, but she knew that was the most important thing. The vortex wanted to take him back, take him to the Dark One world again. And she wouldn't allow it.

Instead, she summoned up a tiny wisp of energy to speak in a torn voice she barely recognized. Her reality was disembodied, the witch's face an illusion.

"Help him, Mina. Help . . . him . . . through. Please."

Through her cracked lids, her eyes streaming so everything was wavering, Lex glimpsed the witch, her long black hair flying with the force of the wind being generated, her bicolored eyes brilliant with the power she was channeling. It was all over the chamber, wherever they were, as suffocating as what she'd first felt in Dante's tower. The being she held and the one trying to bring her home were both Dark Spawn, half Dark One. Mina had to understand. Had to.

Please . . .

Her fingers slipped, and Lex cried out in protest, falling to stone. She scrambled over stiffly, like a fish that had lain too long on shore. Ripped muscles and strained joints protested, holding her down. "No," she screamed. "Don't let him go!"

"He's here. Easy. You both made it. Holy Goddess, Lex."

David, Mina's mate. She choked on her sob and sought Dante. Barely cognizant of her surroundings, she pushed her abilities to the limit and found him. A moan of relief escaped her, but then her brain marshaled where they were. More importantly, who *else* was here.

Breaking free of David's reassuring grip, she surprised him enough to get free and use her wings, broken though one was, to fling herself toward the energy she knew was Dante. She hit him in a half crouch, as if he was trying to get to his feet, and managed to roll them both in a painful tangle of bodies across the stone floor.

A startled curse preceded the explosion. The callback of the energy burst seared her wings enough that she smelled burning feathers. She was rolled over, more swiftly than she could process, making her need to retch again, though her heaving stomach was empty. She scrabbled for Dante, then realized the hard hands that had grabbed her and thrust her over to douse the flames were his. He was on his feet, standing between her and that charge of lethal fire.

"No. Don't hurt him," she gasped, trying to push herself upright.

Stay where you are, Alexis. Do not make me angrier at you. Dante's voice sliced through her mind, quite determined and furious.

"I think the question to be asked is whether he's foolish enough to try to hurt *us*?"

Mina's dry sarcasm brought the volatile energy ricocheting around the room down a notch. Alexis managed to get her back against a stone wall and slowly focused on her surroundings through the vee of Dante's legs.

They were in the underwater caves where Mina used to live, before she and David had moved to the magical Schism line in the Nevada desert. The airbell in here allowed those present to stand on wide ledges of stone, though the retracted water lapped at the edges. She couldn't help but gaze hungrily at the water, her scales aching for the touch of that soothing lubrication. But it would have to wait. She braced herself, hoping she wouldn't pass out from agony or weakness until she was sure she would wake up and find Dante still here.

The electrical burst intended to kill Dante had come from Jonah, of course, which explained the abrupt callback and curse, because he would have had to absorb it. It had hurt him, obvious from Jonah's tight-lipped expression, but it didn't affect his murderous focus on Dante one bit.

The commander was a mere handful of feet away, feet braced, sword drawn. The darkness of his eyes was ebony fire, his face in a hardened battle mask she'd never seen before. While she knew he was intimidating, she had only received resonances and secondhand accounts of it. Her empathy had always reassured her he would hack off his own wings before ever harming her, even when he'd threatened her with all sorts of dire punishments for her adventurous childhood transgressions. She'd never feared him. Always respected and tried to obey him. Her heart twisted as she realized that might be about to change.

There were three other angels in here, as well as Mina and David. While she didn't see Anna, she sensed her mother near, likely in another of Mina's extensive series of caverns. Since her father could speak in her mother's mind, she hoped he'd sent her the message that she was here and safe.

Of course, glancing down at herself, she wasn't so sure of that. She was dehydrated, her wing was broken, as were possibly some other bones in her body, and she was covered in blood. Though it wasn't her own, they didn't know that.

Dante, don't provoke them, please. Just stay still. What if the head-talking only worked in his world?

A harrowing pause, and then his voice flooded her mind, relieving her. *They are going to kill me anyway. What does it matter?*

No, they won't. "The blood's not mine," she managed in an undignified shrill squeak. While she barely had enough energy to move, she wished she could shift to her human form to stand before them, show them she was all right.

Dante had moved his gaze to David. Mina's mate actually stood closest to them, toward the left flank. His one white and one black wing, unique in the Legion, were at a half fold, prepared to propel him into combat as needed. No matter that he was a formidable fighter, David had an inner calm that Lex rarely felt anything disrupt. Even now, those tranquil waters reached out to Lex, cocooning her like a blanket.

However, just like with her father, he bore an expression Alexis hadn't seen before. The daggers he usually kept sheathed were sharp and glittering in each hand. His calm was a frightening calm, waiting for Jonah's order. Marcellus was here, as was Bartolemy, another lieutenant. All angels she knew. She'd grown up under the shadow of their wings, their protection. But the cold rage emanating from them now told her exactly how she appeared, what they were seeing.

"He didn't hurt me," she coughed. *Technically.* "Pyel, please listen to me. Please don't hurt him. He won't harm me."

"If that is so, David will come and remove you from behind him." Jonah's gaze never left Dante's face. The vampire Dark Spawn mirrored his combative stance, every muscle tense, energy emanating from him that pushed against Mina's lingering casting, making the atmosphere a combustible stew.

"She's mine, not yours," Dante retorted. "And she'll move when I say."

The flash of fire was instantaneous. Alexis cried out in protest, but Jonah's sword erupted into blue flame at the same blink that David knocked into Dante, his dagger slashing down. Dante's defensive movement put David behind him, and in the next second, David was over Alexis, crouching to protect her with his body and wingspan as Jonah moved in. Dante spun with the motion of David's daggers, however, and now a concussion of energy struck David in the shoulder, flipping him around so Jonah's sweep of steel and fire slashed through the feathers of his lieutenant's left wing in the close quarters. With a snarl, David completed the turn, tangling himself with Dante so they both went down. Dante sprang free in an instant, but Jonah was already on top of him as well, sword swinging in a deadly arc.

"No!" Alexis screamed.

The explosion, a force of Dante's energy, shuddered through the cavern, cracking the walls and dislodging rock. A stalactite speared the water with a resounding plunge, showering them all. The welcome touch of salt water splashed her needy scales. Alexis gasped as the ledge rocked, dislodged by the blast. At least that was what she thought, but whipping her head around, she saw Mina, already in motion toward the angels, tip her hand. The ledge mimicked the movement to slide Alexis smoothly into the cool grip of the sea, out of range of the combatants. Because of her weakness, she dropped below the surface, and couldn't marshal the strength to surface. As her body sank, she saw flashes of light above her, and struggling bodies. *No. Please, Pyel. Mina . . .*

She was powerless to stop it now. All she could do was hope Mina would. Her tail struck bottom in the cavern below and she wavered there, holding on to consciousness by a thread. There was a flow of water here, warm and cold mixed, as if the destruction had opened another tunnel.

Dante? Are you all right?

There was no answer, but she could feel him. He was still here, still alive. Really, really pissed off. His anger matched her father's rage, making her wonder if the two of them would turn the caverns into a rock pile before they were done and she'd be crushed down here. She should investigate that tunnel.

But when she tried again to pump her tail, get herself off the seafloor, she was hit by another wave of dizziness, a head-pounding pain that made her moan. Goddess, she felt terrible.

As a hand closed on her arm, she yelped. Anna was there, her arms closing around Lex's hips and then shoulders, holding her up. Just holding her. Her mother's hair waved around her, brushing her arms and hips, her soft, singsong sounds of relief and distress resonating in Lex's ear. Alexis clung back, the struggle above momentarily forgotten as the full force of her fears came back to her, the absolute certainty she'd never see her mother again, never feel her like this. Gripping her hair, she pushed her face into Anna's throat, her emotions unchecked as they floated in the water together and battle waged above them.

"I need help, Myel," Alexis spoke in their shared language at last. "I'm weak, and Pyel can't kill him. He mustn't."

Anna stared at her, her maternal eyes logging every bruise, the injured wing, the exhaustion and lingering horror of her ordeal in her daughter's eyes. It made Alexis glad she was in the water, for that meant she was no longer a bloodsoaked specter. If she'd seen her on the ledge, Anna might not have listened at all.

"Please, Myel. Trust me."

Anna at last nodded. Gripping Alexis's waist, they cautiously ascended. Alexis helped with propulsion as much as she could, but she was all too aware her mother was doing most of it, her one good wing and tail no longer responsive.

Anna paused long enough to determine that there were no more energy exchanges going on, at least not the projectile kind, then they surfaced.

The angels were at one end of the cavern, on a broken piece of ledge. Jonah's face was bleeding and there was a nasty burn across his broad chest. Perched on an outcropping from the wall, Dante was on the other side of the chamber. His fists were clenched, body in a predatory crouch. He had a bloody lip and he was holding his arm stiffly. While his wing was going to need repair, David appeared to be all right. Marcellus and Bartolemy likewise appeared uninjured, though from the plethora of feathers floating in the water and the residual fizzing of magical fire, it was obvious the brief fight had been fierce.

Alexis noted the shimmer of a barrier cutting the center of the ledge. Mina stood in the fulcrum of it. Her eyes were blazing, hands on her hips, her teeth pulled back in a sharp-toothed snarl. Overlying Dante's dark magic and the angel's fire was a vibration Alexis had never felt so overtly, though she sensed it every time she was near her fearsome godmother. David had edged closer to her, his eyes watchful, as if gauging that temper and where she was going to go with it.

In a heartbeat Lex understood better why Jonah often feared for his young lieutenant. The concentrated power of Mina's temper alone took away what feeble strength she was lending her mother to keep them surfaced. Anna's arm tightened around her waist. Despite Alexis's resistance, she moved them to the angel side of that barrier, onto one of the remaining narrow ledges.

Seeing Jonah's glance toward them the second they'd surfaced, Lex understood why she'd done it, to give the commander one less concern. But Lex didn't like the visible suggestion she was taking a side, and that side was away from Dante. But when she looked toward him, his gaze was locked on his opponents.

"You will not stand in my way, witch," Jonah snapped. "He does not leave this chamber alive."

"Then you will kill your own daughter," Mina shot back.

That brought everyone up short, including Dante, who spared the witch a narrow glance. Mina turned her attention to him. "I assume that's why you third-marked her. A clever strategy, though it underscores why Jonah should dispatch you in the most painful way possible."

Dante's face went to an impassive mask.

"Explain," Jonah said coldly.

"He's a vampire," Mina retorted. "He third-marked her. In this world, vampires do that to create a human servant, only this one did it to another type of being. If it works the same way, her mortality is linked to his. You kill him, she dies. A servant follows the vampire, even into the afterlife."

None of them could see how Dante felt about that, but Alexis felt his reaction, even buried under that fearfully still expression and ready violence. It startled him, almost as much as it did Jonah.

"He didn't know about that, Mina," she said hastily. "He didn't do it on purpose."

Her vampire gave her a narrow, nasty look, but she ignored him for the moment in favor of her father, who looked dubious. "I know, Pyel. I can feel his emotions. He gave me blood to keep up my strength."

"Damn it, Mina," Jonah snarled. She gave him a venomous look.

"If you had calmed down, and followed my lead, I wouldn't have had to tell you in front of him and given him that knowledge, now would I have? Hotheads, all of you."

"You gave my daughter blood for strength. But a third mark requires that you drink from her three times. Why did you take my daughter's blood?" Jonah's voice was soft, deadly.

"Well . . ." It was ridiculous to be self-conscious, but Alexis flushed as she struggled with the answer.

"I did not ask you the question. Be silent."

He'd been stern with her growing up. But he'd never snarled at her the way he might those in his command, with a thunderous undercurrent that reverberated through the cavern, bringing his angels to attention and making Alexis jump. The only sound for the next few seconds was Dante's hiss as he bared his fangs at the angel, a warning that had Mina's brows winging up.

"Do you have an answer, vampire?" Jonah said again, unaffected, unless one counted the increased tension in his broad shoulders, the hard clasp on his sword.

"I marked her the first and second time through the dream portal spell, to bind her enough to transport her to the Dark One world and to have access to her mind. My reasons for giving her the third mark are my own, but I drank from her that time for nourishment. Such blood is rare there." Curling back his fangs, Dante showed a trace of blue blood that Lex realized must have come from one of the angels he'd wounded. "Unlike a pure angel's blood, hers doesn't burn me." His crimson eyes glittered. "And hers is far sweeter."

"Does it hurt her if something hurts him?" Jonah asked Mina.

Mina shook her head. "It's only a mortality link. It—"

"So I can beat him half to death, and as long as I don't kill him, she's all right."

Dante's gaze intensified, energy gathering around him. "You can try, angel."

"I swear to the Goddess, males are the same in every dimension. The lot of you should be neutered." Mina pivoted on her toe toward the vampire and won a flick of the fiery eyes. "Listen to what I have said. If you die, Alexis dies. You don't have to fight him. He won't risk his daughter."

She turned toward Jonah despite his muttered oath. "I can bind him, send him back to his world with additional protections. It will not make life there any easier, but he will not be killed. Any Dark One who tries to fatally wound him will have it rebound on itself. So he will be away from here, but Alexis will be reasonably safe. He might get desperate enough to threaten to kill himself to win his freedom again, but I doubt it. He's a pure opportunist."

"No," Alexis said.

Her mother's steadying hand was at her waist, another on her daughter's hair, stroking, but Lex felt her watchfulness, as well as the strong link between her and Jonah. She wondered if that was why her father didn't blast her again for speaking out. But his words were clipped like razor blades.

"I told you," he began.

"I can't be silent, Pyel. You can't send him back there."

Jonah glanced at Mina, his lip curling in distaste. "Does this bond create forced feelings of . . . protectiveness?"

She'd been wrong. Her physical energy had been stolen, but the stress of her captivity and the tension in this chamber, the many things not being said that should be and too many things being said that shouldn't, gave her a different kind of strength. A sudden burst of unexpected anger.

"*Stop* talking about me as if I'm an idiot child."

Twelve

SHE captured everyone's attention with the sharp rebuke. Even her mother's hand stilled upon her. When Jonah's dark gaze flickered back to her, she felt something from him, a tightly suppressed emotion that speared her own heart, brought an ache to her throat, but she couldn't react to it now.

Dante sank onto his haunches. The dark hair spilled down his right arm, the left braced on the rock, lean muscle tense in his biceps and shoulders, breath barely moving the expanse of smooth chest. He reminded her of Lucifer there, his dark, sensuous energy and fearful potential. Because of her focus on her father and the other powers in this chamber, she couldn't gauge his intentions or thoughts.

But it didn't matter. No matter his power, she knew his fate rested with her. Mina watched her with almost an identical inscrutability. She wondered if that eerie stillness was a Dark Spawn thing.

Alexis drew a deep breath, prayed she wouldn't faint. "Pyel, I realize how I look. The past two days have been the most horrible of my life. That place . . ." Her voice faltered, and Anna made a noise. At first Lex thought the wave of powerful emotion came from her, but its source surprised her. It was David. Though his stance did not change where he stood at his commander's right shoulder, hands still on his daggers, she felt his reaction.

Seeing the shadow cross his eyes, she remembered. He'd been

nearly tortured to death there. While Mina was often a closed book to her, she sensed the seawitch reaching out to him in her mind, with her heart, her eyes moving toward him.

The bond between them was something innate, hard to explain. Just as this was. But she had to do it, or Dante would be sent back. And that wasn't acceptable to her.

Swallowing, she spoke to Jonah again. "No one should be there. Not him, not anyone. I'm not deceived. I feel his darkness, as you do." She shifted her gaze to Mina. "But perhaps what you don't feel, that I can, is his light. It's there. He didn't want to be born there. He has survived all these years, focusing only on escape, and he used what means he had at hand to do it. He could have treated me much worse, but he didn't."

With relief, she saw Jonah was listening. The father who was enraged and worried was still there, his feelings grasping at her like sharp claws. It made her long to run to him, let him wrap his strong arms and the comfort of his wings around her, let her shudder out all the fear and terror of the past two days. In Anna's embrace, she'd had the barest start of how much of that she wanted to do. But she'd just told him she wasn't a child, and she wasn't addressing her father. She was talking to the being who'd made thousands of judgments on life or death.

"You all know my gift. I can see the core of what he is, and what he can become."

You were given this gift for a reason. She let the thought bolster her where her own physical strength couldn't. *Hang in there. Somewhere at the end of this will be your bed and a long, hot shower.*

"Yes," Jonah inclined his head. "I do not doubt that, Alexis. But I also know it can make you blind to other forces."

"Those were the mistakes I made as a child. I am not that child any longer." She bit back her impatience as he seared her with a glance.

"If you are not a child, you know every being has the potential for good or evil. Which they become depends upon their choices. Their environment may push them, but in the end, it comes to a choice. He made his."

To survive in my world, we kill. To have anything, we kill. Firming her chin at the recollection, she shook her head. "In his world, his choice was only to live or not to live, and to live however he could. There is no morality there, Pyel. No good to protect by making choices against evil. Now he has more choices, and if you let him remain here, he has the chance to make them."

She pressed on, galvanized by the flicker in his expression. "Myel once told me that, soon after I was born, you took me flying over the water. She remembered how you stopped flying, hovered over the waves, holding me up in your arms so the moonlight shone on my skin, gleamed on my wings. She said they were no bigger than your hand then."

Pausing, she let the memory sink in, weave a picture between the two of them. "There were tears in your eyes."

Anna's breath drew in behind her. Jonah's gaze moved to her, then back to Alexis. She noted she'd even captured Dante's cautious interest, though he and the other angels remained far too fixated on one another. "You said you saw everything I could possibly be, all my potential, and you wanted to give me every chance to reach that potential, to achieve the highest pinnacle of happiness in my life. That's what I'm asking for Dante. *This* is his birth. He is an infant, and he deserves that chance."

Perhaps it was ludicrous to compare the tall, muscular vampire with flaming eyes and bared fangs to a tiny infant, but she pressed on. "Please. I understand you have to think about it. But please don't send him back. Give him the chance to have a life here."

Jonah looked toward Mina. Angels at his level could speak into the minds of others, and if a being thought directly at them, they could hear them. It was clear an intense communication was occurring. Lex wished she knew Dante's thoughts, because the only emotions she was clearly receiving from him had to do with impending violence. But since he'd been forced to live by his wits long before he gained the upper hand on the Dark Ones, she hoped he was using his brain rather than testosterone. The cavern was overloaded with it.

"There's merit in her words," Mina said at last. "Perhaps a probation period, thirty days, under supervision. While we sort out all the issues involved."

"He could stay with me," Alexis said.

"When Lucifer decides to build an amusement park in Hell," Jonah responded.

"I'm his surest chance of success here." She turned her appeal to Mina. "I'm the only one who can sense his intentions, help him navigate this world without misinterpreting his actions. He *won't* hurt me. I know it."

Jonah pivoted. Everyone in the chamber tensed, with the exception of Mina, but her father merely used his wings to go to the ledge where she and Anna sat. When he squatted before Lex, she couldn't suppress the full force of his emotions. In his face she saw what these past two days had done to him. That, and his closeness, his strength and familiar scent, undid her. She couldn't help it. Tears came, and her limbs trembled anew.

"Pyel," she whispered.

She was in his arms, those wings wrapped around her and her mother as he brought them both into his embrace. They slid their arms around him as well, burying fingers in his wings and hair, faces in his chest, while he tilted his head over theirs, murmuring incoherent words that Alexis didn't need her gift or ears to understand. He spoke right to her erratically beating heart.

His Legion was his family, of course, but she and Anna, they were his blood, his heart and soul. The emotion from him was overwhelming. Despite all the years of battle experience and training that had kept him focused on how best to bring her back, he'd feared, deep down, he was going to lose her. Because of that, Lex knew that not only was Dante lucky to be alive at this point, it was fortunate the cavern was still standing. It made it all the more difficult to push her father, but with the determined cruelty of the young, she knew she had to do it.

Raising her head to look up into his beloved face, she repeated it. "He won't hurt me, Pyel."

Jonah lifted her hand to his lips. Even as he pressed a kiss to it, his fingers slid over the bruises on her forearms, his gaze taking in the state of her broken wing, her battered face and weakened body. The symbols burned into her flesh, now clearly visible with the blood washed away. "Yes, I can see that."

"There's more to it than that."

"I need no supervision," Dante said. As he straightened to his full height on the ledge, the three angels closed ranks.

Jonah lifted his head, turned it toward Dante. While Lex couldn't see his face, the warm emotions were replaced by something utterly cold. "You would be wise not to speak, Dark Spawn."

When his lip curled back, showing fangs, Alexis spoke hastily in her mind. *This world is very different from the one you left. You know this. You'll need someone to help you get accustomed to it, to avoid pitfalls that might convince them you're too dangerous to be here.*

I do not seek to please them. I will be no one's pet.

His voice in her head was a welcome brush on her frayed nerves, despite the tense circumstances. Lifting her gaze to him, she peered over her father's broad shoulder. *It's not like that. Please give this a chance.*

Mina spoke then. "There is a way to ensure he does no physical or magical harm to innocents while he is here." She glanced at Jonah. "And it won't hamper his ability to explore this world with your daughter."

Jonah blew out a breath. "He is not staying with my daughter."

"Pyel, it's my choice."

"No, it is not."

Alexis set her teeth, but a noise between a tired chuckle and a sob drew their attention to Anna. "I thought I'd never hear the two of you having a battle of wills again," the mermaid said, her voice breaking.

Jonah spoke a soft word of reassurance to his mate. Sliding his hand under her hair to caress, he touched her cheek with his thumb so her face tilted into his palm. Alexis gripped her mother's hand.

Anna swept both of them with a loving look, but then met Jonah's gaze with unexpected purpose. "I don't like this any more than you do. But years ago, when Mina first told us about Dante, it bothered me. I think it bothered all of us on some level."

Though the cavern was a grab bag of emotions, Lex received a sharp spear of surprise from Dante. It was probably no less than her own as her mother continued.

"This is her gift, Jonah. I wish to Goddess it wasn't, but we've seen it grow, and we all knew more significant things would come from it. Perhaps he is too far gone, and it will end in his death. But if all she says is true, he deserves the chance. I can't think of anyone better equipped than our daughter to bring a dark soul back to the Light."

Alexis sensed the weight of memory moving between them. "I can think of one," Jonah said at length, making Anna's mouth curve into a poignant smile.

"I was twenty then," she murmured. "A year younger than she is now."

A muscle twitched in Jonah's jaw, but he turned his gaze to Alexis. "If Mina can figure out a restraint, and the Dark Spawn prefers it to an instant and fiery death at the point of my sword," he said, cutting a glance at Dante, "we will do this. Under my conditions only, and one of them is that I want your word that you believe this is possible because of your empathic ability. Not a sentimental desire to save a stray dog."

Temper flashed through her at the insult, but his mouth tightened. "I am not being sarcastic, Alexis. He is a Dark Spawn, and he has killed before. The scent of the blood on you tells me that, as well as the fact he's achieved power in a world where only violence is respected. You are taking responsibility for him among a host of innocents. We will be close," he added, when she paled. "A direct call from you, and one of my angels will instantly be at your side. But sometimes an instant is not enough. This is no child's game, Alexis. Be very, very sure."

Alexis looked toward Dante. He stood alone, a being of rage and fire. She knew he could do great harm, felt it within him the same way the earth could feel the lava simmering in the volcano or the tsunami waiting dormant below the ocean waves, but he would always have such power. If Mina could do as she said, and the angels would be within calling range, the risk had to be acceptable, because imprisoning him wouldn't change the nature of what he could do with his power.

She turned back to Jonah. "No matter what other feelings I have about him, my request is based on my gift. I swear it on my love and respect for you, and for Myel."

Jonah nodded. When he returned to the other ledge, he strode forward, batting an irritated hand at the barrier. Mina swept it away before his flesh could burn. His wings took him aloft, toward the outcropping on which Dante stood. Jonah hovered before him, his wings holding him steady. "I seek no promises from you, for I would trust none. But know this. I need no excuse to send you back to the hell from whence you came. I will not hesitate to instruct Mina to ward you only so you cannot be killed, and send you back to whatever lesser torments the Dark Ones might wish to inflict upon you. Knowing what you may have done to survive these past two decades, I'm certain they would welcome the ability to make you their slave again."

"Pyel," Alexis gasped, but Dante raised a hand, stilling her.

"I expect nothing less from your kind," he spat.

"*Ahem.*" Mina had disappeared into the adjacent chamber during the interchange and now returned, a silver band of metal in her hands. "Once this is on you, I will charge it with the spell. Any type of violence will rebound upon you, causing you three times the pain you are inflicting. You will also be unable to take a life."

He'd consented to none of it, Alexis realized. Mina's explanation of the collar's effects might as well have been in a foreign language, because when his gaze latched onto it, his rejection was a wall of denial. It would render him helpless, unable to defend himself. It was too much to ask.

"You are not touching me, witch." He dropped back into his crouch, a preparation to attack.

The combustible heat in the cavern expanded, the air much closer. Before Alexis could draw breath, swords and daggers were drawn. Jonah moved back to a position at the head of his angels, while the invisible energy cloud that seemed to float along with Mina wherever she went intensified. Darkness rolled through the chamber, a choking, suffocating reaction of rage, magic being gathered, though Alexis didn't know if it came from Jonah, Mina or Dante, or some fatal combination.

"Both of you leave," Jonah snapped, jerking his head at her and Anna. Her mother's arms tightened on her, but Alexis broke free.

"*Pyel, no.* Please, let me try something else."

The few minutes in the water, and the return to her own world had barely rejuvenated her enough to make the transformation to human form. However, despite the agonizing pressure in her chest, which made her fight to breathe as she rose to wobbly legs, she made it to one foot, then the other. When she managed the awkward hop to the wider ledge, she stumbled against David, since he was the closest.

"You are *really* pushing it," he murmured as he steadied her. But they weren't attacking, and she wondered if Mina had counseled her father to stay his hand, because no way would Alexis's protest have stopped him. As David helped her move forward to stand shoulder to shoulder with Jonah, her father gave her a warning look. She gave him a nod, but turned her attention to Dante.

"We need to do this," she said softly. "It's the best way."

He stared at her. Something shifted in him, so strong her trembling knees nearly gave out on her. Jonah caught her waist. His fury surged over her, but she shook her head. "It's not him," she said.

It was partially true. She was reacting to what she was feeling from Dante, not something he'd aimed at her. Rage and fear, violence and hatred, rolled up in a fetid blackness, expulsed from his psyche like the monster in the child's closet come to life.

"I will be no one's slave again," he said. "I will *not.*"

Still wearing the ragged trousers, he nevertheless managed to still be breathtakingly wild and handsome, the dark hair spilling across his broad shoulders, his fiery gaze intent, darting around the chamber, his upper body taut.

Swallowing, she took another step forward. *Trust me, Pyel. Please.*

She was still within a range where he could reach her faster than Dante could move, another reason she suspected he complied. When she reached out to Mina, the witch laid the collar in her palm. The heavy weight of it pulled against her grip, and she hated it instantly, almost as much as Dante did.

As she made her way on the narrow broken ledge toward the outcropping where he stood, she balanced herself on the wall. Her father stayed just behind her. Myriad emotions ricocheted through the room. Her mother, pensive and worried, but curious as well, seeing things with a mother's eyes Lex suspected her father didn't. The angels, a dangerous fighting force ready to move into action at the least indication by their commander it was needed. David, part of that feeling, but different, too, as he kept his attention on Mina. Mina was a blank wall as usual. But when those disquieting eyes had met hers, as the witch handed over the collar, Lex thought she'd registered approval.

Of course she was too weak and stumbled. Her father caught her waist, but her hands landed on Dante's forearms, his fingers closing on her elbows.

"You are injured," Dante said in a voice that sounded anything but sympathetic, but something emanated from him. Anger at her weakness? Frustration with it? Yes, that was it. Frustration. Something he didn't want to bother him, but did. He couldn't risk a distraction, but he'd vaulted down from the ledge to stand before her now. "You need care."

"I need you to wear this." She tightened her fingers on him. "You know I can do nothing to you without your permission. You're stronger and faster. So will you at least listen to me, before this becomes really bloody and ugly?"

"No." His fingers tightened on her. The ominous hostility behind her made her pulse accelerate. They didn't realize he was rejecting her initial request, not her plea to listen.

"It will only be for a while. Until you prove you're not going to go out there and kill a bunch of innocent people. You've lived your life ready to kill, fight, struggle or escape. You won't have to do that here, but it will take time for you to learn different instincts. Without this, you could really hurt someone without meaning to do so. It's to protect others and help you, not trap you. You can read my mind. You know it's not a trick."

"I know you are not trying to trick me. But you did not produce this item." His gaze turned to Mina. The witch gave him a flat stare.

"Trust has to be given to be earned, Dante. You wanted to be here. Now you are, and how you managed it makes you lucky to still be alive. Don't test your luck. You might hurt him"—she tilted her head toward Jonah—"but I promise you, he *will* end you. And the pieces he doesn't incinerate, I'll finish off."

"Please," Alexis said softly, digging her fingers in to bring his attention back to her face. "I've known them all my life. They are not deceiving you. Please trust me."

In the intensity of his expression, the rest of the cavern disappeared for her. His hands were tight, every finger pressed into the flesh of her arm. *You are mine?*

It was the first time he'd posed it as a question. Though he said it with rough agitation, the uncertainty beneath it tightened her throat, so she answered in her mind.

I'm not sure what you want from me when you say that, or what it means. But some part of me wants to say yes.

His brows lifted as he considered her, as if he was plumbing her mind at the same time she was gauging his emotions. What a couple they made, she thought wryly. They'd be incapable of lying to one another, even white lies. That would be a pain in the ass, in any relationship.

Then she sobered. "Please, Dante." *I know how terribly hard this is for you. But it is the only way. I want you to live.*

A long, tense moment ensued before he inclined his head, so slightly she might have been the only one to see it. He quivered as she opened the latch on the collar and raised her arms. Steadying her weak body, he moved his hands to her waist, or perhaps that was to keep himself from stopping her, because his fingers dug into her flesh with the power to bruise. When he tilted his head down for her, she leaned into his chest to fit it around his throat. Another hard tremor went through him as it latched, making her want to reassure him further. Her father's sharp voice cut in then, the strain in his tone telling her he was at the limit of what latitude he would give her.

"All right, stand back, Lex, so Mina can activate the binding on it."

Dante's hands flexed on her waist, but then he released her with another nod, bidding her to stand back.

As she did, Lex realized something she'd yet to feel from him. Fear. Anger, yes, frustration, concern, but not fear of the type that would make a person retreat before an unwinnable situation or the frightening unknown. She remembered now what she'd felt when he'd thrust her into his circle, allowing her to take his place. A terrible resignation, a deep fatalism like suicides experienced, those who cared nothing more for their soul and were willing to release it to whatever end it sought for itself.

Uneasiness swept her. She sent a prayer to a Goddess that Dante would trust them enough to let her help him. Along with the uneasiness, dizziness returned, another wave from the gray world that wanted to drag her down. No, she couldn't go. She couldn't leave him yet. Not until she had him settled at her place, though she wasn't sure she was even up to the swim to the surface.

Mina gestured. "This may hurt some, but once it's activated, you'll notice nothing other than the weight of the collar." Before Dante or Lex could react to that, she spoke the enchantment.

The steel flared red-hot. Alexis gasped as Dante's body jolted, electricity spearing through it, strong enough to drive him to one knee on the narrow ledge. Lex lunged forward, trying to help him, but her father pulled her back, holding her against his solid immovable force as the magic swirled around Dante, creating a glittering shower of blue sparks that arced off him like fireflies. He didn't cry out, which seemed to impress Mina, whose lips tightened as the spell finished. Her hands came together in a way that reminded Lex of a yoga Namaste.

The magic died away, leaving Dante on the one knee, fingers tented on the ground, his breathing labored. When he lifted his head, Mina nodded to the angels. "Try to attack one of them. I want to make sure it works."

Alexis scowled. "That's not fair. He's already in pain."

Jonah ignored her, putting her behind him and squaring off with the vampire. Dante's eyes lighted with malicious pleasure that Lex was sure her father's expression mirrored. Maybe Mina was right about testosterone needing a babysitter.

"Uh, no." Mina jerked her thumb across the cavern, toward David. "Him you don't have a grudge with, and I know he won't do more than defend himself. Last test. Pass this one, you can immerse yourself in the wonderful world of human vice."

"You are fond of sarcasm," Dante observed. Rolling his shoulders, he eyed David.

"It's actually her native language." David sheathed his knives but braced himself in a defensive battle posture. "Like an accent she doesn't realize is there."

Mina scowled at him, but Dante had already launched himself. He was swift, faster than Alexis could follow, though Jonah turned with the motion, shielding her. Before she could draw in an apprehensive breath, the vampire had hit David midbody. The angel took the blow, using his wings to slow their propulsion backward, but by then, nothing else was needed. Dante was on the ground, coiled around his own midriff, his teeth gritted while he cursed.

"It works," Mina glanced at Alexis. "You can take your new puppy home now."

Alexis nodded, but as she began to make her way back from the narrow ledge, the room tilted again. Her knees gave out, making her stagger. She thought the ledges had shifted again from the earlier damage, but then she noticed she was the only one falling, while her head was spinning like a helicopter's sharp blades. *Oh, no.*

Though she grabbed for consciousness with both hands, it had already eluded her. The ground and water rushed up to meet her, even as she cried out in protest.

Great Lady, don't let anything bad happen to him before I wake.

Thirteen

D ANTE hissed his fury. His rage fought unabated within him, slashing between betrayal and frustration. Where was Alexis? He couldn't get her to answer. He sensed her mind, but either she was unconscious or they were blocking him. They'd said they were going to have her tended by a healer in the Heavens, Raphael. He remembered Raphael from the Mountain Battle. He'd been no healer on that day, wielding a spear that could puncture and thread together three Dark Ones on the shaft before it yanked itself free and returned to its owner.

In the meantime, they'd brought him to Hell. He'd been escorted by all four of the angels. Even Mina joined them for reinforcement. Jonah had said little, but the witch's mate, David, told him that Hell would be the best place for him until Alexis had regained strength and consciousness.

He hadn't been unkind, but Dante didn't like it. He didn't trust any of them. He remembered David only from when he'd come to the Dark One world, years ago. He'd threatened to rip Dante limb from limb then, and now he was expected to trust his words.

But he had escaped his world. Whatever treachery they planned, they were not yet executing it, and he could afford to watch, and wait. He'd done that for many years, and such patience was familiar to him.

What wasn't familiar were his feelings about Alexis's absence, his inability to be near her. His need for her was more unsettling than anything else. He'd told them his reasons for marking her the third time were his own, but the truth was, despite not knowing exactly how to activate it, he'd been thinking of his mother's words. *Use it to bind a soul . . .*

Lex was beyond his reach, and that was simply unacceptable. His cunning deserted him, leaving only the desire to tear, rend, destroy. They'd put this collar on him and then took away the one thing he would fight and kill to keep.

After they brought him to Hell, they left him alone on a spear of rock deep in the bowels of their Earth. It was warm and dim. A deep chasm surrounded his platform on all sides, so he could peer over the edge into endless fire and darkness. Beyond that were endless cliffs of high rock with no visible top point and crevices hard to discern in the shadows, even with his enhanced vision.

Despair rose like smoke from that chasm, but it had a different quality than in his world. It tugged at his memory, made him think about his mother. Perhaps what Alexis had called *regret*? Occasional screams of fear or pain were carried on the air currents.

He sensed no enemy to fight or defend against, to distract him from the madness closing in. Cursing, he shouted out a demand for Alexis, *now*. The echo of it rebounded, mocking him and driving him over the edge, literally.

He leaped, damning the consequences, and found himself slammed flat on his back into the center of the platform. He also found he was not alone at all. The dark-winged angel holding him with only a hand at his throat and knee to his chest gave him a flat, assessing look.

"The chasm is spelled for you. If you leap outward, it would give you an unpleasant jolt, worse than this, and you'd end up back here."

Lucifer. He knew this angel, from the Mountain Battle and the stories of Dark Ones who'd seen others fight him, and lose. No one came back from a fight with him. He was the one dispatched to kill Jonah, all those years ago in the Canyon Battle, the one strong enough to do so if it was needed. His eyes were the only angel's eyes that held red, a crimson glow that glittered through the black void. His long, dark hair draped over broad shoulders and powerful arms tattooed with script that glowed like embers as he moved.

"I do not fear you," Dante snarled. "Get off of me. Where is Alexis?"

"Exactly where you were told. She is safe, and being treated for her wounds. Her life energy was very weak. Your world, and your demand for her blood, weakened her." Though his voice remained impassive, Dante knew what moved under the surface of that unreadable face was not so unperturbed. The merangel had many powerful friends.

"But she will recover."

Lucifer inclined his head, and something loosened in Dante's chest. The Lord of the Underworld straightened and within a blink was on the opposite end of the platform, staring down into the abyss of fire. His wings stretched out slowly, meditatively, his attitude suggesting now that he'd arrived, he did not care for conversation.

Dante rose to his feet warily. Was this the witch and Jonah's plan? Kill him down here and make Alexis believe he'd attacked first? Well, nothing was going to stand between him and Alexis. He wanted to see this world, but he needed her eyes to see it. He needed her energy to interpret the meanings of so many things he didn't understand.

"Many fear Hell," Lucifer said at last. "You do not, because you came from a world of chaos, pain with no end, cruelty with no mercy. There is pain and cruelty here, but it all has structure, a purpose. A purpose that serves the Light."

"I fear nothing."

When the dark-winged angel lifted his gaze, Dante thought if he stared into those eyes too long, he might lose himself in a spinning vortex that was desolate and reassuring at once. "Coming here is a soul's worst nightmare, but an answer to their deepest longings as well. They have stained the fabric of their lives so heavily with their misdeeds, they do not know how to become clean. Until they do, the world above is a painful mockery to them." His wings stretched out further, then eased to a fold against his back. His gaze returned to the abyss. "Forget violence and escape while you are here, Dante. Give yourself time to rest. It may be the last sanctuary you find for quite some time."

———————

THE first time Lex surfaced, she learned that Dante and Jonah nearly knocked heads catching her when she collapsed. Jonah had transported her to the third level of Heaven, where Raphael examined her wings, and healed the break. The golden-haired angel treated her other injuries as well, then recommended nourishment and bed rest to regain her strength.

While she lay in a small pool in a sun-drenched room in the Citadel, the body of water large enough that her wings could stretch unencumbered, she passed in and out of consciousness, her languorous body allowing her brief minutes of awareness. The breeze coming from the blue skies outside. The distant choral voices and instruments as the music angels practiced their craft. Snippets of conversation.

Her fingers passed over her bare skin, bathed in the sun's healing rays. The symbols branded into her skin were gone, likely healed by Raphael's skill. Why did that feel like such a loss? She also heard the seawitch talking, perhaps to Jonah or Anna.

"He has changed from two decades ago. He is no longer the scavenger we knew."

Dante. They were talking about Dante. Where was he? Why wasn't he with her? Underneath the beauty and peace surrounding her, it was a disturbing undercurrent, one that made her sleep fitful.

"The decimation of their numbers from the Mountain Battle tipped the natural balance. Nature does not intend the scavenger to be the alpha."

No. Mina was wrong. There was no natural balance in the Dark One world. What if he'd been an alpha all along? What happened to a leader forced to be a slave before he even knew he was a leader, before he knew he had any power at all?

"Dante . . ."

Her mother's hand. "It's all right, love. He's fine. He's been taken somewhere while you get better."

But he needed to be here. With the third mark, could she stretch her empathic gift beyond those in close proximity, sense his moods wherever he was? If he could reach her in her dreams, why couldn't her reach be at least as far? She hit a wall each time she tried, but maybe she should seek a door, or a window. Even a crack . . .

Her effort drove her into unconsciousness again.

Time passed, but she couldn't follow the events that occurred during it. She was floating, no more than a cloud, lost in a haze in her own mind. So it was startling to wake to full consciousness at last in Anna's cottage by the sea.

She thought of it as Anna's cottage, but of course it was the legacy of the daughters of Arianne, a gift from Neptune. Anna had told her more than once it now belonged to her, as the most recent descendant. Lex knew her mother loved the cottage, though, and she preferred her town house. It was fully hers, separate from any legacies with their preconceived notions. As long as she thought of it as Anna's cottage, it could be a home away from home, because every space of it was permeated by her mother's loving presence.

She was in human form, in the loft bed. At some point, she must have responded to a murmured request from Anna to shapeshift. Her mother was by her side, and the ocean was a soothing rush of noise outside. She wasn't in that awful place. She was home, the most beautiful, priceless word in the whole world.

"Lex, what is it?" Anna was leaning over her, her hand touching the tears on her daughter's face.

"Where is Dante?"

"Your father thought he should wait for you in Lucifer's realm. It's protected—"

"He put him in *Hell*?" When Alexis tried to shove back her covers, the world did a violent, erratic somersault. Fortunately, her mother caught her, else she would have ended up on the floor. "He can't be there, Myel. Why did he take him there? He's suffered enough. He—"

"You said it yourself." Anna tried to ease her to a prone position again. "You need to be with him when he transitions to our world. You're the only one who can read and anticipate him. They thought it would be best to put him in an environment where he could do little harm to himself or others, not that he can do that with Mina's spell, but you understand my meaning. *Alexis*. I may not be as strong as your father, but you are not getting out of this bed until you've sat up for a few minutes. You've been on your back for almost two weeks. Now be still."

Two weeks. Oh, Goddess. He would be going insane. "But Hell? He came from a place like Hell."

"He wasn't put into a redemption chamber, love. He's fine. He's been offered a bath and clothing, blood to nourish him. I sent him the clothes."

Alexis made herself sit up slowly, bracing on the pillows her mother arranged behind her, though her heart continued to thump rapidly. "You've checked on him."

"Often, through your father and David. He's important to you. We all understand that. Your father has more respect for you than you are giving him."

The reproach struck home. But she couldn't relax, not without him near. Watching her, Anna's brow creased. "I've never learned about vampires, but your father and Mina have knowledge of their kind. While vampire–servant relationships are very strong, the bond does allow the servant to travel wherever the Master or Mistress requires them to go, no matter how far it takes them away from the vampire. However, if the Master"—distaste crossed Anna's expression—"does not wish the servant to be away from him, it's possible that displeasure could create the restlessness you feel. We tested it by moving you here. You became far too agitated in the Heavens. When you were brought here, where you are moderately closer to him, you became more calm."

"How is he doing?"

"He's prowling like a trapped animal, but he's fine." Anna squeezed her hand. "Mina said you were very lucky. His blood does not bear the poisoned taint of a Dark One. If it had, you would have died almost instantly when you ingested it. Instead, it was the atmosphere of the world itself that has kept you so weak for so long."

Lex forced her mind away from Dante and onto Anna. Hearing the strain in her voice, and feeling the cauldron of emotions behind it, she laced her hand with her mother's. "You convinced Pyel to listen to me. Thank you."

Anna stroked Lex's hair, which Lex realized was brushed into smooth waves that fell over her breasts and down her back. Anna's fingers lingered on her face. "Being a daughter of Arianne often means difficult choices, obstacles to overcome. You're the first one who didn't have to face them right from birth, so I fooled myself into thinking your life would be normal. Much as I don't want to see it, that strange creature has the mark of your destiny on him, whatever part he will play in it."

Her expression darkened, her lips tightening. "The mother in me hates him for causing you fear and pain. But I see what may lie between you. I saw it in the caverns. I suspect your father did, too, which explains the anger he is carrying now, unable to do a thing with it. His Legion has been overworked on the practice fields these past couple of weeks."

Lex stared at her. "Goddess, I love you, Myel."

"And you think you may love him."

It was a simple statement, but it rocked Lex back on her heels. Anna knew as well as Lex that angels only fell in love once. Up until now, there'd been no indication if she would inherit that trait from Jonah, but the fact that Lex couldn't immediately confirm that she wasn't in love with a being she'd known only from dreams and his brutal kidnapping was worrisome.

"I don't know." She swallowed. "I can't . . . I shouldn't even be dwelling on it. He has so much to learn and understand about this world. I have to help him. I can't get bogged down in my personal feelings. I *know* that."

"Your personal feelings will exist, and be a factor, no matter what."

Lex sighed, freed her hands to rub them over her face. "For so long, I've wanted someone to love me, not just a response induced by my gift. If I was like any other girl who had a first love, or a first date, or a first kiss, I could play all sorts of silly head games and drive myself crazy. But I'm not. *I'm not.*"

She didn't need to feel the sharp ripple of Anna's pain to know her mother well understood what it was to grow up under the shadow of something that kept others at arms' length. To long for what others had, but know if it came at all, it would come in a form far different than expected. Proving it, Anna didn't respond with denials or reassurances, though her hand rested on Lex's.

"While our concerns as your parents tend to get in the way of what we know you must do, your father and I believe in your strength and your intelligence, Alexis." Anna's voice was thick, but her gaze was piercing, steady. "You have your father's determination, his sense of right and wrong, as clear and sharp as his sword blade. We don't wish to doubt you."

When Lex would have spoken, Anna shook her head. "There is something about Dante, though, not only in his past or who he is, but in the way he looks at you. A hunger that is frightening to a parent. As a woman, it would be overwhelming, and it could be deceptive. Believe in yourself, Alexis. You will never steer yourself wrong, and if anything happens, if your heart is broken, know we will be here."

Alexis blinked, nodded. "I've always hoped to have your courage, Myel. I'm so afraid of what's going to happen."

"You stood up to your father, Mina and even Dante to do what you knew was right. If that's the kind of courage I've shown in the past, no wonder Jonah says I give him gray hairs." Anna allowed a twinkle in her blue eyes, lightening Alexis's heart.

"Can he be brought here, now that I'm awake? I swear, it's like having a permanent anxiety attack, whatever's causing it. Two weeks . . ." Alarm took her, for different reasons. "T, and Clara—"

"Marcellus took your cat to a place where he could be tended until you return."

"I'll have to thank him for that."

"Don't go on too much about it. Your father wanted Marcellus to know your building layout."

"Marcellus will be handling guard duty?" Lex didn't bother to keep the surprise from her voice, and Anna inclined her head.

"Jonah wanted to send Marcellus a clear message that he still has confidence in him. These males. If they're only able to slay ten dragons in one blow instead of twenty, suddenly they doubt their masculinity." But Lex felt Anna's worry about Jonah's captain. Even Mina took particular note of him these days, going out of her way to insult Marcellus more often than any other angel in Jonah's Legion, even Jonah.

"I also had him find Clara's phone number. I didn't speak to her, but I left a message on her machine that you'd had a family emergency and wouldn't be home for several weeks. I'm sure that won't eliminate her worries, but at least she won't be calling the police and filing a missing persons report."

"No, it will be fine. Even though she's never met you, she'll know you're my mother, and everything is okay." Alexis swallowed. "Myel, I'm sorry, but can he—"

"He's on his way." Anna covered her nervous hand, her warm grip contrasting with Lex's cold one. "I contacted Jonah while we've been speaking. Why don't I help get you dressed? I bathed you earlier. Do you feel steadier now?"

Lex nodded. Anna slipped an arm around her waist as Lex put her feet on the floor, more carefully this time. When Lex proved she could stand, Anna squeezed her waist once more and took a cautious step away. "Stay there where you can sit back down if you need to do so. I'll go get you the clothes out of the dryer," she said, too quickly.

Lex swayed, not so much from unsteadiness as from what pushed against her filters, strengthening with every rapid step her mother took down the stairs out of the loft. Growing up with Lex as their child, both Jonah and Anna had found they couldn't hide emotions around her. Once they'd accepted that, they'd patiently fielded a small child's questions about what she was feeling from them, no matter how difficulty that honesty was. In return, as Lex grew up, she'd learned when to respect their privacy and let the emotions they had pass unquestioned when it was obvious she should do so.

While this was one of those instances, she couldn't control her own reaction. Not when she looked down at her shiny, clean hair again and the roomy sleep shirt she wore, one of those kept in the cottage for whenever Anna made use of it. It was the first time in the history of the daughters of Arianne that two daughters were alive to use it. Up until Anna, all the daughters died right before the age of twenty-one. The age Alexis was now.

The dam broke then. Thank the Goddess, Anna was already downstairs so Lex wouldn't add to that pain. Lex's knees hit the throw rug, cushioning the sound of her fall. Pressing her face into it, she wrapped her arms around her middle. It all hit her then. What had happened to her, her parents' fear—impossible to process separately because Jonah and Anna were so closely linked—her own terror, things that would be part of her nightmares for weeks to come. But overlying it all was this terrible gnawing need to see Dante . . . Where the hell was he?

It had been a long time since she hadn't been able to filter emotions enough to keep them from overwhelming her. But stress and weakness shoved shields aside, as if they'd waited until she was fully awake to render her raw, defenseless. The need to weep suddenly took everything else over. *Where was he?*

"What is the matter? What is wrong?"

He was a rush of fire through nerves shriveling from cold, and despite the absurdity of it, the flame swept over her, giving her warmth and life again. While it would be easier to believe it had to do with the mark, a simple chemical reaction, the intuition her mother had told her to trust told her differently. Which meant she was far more vulnerable to him than even her father or Mina feared.

When he knelt down beside her, her skin tingled at the touch of his hand on her shoulder, bare because the oversized sleep shirt had slid off it. Then she saw the boot he wore, braced on the floor in front of her knee, flanked by a ragged jeans cuff.

I sent him the clothes.

It hadn't registered when her mother first said it. The magnitude of emotions churning in Anna's wake when she fled the room now made more sense. As Dante had proven to Lex countless times in his world, if the emotions were too complex and strong, she couldn't always immediately decipher their meaning. But when Anna had convinced Jonah to listen, Lex realized her mother had been confronting a much larger personal demon.

One of the traditions of the cottage was that a spare set of men's clothes was always kept there. Every daughter of Arianne had one love, and he was always rescued from the sea. Alexis hadn't rescued Dante from the sea, or had she? He'd come through the sea portal, because she'd pulled him through.

Goddess, she was losing her mind. She hadn't even dated and she was prepared to put all her eggs in the basket of one very messed-up, cosmic-struggle-with-internal-evil, Dark Spawn vampire.

Alexis, look at me.

She closed her eyes more tightly, her hands into fists. Though the curse was supposed to be broken, Anna had still wanted Alexis to pick out an outfit. Alexis had laughed, enjoying the fun of it at first, but sometime during that shopping trip several years ago, another compulsion had taken over. By the end of it, she was leading her mother into the shops. When they returned to the cottage that night, she hadn't known which one of them was more unsettled. She'd put it at the back of her mind, only to have it spring forward now. While it might be proof she hadn't lost her mind when she championed Dante, dealing with pieces of the puzzle falling into place like this might drive her insane anyway.

At last she lifted her gaze, coursing over the faded black jeans she'd picked out before she knew about a vampire born of fire. They creased in the right places, the fading creating an intriguing gray smoke effect on the fabric. She remembered the shirt had been the hardest to pick out, as if she knew whatever man donned it would not look quite right in the tailored, modern clothes of today. She'd found the perfect thing in the vintage shops around the college. The white silk poet's shirt had lacings open at the throat, revealing the line of his sternum, the sculpting to the pectorals. The silver collar lay on his collarbone. Despite its grim purpose, it was a handsome addition to the outfit. When he leaned over her she could see down the open neckline to the jeans' waistband, the terrain of muscle between. He looked as if he belonged to an age of darkness and sorcery, not cars and wide-screen televisions.

He'd had a bath and tending as well, though she suspected Jonah hadn't sponged him down as her mother had done for her. The humor steadied her, particularly when she saw it register in his startled and then speculative expression. *Humor.* He didn't know what humor was. How did someone learn humor? She'd read once that babies learned to smile when their parents were smiling. They'd imitate, and somewhere along the way they'd make the connection between the expression and the feeling.

Washed, his hair was even more of a temptation. She wanted to wrap her hands in it, bury her face in the dark strands that fell over his shoulder as he leaned over her. The strands outlined the slope of proud cheekbones and straight nose. She wasn't brave enough yet to meet his eyes, so she alighted on the firm lips. That was a mistake.

In an instant, she wanted them on hers with a hunger so strong, she thought of him taking her to her back right then and there. Marking her with this new clean, male scent after being away from her for so long.

Holy Goddess, she was here with her mother. *Her mother.* And Jonah was right there, standing on the top step to the loft. She could feel his tense reserve.

Dante's eyes had sparked with reaction to her response. He would do exactly as she wished, because he had no idea they shouldn't.

She jerked back on her knees, so quickly she would have toppled if he hadn't caught her wrists. Jonah's tension ratcheted upward, because it looked as if Dante had frightened her and she'd startled away from him. Though Dante could read her mind, she was sure the unfamiliar images and terms confused him. His expression went wooden, his jaw muscle flexing in anger . . . or perhaps another feeling.

No, it's not you, Dante. We don't do things like . . . what I was thinking, not in front of other people. It's private. Especially when the other people are parents.

In my world, Dark Ones couple wherever they wish, when the urge strikes them. Shadows flickered through his gaze. A feeling, here then gone, touched her with a chilling horror, but she was distracted from that by the hot surge of lust that overrode it.

In this world, we don't, she reinforced hastily.

Then send them away.

She swallowed at the look in his eyes, the demand. Two weeks. Two weeks they'd been apart. The quivering need from him wasn't nearly as shocking to her as her own matching desire, despite her body's debilitating weakness. Trying to collect herself, she got one foot under her, then the other. Dante had stepped back and didn't touch her again. She wondered if he was following her direction, or if he'd removed his touch because he thought she wouldn't welcome it, when in fact her skin was burning for it, craving the flame.

No, he could read her thoughts, couldn't he? She wished she could read his as easily. When he spoke, her gut clenched, terrified he might say baldly what he wanted to do. Her father would murder him right there, leaving a smoking hole in the polished wood floor, boots still standing where his feet had been. Or worse.

"You still haven't answered me. What is the matter?"

She wished she was wearing something different. It might seem illogical, since Dante had seen her in shambles in his world, but she'd wanted the first time he saw her since his arrival to be different.

You are always beautiful, you should know that. His tone was impatient. *Are you going to answer my question?*

"I can't keep up with everyone's thoughts and my feelings at once," she responded, glancing toward the steps. Anna had returned, standing on the stair just below Jonah, leaning into his hip and the curve of his wing. Lex didn't see any other angels with him, so she assumed he'd been the one to bring Dante from Lucifer's realm. That was a distracting image, because of course Jonah would have had to hold him in some fashion to carry him through the sky, and she couldn't imagine either male relishing that. Knowing Jonah, he'd been sorely tempted to drop him several times just to hear him scream. Knowing Dante, he wouldn't have offered that satisfaction, crossing his arms and glaring until he hit the ground with a bone-shattering thud.

She suppressed a giggle, a sound close enough to hysteria to increase everyone's alarm. Biting her lip, she struggled for control, hoping her head wasn't going to explode from the emotional overload. Unlike her parents, however, there was no way to hide her state from Dante. His eyes were narrowed, mouth tight as he watched her.

"I'm still a little bit disoriented. I'm sorry. I don't mean to worry everyone."

"*You* owe us no apologies, Seabird," Jonah said. His tone was sharp, but the familiar endearment was reassuring.

"I'm still sorry." She straightened to her feet, took a deep steadying breath and gazed at both of them. "I'm all right now, truly. Myel, if you could leave me the clothes you brought, I'd like some time with Dante, to start acquainting him with our world, to talk to him a little while, without . . . an audience. I think it will be easier for him. For both of us." She lifted a shoulder. "I admit, I feel a little self-conscious. I've been out for two weeks, and I'd like to try to get back to being myself."

In fact, she'd never felt so awkward, torn between two loyalties. She didn't like the vague sense she was betraying their love. They'd nearly lost her, and here she was, shooing them out of the cottage she'd just acknowledged was Anna's, because she was terrified Dante was going to leap on her . . . or perhaps eager to find out if he would.

"If you feel strong enough, we'll do that." When Anna spoke, Alexis let out the breath she hadn't realized she'd been holding. Jonah didn't move. Anna tugged at his arm, drawing his gaze. "Mina has tested the restraint. He will do no one any harm. As you said"—her blue eyes found Lex's again—"all she has to do is call. One of you can quickly come to wherever she is."

"Instantly," Jonah corrected.

Dante's gaze darkened, but he said nothing, just stood, silent and still. While they'd been talking, he'd moved so his back was to the wall and he had Jonah clearly in his sights. His gaze kept moving, gauging his surroundings. She suspected he'd already scoped out exit and entry points, but he also seemed interested in the array of items here. The lamp on the night table and the light it threw out. The ocean through the large expanse of window to his left.

"There are ways to hurt someone without inflicting a single scratch," Jonah said at last. He altered his glance from Dante to her. "You call if *anything* frightens you. Don't think about whether it's important or not. We'll come a thousand times if needed."

Lex crossed the room, aware of Dante's tension, the weighted scrutiny. He was as good at it as Jonah, so that with the two of them in the room the air nearly crackled. Her head continued to pound.

Nevertheless, she laid a hand on Jonah's wrist guard, curling her fingers to touch his hand. "I would like to spend more time with you both. I'll come to visit you in the next day or so. And I'll check in with you often in my mind. You already know you can talk to me in my head whenever you need to do so. All right?"

Jonah's dark eyes searched her face. "All right. I'll leave you alone with the male who kidnapped you and almost left you in his world to die, since you prefer his company."

"Pyel—"

Withdrawing from her touch, he descended the stairs. Her mother gave her a steady look, reassuring but not revealing, and followed him. As Lex watched them, her heart ached, the pain behind her eyes intensifying. She needed to strengthen her filters, but blocking their emotions seemed another betrayal.

Before she left out the back deck entrance, Anna glanced up, meeting her eyes. Though her face remained somber, Anna blew her daughter a soft kiss. Then she turned away, shutting the door behind them.

Fourteen

ANNA didn't try to keep pace with her mate. When he took to the skies without a word, she shed her human clothes, folded and placed them somewhere she could retrieve them. Then she transformed and dove into the ocean, swimming deep and fast, surfacing far from the shore to view the late afternoon sunset. There was a coolness to the air that gave an edge to the dying of another day, underscoring her own uneasy state of mind. Jonah was likely streaking through the sky at a harrowing pace for the same reason, pushing himself up into the firmament where the thinner air could steal the breath.

She'd seen the hurt in Alexis's eyes at his abrupt departure, but there was nothing to help that right now. Because of how different Lex's life was from others', Anna knew her daughter sometimes forgot her youth, even more than most her age. But her parents never forgot, and perhaps that was what made this complex. Lex was a woman now. In the cavern, amid all the dangerous tempers and energy, Anna had been sorely tempted to convince herself Lex was a child who didn't know her mind. But she'd known from the look in Lex's gaze, the set of her chin. It would have been the height of hypocrisy to deny it when Anna had recognized her own destiny at age twenty, the first moment she'd seen a wounded, unconscious angel, poised to fall into the deepwater Abyss.

Alexis's heart was in her eyes when she looked at Dante, his for the taking. There was no telling what he would do with such a gift, when destruction hovered so thick around him. The angel somewhere in the skies above had dedicated the last twenty years of his life to protecting his daughter. Letting her have scraped knees and bounce out of trees on her fledgling wings had been hard enough. He'd been the first one to tell Alexis that some suffering was necessary for growth, so she wouldn't unwisely apply her gift, but he himself had struggled with the lesson throughout her entire life.

It was no easier for Anna, but she understood a woman's love for a male plagued by demons. All Jonah saw was an enemy, something far worse than a scraped knee or a fall, because Dante might very well turn out to be every bit of the nightmare that he'd so far proven to be.

"Self-conscious."

She rolled to her back to see him hovering above her, wings keeping him in place. Despite the seriousness of her thoughts, she couldn't help but smile a little at the sight of him, his arms crossed and expression dark as a storm cloud.

"Well, most daughters would be self-conscious to have their parents there when what the two of them were thinking about was—"

"Obvious." Jonah dropped down, crossing his legs Indian-style so he appeared to be sitting on the surface of the waves, though his body moved in rhythm with the current, staying with hers. Swimming to him, she curled her fingers over his calves and laid her head on his knee. He sighed, putting one large hand on her head. "I want her as far as possible from him. I want him dead. He deserves to be dead."

"I know." Shifting to human form, she pulled herself up and Jonah helped, catching her waist so she could straddle him. Wrapping her legs around his back, she seated herself in the vee of his lap. She grasped the sword harness across his broad shoulders to anchor herself. "We both know life demands a great deal from us all, especially those of us with gifts. Raphael has said for some time she's only tapped a portion of her abilities. As she gets older she'll be likely to trust herself more, let the filters down, increase her range."

"That I understand. But . . . damn it all." His arms tightened around her body as he pressed his face to her throat, breathed deep, nearly choking on his iron control.

"We can't stand in the way of this. We can only be here if it goes badly. You know that."

"Yes. I want to say the hell with all of it, but I do know." He made a low growl of frustration and lifted his head. "But cheerfully clearing out because he wants to ravish my daughter is going too far."

"You wouldn't have left for that. You left because it was what she wants." She cocked her head. "And you've never done anything cheerfully."

Jonah gave her a narrow look, but she switched topics. "Would you be willing to lead a delegation to talk to one of the vampires?"

"What are you thinking?"

"Mina thinks Dante is about sixty years old. Someone may remember his mother. He can't integrate into the human world, no matter how much he explores it. Like all of us who are something other than human, we need a base of support from those who know who we are." Anna tapped his shoulder thoughtfully. "From the things Mina told me about a vampire's nature, the strict rules of vampire society may help him cope here. And he won't be able to avoid them anyway. Those who try to exist outside Council structure aren't treated well. For that reason, we may want to initiate contact quickly."

"But he's as much Dark One as he is vampire."

"It's the vampire side that will matter here. Remember, Mina is Dark Spawn as well, and she conquered that part of herself."

"She manages it," Jonah corrected. "And David is key to that."

"Yes, he is." Anna held his gaze and Jonah swore.

"I don't even want to contemplate that."

"Neither do I. But you saw how she looked at him."

"Yes. She's infatuated with a handsome vampire with Dark One blood. At best, he breaks her heart. At worst . . ."

"Mina said that just because she is young, and expresses her feelings in a youthful way, we shouldn't mistake immature communication with immature feeling. Love isn't always limited by experience. We both know that."

His jaw tightened. "I can't bear this, Anna. I won't."

Brushing her knuckles against that set jaw, she drew his gaze back to her. "At best, she rescues his heart from darkness, and he embraces the life that should have been his in this world all along. He learns to cherish her for the gift she is, and they discover a love together that makes every sacrifice worth it. At worst, they go their own ways when their feelings for one another run their course. She herself sees that possibility, and that the most important thing is making sure he can survive here."

He shook his head. "You always see the best. You saw the bruises on her. The blood. The—"

"You saw more than that, and so did I. It's why he's still alive." Anna's chin firmed. "If I hadn't seen it, I would have killed him myself."

Jonah made another incoherent snarl. Grasping the back of her neck, he drew her to his chest. When she spoke again, she did so against his firm flesh. "If Mina can find someone among the vampires who will talk to us, are you willing to go?"

"Yes. But it will be a moot point if I murder him before then."

"Even so." She suppressed a smile and straightened. As she did she adjusted her legs around his waist so her heels slid across his buttocks. Leaning back, she arched to put her hair in the water again, fully aware of the upward tilt of her breasts, the jut of her nipples while the seawater waved her hair like fine sea grass across her cheeks beneath the surface. Her lips curved as his hand slid up her abdomen to her left breast, capturing it in a way that caught her breath. His desire for her was evident and reassuring in a way that wrenched her heart and tightened her lower belly. She lifted herself out of the water, came back to his arms as his hands slid over her wet, slick skin.

"You're trying to distract me."

"No." She sobered. "For all its frightening fire, passion often ignites from something deeper and more substantial. Something that doesn't make sense at first, but is undeniable, all the same. I know how you feel about this. I feel no differently. But we have to hope." *And pray.*

He brought her closer to him with that effortless power that made her muscles weaken. She loved surrendering to him, in all ways. He understood her soul as she understood his. In this moment, as with many others, she thanked the Goddess for it. When she told him so in her mind, he took her mouth in answer. A breath from her lips, though, he stopped. He studied her face in that intent way he had, as if she were always something new for him to learn. "I need you," he said.

The joy of it leaped inside of her. Anna remembered that she'd once lived with hope when there was no reason to have any. Now she had a wonderful mate and incomparable daughter, blessings she'd earned. It would be all right. It had to be. She wouldn't despair now. "I know. I need you, too. Particularly right now. I'm afraid, Jonah. So afraid for her, because I know we have to let her do this. Help me be less afraid."

It was the right request, for she knew he would do anything to give her happiness. As his heated mouth closed over hers, she melted into him, taking them both to a place where they could escape their worries, if only for a short while.

———

WHEN the door closed, Alexis stood there. Despite the yearning in her body, she found herself swept by uncertainty. She glanced toward the window and saw late afternoon waning toward evening.

"I believed I'd been tricked, until your sire came for me."

"I'm sorry. I didn't realize."

"You've said that twice now. Your father feels you have nothing to . . . apologize for. I agree."

She looked back at him, met his eyes for the first time. The smile she'd been attempting failed before that crimson penetrating stare. "I went from being your prisoner, dying in your world, to pleading with them not to kill you, to this. Here we are, standing in a normal house, and I don't know what to say at all. Or how I should feel."

"Do you want me here?"

"Yes. No. I don't know. Would it make a difference if I didn't?"

He studied her. "No. Because you would be lying. You fear your feelings more than you fear me."

"Great. A boyfriend who can literally read my mind. Every woman's dream come true." Pushing her hands through her hair, Alexis wished she'd stop feeling light-headed.

"You're very weak still. You defied the magic the witch set upon the portal." His mouth tightened. "I'm angry with you for doing that. You're lucky to have survived."

"You're here because I did it. Wasn't that what you wanted?"

He blinked. "Your answer . . . it strangely fits."

"Yes, no and you don't know?" She was able to smile now, though it was tremulous. "I think I understand that. Yes, because no one would want to be there. No, because it's all unfamiliar and you're out of control. And you don't know because you're torn between the two. Right?"

He lifted a shoulder, but frowned as if that wasn't all of it. "I was told that, while the blood may have hurt you, the mark itself may have helped you survive. Apparently, it is very difficult to kill a vampire's servant."

"Your mother didn't tell you much about servants."

"She told me some things." Dante considered that. "But some things she put in my mind had no relevance to my life there. They made no sense to me, so I just pushed them away. The seawitch said it is a bond that cannot be broken."

As he took a step toward her, she curled a hand in the excess fabric of the sleep shirt. "I was hoping to be dressed when you saw me," she repeated lamely.

His clothes didn't make him less overwhelming, she realized. Nothing human was this magnificently gorgeous, vibrating with power the way he did. Or maybe it was that when he looked at her like this, her body liquefied, making it hard to—

His arm shot out, slid around her waist, catching her to him before she buckled. As she laid her head on his chest, his head bent over hers, his lips nuzzling her hair. His palm flattened, his fingers spreading as he held her tightly against him. "I shouldn't do this," she whispered. "I'm supposed to help you. It would be best if we tried to not—"

He tilted her head up, his thumb pressed under her jaw, close to her pulse. "Now that your body has accepted the mark, my blood is no longer a poison to you. Nourishment and rest will help you recover, but if you wish your energy to return sooner, it will help the most with this weakness."

She remembered that swirling feeling when he'd given her the third mark, as if their souls were being wound together irrevocably. Now she knew they had been. She wasn't sure how she felt about that, but her current reaction was getting much clearer. He held her so close, her breasts were pressed into his chest, and there was nothing under the sleep shirt. Of course, when she had the thought, he had it, too. The hand not around her waist dipped, slid beneath the hem, and found the bare curve of her buttock. In her human form, they could come together face-to-face for the first time, his body stretched out on hers, weight pinning her down, spreading her open and burrowing deep.

He lifted her almost before the thought was completed, and took her back to the bed. As he laid her down, she reached up to his face. He caught her wrist, his face questioning, but she merely stretched out her fingers, asking without words. Slowly, he released her, let her lay her hand on his jaw, slide her fingers up into his hair. Her thumb found his mouth, the tip of a fang, the give of a sensual lip.

"I missed you," she whispered.

There was no reason for her to pretend otherwise. It was how she felt, no matter how insane it sounded, and he could read her mind anyway. With her abilities, she'd learned early that hiding feelings didn't negate their existence, and in fact often just made them worse. Whatever was going to happen was going to happen. If destiny determined that Dante would break her heart into pieces, he would.

"I've never done it like this." His brow furrowed. "In fact, until you, I've never done this with anything but a Dark One."

Lex bit her bottom lip as he slid his hand further under the shirt and found her breast, tracing the curve, making the nipple ache. "You're very good at it, for someone who's never done it."

"My mother's memories were very vivid in places. She did this often, and she had detailed memories of her best lovers. The things they would do to her."

"You know, some people might find it a little revolting to see their parents . . . you know. Oh . . ." She whispered it, emitting a tiny moan as he found the nipple, then dipped his head and suckled her through cloth. *But I'm not complaining. Oh, Goddess.*

She clutched at him, slipping her thumb beneath the waistband of his jeans, her fingers curling and holding on as she lifted her hips to him, rubbed against his turgid length, straining against the denim.

Nervous talking was done. She needed him inside with such a desire she could barely speak. When he opened the jeans, pushed them down his hips with her help to get them out of the way, her fingers clawed at his muscular flesh. He came down on her body, pressing her into the mattress, himself between her legs. Catching her hands in one of his, he stretched her arms over her head, tilting her upper body to him. Even as he restrained her, he continued to suckle her through the cotton, one nipple then the other, as she thrashed and rolled against him. The blood in her temples was pounding, her stomach starting to roil. She was going to be too weak for this, damn it.

He released her hands then, cupping her head to bring her to his throat. *Bite hard, Alexis. Use your canines.*

I'll hurt you.

I welcome pain from you. Bite me now. You will hurt me more if you hesitate and do not bite me as hard as you can.

Because she inhaled his flesh, and it made her mouth water, she obeyed. He let out a growl as blood filled her mouth. Just as in his world, she was amazed at the taste of it, and wondered if having the marks was what made his blood so appetizing. She drank deep, sensing the strength in the nectar he was offering her, and her body's response rebounded. She had her legs wrapped over his back, working herself against him in mindless, untutored need. When he freed her from his throat with a finger eased into her mouth, she latched onto that, imagining doing it to another part of his body. With an oath, he slid deep inside of her. She cried out, but opened up further to him, tilting instinctively to take him deep.

From Clara and romance books she'd sighed over, she remembered foreplay descriptions, of drawing out lazy need until it was desperate yearning. Goddess, being around her parents was like being in the front seat of one long foreplay session. But this . . . she had no patience for anything but his cock filling her, completing her, joining them. Perhaps Anna was right, that his growing agitation at their separation, his influence on the marks, did this, but she rejected that because she didn't want it to be chemical. Whatever the reason was, though, it was undeniable.

Seizing her behind the neck and pulling his hand away, he kissed her, plundering her mouth with ruthless, demanding force. She writhed beneath him, begging for movement, and he answered, beginning to thrust with a force that brought a guttural moan of pleasure from her with every impact.

She could get pregnant. It was a fleeting thought, but the idea of his child growing inside of her only inflamed her in a shocking way, for she saw it as further proof of their connection, of the bond between them.

He stopped, framing her face in his hands. The roaring fire in his eyes was so close, searching her face. That tangled confusion of emotions again, and then he renewed his pleasurable assault.

She was close to climax, but she struggled to hold back, to wait for him. He was having none of it. "Come for me," he whispered, and she was lost, screaming out her orgasm into his mouth as he held her, pumping even harder so she was driven deeper into the mattress. The headboard hit the wall with a force guaranteeing broken drywall. Her cry broke into a series of notes, shrill to pleading, waves of sensation buffeting her and stealing every worry she had.

Thank the Goddess, it took a while for those waves to stop pounding, to become gentle surf that deposited her weak body on the shore of her present reality. Even then she was slow to orient herself, for he was still moving inside of her, and the friction detonated aftershocks such that she continued to cling to his broad shoulders, tease his skin under her lips, savor the lingering taste of his blood in her mouth.

While her tissues were still vibrating, he pulled out. Before she could protest the loss, he brought her off the bed, and pushed her to her knees before him.

"Take me in your mouth as you wished, in your mind," he ordered.

Though she'd never done it before, she drew him in eagerly, her body still jerking with the aftermath of her climax as his hand fisted in her hair, driving her down on him. *Oh, Goddess.* She wasn't sure why she'd wanted this so much, but she had. She moved over him the way he'd moved in her, following instinct and his reaction to tell her the right way of it. As his hand spasmed in her hair, she reveled in his grunts and the tremors through his legs, telling her how close he was getting. Her own response leaked on her calves. She was torn between wanting him to come this way, and having him come inside her, that hot, searing fire branding her, dispelling the emptiness his absence had created.

This was madness. They knew nothing of each other, but could not get enough of one another, a kinetic spell gone awry. Pulling free, he took her down on the floor, sliding back inside her.

It is what I wish, too. I want you all ways at the same time, in the same moment.

Closing her eyes, she pressed her face into his throat as the thought splintered and was replaced by white-hot pleasure when he released. His arms locked around her, and she reveled in his strength, the feel of him all around her.

She hoped this was the way this was supposed to feel, this reckless speed and heat, the inability to think. Otherwise, she was allowing a situation to spin out of control that needed to be kept under a very tight rein, for his sake as well as everyone else's.

Fifteen

AFTERWARD, he followed her to the bathroom, apparently wanting to watch how she prepared herself for her day. She politely asked to be excused, but when she began to close the bathroom door, he caught it.

"I want to see you," he said, his jaw set.

Alexis planted her feet, but it was more likely the wood would splinter than his grip would loosen. Vampire and Dark One strength combined made him far stronger than even vampire lore suggested. Since he'd gone toe-to-toe with her father and three angels, it was a reasonable assumption. But if that was the case, it meant he'd held himself back during their lovemaking when he could have bruised her far more.

"You can. In a minute. In this world, we don't do this in front of one another. As courtesy." She narrowed her gaze as he refused to move his arm. "I am not going to disappear. The sooner you let me do this, the sooner I'll open the door and you can watch me get dressed. You kept the Dark Ones out of your chamber when you didn't want them around."

"You do not want me around."

Her response to that was instant, reaching up to touch his suspicious expression. "You know I do. I just don't want you around for this. If we're going to make this work, you're going to have to trust me when I tell you things about this world, all right?"

He considered her, his gaze shifting around the bathroom, to the one window. The brief flash of emotion startled her, so that she put her hand back on his arm. "Dante, I'm safe. No one is going to hurt me here. This world is different. At least here it is," she amended, having a brief thought of war-torn African countries.

"Someone can hurt you if they wish. I did."

She met his gaze. "And yet, here I am, back safe and sound. Believe me, being kidnapped through a dream portal was not part of my usual schedule. If I need anything, I'll call out. Okay?"

His grip loosening reluctantly, he nodded.

He didn't go far. Dante moved the several steps to the bed, sat down and stared at the door. Distracting himself, he tested the bounce of the mattress, bemused by it, pressing down with his hand. He considered dismantling it to figure out how it came back into its shape that way, but her disappearance behind that door made him too uneasy. He rose, pacing.

Rationally, he knew she was correct. What little he'd seen was a very different world from what he'd known. Even Hell had been different, as Lucifer said. When the time began to stretch out such that he'd considered tearing Hell apart stone by stone to get free and find her, he'd been allowed to explore with supervision, learn about the workings of the Underworld, gain an understanding of the redemption that the souls there had to endure. Dante found a calm familiarity to the pain and suffering that soothed his agitation to a manageable level.

He was not soothed now, even though, being inside her mind, he could know everything she was thinking. Any threat to her would be known to him instantly. Yet he'd said it himself. The greatest threat she'd experienced in her short life had been him. He'd caused her the most pain and terror. As such, Jonah and the others hadn't perceived his agitation as a desire to confirm she was all right, that she was recovering properly. To give her blood if she needed it.

Truth, he couldn't understand his feelings right now, either.

He'd returned her to her world at a risk to his own objective, in order to preserve her life. That entirely unexpected compulsion had turned him on his axis. Given that, this inexplicable protectiveness was merely a bump on that same road.

It was also irrational. This was her world. She had powerful allies. Jonah, the seawitch, David. She thought of them as her family. But Dante didn't know about family or allies. He knew about minions, those forced to serve through fear, trickery and threat. Alexis's perception of how he felt to be here had been startling. *Yes, no, I don't know.*

In the Dark One world, he'd understood how things worked, and Alexis had been completely his. He'd fought his way up from the bottom, and knowing the road behind and ahead had a comfort to it. From his brief time here, he was uneasily aware this world might require a different skill set than the ability to kill the strongest rival and therefore bring the others into line. If that was all he knew, how was he going to succeed, find a position of strength and hold it? Who would take advantage of his weakness if he couldn't find such a position?

While he was aware of the metal band on his neck, he also knew the threat of pain would not stop him from fighting or killing if it was necessary. Pain was only a deterrent to someone who feared pain. But he didn't like her being behind closed doors. Where was she?

The door opened then, and Alexis was there, smiling at him and bringing that unfamiliar warmth into his chest. The warring factions battling in his mind stilled. He could tell she was worried she couldn't stay balanced, help him the way he needed to be helped, because she was too overwhelmed by her desire for him. He had no problem with her desire. It was a weakness he could exploit as needed. The problem was he had a similar difficulty when he inhaled her scent, touched her body, sensed her willingness to be with him. Her openness made him feel . . . not in a cage. After being trapped for so long, it was as if he had wings like the angels, capable of stretching as far as he wished. As far as he dared. Perhaps that was the problem. In his world, only one kind of fear had to be conquered.

"It's soft, isn't it?"

He noticed then he had one hand clutched in the quilted coverlet. He glanced down at it, then at the other things he hadn't taken time to notice, too caught up in her body, soft and available to him. Pillows. His mother had given him so many images in her mind, words to go with them, so he knew these things. Things had also been brought to the Dark One world, reinforcing that knowledge before they were inevitably destroyed. But knowing and touching, experiencing, were entirely different.

"Why does your father call you Seabird?"

"It's a nickname. A term of affection," she amended, "because I'm an angel and a mermaid both. Nicknames come from looking at someone and thinking they're like something or someone else." She gave him a half smile. "Do you look at me and think of something from your world? A marsma, for instance? I can hop."

"You are like nothing else I know."

Her cheeks pinkened, and he sensed that had pleased her, but she crossed the room to pick up the folded clothing her mother had left her. "Feel free to prowl around and look at things while I'm getting ready," she said. Rummaging in a dresser, she pulled out some more things. When she went back into the bathroom, she left the door open, so he cautiously did as she suggested, rising and touching the pillow, picking it up to squeeze it, turn it over and examine it.

"When I was young and stayed over with human friends, what we call slumber parties, we'd have pillow fights." She looked up in the mirror, seeking him, then her eyes widened. She turned. "Wow. So that one's true, too."

He raised a brow, and she gestured to the mirror. "No reflection. Guess that's why vampires are so good-looking all the time. Since you have no way of checking if your hair is out of place or you have something smeared on your chin, genetics makes you out of Teflon. It all slides off or falls back into place." When she gave a quick, easy grin, the surge of warmth came again, though he sensed something more tentative and wary behind the pleasant façade. He left it alone for now, since he felt a similar way when they were not coupling as they'd just done.

"Pillow fight?"

Putting down the brush she'd been working through her hair, she picked up an extra pillow that had been left in the chair by the bathroom door. Clutching the top two corners in her slim hands, she took a swing at him.

He blocked it, halting her follow-through and shoving her against the wall in the same flow of motion. Taking her off her feet earned a startled cry, but he held her there, searching her mind. What she'd thrown at him had been harmless. Soft. Why would she use that as a weapon?

It's a game. It's not meant to harm anyone.

She was trembling. He'd frightened her with his speed. Her hands, so fragile and breakable, were clutching his shirt at the shoulders, her pulse racing. Dante swallowed, brought her back to her feet. "I do not know about games."

"It's play. Let me show you." Giving him a searching look, she bent and picked up the pillow, holding it out for his examination before she took the open end of the covering over it, twisting the excess fabric into a handle. "See, when you're at slumber parties, you grab up pillows and hit each other with them." She gave him an arch look, still tremulous at the corners of her mouth. "Okay, don't go crazy here, but I'm going to swing it at you, to demonstrate."

She let it hit him in the side. Then, with an impish grin, she took a stronger swing at his head. Dante ducked it, but she was already turning and managed to hit his hip with more force. He circled the bed, considering, and picked up the other pillow. "What's the goal of this . . . game?"

"Just to have fun. There's no scorekeeping in pillow fights. Technically. I've known some people who think it should be an Olympic sport." As he probed her mind, she quickly picked up his intent. Images appeared for him, filling in the blanks. Then she decided to hop up on the bed, giving herself a height advantage, and took another swing at his head.

He dodged it, retaliating with a swipe that hit her thigh and knocked her legs out from under her. He'd attempted to hold his strike, but she landed with a decided bounce on the intriguingly springy mattress. "*Oof.* Good thing I went for the bed."

He peered down at her, then his gaze went lower, to where her nightshirt had slid upward, nearly revealing her pretty sex. Thinking about the soft give of the mattress and pillows, he recalled the way those tender lips had spread for his cock, taking him in deep. Though his mind was not open to her, Alexis obviously read his emotions, for she scrambled back to the other side, leaving the pillow. "I'll get dressed," she said hastily. "Otherwise, we might never get back to my place today. Have you walked down to the beach yet? Oh . . ." She turned around again. "Can you go out in sunlight?"

"I was told by Mina that I could, that my Dark One blood dulls the effect that sunlight normally has on vampires. I can't stay out in it long, though, and she recommended something she called *sunglasses*. Very dark ones," he added.

"Good point," she agreed. "We'll stop somewhere to get those first thing. You're going to be unsettling enough without someone seeing your eyes."

"Humans don't know about beings other than themselves. I find that odd."

"So do all of us. I mean, the nonhumans who live here." Alexis shrugged. "For some reason the Goddess allows humans to decide whether to believe in angels, mermaids or worlds like yours as a matter of faith. After the Mountain Battle, it was weird how many of them rationalized it into something else. They decided they'd imagined seeing angels because of the trauma of fighting off *alien* attackers."

She rolled her eyes. "Since then, there've been stories that the Dark Ones were bioengineered soldiers being tested out by some country. I guess it works best for us to hide our identities, except from the few humans who would understand. As a whole, they really don't. They need to control what they don't understand, or they destroy it. Even my closest friend doesn't know what I am, and she's clairvoyant."

"Yet you prefer to live among them, while your parents do not."

"Well, Myel has lived among them before, for short periods of time. I just . . . it feels like where I'm supposed to be, for now. I like it. They're very busy, you know? Active. Always something going on. But I do love the ocean and sky. They're active, too, in a different way. Pyel says I straddle the boundary between sky and water because I feel most balanced here."

After a brief hesitation, she shed the sleep shirt, revealing the fragile slope of spine and sweet curve of buttock. He still saw bruises fading under her skin, the result of the rift energy's bludgeoning, and her fight against the circle's shields in his world. Only a handful of days ago, he'd been in that world, the place he'd been all his life. Now he was here. He was certain in some ways it was a dream, only he could not have imagined some of the things in this dream, having never experienced them. The fragrance of the lotion she smoothed into her hands and on her face. The crumpled look of her clothes on the floor. The smell of salt water drifting in through the open window and the sound of the ocean. Even when he'd had the rift windows, sounds had been muted, distorted, and there'd been no ability to smell, taste.

She stepped into her undergarment, a quick hitch, then she was putting her arms into the straps of her bra, hooking and working it around to cradle her breasts. It commanded his attention, the erotic movements of her body performing such a simple task, the wriggle of her hips as she pulled on a skirt that hugged them, arching into a shirt that clung to her curves. The V-neck showed the valley between her breasts. He knew enough to know it was not a deliberately provocative outfit, but his palms heated with the desire to touch regardless.

Alexis twisted her hair up and stuck in a pair of dark shiny sticks topped with glittering sapphire stones to hold it. "All right. Why don't we go to my place, get you settled there? Is that all right, or is there something else you want to do right away?"

When she turned and faced him, color rose in her cheeks. "Other than that. I'd feel more comfortable being with you where I live. My parents may decide to stay here tonight."

Her gaze went to the wall behind the headboard. "I'm hoping they'll think they did that. The one advantage to having immortal and amorous parents."

Clearing her throat, she continued to stare fixedly at the head-board. "Can you stop looking at me like that?"

"Why? Because it makes you want to do exactly what I'm thinking?"

She shot him a narrow look. "You get a free pass on comments like that because you don't know what a smart-ass is. For now."

No image in her mind explained that, so he simply studied the enigma that was her. "Do you want to see my home?" she asked, a note of desperation in her voice.

"Yes."

Since he stood by the dresser at the stairs out of the loft, she had to draw closer. When she looked up into his face, touching his arm, it made the nerves under his skin ripple, his body tighten. But because she seemed determined to take him somewhere else, and he was curious to see more, he tried to mute his lust so she would relax.

"I won't take you to places with lots of people, not until you're used to them. And remember, you don't have to see and do everything at once. Whenever you get overloaded, or tired, just tell me, if I don't sense it up front. You're harder for me to read than most people."

She was still wondering if that was because of the interference of her own feelings, or something else. Since he had no answer for her and his mind was elsewhere, he put his hands on her hips, drew her closer to him. Her palms settled naturally on his chest as his fingers curved into the shirt, finding the tempting give of her body beneath. Her forefinger moved in a single stroke over the base of his neck. "It's going to be okay," she said.

"Alexis, I am not a child you need to reassure. Do you understand this?"

She frowned. "Now you sound like my father."

"Perhaps he and I agree on one thing, then. If something happens out there, and I feel threatened, you will not be wise to get between me and that threat."

"It may not be wise, but I'll do it, because nothing you're going to see today is a threat. I don't want you hurt by that collar rebounding, or have you accidentally hurt someone else. You have to trust me." Her fingers dug in a little, with insistence and sharp edges. The sudden set of her jaw was matched by the determination thrusting forward in her mind. "So if you're wise, you'll pull your punches."

"You will not command me," he said testily.

"It's not a command." She blew out a breath. "Geez, the testosterone factor. You do realize how much my father wants an excuse to obliterate you, right? We have to show him, prove to him, you can get along in this world without maiming, blowing away or ripping anyone's head off. I know you hate that. I know you're very proud, and you think by trying to get along you're somehow becoming a slave again."

He stepped back from her then. "Because you know my emotions, do not think you can dictate to me."

"I'm not trying to do that. Dante, it's going to take time for you to understand." Her fingers curled into tense balls at her side. He saw the jumble of thoughts in her mind, her struggle to describe what was beyond his immediate understanding. "You can be what you want to be here, as long as you don't harm others to be that."

He hooked the collar with two fingers. "You put this on me, which keeps me from being what I am."

"You let me," she said, though she flinched at the accusation. "Dante, you remember how you set up the circle shield to keep me in the chamber, until I understood why I couldn't leave it? To protect me when the Dark Ones came in?"

He nodded, reluctantly. "You want me to believe this is like that."

"It is." She stepped to him again and the return of her closeness was welcome, despite the discomfort her words were causing. Stopping between his boots, she tilted her head. "I understand about the collar. I know that pain won't stop you. It breaks my heart, knowing why that is. What you've endured. Those emotions are a well inside of you, and that well is way too deep and dark to go all the way to the bottom, even for me. But you worked so hard and long getting here. Can you have enough patience left to trust me a little, enough to get through today? That's not so bad, right?"

He looked down at her. Pulling those sticks out, he made her hair tumble down onto her shoulders. He framed her face and brushed his mouth over hers, a brief taste. "I like your hair better like this."

"Then that's how I'll wear it." Her fingers made another shy pass near the base of his throat, a stroking. "Are you ready to go?"

"I am ready."

Sixteen

AFTER classes that day, Clara went to Lex's place, letting herself in with her key. It had become a daily ritual, hoping she was there, and embracing the tactile comfort of being among her things when she wasn't. The clothes they'd picked out together, the ugly footrest shaped like a huggable sea urchin. Lex had fallen in love with it at a dorm yard sale. The food in her cupboards included candy bars she kept specifically for when Clara came, as well as her favorite soda. She got one of each now and wandered back to Lex's bedroom, to the waiting pile of stuffed animals.

Clara desperately wished Lex had a cell phone so she could call and find out what kind of family emergency she'd had. Lex had always had a habit of disappearing for a few days at a time with no real explanation coming or going, so it wasn't the absence that had caused Clara's worry. Things felt okay now, but for the first several days she'd been gone, Clara had experienced such cold fear, she'd nearly lost her mind. Knowing that the police didn't look for an adult until forty-eight hours had passed, particularly one with a habit of disappearing, she'd had to settle for checking out all of Lex's normal haunts, asking who had seen her and who hadn't. Branson at the Conservancy hadn't, but again, Lex rarely kept a set schedule with them. When she was around, she was as regular as clockwork and immensely useful, so they'd adjusted to her periodic, unexplained absences the way everyone else who knew her did.

"I don't want to lie to you," Lex told her once. "You know my life is different from most. Please don't ask me to explain what I can't. I'll understand if that means you can't be my friend, but I hope that won't be the case, because I really need you to be."

The friendship had become a permanent bond, because Clara knew Lex meant to say "want," but "need" was closer to the truth. A lot of people considered themselves Lex's friends because of that vibe she projected, but they were too dazzled by the light to delve below the surface to find out what Lex truly liked or needed.

Before Lex, Clara herself had made a conscious decision not to be true, heart-to-heart friends with anyone because of her clairvoyance. It was too difficult, seeing things about another, their present and future, in stereo simulcast with their spoken hopes and dreams, the things that made them laugh or cry. But she could only read vague things from Lex, no clear pictures of her present and future. It was like the reassuring hum of a radio turned down low, instead of blasting music all the time. If she probed, Clara hit a wall. She'd accepted that block, and they'd been close friends since, even though Lex's aura was unclassifiable, and that light . . . well, it wasn't exactly human.

On the third day, when she was determined to go to the police, the cold feeling ebbed and she received a phone message from a woman who said Lex had a family emergency. Though Lex's psychic signature was strong, her mother's surpassed it, leaving no doubt in Clara's mind the woman was who she said she was.

Something bad had gone down, she was sure of it. It might be over now, but as her friend, she wanted to see Alexis, wouldn't feel comfortable until she did. Which might be why she found herself at Lex's town house, lying on her bed, staring up at the ceiling, thinking and dozing by turns when the sugar crash kicked in. Groggily, she turned her head, startled to see she'd been here for two hours. She'd dozed off longer than she'd expected. Best to get up, find her Chem-Lab book and do some work. Maybe she'd stay here tonight instead of walking across the green to her own town house. But she was so sleepy . . .

She let her eyes drift closed again, but a sense that something was not quite the same in the room made her open them again. She blinked, her lips curving in amazement. "Wow."

As dreams went, he was something else. Tall, winged, dark-haired and dark-eyed. The red silk half-tunic he wore stopped at midthigh and did a great job of not concealing the length of powerful leg, the bare chest and striated abdomen above the wide belt. A deep scar on his chest tweaked a thread of pain in her heart. Angels must be more mortal than advertised. He had gorgeous dark green wings that caught the sunlight filtering through the blinds. Though they were spread enough to frame his broad shoulders, they folded as they tapered down, crossing at the tips near his bare feet. He was studying her closely.

"This is a dream," he said. The power in his voice rolled over her, making nerves tingle all across her flesh.

"The best dream ever," she agreed, pushing herself to a sitting position. His eyes widened fractionally, as if that was unexpected, but it was her dream, wasn't it? She rose and walked toward him, through the bands of sunshine streaming through the slats of blinds. Though they briefly obscured her vision, she reached out anyway and encountered hard male flesh. Oh, a really real dream, and she had more vivid ones than most. She usually recognized the difference between a dream and a vision that might come to pass, her clairvoyance joining with a touch of the fortune-teller, but this seemed like both and neither, at once.

She'd almost say it was real, but of course it was an angel standing in Lex's bedroom, an angel with a strong, heated aura and a touch of darkness. That darkness was a small shadow on his soul, revealing a sadness there, but she could make it go away, all she had to do was touch his lips. She leaned into him, smiling at the idea of kissing away an angel's hurts in her dream.

But it would take more than that. As she gazed up into his eyes, she saw it. The physical scar went so deep, it had damaged the muscle, made it harder to fly. Not impossible, no, but he couldn't do it as well as he'd always done it, and that hurt his pride. The memory of the battle where he'd gotten it made her draw in a breath, seeing his fierceness, the flashing sword, the warrior light in his eyes as he spun and slashed, even after he was struck. Grazing her lips across it impulsively, she slid her hands over his ribs, palms coming to rest on the wide belt. Hooking her fingers there gave her the leverage to lift to her toes and raise her face for the kiss she wanted. But darn it, he was still too tall.

Leaning in to experience every delightful inch of his body, she pressed her thigh against his and shifted onto his foot. She slid one hand over the scar, following it to his shoulder. Tangling her fingers in his hair, she found his nape. His strong neck would give her the needed hitch to reach his lips. But if it was her dream, he should be a little more accommodating and bend down, meet her halfway. Shouldn't he?

"Marcellus? Clara?"

The angel touched her. He gripped her upper arms with a strength that was knee weakening, but not bruising. Easing her off his foot and back onto her own, he held her there as she blinked. Focused. That was Lex's voice, Lex's real voice.

She pivoted on her foot, slow and careful, and saw her standing in the doorway, eyes wide, brows raised. Clara shook her head, trying to figure out why she wasn't looking up at Lex from the bed, which was where she'd be if she'd just woken up. Of course, sometimes during her more powerful visions, she sleepwalked. Once she'd made her way to a flight of stairs and woke by tumbling down them. Since she'd been mostly asleep when it happened, she'd been limp, like a drunk, and had arrived at the bottom with nothing but bruises and rattled nerves.

"Lex," she said. "*Lex.*" Her friend's instant, reassuring smile warmed her, inside and out. "You're okay."

Clara ran forward then, heedless of her groggy state, and threw her arms around the other girl, squeezing her close, breathing in the amazing vibrating energy that was Alexis. She'd always known Lex was glad for their friendship, that it made her feel less alone. She wondered if Lex knew she felt the same. She should really tell her that, but—

Something was still off. Clara frowned, easing back but still petting Alexis absently as she turned her head. And blanched. "Okay, I'm really awake, and he's still there. Lex?"

"You thought he was a dream?" It was the barely repressed laughter in Alexis's voice that brought Clara to a fully awakened state. "Well that explains it. I knew you were pretty forward, but I thought it was a little blatant, even for you."

Clara squeezed her once more for reassurance—*Lex was okay!*— then retraced her steps to the angel, whose dark eyes made it impossible to tell what he was thinking. Though if she had to guess, she'd say he was poised between agitated and . . . irritable. He *had* to be a dream. This was crazy. Putting out a hand, she touched his chest again and sucked in a gasp as he much more readily and quickly took hold of her wrist, stilling her. "Holy shit. He is real."

"Yes." He spoke in that distant thunder voice again, changing his attention to Lex. "I told her not to see me, to view me as a dream. She didn't."

"Clara has exceptional clairvoyance. Pyel knows, which is why he never comes around me when she's here. But I wasn't expecting her. I wasn't expecting you, either." There was fondness, but a mild reproof in the tone, and this time his brows drew together, his grip tightening perceptibly. But Clara was pleased that his grip was tightening on her, whether conscious or not.

"Your father asked me to watch you."

"I know. I'm sorry, Marcellus. I didn't mean to sound snappish." Alexis looked between her friend and the angel. She was receiving a curious mix from them both. Well, not so curious from Clara, because she knew her friend's irrepressible appreciation for men. Marcellus, however, seemed almost reluctant to let Clara go.

"So, if he's real"—Clara cleared her throat and attempted to look nonchalant, something Lex knew was entirely bogus, since her friend was bouncing between disbelief and amazement like a Ping-Pong ball—"did he show up in your bedroom because you're shamelessly using him? And if not, can I have him?"

Lex couldn't help it, she laughed out loud at the expression that crossed Marcellus's face. Oh, Goddess, this was why she'd missed Clara so much.

"*Er*, he's like an uncle to me, Clara. He and my father are very close. Which is why he's looking so horrified. Trust me, he's way too much trouble. Angels always are."

Marcellus stepped back then, releasing Clara, and gave a slight bow. "Where is Dante?"

"Right here." Dante stepped out of the shadows behind Alexis, where he'd obviously been gauging the situation. Lex knew he'd been prepared to counter the potential threat the angel posed, so it had been tricky there for a moment, coordinating between her conversation and the reassuring thoughts she was sending to him, filling him in on who Clara and Marcellus were.

All the blood left Clara's face and she backed up two steps, right into Marcellus, who put his hands on her shoulders. Whether to stop her from squashing him in the corner or as reassurance, Lex wasn't sure.

"He's . . . He was what was all over you that day, when your aura was strobing like Christmas lights. Who . . . what is he?"

"Clara, this is Dante. As far as what he is, I think maybe you and I need to talk some." Alexis shifted her glance to Marcellus. "I don't think there's really any choice but to tell her some of it now, right? I trust her."

"I trust your judgment regarding her." Though his tone said he found her judgment about Dante far more questionable.

Lex suppressed the urge to stick her tongue out at Marcellus as she had when she was younger and he was being too overbearing. It didn't matter, because she was being ignored, the two males eying one another with mutual dislike.

Despite that, Alexis discovered something unexpected. Marcellus didn't have the same vibe toward Dante that her father did. Not that Marcellus trusted Dante, but she felt more of a wait-and-see than obliterate-him-now attitude. He brought his attention back to her before she could digest that. "Tread carefully, Alexis. I will inform your father of this new development with your friend, if you are truly fine."

"I am," she promised. "Thank you, Marcellus, for checking on us."

"You," he corrected. "I was checking on you."

Okay, so he wasn't entirely different from her father. She bit back a sigh and nodded. "Tell Pyel we're doing fine."

Marcellus nodded, and then he was gone. Alexis knew angels moved quickly enough that they appeared to dematerialize. From the way Dante stepped to the right, clearing the doorway, she knew he had seen him, but Clara swayed at the sudden lack of support. Lex leaped forward and caught her hands.

"Come and sit down," she said. "We'll talk."

———

As she and Dante had discussed, humans had difficulty processing drastic changes to their reality. Clara was more attuned than most, but Lex still proceeded cautiously, knowing part of it was her own selfish desire not to lose Clara's friendship by forcing a direct confrontation with Alexis's "otherness."

After she'd told her the basics—what she was, where she'd been the past week, Dante's presence—she subsided, waiting for questions or reaction. Clara had remained quiet throughout, her large eyes fastened on Alexis's face. During that time, Dante had prowled the town house, but now he returned to her bedroom and settled on her incongruous vanity chair. It felt like a show of support, an acknowledgment of how difficult this moment might become. She hadn't had to ask him to give her the uninterrupted time with Clara, either. Was it mind reading, or just chance? If it was the former, he was actually being considerate, which was intriguing on its own.

He didn't speak in her mind or say anything to confirm or deny as he returned, but she'd already noted how little he spoke unless addressed directly, or he felt a command or directive was needed. Where Dante had been, idle chitchat wasn't a way to pass the time; scoping his surroundings for threat and information was. While she wondered what he gathered about her place, she considered how many years it would take him to relax and enjoy a setting, rather than assessing it. She'd seen police officers from urban war zones do the same when supposedly relaxing with family at a park or restaurant.

If Clara didn't speak, she was going to scream. There was nothing definitive coming from her yet, though. The girl had curled up in Lex's papasan chair to listen while Lex sat on the bed. She had her arms wrapped around her knees, her chin on them, eyes downcast as she thought.

Lex turned her attention back to Dante. The sunglasses they'd picked up, along with the silence of his emotions, made him disturbingly unreadable. *Are you okay?*

Instead of replying, he rose and moved across her room to the pile of stuffed animals. Squatting in front of them, he reached out and touched Eeyore's wide, pink plush nose. Then he closed his hand over the creature's entire face and lifted the toy, holding it in both hands. The two stared at one another, Eeyore with soulful, sad plastic eyes, and Dante in sunglasses, just as monochrome in his expression.

"I always knew it was something." Clara spoke at last. Alexis snapped her attention back to her. "I'm glad I finally know."

Easy as that, the girl uncoiled from the chair to lean forward and cover Lex's hand with her own. "Mind you, for the next few days, I'm going to be thinking 'no freaking way.' It'll take a little bit to get my mind around it. But I think if that angel comes and stands in the corner of my bedroom, it will help me accept the situation more quickly."

Lex grinned, squeezing her fingers hard in response, holding her friend's gaze long enough to convey her gratitude. What came from Clara were the same waves of friendship and love she'd always shared, laced with a liberal curiosity Lex was sure meant she'd eventually have a million questions to answer. "Trust me, stick with Greek professors. Much easier to deal with."

Clara smiled back, but as her gaze moved to Dante, her sober expression returned. "Lex . . ." She bit her lip, obviously realizing there was no way to speak her concerns, because Lex had made it clear that Dante was in her head. Not to mention he was in the same room.

"I know what you see, Clara." Lex retained her hand. "Trust me. The Dark Ones are terrible beings. Until about twenty years ago, it was assumed that any of their offspring were just as evil. But my godmother is a Dark Spawn. There is a terrible darkness to her, but a great goodness as well, a strong power she used to save the world before you and I were born. My gift is feeling emotions. Most of the time I know what he feels as he's feeling it. He's not evil." *Just a tad dangerous and unpredictable right now*, she added to herself silently.

"So when he gets a sudden urge to murder you, you'll know right ahead of time?" Though Clara muttered it, the ominous presence behind Alexis flickered with warning, no matter his apparently harmless examination of her stuffed animal collection.

"Dante won't hurt me. Not on purpose."

"He's . . . like you. I can't feel anything from him. He's got psychic shields like Fort Knox."

"I know. Sometimes I have a hard time reading him as well. It's like his emotions are all there, but they're a big ball of yarn."

"Leave it to you to pick the most complex male in the whole universe." Lex was relieved to feel Clara push back her worry. "What can I do?"

"Well, I'd kind of like you two to meet each other formally." But when Alexis shifted around, she stopped, blinking.

He'd picked up several more animals, and was bringing them to his face, rubbing the soft fur there. Giving Clara a reassuring look, she rose, circled the bed and kneeled next to him. As he looked toward her, she slid the glasses off his face, because she wanted to see the swirling flame of his eyes. "These are toys," he said.

She nodded. He held Tigger in one hand and Pooh in the other, Eeyore balanced on his knees. Alexis took the Eeyore and closed her arms around the donkey, giving him a hug. "I sleep with him sometimes. His sad eyes make me feel better if I feel lonely."

He took that one back from her. It should have looked odd, the tall man with a stern expression and frightening eyes holding a trio of stuffed animals, but the wave of jumbled responses from him told her differently. He studied Eeyore. "You hold him while you sleep. In one of those large shirts that hides your body." His distaste for that was so obvious she caught Clara's surprised quirk of mouth.

"Yes. They're comfortable."

"Mmm." He brought the Eeyore back to his face, stroked the

plush once again across his jaw. When he leaned forward, Alexis held still as he rubbed his jaw against her skin, his nose teasing her hair.

"I'm not as soft and furry," she attempted to smile, though her heart was in her throat.

He shook his head, leaned back. "Just as soft, a different way. There is nothing soft, where I am from. The closest to it are not close at all. They are . . ."

"Squishy?" she supplied helpfully. He nodded.

"Yes. Many of them bite, or their skin is poisoned." Dropping Tigger to the floor, he ran a thumb over her bottom lip, then down her throat to the vee of her shirt. As if Clara's presence was inconsequential, he grazed his knuckles over the rise of her breast. "If I sleep with you in my arms, will I feel less lonely?"

"I hope so. I don't want you to be lonely anymore. Ever again." Her passion surprised her, rising hot and sure from her heart. Also unexpected was a sudden surge of anger toward Mina. Why had she left him there?

"She owed me nothing." He cocked his head, his gaze penetrating. "Neither do you. Why do you help me, Alexis? What is it you wish from me, other than the pleasure of my body?"

Alexis's face flamed. Clara cleared her throat. "*Er*, do you want me to take off now? I do have a Chem test, but if there's anything you need from me . . ."

Alexis straightened, and Dante rose with her, blocking her way. "You did not answer me." The crimson eyes flamed in warning, though she'd already felt the darkness swell within him, goaded in some way by the direction of his thoughts, his question. Clara registered it as well, for she was casting about for something to use as a weapon.

Dante turned on his heel. Lex caught his sleeve. "No, she doesn't mean you any harm. She's—"

Curling his lip he hissed, showing off the prominent fangs, and giving Clara a direct view of his otherworldly gaze. The girl gasped, but she held her ground, closing her hands into fists. "You try to hurt her, you'll have to take us both."

"No one is hurting anyone." Alexis kept a firm grasp on Dante's sleeve, though she knew that would be no physical deterrent at all. Fear flooded her. *Please, don't hurt her. Dante, why are you angry?*

He vibrated with barely leashed violence, so malevolent everything in Alexis demanded she withdraw her hand and escape the room with Clara. Instead, she tightened her grip. *You're scaring me. Scaring us both. We've been through this before. You're much stronger and faster than either one of us. You could kill us before we could blink. We're not a threat. Please stop.*

Slowly, some of the tension left the arm beneath her grip. He held his gaze on Clara's pale face another second before he turned his attention back to Lex. "I want her to leave," he said.

"She's my friend. She wants to be sure I'm okay, and safe."

"I will protect you."

"Yeah, that's definitely the impression I just got. You can't control what's in you," Clara retorted. "She just told me Dark One blood is hard to contain. How do you know for sure you won't hurt her? What's stopping you?"

"Clara," Alexis said sharply. "Don't." Goddess, why was Clara goading him?

"This." He tapped the steel on his neck with a short, jerky movement. "A collar to contain the beast's madness, until she decides I am useless and they kill me. That is why her motives are important to me."

"Please look at me, then. Let me answer you." Alexis held her breath until he stared down into her face. Those eyes could laser right through her flesh, open her up, but she held his gaze. "You have a right to live here, not to be trapped in a Dark One world. The collar is for your protection."

"I need no protection," he snarled, and Clara jumped. "I need nothing. I got here—"

"Because I risked my life to pull you through," she shot back. "Because I believe you have a right to live. Why isn't that enough of a reason for you?"

"Because no one risks their life like that. No one."

"You did. For your mother."

He went still then, his body turning into a rigid statue. In contrast, the energy building around him eased off enough that Lex dared to look at Clara. "I'm all right," she said calmly. "I'll call you tomorrow if I can. Okay?"

Please don't argue, she thought, not sure if she could talk Dante down from that ledge when he was still standing so close to it. "Okay," her friend responded after a tense pause. "But I'm close by if you need me."

"I know." Alexis sent her a distracted smile. She held her focus on Dante as Clara left the room, and they heard the door close.

"You know nothing of that," he said.

"Yes, I do. I felt it, when you spoke of her, when you said you killed her. Feelings are a map, Dante. Even though yours are pretty tangled, a few of them come through so strong they practically come with pictures. They chained her, you said. She kept you alive by letting you feed on her. They tortured her, used her. And one day, despite the fact you knew you would be punished for it, you couldn't bear it any longer. Her mind was gone, broken, and so you ended her life. They hurt you badly for it, but they didn't kill you, though you wished they had, for a while. You had nothing to gain for yourself by taking her life."

"You are wrong. I did not like the way her pain made me feel. So I killed her, and felt better." But Dante shifted his glance back to the stuffed animals. *Toys. Things given to children and even adults for amusement, comfort.* Earlier, he'd heard Lex's thoughts, wondering how to teach him about emotions he'd never experienced. Some of them were apparently imprinted on the soul at birth, because coming in contact with them now was like the return of sensation in extremities long ago frozen, burned or even amputated. The thawing of this memory brought sharp agony, almost worse than physical torment.

He hadn't wanted to remember the reasons he took his mother's life. He'd blocked out everything but the actual deed, that savage thrust into his mother's heart with the blackwood stake he'd sharpened. He'd hacked off her head as well, using his fangs as needed, so there was no way they could revive her. They'd likely eaten her, but he never knew. They were removing her chains when he was first beaten to unconsciousness, the last escape he experienced from pain for a long time after that.

She hadn't been lucid in months, his mother. The last time she'd spoken to him, recognized him as her son and not one of the Dark Ones, she'd said little. Simply shuddered with pain and repeated the name he'd chosen for himself, over and over. He'd curled up at her feet, laying his head against her bare thigh. She never minded him staying close, though most times the Dark Ones drove him away from her. They only let him feed off her blood while they violated her, and they made sure he was so ravenous he couldn't refuse his own hunger. He'd had to shut his ears to her cries of pain as he was drinking, the grunting of the Dark One and rapid flap of leathery wings. She would speak in his mind, the one thing they couldn't take from them, and tell him it was all right, to take his fill, even though her thoughts were broken into halting pieces by her own agony.

Why had she never given him a name herself? Or had she, and she just refused to tell him, not wanting to give him something else they could take away?

"Dante."

Somehow he'd gone back to the stuffed animals. Alexis was kneeling next to him. He gripped one of the toys, the yellow bear with a red shirt and a bewildered expression.

"I'm hungry," he said without inflection. It was the only certain thing.

Taking the bear from him with gentle hands, she rose to her feet and drew him with her. Sitting down on the bed, she moved her lustrous fall of brown hair over her right shoulder, baring the left to him as she pulled her shirt off of it.

Instead of accepting that offer, he put a knee on the bed and took her to her back. He curved a hand over her throat, holding her down and feeling the pulse of her life beneath his palm as she stared up at him. She didn't know what he was going to do, and that worried her a little, but she was choosing to trust him, a decision that angered and aroused him at once.

"Lift your skirt so I can see your cunt," he said crudely. Her flush, the way she moistened her lips, goaded him further.

"I like your touch," she whispered against his hold.

"Do as I say."

Gathering up the hem of her skirt, she worked it up until he saw the swatch of panties covering the plump line of her sex. As he watched, a drop of moisture bloomed on the silken crotch.

It inflamed him, her trust, her desire. He bent, increasing his grip at her throat as he closed his mouth over the filmy cloth, tasting her through it. Emitting one of those gasps that rippled through him, hardened his cock, she arched up into his face. He rubbed his cheek along the tender flesh of her inner thigh, pressed the points of his canines into softness, hearing the rush of the femoral artery.

Spread your legs wider for me.

She trembled, but complied. Savage monsters rose from the darkness of his subconscious, but they didn't intend to harm or kill. They simply wanted, with an avarice concentrated on this moment only, this room. They wanted to drain not only her blood, but the life energy that swirled through her, warming him, confusing him.

Lack of control made him vulnerable to attack from any direction; his wildness blinded him, so he'd learned never to give full rein to his desires. Until he'd mastered such iron control, there were times he'd gone mad trying to hold the reins on himself that tightly. For days he might caper around the Dark One world like a rabid creature, half remembering everything he did or experienced. The Dark Ones had found that amusing, taunting him but doing less damage than when he was self-possessed.

She'd spread herself wide for him, her arms out to her sides, fingers clutched into the coverlet. "Will this hurt?"

"Yes," he said, "But only for a moment."

He bit, and she sucked a cry in through her teeth as he found the bloodsource he wanted. The heat of her sex was throbbing against his face as he suckled and licked, his head moving in slow, rhythmic motions that rubbed his temple over her swollen clit behind the tight, damp fabric. She moaned each time he did it, lifted and dropped.

When he was done, he pressed his mouth upon the puncture, laving it with his tongue until he'd stopped the blood flow, then he turned his mouth to other hungers. She almost came off the bed as he sealed the wet heat of his mouth over her, marking the fabric with her blood as he flicked his tongue over the soaked panel, inhaled her deep through flared nostrils. She quivered, hard and deep in her belly. She was so close, he could see it in the spiraling, chaotic tumble of thoughts, images and sensations. It overwhelmed him.

Turning her in an effortless move, he brought her up on her hands and knees. Pulling open the pants he wore, shoving the skirt to the small of her back and tearing off that swatch of silk, he entered her from behind. The way Dark Ones did it. He despised the visceral satisfaction, even as his body didn't care, surging into hers, claiming, needing.

Your wings. I want to see your wings. He tore the shirt down the middle just as her wings came forth, spreading wide and then angling up, as if he were pressed against a butterfly, her soft feathers brushing his skin as he thrust into her, hard, greedy, feeling her spasm and writhe, so close, milking him deeply. The legs transformed at the same time, increasing that divine tightness, her tail sliding off the bed as he adjusted to straddle it.

She screamed, her climax galvanized by the different sensations, and he released as well, that quickly. Her blood coursing through his system, his seed jetting into her, was a painful yet pleasurable finish that had his face pressed into her nape, lips in her hair, while her wings trembled out to either side of him. As she slowly came down from her pinnacle, wracked with tiny convulsions, the wings went to a half fold, brushing his shoulders and hips, tips tickling his calves.

Gradually, she transformed so he was holding a human woman again. Still drained from her time in his world, something such as this could rob her of strength as quickly as the climax itself. His knowledge of her exhaustion had him turning her onto her side on the bed. Loathe to let go of her, he fitted his body behind her. Making a noise of contentment, she closed her hand with an intriguing possessiveness on his forearm, nestling her head into her pillow and under his jaw.

———

Why are you helping me, Alexis?

She was asleep already, he knew. She'd answered the same question earlier, but he could neither believe her words nor comprehend the emotions in her mind when she spoke them. Too many unfamiliar impressions and feelings.

She'd had no male in her life, no sexual experiences before him, so it could be explained by that. It was plausible for one so young. The first time he'd had an actual orgasm, forced as it was by his tormentors, the pleasure of it had been addicting. A way to escape everything for a few seconds.

He'd told her he was ready to go from her cottage to this location. He'd been partly wrong about that. All those images he'd dissected a thousand times in his head were nothing next to experiencing them firsthand. Alexis had described this world as busy, always moving. He was used to that in the Dark One world, but the variety of activities here were different, often not violent or dangerous, but disconcertingly unpredictable. In the Dark One world, all activities came with danger or violence. Base needs—lust, hunger, thirst, fights for dominance.

Sequestered in this snug, warm bedroom, thinking of the love and devotion of her parents and those who served them, he had a hard time thinking she sought escape through sexual passion as he had. But his presence in her life could very well be riding on the goodwill of her youth and sexual self-discovery. When that passed, she would have no use for him and the others would try to kill him, as he expected.

They could try. And she could tire of him all she wished, but he would let her go only when *he* was ready.

Seventeen

S HE woke famished. She was going to have to start keeping Red Cross blood donation supplies in her nightstand. Cookies, juice, crackers. Then she realized Dante was not in the room with her. Amusement turned to panic. It hadn't occurred to her he would go somewhere without her. They hadn't really set any ground rules, or even established how he would react to ground rules.

Scrambling out of the bed, she ignored her growling stomach and wobbly knees, made it halfway to the door and realized he was in her kitchen. Either that or she had a very large rat emitting multiple sonar pings of curiosity. He was likely going through cabinets, examining each kitchen utensil.

Determined to start today halfway decently dressed and put together, she resolutely about-faced and headed to the shower. The bite area on the inside of her thigh was healed but still tender. As she passed her fingers over it, the memory made her shiver, the heel of her hand brushing her sex. Goddess, he'd been so urgent. So hungry. Rather than her being dismayed by his violence, her own hunger had almost eclipsed his.

That thought put a damper on her recollection. She'd let her own lust take precedence over the possibly destructive state of his mind, and that wasn't good. Hadn't she confessed such a worry to Anna? But it was harder than she'd expected. Even with her empathy, she'd always been an outside observer to the emotional fluctuations of young women who'd experienced sex for the first time. That mad flush where physical reaction was confused with emotional because of the intensity of the experience. Of course, it was hard to compare what occurred in candlelit dorm rooms, a sock hung on the doorknob to warn away intrusive roommates, with a seduction that began in her dreams and was consummated in a fiery world where her life had hung in the balance.

However, she was aware of what might be the same as some of those women's experiences. It might have meant something far different to him. She was honestly too swept away by her own feelings at the time to register his. But he had felt something. She would have sensed a physical reaction devoid of feeling.

Goddess, the truth was she was in over her head and afraid to admit it to anyone who could help her, because she *was* certain about one thing—right now, she was the only true ally he had, and he couldn't afford to have her taken away from him.

The water was running hot, so she stepped in, letting it wash away her uneasy thoughts for now. Hopefully Dante was too busy discovering the delights of cookware to have tuned in to her dilemma.

At least it wasn't too difficult to focus on this instead. Though her mother had bathed her, it was of course not the same as a full scrubbing. Plus, the washing brought the musk of their lovemaking to her as she cleaned those private crevices. She shuddered anew, remembering how he'd taken her over. If nothing else, she could be sure she was anatomically more pleasing than what he'd had before.

"Infinitely."

She yelped, opening her eyes, and found him standing at the shower door. He was still naked, the same way he'd slept with her. The sight of his tall, muscular body, so imposing and appealing at once, the cock semierect already, made her libido stomp out her attempts at self-control and rationales like a lumberjack with size sixteen boots.

It didn't help that he was studying the way the soap slid down her wet body with intense interest. He lifted a candy bar. "This was in your mind when you woke. Along with many other food items I couldn't match to what is here."

As she watched, he peeled back the wrapper and tossed it away, then extended it toward her mouth. "Eat, before you fall down."

Chocolate with the flavor of water running over her face had a sensual appeal, particularly with him feeding it to her. Her body vibrated. They had things to do. They . . .

"It does not have to take long," he noted, his eyes darkening in their flames. Before she could think of a protest, or whether she even wanted to try, he'd stepped into the shower and caught her under the arms, holding her up against the shower wall. The chocolate melted in her mouth as his closed over it. She clung to him as water poured over them both and he entered her again, cock now ready for her such that she gasped as his fullness invaded. Her legs wrapped around his back, welcoming him eagerly.

SEX with Dante was exhausting, but it was nothing next to teaching someone who'd only had a bird's-eye view of the earth everything that could be crammed into one afternoon. He never ran out of questions. They started with her kitchen, and the various assortment of things he'd taken out of her refrigerator and lined up on the counter. With some amusement and dismay, she noted he'd dismantled a bunch of items. He'd ripped the seams out of one of the couch cushions to touch the filling, opened the cover of her movie player to study the wiring. Unscrewed lightbulbs, even tested the rarely used dead bolt on the door, but thank goodness he hadn't tested its strength or she suspected she'd have been calling a carpenter to replace the frame. Or repair the drywall that would have been ripped loose by the force.

She didn't turn on the TV yet. That would be a good choice for later tonight, when she could lie on the couch, nurse her tiredness and yet keep answering the endless array of questions she expected cable programming to incite.

Plus, as much as he liked to ask questions, she noted he was increasingly restless, wanting to get out of the confines of four walls. When he took her organic eggs out of the carton and arranged them on a plate in an amazingly balanced pyramid, it reminded her of his garden and gave her an idea of where to take him.

Getting him into the car was smoother than the first time. At the cottage, he'd circled it, studied it from all sides. He'd had Alexis roll down the windows, not liking the closed feeling. Cars had been new to his mother when she was taken, but not entirely unfamiliar. He'd seen them through those rifts before Mina closed them, as well, but being close to them of course was different.

This time, she was the one who needed an additional steadying breath, standing in the open car door. This would be the first time she'd be taking him out in public, around others. After the past twenty-four hours, she was very aware she was more a guide than a guardian. Did she really know what she was doing? How had she convinced her father and Mina of this madness? Maybe it was best for them to go back inside, and . . .

He stood on the opposite side, gazing steadily at her. Fortunately, there was no anger in his gaze. "What do you fear, Alexis?"

"You know. That you'll think someone's attacking me or you and incinerate a city block. Then my father and Mina will come and take you away . . ." *From me.* She bit it off, realizing anew how possibly counterproductive her own motives were. "Dante, I'm not sure if I was right. Maybe I shouldn't be doing this without a couple of the angels along."

"You were sure last night. It is only your fear making you doubt yourself." His straight hair, loose on his shoulders, lifted and swept across his face, his sensual lips. She wished she could see his eyes, and he accommodated her, removing the glasses so she could meet them. He was eager to get out, see this whole new world. And why wouldn't he be? He didn't want to kill and maim. He wanted to see how a car worked, walk amid people who wore different-colored clothing, smelled of different fragrances. See the sun shine, even if it was from the safety of a table umbrella at a sidewalk café.

Those weren't his thoughts of course, but the emotions he was emitting had hints of that in it, like a hummed song where the listener could almost understand the words from the feelings evoked by the notes.

He slid a hand across the top of the car. Intrigued, she reached out, met his fingers tip to tip, since her arm was shorter and couldn't quite reach. "What was that for?" she asked softly when he pulled back.

"Touch eases your mind," he explained. "And I like touching you."

He could relax with her. He couldn't do that with an angel escort. She'd survived the Dark One world, for Heaven's sake. She could survive being a vampire's tour guide.

"Okay, let's go."

———

ALL right, maybe she couldn't. "Dante," she explained for the tenth time, "I can't answer questions about everything you see, because I'm driving. If I look to see everything you're pointing at, I'll wreck the car. Though you may be indestructible, it won't be pleasant. And I like my car. We'll walk later today, and that way I can tell you about things right when you see them."

"Why can't we stop and walk now?"

"There will be time to do it all," she promised. "I just have somewhere I'd really like to take you first. There are too many people on the sidewalks. I'd rather you get used to having people around you in a more . . . low-key environment."

He seemed dissatisfied with that, but subsided, though he continued to watch the passing scenery with intense interest. She was beginning to think her comparison to an infant was not inaccurate, though it was still amusing, given that the last thing she wanted to do when she looked at Dante was shake a rattle at him or coo.

Of course, he was plundering all information around him, including her mind, so she was pressed into an explanation about babies and their entertainments.

Maybe she was more like a new mommy than she wanted to acknowledge. She was intrigued by his reactions to everything, and still nursing a nervous flutter about having him out on her own. No mother had ever been so distracted by her infant's profile or how his jeans fit his thighs, though. Plus, an infant would have been behind her, strapped in a child safety seat. She suppressed a smile as he turned a narrow gaze to her.

"Oh crap." The fuel light. In her distraction, she'd forgotten to stop and get gas, and Heaven only knew how long that had been blinking. If Dante had been practically hanging over her shoulder, as he'd wanted to do in order to watch the way the instrument board worked, she was sure he would have noticed it earlier.

They weren't far from her destination, the community center, so she pulled into the Korean grocery on the corner. The bars on the windows and door, the graffiti on the cinder block side walls and concrete island, advertised this wasn't the best neighborhood, but that didn't concern her. Her gift protected her from unfriendly advances.

The community center had been built in such an area to be accessible to low-income families, and she didn't mind supporting the Korean grocer that stuck it out here, despite constant robbery attempts. She enjoyed showing Dante how to pump the gas, talked him out of pouring some on his hand to smell it and left him leaning against the car, watching the numbers tick by, while she went in to pay. She'd told him how to finish up and put the lid back on, so that gave her an extra minute to pick up another candy bar and a bottle of juice. The healthy breakfast she'd consumed while explaining everything to him had helped steady her, but she wanted to be prepared, just in case.

However, her pleasure that things were going so well was disrupted by the storekeeper waving her back up to the front. "Your friend may have trouble," he said.

Leaning across the counter to see out the window, she swore under her breath. A car full of gang members had pulled up to the pump on the other side, and the members had spilled out, a couple coming toward the store while the others propped on their vehicle, engaging Dante in conversation.

"I can't leave the register," the grocer said, a worried look on his lined face. "I'll call the patrol officer and ask him to drive by for your friend, but he may take a few minutes."

"It's not my friend I'm worried about." Paying for the gas, Lex grabbed the items she'd bought and hurried back out toward the car.

Dante was still leaning against their vehicle, his arms crossed, sunglasses hiding his expression, but from the stillness she felt from him, he was aware he faced trouble.

"It's a pretty white boy. A *really* white boy," one of the gang members was taunting, as several others circled her little hatchback, hooting at her fairy and flower static clings. "Got any money to pay for our gas, pale boy? Hiding under that cute shirt you're wearing? Look at all that pretty hair."

Dante glanced down at himself quizzically and then back up. "No. I do not have money."

"Sure you don't. Think you ought to let my friends here check."

"Stop this," Alexis said. She pushed past one of the boys to move in front of Dante, ratchetting up the angelic light of her aura. While it would momentarily confuse their intent, she was touching excessively battered consciences jacked up on chemicals, clouding their receptors. "We're just going to visit the community center. Please let us go."

"Oh, one of them do-gooders. How about you give us some money for our gas, pretty boy's bitch?" The one in charge gave her a raking glance and rubbed his crotch suggestively. "You fine looking, girl. You let your bitch do your fighting for you, pretty boy? She looks tougher than you, that's for damn sure."

She had a tart response for that, for she already sensed this was more show than intent, performing for his boys, but she'd forgotten how fast a vampire could move. She didn't even know Dante had left her side until the gang member squawked for air. He was being held off his feet, his back slammed against the gas pump. As his face went red, headed toward blue, the boy's sneakers kicked ineffectually against Dante's legs.

Dante, please don't hurt him. We can't let you—

Even as she began the admonition, she registered the tremor in Dante's back, smelled burning flesh. Dropping the sack, Alexis lunged forward, caught hold of his shirt. "Put him down. Stop hurting yourself!"

Dante complied by tossing his victim away from him, which took the young man twenty feet across the parking lot. He landed on the broken asphalt with a bone-breaking thud and a shrill shout of pain. As two of the gang ran to his assistance, Dante closed a hand on Alexis's arm, holding her at his side as he removed the sunglasses. The other three closing in confronted pure flame. His mouth was taut with pain or rage, she couldn't tell, because both vibrated from him.

Lex saw dark rivulets running under his skin, burns from the steel collar. The metal was dull orange, but a moment ago it had been stove top red-hot, like sword steel pulled from a smelter's fire.

"She is not yours to touch or threaten," he said, and the coldness of his voice should have chilled that steel to ice. Then he bared his fangs.

She thought they set Olympic records, scrambling away from him, piling back into their car. The two who had the gang leader didn't come back at all, helping him up and taking off toward the street, the car peeling out and picking them up before they sped down the road.

At least they wouldn't be scurrying to the nearest police officer to report their strange encounter. She told herself that, hoping to calm her shaking. She'd been right. They couldn't do this. It was too close a call. Taking lives was a simple thing to him, not even creating a ripple in his conscience.

She watched numbly as Dante knelt, picking up the items that had fallen out of the grocery sack, examining the candy bars, sodas and juice she'd chosen. When he brought them to her, he closed his hand over her trembling one.

"You are correct, Alexis. You're my guide, not my keeper. If this is distressing you, I will explore on my own and come back to your place later, when I am ready."

"You can't. They won't let you do that. They said—" She blew out a breath at his expression. "Why are you staying with me, then, if you don't feel like they can keep you here?"

"Because it is easier to do this with you."

Of course. It was easier to have someone to translate and explain what he was seeing, and be a ready-made meal when needed.

The paper crackled between them as he moved close to her. She was standing on the island, so her eyes were almost level with his. Sliding a hand into her hair, he wrapped it around his fingers, tightening so he brought her to her toes and pressed his mouth over hers. Slow, devastating, but hot and needy as well, so that the paper complained further as she clutched it. By the time he lifted his head, she was leaning into him for balance.

"I translated magical texts in a Dark One world. Figured out how to create a new rift there, deep in the earth. Conjured a dream portal to capture you. If I wanted to understand the things in this world, I could. I prefer you at my side."

She swallowed. "I can't be objective. It's not safe."

"That is not something you can control, so that is irrelevant."

He was right, but it didn't make her feel any more comfortable with herself, or at ease with the situation. She couldn't stop thinking of his words and what they meant. *I prefer you at my side.* "Your sunglasses . . . you really should put them back on."

Lifting a brow, he brushed a thumb across her mouth. She couldn't help it, she parted her lips, bit down. He held the digit there, pushed it a little more aggressively against the corner of her mouth, like a horse's bit, stretching her lips as his other fingers curved around the side of her throat, holding her in a way that made every nerve ending electrify. "I assume it is not appropriate to take you here. That this is also public."

"Way public," she whispered. "But I wish it wasn't."

"There are a few things I definitely do not like about this world," he commented, and released her. Alexis drew a steadying breath.

"Dante, you can't . . . I appreciate you defending me, but you need to let me take the lead in situations like that. I could feel what he felt. He wasn't going to do me any harm—"

"He intended to frighten you." He shook his head. "I did that, and I didn't like it."

"I already forgave you for that." Placing her hand on his throat, beneath the collar, she touched the black marks. "Are you okay?"

He wouldn't be distracted. "That is not something to forgive, Alexis. When someone harms you, you ensure it does not happen again. The burns will heal. All my wounds heal."

Not all of them, she thought, touching that black knot of emotions from him. "I'm just saying, since they weren't going to hurt me, it would have been best to let it go. They tried to frighten me, yes, but I wasn't going to be afraid while you were here."

"I am not being clear. I will not tolerate anyone having a thought of harming you, whether they accomplish it or not. You are not strong enough to change their behavior, so it is the only way."

"No. There are other ways," she said softly. "You could have hurt me, in your world. You didn't."

"That was because you . . . my intention was not to hurt you."

"But you would have if you needed to do it, to free yourself. That's what you implied. But when the time came, you didn't. And it wasn't because I was stronger or more powerful than you, more capable of causing you pain. We found another way."

He studied her. "Perhaps. But violence is still more reliable."

"You and my father have more in common than you realize," she muttered, but she ran her knuckles along his cheek. It made his brows furrow as he analyzed the gesture, the way he seemed to do all her actions. Before she could think of something else to say, he'd glanced down at himself again.

"Is there something wrong with my clothing?"

"Yes and no." She allowed herself a small smile. "I love the shirt on you, but it's a bit more romantic than what most men wear, outside of a Renaissance faire. Stay here. I'll go back in and buy you a nice, manly T-shirt so no more local gangs decide you're a sissy girl and get dismembered for their poor judgment."

"You chose it. I will wear it." He opened her car door, peering at the control panel again. "I want to drive this."

"One thing at a time." Moved by his simple declaration and amused at the speed at which his mind was working, Alexis got in and nodded toward the passenger seat. "Tomorrow we'll go to a parking lot so I can teach you to drive."

Eighteen

THE community center was quiet, since it was a weekday during business hours. It was located in the middle of Fortram Park, frequented by adults or sitters letting their young charges enjoy the maze of playground equipment.

She'd given it a great deal of thought, and come to the conclusion children would be the safest ground for him at the beginning. To help him assimilate into his new world, he had to be in a less defensive mode. All predators recognized the young. Children had a greater chance of being accepted as nonthreatening.

Exposing Dante to children might seem a terrible risk to those who only understood him on the surface. It was a steadying reminder of why she'd wanted to be the one to guide him.

As they got out of her small car, he stretched his long legs and looked around him. She'd brought a light jacket for herself, but he didn't seem to be bothered by the nip in the air. The playground wasn't overly busy, which was good, because he didn't blend in in the slightest. The dark frames she'd found for him swallowed those exceptional eyes but emphasized the sensuality of his lips, the sculpting of his jaw. The wind swept his hair over the broad shoulders, drawing the eye to the loose lacing in the shirt front and the tempting chest revealed. She suppressed a sigh. Okay, a common-looking Henley pullover and a haircut might not be amiss. Though she remembered the way his hair slid across her bare skin as he put his lips on her breast. What if he'd gone downward, over her belly, teasing her navel piercing with his teeth . . .

"If you do not stop doing that, I will have to block your thoughts. Or we will have to go back to your home, since you insist on privacy." He spoke without looking toward her, still studying the playground.

"It's not my fault." She closed her car door. "You could try looking less attractive." He'd caught the attention of almost every female in the park, and a couple of the males who obviously preferred their own gender. She came up to his side. "Want to find a bench and sit for a while before we go inside?"

He glanced down at her. "I am not interested in males."

"What about females?"

"Would that anger you?" When she didn't respond, he lifted one perfect brow. "It would. Not anger, but it would . . . hurt you. Make you upset. You are . . . possessive."

Lex turned her gaze away, studied the park herself. "I have no claim on you," she said, knowing it was the truth. In thirty days, if she was successful, he would go and do anything he wished. "But a lot of women have this funny quirk. When we're . . . with a male, we prefer that he only be with us, while we're with him. Physically. What we were doing earlier."

Those dark glasses were still trained on her face. From the heat sweeping across her skin, she knew she was flushing. "Females prefer one male only," he said slowly. "If he wishes another female . . . physically, she no longer wants him."

"Close enough. So if you decide you want to . . . with someone else, I'd prefer you not do that with me anymore."

"When I make that decision, I will remember your request and consider it. Now where is this bench?"

He took a couple steps from her, stopped and looked back at her. "You ask me not to do harm, but you are thinking of skewering me with a stake."

Alexis closed her eyes. When she opened them, she started, because he was back in front of her. Before she could speak, he'd drawn her to her toes and laid his mouth on top of hers. This kiss demanded she melt into him as his arm cinched around her waist, fingers sliding under the knit shirt so he caressed her skin below her bra strap. The position pressed her against his groin, which even under denim and the untucked white shirt made it clear where his thoughts were.

When he lifted his head, his mouth was wet from hers. "If the other females here are the way you say they are, they will not want me now, because they see I am with you. Does that make you feel less angry toward me?"

Actually, after that kiss, she thought they were imagining their curled toes standing right in her shoes. "Your mom had some outstanding memories. You're too good at that."

He lifted a shoulder. "Vampires and Dark Ones are very lustful creatures. Since I have both their blood, I found those memories the most fascinating, and I learned. You are the first I've practiced upon. I had no desire to touch a Dark One like this."

"Oh." She cleared her throat. "Maybe you *should* block my thoughts for a while, at least while you're learning about other things. Less distracting to both of us."

He smoothed her hair. "As you wish. For now."

Backing away from that intense look, she took him toward an empty bench near the playground. She assumed he was following, but was surprised when he clasped her hand. Glancing over, she saw him looking toward another couple who had entered the park, strolling hand in hand. He intertwined his fingers with hers as the two lovers had and then examined the fit. That jumbling of emotions bounced against her mind, what she was beginning to recognize as his reaction when he wasn't certain exactly how to feel about something. He seemed satisfied with it, though, for he moved forward with her in that fashion.

When Alexis sat down with him, she steadied herself. *It doesn't mean anything, Alexis. He's just learning.*

It really was aggravating, to be mature far beyond her years in so many ways, and yet have the emotional yearnings of a twenty-one-year-old who'd never even had a real, romantic kiss before Dante entered her dreams. She wanted to capitulate to the fantasy, not the reality. If she was the only one who'd be hurt, she might risk it, but she had to keep her head on straight. At least until those thirty days were up.

Renewing her resolve, she tuned in to their surroundings, and found a problem, albeit a fixable one. Communicating her intent to him so he would release her hand, she rose to amble among the adults and children. The handsome but sinister-looking stranger watching them and their offspring was making them nervous, so she made sure her angel light was dialed up to ease their worries, smiling gently as she passed by each knot of humanity. Rather than immediately returning, she leaned up against the frame of the swings to watch him.

Back when she'd learned to manage her empathy, what had been most difficult wasn't feeling what a lost soul was feeling. Rather, it was accepting the inability of others to feel the way she did about that person. Instead of understanding, they viewed him or her with suspicion or hatred. They would shun a lost soul, thereby making it even more lost.

As much as her female heart was drawn to the enigmatic vampire, the empathic part of her was consumed by his utter isolation, as he looked at something as alien to him as his world had been to her. Parents playing with their children. Enjoying leisure time, and the beauty of a sunny day. He knew what he was seeing was an accepted standard here, something he'd been denied.

How would he react to that? She assumed his concept of gods and goddesses, faith and cycles was vague at best; everything was capricious fate, luck or the ruthless application of the strong survive. Maybe there'd been a blessing in that. Someone believing in a benevolent higher power, all powerful and all seeing, would have shredded his soul trying to understand his circumstances, wracked with blame, rage, guilt or any combination of the three. But the only higher powers he'd known had been Cruelty or Indifference, so he had no expectations for mercy from either of them.

He saw himself as ruthless, but she was carefully collecting instances proving that wrong, building on it. His decision to save her life, even if it meant his freedom. His mercy killing of his mother. Then, this morning, as she'd showered, she'd realized something else that she'd missed during their intense lovemaking the previous night. He'd said he'd never had sex with anything other than a Dark One, which meant he hadn't raped any of his female sacrifices, or human victims the Dark Ones had brought with them before the rift closing.

His physical appetites were extreme. Even without experience, she recognized that. Using a sacrifice for sexual release wouldn't have interfered with his magic, obviously. The recollection of the female's empty, suffering eyes twisted low in her stomach. While perhaps he hadn't wanted the Dark Ones' leavings, she thought it was something else. He'd been sodomized by the Dark Ones repeatedly. She'd felt the terrible flashes hinting at it. While he didn't hesitate to take a life, he had a line he didn't cross. It wouldn't nominate him for Humanitarian of the Year by a long shot, but it meant something, all part of the puzzle.

He could change, because somewhere under all the debris of his wrecked soul, he wanted to change. She knew it. Which meant this was where she was supposed to be, what she was supposed to be doing, no matter the risks.

As she moved back across the playground to him, she knew when his attention focused on her again. Despite the weight of her previous thoughts, she couldn't stop a rueful smile. Physical appetites, indeed. He was watching the way her hips moved. How the breeze innocently molded her shirt to her breasts and the slope of her abdomen. Then his jaw lifted and she knew those fiery eyes were on her throat, the press of her lips, meeting her eyes at last.

He'd suggested vampires and Dark Ones were very carnal. Perhaps that was why his emotions were so tightly intertwined with his physical responses. He was being overwhelmed by what he saw, with every direction he turned. Maybe the spinning only stopped when he was inside of her, a temporary drug that helped steady him, while knocking her off her axis.

She sat next to him again. He was leaning forward, his hands gripping the edge of the bench seat, so she curved her palm over one of them, fitting her fingers into the spaces between his. Glancing up into the sky, she studied the cloud formations. "Did you ever do that? Cloud pictures?"

He shook his head. "I don't know what that is."

"In your world it would have been different, because the sky was like fire. But here, to pass the time, sometimes we gaze up into the sky and pick out pictures in the clouds. See, over there. That's a pig, with a snout, and a round head. It could also be a bald man with a pug nose. Actually, that fits better. See his double chin?"

He leaned back on the bench, stretching his arms out so one was behind her. Alexis laid her head on his biceps so they were studying the same thing. "Sometimes I saw dragons in the flames," he said at last. "Blue and green, or gold and silver." His arm flexed beneath her head, and she closed her eyes as his fingers stroked her upper arm during a long pause. Finally, he spoke again. "I was willing to hurt you, but you think I would not hurt a child."

"I'm not a child."

He cocked his head, gazing down at her. "You are as fragile. It is the same."

"That's condescending, but I think that comes along free with the arrogance package." She pinched his hard thigh and earned a bemused look. "All right. It's because you're like a child. You've seen a lot of this, but that doesn't necessarily mean you understood what you were seeing. What it meant. You have to touch, feel, interact, to get that. You don't trust anyone right now, but you'll trust a child, because usually a child's motives are harmless and easily understood. Am I right?"

"Except for the part about perceiving me as a child." He lifted a brow. "I think that was . . . condescending."

"Well tit for tat." She smiled. When he sharpened his gaze on the curve of her lips, she held the expression an extra few seconds. His mouth lifted, perhaps to emulate it. Was it conscious, or was something in him responding, learning? Straightening, she closed her hand over his tense fingers, now resting on his knee. Before she could speak, he surprised her.

"Alexis, what can I be in this world?"

"Whatever you want," she responded. But then she shook her head at her own automatic response. "I guess that's what we all say," she admitted, "so people will reach for their dreams. The truth is we often don't get to be what we want. But sometimes what we end up being is better."

The answer didn't satisfy him. For that matter, it hovered uneasily in the pit of her own stomach, like undigested food. She squeezed his hand. "You don't need to worry about that yet. Getting accustomed to all this is enough for now. The rest will come. Want to go see the community center?"

"Yes."

As they strolled in that direction, he copied the body language of those around him, adapting so quickly she knew if it weren't for his extraordinary appearance he'd be a true chameleon. Once, he'd been a scavenger. The skill showed, even now.

She checked them in at the front desk. Her destination from there took them through the main gym area, filled with echoing noise and the movement of young bodies. The scent of sweat and wood cleaner added to the atmosphere. As she guided him around the edge and up the stairs to the second level, she stopped on the top step so he could look down at the entire floor. Boys and girls alike were learning to box from a volunteer coach, and a handful of teen males were busy on a basketball court. Weight training, dance and all sorts of activities were happening, volunteers dedicating themselves to nurturing self-confidence in the hopes it would carry the kids to the top of the heap in their world. Or at least a place that kept them from being crushed.

As a door opened behind them, Dante faced it, putting himself in front of Lex. A mother had a small girl covered with blue paint in tow. The child gave Lex a wide smile as they headed for the washroom. Fortunately the mother missed Dante's forbidding expression.

"Look less intimidating," Lex advised, sliding to his side and tugging him by the hand. "Come in the craft room. You're going to love it."

As they stepped in, Alexis breathed in the comforting aromas of clay, paint, glue and construction paper. The large area had cubby-holes and cabinets stacked with art supplies, everything from buttons and Popsicle sticks to fuzzy, brightly colored pipe cleaners and pom-poms. One of the things she liked best was the large mural on the back wall. It depicted a rainbow-colored Goddess creating the world at a craft table much like these, pondering tiny animal creations, every-thing from the elegance of the swan to the whimsy of the porcupine.

Dante slanted a glance at her. *"Porcupine?"*

When she gave him the image in her mind, his brows rose further. "The seawitch comes to mind."

She almost laughed, but then she caught the bitter undertone to the observation and remembered Dante didn't make jokes. He'd changed position so he was next to the door, his back against the wall, and was continuing to keep her on the far side of him, where she'd be harder to reach by anyone passing by. Giving him time to assess his surroundings, she did the same.

About six sets of children with parents were working at various projects. A sugar cube castle, a knitting lesson, clay sculpting and a couple of paintings were in progress.

"You can create whatever you wish in here," she gestured. "Just like your garden, only here you have all the supplies you can imag-ine." Drawing him with her now, she took him to one of the cubbies and pulled out a fat wad of direction manuals. "Here are lots of ideas, pictures of the things you could do. Hanging out in here for a while, watching the kids and parents, will help you understand human behavior a bit more, and get you used to the noise humans can make in a relaxed environment. I thought the crafts would give you something to do with your hands, if you get restless. I can cram your head with a million facts, but it won't mean as much until you spend time seeing things in action, mingling."

"What is their purpose for doing this?" He nodded to the groups.

"It varies. Some people come here as a way to unwind. Or to spend time with their kids, or with friends who like to do crafts as well."

Spotting an empty place toward the back where they'd be in a corner facing the door, she gestured. "Why don't we sit there? You can watch and think about what you'd like to do."

He nodded. Halfway to their table, he stopped by the child and mother making a castle out of sugar cubes. The boy was adding glitter to the upper turrets while the mother cut out construction paper flags to put on the top ramparts. She glanced up at Dante, did a double take, and Alexis moved in smoothly to his right. "That's lovely," she told the child, a boy with rumpled red hair and long-lashed green eyes. "Is it your castle, or someone else's?"

He produced an action figure Alexis recognized from television. "Well, I think he'll be very happy with that."

When Dante squatted down to the child-sized table to touch the castle, it placed him well within the mother's personal space buffer. She inched away, but Dante ignored her.

He'd assessed her and determined her as harmless, Alexis realized. On top of that, he'd done what any dominant animal would do. Taken over her space and made her move, acknowledging his superiority. The child, not as attuned to such nuances, was across the table, studying him curiously. Dante picked up one of the cubes to examine it. Digging into the box of sugar cubes, the boy handed him one. "Eat this one instead. That has glue on it. Though be careful, cause if you eat too many, you can go crazy and drive your mommy into a loony bin. That's what Mama says."

"Will," the mother began, but Dante took the cube. When he did, his larger fingers closed over the child's smaller ones. He stopped, going very still, and then closed his hand over the child's wrist, turning the palm.

"Sir—"

"My friend means him no harm." Alexis laid a hand on the woman's shoulder, giving her a strong push of calming energy. She was a fortyish woman with green eyes like her son, and laugh lines. Lex sensed a busy life, stresses over money, childcare . . . in short, a normal human, well balanced between the forces of good and evil. She was a good parent. "My friend has been in a special home, and hasn't seen a child in a very long time."

"Why are your sunglasses so dark?" Will asked. "Are you blind?"

"No." Dante stared at a scratch on the small palm. "How did that happen?"

"School. I was playing kickball and fell down. But I kicked it really far. I get picked at least third when they're choosing teams. Try the sugar." He disentangled his hand from Dante's and extended it toward his mouth. "It's really good. I like sucking on it until it melts."

After a pause, Dante opened his mouth and let Will put the sugar cube on his tongue. Alexis was relieved to note the gesture didn't noticeably expose his fangs. He closed his mouth, and his jaw moved, rolling the cube over his taste buds.

"See? But remember, too many and you go craaazy." Will giggled. "Right, Mama?"

Alexis smiled at him. Dante rose and jerked his head at their table, moving away toward it. Lex nodded to the boy and his mother. "He doesn't talk a lot, but he's happy to meet you." With a last bolstering shot for Will's mom, so she didn't run to the front desk and tell them there was an odd adult male touching the children, she followed Dante.

The metal chairs were far too small for his large frame, but he perched gracefully enough, reminding her of how he'd looked like a hunting raptor when he crouched on the wall in Mina's cave. Alexis sat next to him. Cupping the back of her neck, he drew her toward his mouth. Knowing he intended to weaken her knees and flood her mind with warm molasses, she had a brief thought to stop him, not wanting to incite any more interest in their presence. But she suspected he would never permit her to deny him on this, which actually weakened her knees more. When he teased her lips apart this time, though, his kiss was mild. For him. Merely incendiary instead of full conflagration. She made a surprised noise as he tumbled the partially melted cube of sugar onto her tongue, bringing sweetness with the heat. He pulled back. "It is a different taste. But I prefer your blood."

Alexis took in a steadying breath, wondering how many of those she would need before the end of the day. Hyperventilation was a real possibility. "I think meals should also be a private thing. Else they'll be calling the police."

She had to explain how law enforcement worked, then, which he viewed with great suspicion. Soon after, she had him distracted with other things. He investigated glue, felt, sequins, pipe cleaners, clay, yarn. As he took things out of the cubbyholes, he left them wherever he put them down, moving on to the next thing which caught his interest. Alexis patiently returned them to their proper place, except when he said that he wanted to use something. Then she took it to their table.

As she moved around, she noticed that when others came near him, even the children, he tensed, watching them closely and determining their intent before he returned to his own rummaging. In contrast, however she approached him, there was no tension when she laid a hand on his back or arm, as if he always was aware of her presence, no matter where she was.

Bemused, she saw a small girl slip into the child-sized space between his body and the cubbies to squat down and pull construction paper out of the lower area. He watched her, tension turning to curiosity as she bit her lip with the effort of pulling the yellow out from beneath the red and brown. The curve of her young back pressed against his shins. Unconcerned by adult presence as children were, she rose after obtaining her objective, returning to her table.

Shaking her head and holding on to her smile, Lex turned to organizing the items he'd wanted thus far in a way that ensured he had a clear work space. But when she returned to him, he'd changed tactics. He was putting away the things he'd been looking at while she was busy. As she approached, he looked toward an older girl working on a clay bunny. She gave him an approving nod, her multiple pigtails and bows nodding at different velocities.

"She told me I had to put away my own things." He gestured at a rule board on the wall. "Every person cleans up their own mess. Not mommy or daddy, or even my friend. You."

"Oh." She lifted a shoulder, not sure what to say to the faint accusation in his tone, even as her mouth quirked at his dutiful obedience to an imperious nine-year-old. "I like being considered your friend."

He gave her an assessing look. "My mother said vampires have few close friends. She said we do not trust easily, and we are very territorial. A close friend was someone who could be trusted, relied upon to help if there was trouble. When I asked why her close friends didn't help her now, she said they were too far away to help. That they might not even know she was in trouble, because vampires often disappear for long periods of time."

Looking down at the multicolored pom-poms he held, he closed his fingers over the soft give of the balls. "So far, it seems you are my friend."

Her humor gone, Alexis nodded, closing her hand on his forearm. "I hope I am. But a close friend also looks out for your best interests, even if you don't agree with them. They have to be brave enough to risk the friendship, tell you the truth when you need to hear it."

He gave her an ironic look. "So why didn't you tell me the rules? Why did you . . . clean up my mess?"

Alexis sighed, gave him a helpless shrug. "Sometimes a friend also knows when to ease up. When you need room to figure things out, without a lot of interruptions."

"All right." He digested that, turned toward their table. Before they got there, however, he stopped again, drawing her face up to meet his eyes. "A softhearted friend may give too much. Make herself too vulnerable, causing me to be more protective than she thinks I need to be."

Alexis narrowed her gaze. "I'm sorry, we're only psychoanalyzing *you* today. You're the one from an alternate dimension."

He raised an eyebrow, but before he could say anything else, the nine-year-old piped up. "You can't fight in here. That's rule number eight." She pointed to the board for emphasis.

"No fighting," Dante agreed, glancing at Alexis. "You must accept my opinion, so we will not fight."

Alexis had a colorful response to that, but she issued it in her mind so she didn't break rule number four. His mouth twisted, and she waited, hoping she might see his first smile. Instead, he gave her a quick look over the top of his glasses, his red eyes glinting with the promise of a retribution so adult, it wasn't covered on the rule board.

"Behave," she whispered, though she couldn't help the shiver as he slid his knuckles down her arm.

Fortunately, he did for a time. While he tried paints, clay and other mediums, each scrape of a chair on the floor, a higher decibel of laughter, would earn a quick tilt of his head, a flicker of the extraordinary eyes behind the glasses. When five women entered, a craft club who wanted to work on their scrapbooking, there was a new level of chatter and gossiping to assimilate. As she hoped, he appeared to be analyzing how children and adults alike interacted with one another.

But none of that stopped the nimble movements of his fingers. He worked with the clay, then moved to drawing paper, becoming familiar with the pencils and charcoals. The weaving was pushed aside, unable to claim his interest after he figured out the way it worked.

As time passed, the hum of relaxed, creative activity spun its tranquility such that some of his guarded wariness relaxed, though it didn't abate the intense interest he was creating among all of them, particularly the women. While the presence of an adult male like Dante making crafts might be curious, it didn't explain her own fascination. So she wouldn't stare at him like a besotted idiot, Lex had chosen a foam cutout kit and created a cat out of the brown and orange pieces, complete with a pipe cleaner tail, big silly eyes and whiskers made out of fishing wire. She'd give it to Clara, who loved T.

When she was done with that, she perched on a stool behind him so she could lean back against the wall and indulge herself. Despite the flow of the poet's shirt, it stretched taut over his wide shoulders. He was used to dealing with his hair, for he'd used a black pipe cleaner to pull it back into a tail so the strands wouldn't slide forward into the paint or clay, or obscure what he was trying to do with the pencil. It let her see his profile better, the concentration of the glowing eyes behind the glasses, the hard press of his lips.

Oh, hellfire. It was against her nature to restrain her impulse to touch what she wanted. She'd never felt any inhibitions about it before. It was natural to connect with other life. Keeping herself from it now was an impossible effort, because his scent, his appearance, the strength and grace of his body, the way his hands moved over his task, took it past pleasant indulgence into obsessive desire. Leaving the stool, she slid her arms over his shoulders and around his chest, pressing her cheek to his temple. He stilled beneath her touch. Where her breasts pressed into his back, she could feel his heart beating. When she stroked his chest, it accelerated.

You told me to behave.

This is just affection, not seduction. But she suppressed a smile at his mental snort and made herself straighten. Studying his hair, she eased the pipe cleaner free, separated the strands and began to braid, imagining muscular Indians in war paint and brief loincloths. "What are you working on?"

Reaching back, he followed her fingers. When he glanced toward the young girl with braids, she was impressed, as always, with his quick connection. She was even more impressed when she looked over his shoulder and found the answer to her question.

A woman's face stared up at her from the pencil drawing. He wasn't as accomplished with the pencil yet, having never held one before, but it was still a lovely face, though the mouth was drawn tight, the eyes stark and darkly lined to show pain. She wondered if he'd drawn in the ice or muck of the Dark One world. Shifting her glance to the clay, she found he'd flattened the clay down and was pinching and stroking it into the woman's face, so the pencil drawing was a rough study for the sculpture. As he resumed that project, she bent forward and realized his eyes were closed behind the glasses, letting his mind guide his hands.

Her gaze drifted across the table. Earlier, he'd used tissue paper and created what appeared like the geraniums in front of her town house in vibrant fuchsia, blue and yellow, a scattered bouquet. Wire and his new knowledge of scissors had added stems and jagged leaves that looked natural due to their lack of uniformity. On another side of the table he'd formed a vase out of sugar cubes, using a razor blade available only to the adults to sculpt the edges and create a rounded surface on the outside. Studying Will's castle, he'd then employed glitter.

Done with the braid, using the pipe cleaner to hold it, she reached around him and put the flowers in the vase carefully, so they didn't dislodge the cubes still drying. Not wanting to disrupt his concentration, she returned to the stool and leaned back, dropping her shoes to the ground to wiggle her feet under his buttock through the chair's open back. Her toes were cold, as were her hands. When she put her head against the wall, she thought about letting the room's rhythmic noise lull her into a very short nap. The frustrating fatigue had caught up with her again. Whenever she most needed her energy, it seemed to be deserting her.

It is because you have not allowed yourself time to fully recuperate. Dante straightened, and turned in the chair, flexing his taut backside on her feet. When he rose and touched her face, he brought the soothing smells of clay, paint and sugar. *Lie down right there, Alexis.*

She followed his direction and saw one of the mats that were scattered about the room for the children to play on, or in this case, nap. "I'm fine," she assured him.

"It was not a question or a request." He pointed. "Down there. Now."

She met his gaze, though it was obscured by the glasses. "I'm not yours to order around."

"Are you not?" The question was soft, dangerous and sent a thrill running through her veins, even as she struggled to be offended.

"No."

"*Hmm.* Then come here." He tugged her off the stool and brought her to sit next to him at the table, only he didn't put her in one of the small chairs. Instead he had her sink to her knees on the floor next to him. She wondered if he was going to let her lay her head on his thigh and stroke her hair, but that was something she'd want, not something he would know how to do.

"Until I saw it in your mind," he commented. "But I will do that later. Be still."

He'd dipped his finger in one of the open paint pots. Tracing paint along her temple, he moved down to the middle of her cheek. She thought to pull her hair back and held it in a tail as he brought several other pots closer. It felt like he put a dot at one corner of her mouth, then turned his finger, dragging it in a jagged line. It was soothing and arousing at once, to be under the stroking touch of his fingertips and the total focus of his attention. She wanted to take his glasses off, yearned to see his eyes, but since she couldn't, she focused instead on his expressive mouth, even reaching out to touch him there. He nipped her finger, then caught her wrist and took her hand to her lap again, caressing her palm before going back to her face.

He didn't stop there, though. He trailed paint down her throat, made her tilt her head back so he teased the firm line of her esophagus, then along her collarbone. Unbuttoning two buttons of her soft knit shirt, he widened the collar to slide it to the points of her shoulders.

"Dante . . ." She warned, not daring to look around, even though he'd exposed nothing inappropriate.

"*Sshh*." He kept on with his work. A few minutes later, she realized he'd drawn a different kind of attention. The girl with the pigtails and Will were on the other side of the table, staring at his handiwork. She could tell he was aware of them, but it didn't seem to bother him. When he wiped his hands with a damp towelette, a box of which were kept in the center of each table, the girl spoke. "Will you do me next?"

Alexis looked toward the large mirror, placed on the back wall to help parents keep track of where their children were in the room. In her mermaid form, Anna had elaborate, silver markings on her flesh. When she was younger, Alexis had traced them with small fingers, following the Celtic-like curls over Anna's arms and wishing she had them. Her father often did something similar to her mother, with a far more sensual intent.

Dante had decorated her with as much artistry as Nature had decorated her mother. He'd used a dark blue and brown with touches of pink to swirl a design down her right cheek, a slash of color on the opposite cheekbone, and then further twists down her throat. She looked like some mystical earth fairy, her face peering out from the vines and flowers of the plants she cherished. It was not too much or too little, a perfect design to attract his admiring fans.

The little girl was taking a seat on the table at his direction so he could examine her face. When Alexis rose to return to her stool, he caught her wrist. Rising, he guided her toward the mat, putting a hand on her shoulder. She resisted, despite his height advantage and intimidating expression. *I'm fine.*

Lie. Down.

She set her jaw. She was really, really tired all of a sudden, but that wasn't the point. *You can't order me around. And you shouldn't force mothers out of your way with your weird alpha dominant male routine. It's . . . rude.*

He lifted a brow. *Is there a "not rude" way to make you do my will?*

You're missing the point. But yes, you can ask me to lie down. Tell me you're worried and it would make you feel better if I lie down and take a rest.

Dante's impassive expression didn't alter. "Please lie down. I'm worried because you look tired and it will make me feel better if you rest."

Then he took another step, and damned if she didn't do just as the mother had, shifting back so she was standing on the mat in her bare feet. His hand rested on her hip, tightening with proprietary intent. As he stood there, she realized he was waiting to see if her way would work, or if he would have to resort to his own measures. From the pulse of lustful aggression she felt, he was hoping for the latter.

"Fine. Thank you. I'll rest," she said ungraciously, plopping down on the mat at his feet.

Nineteen

D ANTE considered her mutinous expression, but since she was doing what he'd told her to do, he returned to his chair.

The little girl giggled. "What?" Dante asked, his fingers poised over the paint.

"She made a face at you," Will informed him, and demonstrated, sticking out his tongue and putting his thumbs in his ears to flap the other fingers at him. He also crossed his eyes.

Dante twisted around. Alexis was the picture of innocence, though her smile was quivering at the corners of her mouth, and he saw the imprint of her act fading from her mind. "Why would she do that?" he asked his new companions.

"Probably because you did something to make her mad," the girl told him, adjusting the pink marbleized balls that held one of her pigtails. "I got mad at my mommy once, but she caught me making the face. She spanked me."

"Really? What is spanking?"

"Nothing you need to know about." Alexis sat up in alarm, but he'd already gotten the visual from her mind. Or rather, the visual the child's suggestion gave her, for as little as he knew about spanking, he somehow doubted the parent had administered discipline to her little girl in the manner Alexis's mind had just conjured. Herself naked and helpless across his thighs while his hand left a red print on her backside and she struggled against his lap, arousing her and him both.

If she did not want him to do something publicly offensive, she was certainly pressing the limits, though from her embarrassed flush, he was certain her imagining was involuntary. The blush added an interesting color contrast to the face painting.

The women at the scrapbooking table seemed to have gotten the gist of it, because they seemed discreetly amused at Alexis's discomfiture. In fact, with his enhanced hearing, Dante was fairly certain he heard one murmur, "It'd be worth it to be that bad," before she flicked him a quick once-over beneath her lashes.

It was a confusing world. He made himself turn his attention to the children, even though his body was simmering, not just from the titillating picture Alexis had given him. Painting her skin as she submitted to his touch had conjured his own vision. Laying her on the mat, stripping off her excessive clothes and painting her whole body. Ticklish circles on the bottoms of her feet, so he could chase her around the room and let the circles dot the tile floor. Tiny leaves and flowers all the way down to the delicate crease between sex and thigh. When he caught her, he would smear the designs as he rubbed his body over hers, transferring the paint to his own flesh, making them both a canvas.

Will's mother had joined them and was studying the clay sculpture. "You're very good," she offered with some hesitancy. "She's beautiful. Are you an artist?"

"No," Dante said.

"You should be. I've seen things in galleries that aren't as good as that." She cocked her head. "There's a loneliness to her. Desolation. But a savage beauty, too." Her gaze rose to his face, her brow creasing, then she looked away quickly at her son.

"It is how I remember her," Dante said. Then he leaned toward Will with paint-coated fingers.

HE gave face paintings to every child there. While Alexis noticed his touch was not gentle or sentimental, he was careful of his strength, so it was fascinating to see him hold a small chin to keep a child's face steady, or apply pressure to turn from one cheek to another. Unfortunately, she couldn't help but remember how he'd wielded a knife with similar precision against his sacrifice's throat. Two sides to a coin, though the sides kept changing into something altogether different with every flip, giving the coin far more than its apparent two sides.

On a more sensual note, Alexis could tell only the tenuous bounds of propriety kept the mothers and the scrapbook group from asking for their own decorations. She couldn't blame them, since her body was still restless from when he'd been painting it. She dozed, drifting in half dreams of his hard flesh and muscles moving against her, the smell of his skin and hair as she buried her face in it. When she woke and scrubbed sleep out of her eyes, her eyes alighted on him with need.

Whether it was her thoughts goading him, or a spiraling effect that kept them both in this churning ache, his grip on her hand as they left the community center was hard, his forefinger crooking inward to fondle her palm and accelerate her pulse further. "I want you now," he stated bluntly when they reached her car. "Take me somewhere that is possible, without breaking your world's rules. Your town house is too far," he added before she could say it. Gripping her shoulders, he pushed her against the car door, letting her feel his hardness against her belly as he nipped the tender flesh beneath her ear.

"Now, Alexis. Or I fuck you right here, your rules be damned."

It was the first time he'd used the term, but she was so stirred up, it only drove her higher. She fumbled open the door, unlocked both sides. When he got in on the passenger side, she turned the engine over and accelerated with a jerk.

As she turned out of Fortram Park, his hand slid over her thigh and between them, tugging her open. "Dante, don't. I could wreck the car."

"Then find us somewhere to be. Quickly." He was under her skirt, and his fingers flicked her clit beneath her panties so that she spasmed, her breath catching in her throat.

Would it ever be easy and gentle between them? Did she care?

Candlelight and rose petals, slow and easy lovemaking to soft music were a romantic vision, but he kept her blood on high simmer, such that whenever he demanded it, she could boil over. Earlier, she'd made it clear she didn't like being ordered about, but when it came to this, he could steamroll her without a murmur of protest. She was incapable of refusing him.

Pulling into a diner parking lot she knew was likely deserted this time of day since they didn't serve dinner, she drove around the back. Clicking off her seat belt, she nodded toward the backseat. "There. Easier to . . . just easier."

Instead, he caught her waist and lifted her over the console to his side of the car in a smooth movement that demonstrated how easily he could have crushed one of those tiny faces. Holding her in his lap, he stripped off her panties with the same firm efficiency, not tender nor rough, just intent on his goal. Guiding her legs to straddle him in the narrow space, he opened the jeans he wore. She barely had time to gasp before he'd driven her down on him, all the way to the hilt. She was soaking wet, eager to take him, so that her tissues rippled in response, wresting a cry from her throat. His hand caught the back of her neck and he bit, sinking his fangs in as deeply as his cock. She fumbled for the handle of the seat and reclined them, taking him even further inside her.

It was pure, hot possession, underscoring what he'd barely held in check earlier. He'd called her his friend, but he'd also called her his. In a very non-twenty-first-century way, he considered her just that. He wouldn't be pushed too far away from that idea before he would retaliate in ways like this, which she feared proved his point. She welcomed this kind of assault on her will.

But there was a power to it, too, for as she moved on him, the waves of his own need and desire crashed against her. She found his face with fumbling fingers, pulled off his sunglasses so she could be bathed in the hellfire of his gaze. The glasses clattered against the console as they fell, but she was already touching his face, the brow, the shape of his eyes. His thick lashes fanned his cheeks as her thumb passed over them, learning him while he took from her throat. When he drew back, on instinct she went for his mouth, using her tongue to delicately lick at his fangs, taste herself.

He growled and increased his rhythm, bludgeoning her with the powerful thrusts, but it was also an unfathomable pleasure, out of control, frightening and exhilarating at once. As her clit smacked down against his pelvis each time, he dragged her to the precipice, leaving her no sense of direction at all.

He opened the front of her shirt, his mouth on lace and flesh, teasing her nipple under the hold of the cup before he shoved that out of his way and suckled her. Impaled and quartered between all the different sensual weapons he had, she was a helpless doll, tossed upon the waves of lust, only able to grip his shoulders and mewl, plead.

The climax grabbed her by the throat, tearing a scream from it as it rocked her forward on him, shuddering. His seed seared her channel, his face contorting, a grunt becoming a groan and then a snarl as he pulsed inside her, legs jerking and trembling beneath her buttocks, muscles flexing in his arms and shoulders.

They careened to a stop like a derailed train. When she collapsed against him, his arms slid around her, holding her to him as she dropped her face into his shoulder. She shuddered. He hadn't been taught to do that, hold a woman to him after making love to her. It had to be what his heart told him he wanted to do. It was a nice thought, even if it wasn't true, since he could have read it from her mind as well. But his arms were firm and sheltering, protective and possessive.

Sliding his fingers along her spine, he traced that fragile part of her, then down to the flare of her buttocks. He stopped abruptly, tracing something there. Something that felt different, thicker somehow.

"What is it?" Alexis asked groggily, too tired to reach around.

"It is a mark. A mark that I left."

"Another one? I thought there were only three."

"The three markings are internal in their effect on you, but the third mark comes with a brand upon the skin, a mark of the vampire's ownership of the servant. I had not thought of it until now, because you are the first I've ever marked three times. You did not notice it?"

"I'm sure Myel saw it when she bathed me, but she didn't mention it." Though Alexis wondered if that was part of why her mother had been so emotional. "What does it look like?"

Dante surprised her by showing it to her in his mind as clearly as if she was looking at it herself. A benefit of the second mark she hadn't realized fully until now. Digesting that, she focused on the image. The mark, a cross between a tattoo and a scar, was shaped like a tongue of flame.

"My mother mentioned it, but I don't know why it occurs, or the significance of the design." He frowned. "Does it bother you?"

"Only because it doesn't. I missed having the other marks . . . the ones you put on me." Knowing it was crazy for her to feel that way about the magical brands that had pulled her into his world, Lex laid her head back down on his shoulder. Having him look in her face when she felt so vulnerable was somehow more difficult than knowing he could plunder her mind. "We'll find out more about vampires, don't worry," she added hastily in the weighted silence. "When you were face painting, I checked my cell messages. Myel said that Mina and Pyel have initiated contact with a vampire who might know more about your mother."

Not responding to that, he lifted her to look at her upper body, the clothes he'd torn away to reach her flesh. "I am also glad you still carry my mark upon you."

Under his intent scrutiny, she held still, but she felt that confusing mix of emotions . . . and something else, too. On instinct, she twisted around, looking out the windshield. There was an abandoned field behind the diner, littered with trash, of course. The sun had gone behind a cloud, giving her a shivery cold, though the day had warmed up and the car more so because of the things they'd been doing in it.

"What is it?" Dante's attention sharpened, picking up on her mood or thoughts, she wasn't sure which.

"Nothing, I guess. I just felt, for a minute . . ." It had been a malevolent presence, a wave of vengeful anger, but she couldn't isolate it. In this section of town, it could be a random wave, except the intent had been firmly fixed on her. Or Dante.

Almost before she finished the thought, he'd lifted and placed her back in her seat and was scanning the area, his expression intent. "I think they're gone," she said, probing their surroundings herself. "Whatever it was. Let's get home. Maybe it was just somebody who saw what we were doing and got really upset. People can be like that about public sex." She tried for a smile and failed when he turned his gaze to her.

"It was more than that. But you're right. They're gone, whoever they were. It could be one of your father's Legion keeping watch on us."

"I guess." Only what she had felt was a malevolence that transcended paternal outrage, or a vicarious sense of it. She started the car. Whatever it was, she didn't want Dante facing it and forcing an evaluation of his probation before it even started. She didn't want to contemplate any confrontation between him and the angels, or Mina.

"You think of their lives or mine. Do you not value your own life?"

"It's not that. I thought we agreed you'd stay out of my head. Dante, you're doing fine. There's no reason to think . . ."

"There's every reason to think it," he said. "You *should* think of your own life first. I will not go back to that world, even if they have to destroy me here. Your fate will be secondary."

When Lex spoke again, she had to do it in a low voice to keep it steady. "You put my fate first, earlier."

"Because you cared about mine, and it was the first time anyone had done so. It took me off guard. Such things are temporary, and only useful for certain periods of time. As I said before, when your arousal for me cools, or I have done something that makes it too difficult for me to be here, you will not care as much what your father and godmother do to me."

She stared at him. Putting the car in park, she opened her door and left him sitting there, though she slammed the door hard enough to rock the vehicle. While it didn't surprise her that he was at her side in an instant, her own reaction did. She slapped him, a solid *thwack* that hit his perfect jaw. He hadn't anticipated it from her mind, because he didn't jerk back in time to avoid the blow, though he caught her wrist to prevent a follow up. If she'd used her fist, she suspected he would have knocked her on her ass, but like a spanking, a slap was confusing. It wasn't intended to injure, but to express an emotion in physical form, in a way most males would read loud and clear. While she wasn't sure if he had that radar, she didn't particularly give a damn.

"I get it. You've lived in this awful world where you couldn't count on anyone. But you do not get to do what we just did, and then sit there with that stupid, horrible arrogance and calmly state that my feelings are a phase of lust and shallow infatuation. Like I would abandon you like that. Look at me." She jerked away from him and gestured to her shirt, still in dishabille, breasts nearly exposed. She'd pulled her skirt back down when they'd sensed the disturbing presence, but her panties were in shambles in the car and his seed was damp on her thighs. His fingers had speared through her hair, mussing it, and his paint was stiff upon her skin, like a light rope restraint twining around her throat and arms. "You are a complete . . . ass."

Turning, she stomped away from him. Rationally, she understood he couldn't help it. For Goddess's sake, he put the capital letters in Dysfunctional Childhood, and had been exposed to a semblance of normalcy for less than forty-eight hours. If her feelings weren't far more involved than they should be, she could accept that. Trust took time. Even when rehabilitating a manatee, she had to win that to heal his or her wounds. Huge leaps forward could be followed by huge leaps backward.

But she wasn't detached. She knew his feelings, and his marks had tightened those ropes even further, binding her to his mind and body. Half the time she embraced his thoughts and emotions, reveling in their dark pleasures, and other times they frightened her. Anger fell somewhere in between, but she preferred it to the fear.

She was the only one who sensed that one spark within him. No matter how faint its flicker, its very existence was an indication of how strong it was, how strong it could be. She knew evil could triumph over a spark of good, no matter her influence, if the person's will was already drawn irrevocably toward that darkness. But she wasn't losing Dante to that.

Ah, Goddess. This was impossible. She needed some way to vent. Unfortunately, she didn't have the option Clara did, arriving at Lex's town house with ice cream and Kleenex to spend a self-indulgent night lamenting a boyfriend's betrayal, berating him as a complete bastard. Yeah, she could see that happening.

See, I brought this guy back from this horrible hell-planet and he's got enough baggage to fill up a 747, but the sex is so hot I'm having a hard time kicking him to the curb. And even if I could, I can't, because I'm supposed to make sure he doesn't wreak havoc on the world . . .

When his hand closed on her wrist again, she stopped, stiffly facing away from him. He stepped around to her front, and she pivoted on her toe. Yes, it was childish, but her feelings were going to strangle her. She was all alone in this. Her father was hoping to see Dante a corpse before it was all over. Her mother was supportive, but too worried for Alexis to burden her. And Dante, he was the problem, wasn't he? It was hard to lean on the problem.

"I've upset you."

"You think?" She managed the sarcastic reply through a throat thick with tears. "Just go back to the car for a few minutes. I'll pull it together. Just leave me alone."

"No," he said. "I've upset you, and it bothers me."

She lifted her face to him then. *Damn it, Alexis, be better than this. Stronger.* Fighting out of the thicket of her own feelings, she focused on his. Confusion again, and a tugging that could be regret, if he knew to call it that. "When someone does something here that hurts your feelings, they say they're sorry." She swiped at her cheek, frustrated with more stupid tears. "And really mean it. You don't say it just so everything will be less awkward."

"Does being sorry mean I am admitting I was wrong?"

She choked on a chuckle and a sob together. It made her lungs hurt. She bent her head, pressing her forehead against his chest, and drew a deep breath. "Sometimes. Sometimes not. You can think you're right, but still be sorry that you hurt someone. I wish you didn't think you were right, though. I wish you had faith in me, in my father."

His arms slid around her. He was somewhat stiff, as if he wasn't sure how this nonsexual gesture would be received. She recalled then how he'd watched the children and parents at the craft room, and in the park. He would have noted how parents hugged their child if he fell down and cried, or was getting fussy, and as she'd said, he was quick to adapt. Swallowing, she slid her arms up his back, clutched his shirt. His arms were a comfort, as long as she could push aside the reality that he was imitating the behavior, rather than understanding what a hug was supposed to convey.

No, that wasn't true. He did have an indefinable need to soothe her, to make her happy. He truly didn't want her to cry or be angry with him. Thinking about his world, that might be a first as well, because the only reason to avoid anger in his world was to prevent physical retribution. He knew he was in no danger of that from her.

Dante eased her back from him and traced the track of a tear. "I was cruel."

When she nodded, a muscle flexed in his jaw. "I am sorry, Alexis. I . . . It is difficult for me. Your world . . ." He glanced around them. "It's so quiet here."

Alexis tuned in to the sounds of birds, the light whisper of the wind, a far away murmur of traffic. He shook his head. "You remember the roaring in the Dark One world?"

A low, incessant current of thunder, the sound of flames, punctuated by screams and shrill cries from the Dark Ones. She remembered. It was part of what had frayed her nerves while she was there, like a horror movie soundtrack on a continuous loop.

"In that world—" That muscle jumped again, and she sensed a struggle going on inside of him, something he didn't necessarily feel comfortable saying. "It was as Mina said to you. I was different, for a very long time. I was always . . . afraid. Or hurt, from whatever they were able to do to me when they caught me, which was often. But because of the Mountain Battle, many of them were gone. So I grew stronger, more determined, more clever. Eventually, I hurt them. Made them afraid of me."

His hands flexed on her arms, and when she shivered, he stepped back. "But I never stopped being on guard. Expecting to be hurt and afraid again made me determined to do whatever was necessary to keep that from happening. You don't live like that, so I can't believe you would endure much discomfort on my behalf, for no gain to yourself. But there are many things about you I have never experienced before."

He raised his hand as if to touch her, but then, as if he also remembered her flinch, he dropped it. Alexis not only felt his mental struggle, but saw it, in the flexing of his jaw, in how long the silence drew out between them before he spoke again. His voice was rough. "I have no experience with asking for anything. But I need to ask you . . . to have faith in me, as you say, until I learn what that is myself. And," he added, his voice lowering, "I may be wrong. I think it is possible your fate does matter to me. Very much."

Alexis had seen her share of male and female relationships. With her unique insights, she knew that men and women had difficulty being entirely truthful with one another, and sometimes lied to keep peace between them, to push away the problems or worries when they rubbed one another the wrong way. But even if she couldn't sense his emotions, she knew Dante didn't lie. Not about things like this.

What was the matter with her? He was struggling with feelings he'd never handled, and she was being almost as self-absorbed as he expected. She needed to—

"Do exactly as you are doing." His eyes sparked, and now he tilted her chin up to hold her gaze. "I learned how to fight by being beaten, Alexis. I learned how to steal by being hungry. I learned how to seek out power by being helpless. Perhaps the only way I can learn about these emotions you experience is by running afoul of them. And," he added, his face hardening, "I strongly dislike the idea of you treating me like one of your wounded animals. I allowed this." He touched the collar with distaste. "But I will not be treated as inferior or weak, someone not deserving your full respect. You will not be successful in being emotionally detached from me. I will not permit it."

He was so difficult to keep up with. It was a struggle to get her mind around the alternating currents of emotions, some anger, some far deeper, coaxing her into the darkness of his soul where she sometimes became as lost as he might be. He was on target, though. To do this right, she couldn't be emotionally detached, so she had to accept and deal with her own turbulent surf. The hug had been new for him, but she'd sensed he'd liked it.

"I like the way your body relaxed into mine," he confirmed. "It was different from what we did before."

"It's affection," she explained. "The desire to touch for emotional connection. Which the other has as well," she added with a touch of a flush rising in her cheeks, "But this is . . . quieter."

"Like holding hands," he said shrewdly. She nodded. "What other things show affection?"

"You saw some of them today, between the parents and children."

"I am more interested what those who know each other as we have do."

"Oh. Well, all right. Can you hold still?" At his amusingly wary nod, she rose on tiptoe to reach his face. Putting a hand against his cheek, she slid her fingertips into his hair, slow and easy. Then she laid her lips on his. True to his word, he remained immobile as she brushed his mouth in a tender caress and then went back to her heels again. "Gentle kisses like those can be another way. Then there's lying together, without sex. I see lovers all the time lying on blankets on the beach at sunrise, watching the tide roll in and out. Spooning together, dozing." She gave him that image in her mind, and was intrigued by the flicker of interest in his eyes. "Lovers also do things for companionship. Read or watch TV, playing games and sports together. If there's emotion beyond merely sex, you want to spend time with that person."

"Like us at the craft room?"

"Yes and no," she said, managing a strained smile. *Keep the fantasy away from the reality, Lex.* "In our case, that was getting you used to things here, so it's functional first, rather than romantic." As his gaze strayed lower, Alexis cleared her throat. "I guess I better put myself back together if we're going to go other places today."

"That might be wise," came a voice behind them.

Twenty

D ANTE and Alexis turned together to see Mina leaning against the car. The black-haired witch was in human form, of course, clad in a velvet skirt and a T-shirt printed with two lop-eared rabbits sleeping amid a cluster of purple violets. Her long hair was braided down her back. She looked like a college student with a bohemian fashion sense, as long as one didn't look at her bicolored eyes, or the fathomless layers of power residing in them.

Her glance passed over Alexis, dismissing her state of dress, though Alexis self-consciously refastened her clothes and gave a tug to bring her bra back in place. Mina focused on Dante instead.

"We've located a vampire who might have known your mother. We're here to take you to her."

Dante turned defensively as David landed a few feet behind him. While the angel spent enough time with Mina in Nevada that Alexis often saw him in casual human clothes like the witch was wearing now, today he was with his Legion, for the short red half-tunic he wore as a battle skirt and wide belt were his only garments. Unless one counted the weapons harness that held his daggers. Alexis wondered if the display was to keep Dante mindful of his manners, or something else.

"The vampire we're going to see is one of the most powerful of her kind," Mina said, picking up the direction of her thoughts. "It's important at least one of us appears worthy of the audience."

David's mouth tugged in a slight smile. "I tried to convince her to wear striped stockings and a pointy hat."

The humor eased Alexis's concerns, but she could see the tension in Dante and slid her hand into his. "I'll go with you."

"No, you won't. Your parents want to see you." Mina straightened from the car. "Dealing with your father is a pain in my ass. Go ease their concerns."

"She is not yours to command, witch," Dante said sharply.

"As my goddaughter, the right is more mine than yours." Mina's gaze flashed. "Do not press me, vampire."

"Stop," Alexis interrupted. "Mina, my parents will certainly understand if I go see them tomorrow. How can I help if I'm not allowed to be with him when he learns more about who he is?"

"He can tell you when he gets back. There is some danger involved in this." Mina's expression reflected irony at Dante's forbidding expression. "Vampires are not highly social outside their own kind, and can be unpredictable, the oldest ones most of all."

"More than a witch with Dark One blood?"

Mina's gaze snapped back to Alexis. Some of her courage withered under that stare, but she managed to keep her chin up, her expression resolute. She thought she heard a muffled chuckle from David. "You'll be with us, right? Please let me go with him, Mina. This is about Pyel, isn't it? He didn't want me to go."

"You underestimate the power of your mother's guilt. When she wields it, it's a weapon even more formidable than your father's overly eager sword." Mina sighed irritably. "Fine. Go, then. But you go as an observer only. Be silent unless spoken to."

"I will permit no harm to come to her," Dante declared.

The witch gave him a gimlet eye. "You know nothing of what you are about to face, so you have no idea if you can protect her or not."

"He can," Alexis said firmly. "With the three of you, I couldn't be safer."

"We go to see the eldest of the vampire kind. Assume nothing."

Mina began to etch a circle around them, presumably to transport them to the vampire in question.

As Alexis retrieved Dante's drawing, locked the car then returned to the circle, she sensed Dante's tension had moved to what lay ahead. She took his hand again, risking that he might pull away. While he didn't, his fingers were tense, unresponsive, his body prepared for the possibility of another threat. It made it all the more critical she go with him.

You're going to find out more about your kind, Dante. That's a good thing. And I will have faith in you. Try to have faith in yourself.

It will not be my kind. No species welcomes half-breeds.

Mina grouped them around her and ordered everyone to grip her arms, Dante and Alexis's hands on her right, David's on her left. Alexis noticed his thumb caressed his mate's elbow, then Mina uttered a short enchantment and the world spun.

She knew the witch was powerful, but her command of magic was always breathtaking in its effortlessness. While there was the brief sensation of traveling in a tunnel, it was barely a blink of time, before it was over. Alexis swayed, disoriented, as they materialized outside a wrought iron gate.

"We're at Lady Lyssa's Atlanta home," Mina explained. The gate buzzed, as if someone was watching for their arrival, and she pushed it open, guiding them in. Dusk was drawing in, but the drive was well lit, leading them up a paved, long driveway to a plantation house with graceful columns and stunning roses clustered along the borders and against the foundation of the estate. "She's of royal blood," Mina was continuing, "the last queen of the Far East clan of vampires, and over a thousand years old. I'd be careful of that attitude of yours." She shot Dante a warning glance. "Much as I'd enjoy seeing her knock it out of you, the point is to find out about your mother and background. Her willingness to help can vanish if she's provoked."

In response, Dante stopped and spun on his heel, bringing Alexis behind him in the same movement. He'd removed the sunglasses for the transport, and now his eyes glowed like embers in the shadows of twilight, light glistening off bared fangs.

When an ominous pair of growls answered out of the darkness, David put his hands to his daggers and stepped in front of Mina, presenting a solid male front.

A short command and the growling subsided. A man stepped out of the darkness with two Irish wolfhounds at his heels. Tall and handsome, with reddish-brown hair and blue eyes, his aura, similar to Dante's, told Alexis they were facing a vampire. While he wore jeans and a T-shirt, it was deceptively casual, like Mina's. It would be unwise to overlook the vibrant focus of his eyes, the otherworldly strength emanating from the lean body.

"You asked to meet with my lady as guests, but your behavior suggests something different," he said, a faint Irish lilt in his voice. Though there were a variety of powers before him, he accurately kept his gaze pinned on Dante as the most unpredictable threat. "I'd take the witch's advice and tone it down, if you have any desire to meet with her."

"He's new to your ways," Alexis spoke up. But when she moved to stand beside Dante, he blocked her.

Stay where you are, and do not speak, Alexis.

"Which is why I gave him the courtesy of the warning," the other vampire replied. He changed his attention to Mina, though he paused for an intrigued assessment of David, particularly the one black and one white wing the angel possessed. "I'm Jacob, Lady Lyssa's servant. We spoke before."

"I figured." Mina nodded. "She's correct. Dante isn't used to being around your kind . . . or anyone much other than Dark Ones. He's not housebroken."

"Which means, like the dogs, he won't be permitted into my house until he learns manners." The shadows moved, and materialized into a woman.

Lex, still getting her mind wrapped around the idea that Lady Lyssa had a vampire as her servant, rather than a human, tilted further on her axis. The woman in front of her had a vampire vibration, but it was like a memory. Something far different and more conspicuous ran through her veins.

Lex was used to being around powerful entities. Mina was probably the strongest, with her father a close second, close enough she'd always hoped they would never be on opposing battle lines. While the vampire queen was not on par with those two, there was a heady, exotic perfume to the forces that swirled around her that gave Alexis pause. Jacob's energy imprint meshed unexpectedly with them, as if they shared the same power source. Apart, she wouldn't want to anger either of them. Together, she suspected they could have an impact similar to a category five hurricane.

Aside from the powers of destruction she might harbor, Lyssa had another potent weapon. Long black hair and jade eyes with a hint of Asian ancestry complimented a petite, graceful frame that emitted an overwhelming wave of sensuality. While the two males remained in alert posture, a simmering violence from Dante and calm readiness from David, Alexis picked up an additional attentiveness toward the vampire queen that made her grimace.

Surprisingly, Lady Lyssa ignored Dante and Alexis, riveted on David instead. Lex remembered how Jacob had paused on his wings, and now her jade eyes focused there as well, only for a more lingering regard. "How amazing," the vampire queen noted at last. "A thousand years, and there is always more to see. I remember the Mountain Battle, of course, and saw your kind then, but there was little time to observe you before you were gone. Would you be offended if I touched one of your wings?"

Her tone remained as royal and remote as if she'd commanded it, but David shook his head and stepped forward several paces. He stretched out the white one, so it curved forward over his bare shoulder. Alexis noted that the position kept him facing both Jacob and Lyssa. His left hand remained on the hilt of one of his daggers. Jacob noted it as well, for he stepped forward, closer to his lady.

"I mean her no harm if she does none to me or mine," David said.

"I would say the same."

David nodded, the two males apparently in accord. Lex glanced at Dante. He was radiating the most tension of the group. It wasn't hard to understand why. They were surrounded by incredibly potent energies. Dante's might be at a lower decibel, but possessed a far more erratic tempo, which she suspected was why Jacob's regard remained on him, even with a watchful eye on David.

Lyssa laid her hand on the wing, stroking her finger through the feathers. A look of wonder appeared on her face as she glanced toward Jacob. "You can feel the heat coming from them, the light energy." Drifting down, she followed the feathers to the ends and grazed David's forearm, the silver arm brace he wore there, engraved with praises to the Goddess. The opposite one had a dragon engraving, which Alexis knew was his tribute to Mina. Lyssa cocked her head, as if someone had spoken to her, and her eyes glinted.

"My mate says I cannot resist touching," she said.

"Try."

Mina's voice was every bit as remote as the vampire queen's, but there was a power resonance to it that shuddered through the ground, sending a chill breeze rippling through the trees above them. It shifted Jacob's attention from Dante to Mina instantly. Alexis was so accustomed to Mina's general scariness, it was a surprise to see Jacob had assumed David and Dante were the ones to be reckoned with, overlooking who the strongest force for destruction was in this gathering. Lyssa's gaze had locked with the witch's. After a long, testing moment, she inclined her head with a feral smile and withdrew her hand. Alexis admired her unruffled demeanor.

"You are most fortunate. Things are not always as they seem." The vampire queen gave David a second, more assessing look. "But then, who holds the reins isn't always about who has the most power, is it?"

Mina blinked once. "No, it's not. But either one of us is more than capable of curing you of your need to touch."

The queen laughed then, a silvery sound that whispered along nerve endings and made Alexis think of secret desires, caresses in the dark. "Your power is great, witch, but you cannot have a jewel like that and not expect him to be desired." She glanced then toward her mate, meeting Jacob's intent blue eyes, her gaze lingering on his serious mouth. "I have no designs on your mate, except for how the pleasure of his body makes me think of the pleasure of the one that belongs to me."

Now her gaze returned to Dante, and Alexis's stomach tightened with anxiety. "You are vampire, and yet other," she observed. She glanced at Alexis. "And you are his fully marked servant. The form of it is different, because of the Dark One blood. Or perhaps because of what *you* are."

Dante shifted, blocking her view, and Lyssa came back to him. "Your face is familiar," she said.

"We have a drawing of his mother." Alexis spoke up again, but when she tried to move out of Dante's shadow once more, he recaptured her arm, only this time his grip was less controlled, biting into the bone like a bear trap. She gasped, and if she'd held the paper in that hand she would have dropped it.

"Ease off." The warning came from Jacob and David at the same time. Lyssa stepped forward, but whatever she communicated to Jacob stayed his forward progress. Alexis bit her lip against the pain, trying to control her reaction so things didn't escalate. The challenge from both males had Dante's power rushing to the forefront like an approaching torpedo, alarms blaring louder and faster in her head. Mina might have been correct, that her presence was more detrimental than useful here. The smell of singed flesh told her the collar was working. She wasn't sure if she was more concerned about it hurting Dante, or Mina realizing how little of a deterrent it was to him.

Lyssa cocked her head, her expression that dispassionate mask that Alexis knew could hide so much. She felt little from the queen but calm readiness, however. "A vampire's servant is his to command, Dante. To punish if he sees fit. But there is a bond there that should never be abused. It is the one constant in a vampire's life. Do you understand me? Of course you don't. But you will." She held out her hand. "You are trying to protect her, but maiming her is not the way to do it. Release her and let her hand me this picture."

"I want her out of here," Dante hissed at Mina. The witch moved forward another step, so she and David were both close to Dante, close enough to act against him, Alexis realized. They felt the imminent violence from him as she did.

"You insisted she come along. So did she. Now let go of her, before I take your arm off at the elbow." The witch's voice was frost.

Dante, they're trying to protect me. That's why they're acting this way. They see you as a threat, because of how you're holding me. Believe me. Please let go of my arm.

A long pause, and then she heard his grudging response. *Very well, but do not move from my side. Agreed?*

Agreed. Please, you really are hurting me.

His fingers loosened and she drew a steadying breath, cradling the arm against her in the hopes the throbbing might subside. She might have lost her nerve entirely then, but her attention was caught by Jacob's emotions—encouragement and surprising wry commiseration. When she met his direct blue gaze, it was as if he'd said it aloud: *Vampires. What can you do with them?* The quirk at his lips made him seem almost human. Thank Goddess, it also gave her the necessary fortitude to hand the picture to Lady Lyssa.

Slim, elegant fingers bedecked with rings took it. Lyssa studied it, her hair falling forward over her shoulder. With the ease of long habit, Jacob came and slid her hair back so it wasn't in her way. As he did, he placed a kiss on her throat, below her ear. Tilting her head away, she gave him that access, murmuring as he straightened and they looked together.

She looked up at Dante. "I did know your mother. Come inside."

"SHE was nearly two hundred when she disappeared. Not very old for our kind, just embracing her adult years, really."

Jacob had taken them to a library, which held a circle of comfortable chairs and an impressive compilation of hundreds of books lining the walls. On the desk, Alexis was bemused to see a small stack of superhero comics. They rested in skewed fashion on top of a copy of *The Velveteen Rabbit*. Under the desk was a small rubber bear, a toy an infant might use for teething.

Lyssa sat down in the desk chair and Jacob took a position on the wall behind her, arms crossed. While he wouldn't move in front of his lady, Alexis had the same sense she'd had when David imposed himself between Mina and the male vampire. He was protecting what he considered his to protect, and would do so, even if it cost his life.

Dante had been directed to take a chair across from the desk. While David stood behind Mina's chair in similar fashion to Jacob, Dante apparently did not want Alexis at his back where he couldn't see her or control her movements. Easing her down to the floor between his knees, he kept a hand on her shoulder there. Lyssa and Jacob did not seem to find that unexpected, but David gave her a quizzical look, confirming that Alexis was all right with the position. She gave him a slight nod.

Males were strange animals, she knew, and it seemed when a girl was dealing with one closer to his primal roots than others, he became even stranger. The atmosphere wasn't quite as charged in the library as it had been out in the courtyard, but there was still a wariness among the males keeping everyone on alert. They were too far away from the craft room environment of earlier in the day, and suddenly, she'd had enough of it.

"Lady Lyssa," she said politely, "do you have a child?"

Lyssa's jade eyes riveted onto her face. Alexis held her gaze until Jacob made a slight noise, gaining her attention and breaking the contact. The intent regard had been unsettling, but more than that, she felt some shift had occurred, possibly not a good one.

"She doesn't know, my lady," Jacob noted quietly, and Lyssa lifted a shoulder, expression unreadable. He glanced at Alexis, and then at Dante. "Human servants don't meet the gazes of vampires unless invited to do so."

"Oh. My apologies, my lady," Alexis said, then discovered the difficulty of speaking to someone without looking at them. She recalled Jacob had not seemed concerned when she'd met his gaze earlier, but he was also a vampire serving as another vampire's servant. It was confusing, but from Mina's sharp glance, she realized now was not the time to get mired in speculation.

"Er . . . was my question inappropriate?" Damn it, unless they could all unbend enough to have a real conversation, this wasn't going to go well.

"No," Lyssa said at last. "You may look at me, child. It makes me dizzy, your eyes darting all over the place. We have a son." She glanced up at Jacob. "His name is Kane. Right now he is with the majordomo of our estate, Mr. Ingram, probably being allowed to wreak havoc in my rose garden."

"But you're both—I thought, two vampires couldn't . . ."

"It's extremely rare, but it does happen. Jacob is a made vampire. We conceived Kane when Jacob was my human servant."

"I still serve you, my lady," Jacob replied, his hand curved around the back of the chair, fingertips brushing her shoulder. Lex felt the unmistakable bond between them. The vampire queen loved this male with all she was. This, despite the reproving look she sent him.

"When it suits you."

His grin loosened the knots in her gut. But before Lex could draw an easy breath, Lyssa returned her attention to Dante. The muscle in his calf was taut beneath Alexis's fingers.

"Were you old enough to know your mother's name before she died?"

"She never told me her name. She never named me, either." Dante's impassive expression deepened.

Lyssa nodded, considering that. "When I knew her, she called herself Lana Devereaux, though I suspected she changed her name. She was a made vampire, sired in the early 1800s. She stayed with her sire for some time and then went on her own path, as vampires often do. She liked to design clothes. Before she was made, she was a seamstress for a royal tailor who took all the credit for her design work. But after she became a vampire and gathered more resources to her, she opened her own dress shop. She was accomplished, intelligent and overly romantic, hence the name. In the early twentieth century, she had a fondness for the cinema."

Lyssa lifted her hand to intertwine with Jacob's. "Lana was in love many times, but she thought she'd found her soul mate in Lord Willingham, who was a vampire overlord in London at the time, and is now a Region Master. Unfortunately, he was torn between two female vampires, one of them being your mother. The other was Eleanor. She kept a female servant whom she shared with Lord Willingham on occasion. When he conceived a child with Eleanor's human servant, his choice was made, for vampire children are so rare they can be considered a compass direction for Fate. He bound himself to Eleanor."

Alexis looked at Dante. He was staring fixedly at the queen, but he could have been a statue. The tension in him had changed, become something she couldn't define, which she now knew meant he was feeling something he probably didn't understand himself. She tightened her grip on his calf.

"Lana fell into a deep depression when he rejected her. When she disappeared soon after that, it was assumed she'd chosen to meet the sun." Lyssa passed her free hand over the drawing in an attitude of regret. "Vampires do that at times. Though she was young for such a decision, she was romantically inclined, as I said. It was not improbable. She designed a dress for me, all those years ago. That is how I knew of her. We were not friends, but she spoke during my fittings, as women will, revealing more personal things about herself. It is also my business to know a great deal about many other vampires."

She angled her attention back to Dante. "Mina has told me things I did not know, and likely did not want to know. About angels and Dark Ones, and rifts in our world. Unlike the humans, we of course did not forget the Mountain Battle, but still we knew little of what had actually happened. While I will say it's useful to have a greater understanding of these matters, the knowledge may bring me more nightmares than comfort. I don't know how your mother was taken by Dark Ones, though her depression likely lowered her guard, made her more vulnerable to predators."

Lex pictured an elegant woman who would have been besotted with Greta Garbo and Lana Turner, Hedy Lamarr. Had she not been taken by Dark Ones, she could have designed their gowns, a fashion designer renowned by Hollywood and fitting into their eccentricities perfectly by only working during night hours.

"The question now," Lyssa considered, sitting back, "is what to do about you. There are few loner vampires out there, Dante. We are very structured. We belong to territories, Regions. We have overlords and Region Masters for these areas, a protection for all of us. Having you roaming free with no sense of what a vampire is or does could become a liability for us all."

Mina spoke up then. "Right now, he's on thirty days' probation here. The enchantment on his throat also prevents him from causing harm to others."

"I am more concerned with him exposing our world to more scrutiny than we desire. Not what harm he can cause to humans. That is far more easily controlled. Beyond that, there is his own well-being, if that is of concern to you." She gave the witch a shrewd look. "It is not wise for him to be in a territory without the overlord or Region Master's awareness of his presence there. It's surprising no vampire has yet found and challenged him. A loner is quickly attacked."

Lex remembered that malevolent presence near the diner, but Dante had his attention on Lyssa. "I am told humans prefer ignorance of our existence," he said. "But I do not necessarily belong to your world, any more than I belong to the Dark One world. I will choose where I belong."

"Really?" Lyssa studied him. Heat sizzled between the two vampires like a laser line. "How will you do that, youngling, if you have no idea who you are?"

"How would you propose to teach me?" The derisive challenge was blatant.

Dante, I think she's trying to help.

Lyssa cocked her head. "I could force you to concede my power over you. Is violence what you require to learn, to listen?"

I learned about power through being helpless. I learned to fight by being beaten. Alexis blanched as his words came back to her, his ability to learn through conditioned response and reaction. And he was prepared to prove it right now. His emotions were clear on that. She felt the heat gathering within him, ready to strike.

"No," she said. Before he could anticipate her, she'd lifted herself up on his legs and wrapped her arms around his shoulders, pressing her face into his throat, her body into his so he was cradling her in his lap. His only choice was to hold her or toss her to the side as unceremoniously as a sack of potatoes.

Which he might very well do, so she tightened her arms, holding on to him. *Let them help, Dante. Please.*

Dante's body quivered beneath hers, but his fingers curled into her back, the other hand sliding over her thighs, a protective rather than a dismissive gesture, thank the Goddess.

"How can you help me learn to live here?" No less argumentative, but the phrasing made the difference. Lady Lyssa sat back, her eyes sliding over Lex curled in his lap.

"I likely can't. Not right now. Mina is right. You are more savage beast than student, and to conquer that requires something different. Perhaps what's in your arms now, a balance to your darkness. But if you win that battle, then you would do well to consider spending some time here. We can help you understand the vampire side of yourself, what rules govern our lives, and where you might fit into that life. As I said, vampire children are rare. It automatically wins you a title, *Lord* Dante." Though there was mocking humor in her voice, it wasn't entirely unpleasant. "Whether you earn the respect that goes with it is up to you."

She shifted her gaze to Mina. "I will speak to Dante alone now. Jacob will show you my roses and let you meet Kane."

Twenty-one

DESPITE the fact she was a queen, getting everyone to comply with that directive was not so easy. Dante did not want Alexis out of his sight. Jacob didn't seem overly enthused leaving Lyssa alone with an unknown Dark Spawn male vampire. But in the end, her will prevailed, as did Mina's, who supported the Queen's request.

Alexis found the roses even more beautiful than the ones on the front drive. Kane likewise was a gorgeous child, perhaps two years old. He had his father's still, vibrant eyes and mother's silky black hair, as well as kittenish fangs.

The baby found David as fascinating as his parents had. When the angel squatted down, his wings curving across the ground, Kane went right for them, losing his balance on the uneven surface and plopping down upon them. As he laughed and sunk his fingers into the feathers, David twisted around, watching him play with amusement.

Angelic energy put most parents at ease, and Jacob was no exception, despite his obvious concern about what might be happening in the study they'd left. He wasn't alone in that. Alexis paced uneasily until Mina's fingers closed around her arm. The witch sat her down on a bench beneath a heavy canopy of yellow fragrant blooms highlighted by the rising moon. "She's not harming him, Alexis."

"I know."

"Of course you do." The witch gave her a sardonic look. "You're in his mind. You know what he's capable of. You aren't worried about what Lyssa will do to him. You worry what *he'll* do if she says the wrong thing, makes the wrong move. You want to believe in him, but you know belief isn't always enough."

Alexis bit back a retort. She was far more prepared to reassure her parents than to fence the far-too-accurate observations of the Dark Spawn seawitch. She was tired, hungry and her nerves were frayed, but she could hold it together. She would. "He doesn't understand a lot of things yet. He might interpret something simple as a threat."

"*Hmm.* Sounds like it might have been better to keep him in Hell, let him learn about Earth in a controlled environment for a few months before releasing him on the world. Why didn't *anyone* think of that?"

Surging up from the bench, Alexis faced her godmother. "It needs to be his choice. He's not going to do well anywhere he feels trapped. He's been trapped long enough. If it weren't for you, he'd have been here twenty years ago."

She stopped, biting her lip, heat flooding her cheeks. Jacob and David paused in their conversation, but Mina ignored them. "You feel his feelings," she said, "but you don't necessarily know everything about who he is, who he was."

"I know more than anyone has tried to know," Lex snapped. "Except maybe you. You didn't have to try. You *knew*. You gave up on him, left him there. The person who understood him better than anyone."

"Perhaps that was why I left him there." Mina's eyes sparked. "Change can be very difficult when you've chosen your path."

Alexis fought to contain her emotions, cognizant of their host's scrutiny. When she nodded to David, feigning reassurance, he gave her an even look, but spoke a word to Jacob. They returned to entertaining the baby.

"I overheard you talking, when I was under Raphael's care," Alexis said quietly. "You said Dante *had* changed. That he'd been a scavenger, but now he was different."

When the seawitch's expression altered, the truth of it clicked into place. "It was the closing of the rifts. You shut down the one avenue he had. Life became even more unbearable."

"Rather than giving up, he became angry, and his rage overrode his fear." Mina shrugged. "It can happen. It says something about who he is. Whether it will be his salvation or the avenue to his own destruction, only time will tell."

"How can you be so callous? I know you feel things. I may not understand all of them, but when you and David are together"— Lex's gaze traveled between the two of them, and back to Mina's face—"I know how much you feel."

"You know many things." Mina rose and met her toe-to-toe, the spark in her blue and crimson eyes becoming something far more dangerous. "You may feel what I feel, or Dante feels, but don't make a child's mistake of thinking that brings you full comprehension."

Alexis tried to draw back, but she couldn't. Mina's energy poured over Alexis's skin like hot oil, holding the girl in a tunnel of suffocating heat. That Dark One blood Mina carried, so much like Dante's, was raging over her. She couldn't speak without whimpering, but Mina wasn't done yet.

"You don't know what it is to grow up without any love, except for a mother who lived her life in torment until she couldn't bear it anymore. You don't know what it's like to be tortured by those who are amused by your pain, who revile you as a thing, not a living being. Not just one day, or two, but from the second you're aware of your own existence. To have that suddenly be different . . . it takes a long, long time to believe it *is* different. It's safer to believe it isn't." Her lip curled back, showing Alexis a hint of the witch's fangs, a sign of her own Dark One sire. "Your job is to give Dante courage through your understanding, courage to make his own decisions and face the consequences. Not to shelter him with soft feelings and wishful imaginings. Because if evil has gripped his soul deeply enough, it will take him in the end.

"You've already seen what he can do physically, and some of his magical abilities. Unlike you, I am far less concerned about his feelings, or yours, than the swath of destruction he could cut here if his mind succumbed to the desire for power and control. No matter how many bodies he has to stack up to achieve it. You sense where he is vulnerable, but you do not see those same areas are like volcanic lava, ready to explode with fire and destruction."

Alexis shook her head, flinching when Mina's hands gripped her biceps, claws digging into her tender flesh. "You've known loneliness, Lex. Some rejection, some fear about who you are and what you'll become, but you've never in your life experienced isolation, except for your brief time in the Dark One world. Even then, you made a connection to Dante's mind. Every bad thing you've experienced has happened against a backdrop of love, friends, a family who will sacrifice anything for you. You grew up playing in the sparkling waters of the ocean, close to the surface where you never lost the warmth of the sun except by choice. You flew in the skies safe in your father's care, adopted by practically his whole Legion."

"It doesn't make my gift worthless," Alexis managed, glaring through a haze of heat at the witch. "I've just never used it like this." Hell, faced with a challenge like Dante, she was realizing she'd hardly used it at all.

"It's not worthless, but it is limited, if you refuse to understand its weaknesses. Take yourself past your own experiences and reactions. Don't translate someone's feelings into your own language. Understand it in theirs. Then your gift will truly find its potential."

Just as abruptly, Mina's hypnotic gaze released her. Alexis would have fallen, but David was behind her, his hands on her shoulders. Mina jerked her head at the bench. "Sit her down before she falls down." She adjusted her attention to Jacob, watching the proceedings with intense interest from the steps, Kane now playing between his bent knees. "Can that majordomo of yours make a sandwich for her before she passes out?"

Alexis blinked through the pounding in her head. She hadn't realized how angry she'd been with her godmother about Dante's imprisonment. Now that anger swirled inside of her, confused and unsure of its target, because for once, the witch's feelings weren't incomprehensible to her. Despite her sharp tongue, Mina wasn't angry with her at all. She was frustrated . . . afraid. Afraid for her goddaughter. *Goddess*. Mina was as afraid Lex was going to make a bloody shambles of this as Alexis was herself.

Jacob had risen at Mina's request, Kane toddling forward just ahead of him. The child initially had been heading for Alexis and David, but at the last moment he bypassed them and tripped, falling against Mina's legs.

The witch glanced down as Kane landed on her skirt, both his fists grabbing onto the velvet as he tipped his head back and gurgled at her. "Shoo," she said in a practical voice and twitched a leg, an unsuccessful attempt to dislodge him. "Pink leech."

David sent Jacob a pained expression. "She's very maternal."

"My lady calls him *the parasite*, and that's one of the kinder names. She'd also do anything in the world to keep him happy. It's not in the ear, but the heart." Jacob smiled, nodded respectfully to Mina and plucked his son off her skirt, settling Kane in the crook of his arm. "Let's go find the pretty girl some food, *hmm*, Kane? Best way to win her affections."

Alexis attempted a wan, polite smile, but when he moved away she put her head down in her hands. Goddess, all of this would be easier if she just felt better. She wasn't sure if she was going to throw up a sandwich or devour it like she hadn't eaten in months. She knew Dante was right, that she wasn't giving herself enough recuperation time, but what choice did she have? Take a vacation to Tahiti and let him fend for himself?

Mina and David stood near, for she saw their feet. David's were bare, as most angels, and Mina wore black canvas sneakers with unicorns printed on them in hot pink outlines, like neon equine ghosts.

"So what *is* Lyssa doing with him?" she said in a monotone, wondering if she could bear another catty remark from Mina.

The witch sat down next to her, stretching her legs, crossing her ankles between David's feet. She rocked her toes, scuffing his calf as he gave her a narrow look.

"I expect she wanted to get a sense of him alone without all of us in attendance. Or, if she really does have to slam him to the floor to get him to listen, she felt it was best to do that without an audience witnessing his humiliation. Particularly you." Mina put a hand on her arm when Alexis started to rise. "Alexis, are you listening to me at all? It's as bad for you to assume he's a misunderstood puppy, as it is for others to assume he's an untrustworthy monster. The truth lies somewhere in between."

Alexis winced as Mina altered her grip to press on the area that Dante had gripped so brutally. "Don't forget that. You don't have to worry about Lady Lyssa. She can hold her own against him, even though I didn't configure the restraint for vampires. Humans and one merangel were my major concern. Plus, I didn't expect him to encounter many vampires. I also didn't want to leave him at the mercy of the species among whom he's most likely to make his home. Vampires only respect aggression." Her brow lifted. "Now, would you like to hear more about vampires, or do you want to keep acting like a cranky baby?"

Alexis scowled. "I think David's right. You're fluent in sarcasm."

David's somber lips curved, drawing her attention. "At least it's remarkably easy to translate."

Alexis set her teeth. "I'd like to hear more."

Mina gave David an annoyed look. He simply went to a squat, his hands falling on her bare ankles, caressing them and the small sneakers. "Vampires are clannish, as Lady Lyssa implied," the seawitch said at last. "They consider humans inferior, and view most other species with suspicion. Their respect for power and hierarchy is innate to them, which may explain how Dante accomplished what he did in the Dark One world. Vampires are also very dominant in their relationships with others."

"Well, domineering I know." Lex snorted. "Look at my father."

Mina nodded, inscrutable. "Yes, he is. But the type of dominance I'm discussing is something more like what he shows toward your mother. Since you're an adult, I know you're quite aware of it."

"Pyel doesn't . . ." Lex drifted off. "Oh. *Oh.*" Despite herself, a warm shiver ran up her spine, because she did know what Mina meant. It had been that way even in the Dark One world. It was too primitive and visceral to be a compulsion magic, but something elemental in her responded to Dante's sensual commands.

"No shame in it," Mina said quietly as Lex's cheeks flushed and she avoided direct eye contact with either one of them. "Your mother has it, too. It's in your nature to submit to the man you love. With vampires, it's essentially a requirement of bonding with them. If you hadn't had it, it's far more likely he would have killed you."

The witch sighed. "A submissive personality seeks the best in the one she loves. She will seek it in the darkest part of her soul if she has to, because she must find it. Her heart and sanity depend on it. It's why your mother was able to call your father's soul back from the Dark Ones, when no one else could have. Dante . . . his soul is far darker than your father's ever was."

"You're making him sound like a monster again." Alexis shook her head. "He's not."

"No, he's not," Mina surprised her. "He's a predator. That's different from humans. Humans aren't natural predators. They're aggressive and opportunistic survivors. If something threatens them, they won't hesitate to use what their intelligence provides to fight back. But a predator's primary directive is to evaluate every life-form as food, foe or family. And the last category is a very small one." At Alexis's frown, Mina gave her an impatient look. "Why do you think your father didn't want you coming with us? He knows vampires, Alexis. Lady Lyssa is more complicated than most. She's practically responsible for creating an overarching Council that keeps the small number of vampires on this planet observing basic rules of civility, like killing no more than twelve humans a year in the pursuit of blood. But within their ranks, the vampires slaughtered by their own, or human servants sacrificed to their interests, isn't limited."

"And I'm his human servant."

"You bear the marks. Have you had trouble reading him as easily as you have others?"

Alexis nodded, and Mina grunted. "I figured as much. You probably thought it was because your girlish head was spinning under his seductive charms. But it's very possible that he's able to keep some of himself shielded from your gift. Fortunately for us all, he's not been entirely successful at that. Dante doesn't yet understand the full significance of what third-marked means in the vampire world. But he will. Your father already does."

Mina gave her a direct look. "If the bond between vampire and servant is willing and understood, it's a moving and intense relationship, but there are aspects of it that are very disturbing, unless that strong bond is there. Vampires share their servants. Sexually, as part of their games of pleasure and power, because vampires are an extremely carnal species. As I'm sure you've noticed."

Ignoring Alexis's renewed flush, she continued. "But being human servant to a vampire means more than that. At least in the mind of the vampire, he owns that human—body, mind, heart and soul. Lady Lyssa is correct. As a vampire, Dante needs to understand their world, and it is likely he can only understand it by living as part of it. If he does, it is likely he will desire to do it with you at his side."

"Does my father . . ." Alexis closed her eyes. "Of course he knows. That's why this is driving him crazy."

"Oh, there are a variety of things that have his feathers in a twist, I can promise you," Mina observed dryly. "But that's one of his big concerns. Vampires are not evil, per se, but if you do not know the proper way to deal with them, they will literally have you for lunch. We are fortunate that Lady Lyssa has lived so long, long enough to see the consequences of excessive violence. And that her servant and mate, Jacob, straddles the world between human and vampire so easily."

Mina lifted a shoulder, sighed and twisted so she was facing Alexis on the bench, commanding her full attention. "We are who we are, Alexis. Change is very difficult for all of us. All I want is for you to understand."

If Lex had been sitting with her mother, she knew Anna would have stroked her hair, explained all of this in gentle if inexorable terms. Nevertheless, Mina was giving her a different form of the same. Support, guidance and the truth, no matter how difficult it might be to hear.

Knowing everything she knew thus far, she couldn't deny Mina's logic for leaving Dante in the Dark One world, but she hated it. It would have been a difficult choice for anyone, but that didn't make the decision correct, right? Under her godmother's piercing stare, Alexis forced herself to consider what would have happened if Mina had released him, and someone like Lex hadn't been bound to him, translating his needs in a way that helped him cope with the transition to a world so different from the Dark Ones' desolate planet.

Had the seawitch's decision to leave him locked in his personal hell for twenty more years, whether intended or no, been an act of mercy?

"WHAT is it you want, now that you are here?"

"Not to be there," Dante said simply.

Lyssa's jade eyes narrowed. "That might be the truth, for now. It's not in our nature to be passive, Dante. You will want something in time. What questions do you want answered? The ones you did not ask in front of the others."

"What questions do you think I have?"

Lyssa leaned back in the chair, templed her fingers. "There's a fine line between intelligent caution and wasting a resource offered to you."

"*Hmm.*" He considered the books on the wall, the stained glass design of the windows, the lights behind them, which made the glass sparkle. Then he was in motion.

He came over to the desk at his full speed, only to find that his target was not there. He hit the chair, but arched lithely over it, spinning it in front of him so it hit the desk and formed a bulwark against rear attack.

Lyssa sat in his chair, as relaxed as she'd been in her own. "Care to try again?" Her gaze sparked fire. "I will not be as tolerant this time."

With a snarl, he sprang. He never reached her. Instead a powerful energy rolled out from her body and slammed into him, meeting him halfway over the desk. He was catapulted backward, hitting the wall such that the wood groaned at the impact. He landed on his feet, but had to shake his head to clear the concussion. When she rose, the wind from the magic she'd used was still rippling her black hair over her shoulders. "Try again," she said, showing a hint of fang. "This time I will let you reach me."

Bloodlust clouding his mind, he leaped. As she'd said, he reached her, but when he expected to tumble her backward, instead she was moving with him, a turn and twist like a dance where she had all the balance. She put him on his knees, his fingers gripping her waist, his other hand caught in hers, unable to shake off the weight of the power she pressed down on him. He cursed and struggled, but it was obvious she outmatched him. She didn't appear to even be making an effort. Tossing her hair to one shoulder in a graceful move, she bent and sank her fangs into his throat.

Being helpless was something he'd sworn he would never again be, and yet, from that first bite, it was obvious there was something very different about this. It wasn't like the Dark Ones who'd over-powered and brutalized him merely for the vindictive pleasure of it. First, like him, she wasn't all vampire. In fact, he wasn't sure if she was vampire at all, though there was a lingering sense of the species about her. She had fangs to use on him, but her scent was different. Though she'd put him down, her free hand slid up to the back of his head, stroked through his hair, a sensuous, almost reassuring caress, as well as a reproof. He thought about using the hand at her waist to try and shove her away, break the hold on his throat, but something about the power of that bite, the way it stilled things inside of him, left him undecided. The rage he carried was there, but somehow she'd thrown a silken tether around it, kept it trembling but still, as if wait-ing for her command to unleash it.

She took several swallows, then licked his throat delicately, re-moving the excess blood and staunching the flow. When she lifted her head, she was still stroking his hair, but she tilted up his chin to meet her gaze.

"As you may have sensed, I no longer hold vampire powers, but I do observe the rituals when needed. My mate can connect to you through my blood, like a first mark. I can find you now, and sense something of your state of mind."

"Why would you do that?" he said bitterly. "To prove your power over me?"

"Yes," she responded evenly. "Because you need that. You would respect nothing less. You understand that, whether you admit it or not. Now, if you choose to attack me again, I will prove to you that broken bones are very painful, even if they do heal."

"I already know that."

"*Mmm.* I suspect you do. To our kind, you are very young, Dante. Keep that in mind."

When she at last let go of him, he put himself across the room, though he knew that was a false reassurance. While he stood straight and tall, his jaw clenched, some small, ridiculous part of him was glad Alexis had not been here to see his humiliation.

Lyssa's gaze flickered, giving him the impression she was communicating elsewhere. She allowed a thin smile. "My mate picks up on my mind far too well at times. He was concerned. I let him know it was nothing I could not handle. Normally, I expect he'd disregard my assurance and come to my side, but he will not leave our son alone with strangers, no matter who they are."

"Alexis would never hurt a child," he said.

"Intentions are not always the same as reality," she responded. "I've lived long enough to leave nothing precious to fate or chance. It often takes choices away. But you know that too, don't you?"

When he chose silence, she took a step toward him. He held his ground. His bloodlust told him to try again, to seek a weakness, some way to undermine her. His mind tried to hold on to control, but deeper, darker things fought it. She wouldn't subjugate him, even if it tore him to shreds to prove it. He curled his hand into fists, his fangs pushing against his lips, trying to elongate further.

"Your mother hoped for children," Lyssa said, as if she was unaware of his dangerous state, though he knew she wasn't. "Though of course she knew they were rare. She had vampires, other than Lord Willingham, that she loved and lay with, for that is our nature. But she never conceived. I lived for over a thousand years before I had my son. Perhaps fate chooses a specific pairing for vampire children, and until that pair is drawn together, a child will not be born."

He struggled to focus. "You're saying my mother was supposed to be seeded by a Dark One male?"

"The pairing was perhaps less important to Fate than the result that came from it." Her gaze wandered over him, and he realized he was limned in the red and gold light from the tall stained glass window behind him. "You are unique, Dante. I sense many latent powers in you, as well as overt ones. If you learn who and what you are and make peace with that, you may become far more than you ever expected. Or"—she curled her lip again—"you are simply an accident and your own savagery will consume you so that Nature can fix its mistake."

Returning to her desk, she perched gracefully on it. "Set aside your anger and ask the questions you have. Don't irritate me with your stoic male silence."

Dante considered. "Was she like you?"

"No. Since she was human, a made vampire, she did not have any exceptional powers, though she came from Native American blood and confided there were some shamans in her ancestry." Her attention roved over his sculpted cheekbones, the set of his mouth and the long dark hair on his shoulders. "Before her turning, she had to hide that fact, since at that time her rights to own property or decide her own destiny would have been severely curtailed."

Lyssa pursed her sensual lips. "She handled herself well. In our world, power and violence are necessary to hold your own, but if you do not have much of those, you cultivate other talents. She understood how not to be a threat, and at the same time not be a doormat. There was a loveliness to her core that attracted male attention, more than most. She seemed . . . decent to me. She wasn't overtly strong willed, but she would not go against her principles, either. Did she . . . how long did she live in the Dark One world?"

She gestured at the chair in front of her. When he didn't move, she raised a brow. "Not afraid I'll bite you again, are you?"

He saw that quirk to her lips he now understood was a near smile. He was also beginning to understand there were many types. While this was not the open freshness of Alexis's smile, it wasn't malicious in nature. He crossed the room and sat. She was only a foot or so in front of him now, and he suppressed the desire to back the chair up several feet.

"I didn't understand about time then," he said. "But I was half as tall as I am now. She transferred her memories to me when she died."

"*Mmm.* Not yet matured, likely around eleven or twelve." Though her intent expression didn't change, he realized she was not unmoved by his mother's fate. "Perhaps she had some magic after all. There are many types. From what Mina told me, she had great fortitude to survive that long. I hope her end was merciful."

"Any end in the Dark One world is merciful," Dante responded.

Lyssa's mouth tightened and she inclined her head. "I wish I had known her better, so I could tell you more. But I can inquire for you and see if I can find others, if you'd like to know more. Would you like me to do that?"

Dante gripped the chair arms. "What would you want in return?"

The vampire queen leaned forward, her hair whispering off her shoulder to fall against his knee. Her extraordinary eyes locked with his. "She told me if she had a child, she would have named him Patrick. It's from the Latin, meaning *nobleman*. Noble man. Learn to conquer your pride and fear, Dante, and live up to the name. Then you will have given me what I wish. What she would have wished as well, I expect. Would you like me to look for others who knew her?"

He lifted a hand before he thought, so he stopped in midmotion. Something in her face told him it might be all right, though. Slowly, aware of her power, he closed his fingers over the skein of hair, remembering his mother's. They'd often torn it out, but being a vampire, it grew back quickly, down to the small of her back in a matter of days. Soft, silken wisps of it had fluttered over his face when he pressed to her side.

He closed his eyes, a hard shudder running through him. Lyssa touched his temple, gentle, easy, her exotic scent cocooning him, the dim lights of the windows closing in. A vampire home, a place where vampires knew who and what they were.

Bolting out of the chair, he put the distance of the room between them again. Lyssa remained where she was, watching him breathe hard. He had his fangs bared, and he knew the crimson light of his eyes was likely like a demon's in the shadows.

"No," he said. "She's dead. There is nothing else I need to know." *Nothing else I can afford to know.*

Twenty-two

MINA returned them to a wooded area close to Alexis's home. Dante had said little when he emerged with Lyssa. Mina and David had made the appropriate farewells and thanks, and Lyssa had reiterated the invitation—though Alexis sensed an underlying command—that Dante should consider staying at her estate for a time to be tutored in the ways of his vampire kin. When she added that his servant would of course be welcome, Alexis detected emotion from Mina and David that suggested *they* would not necessarily welcome that idea.

Remembering how Mina had described the relationship between vampires and their servants, she shivered a little. Slaves, made to serve sexually . . . But then she thought of what Mina had said about Jonah and Anna. *It's in your nature, to submit to the man you love . . .* And then Lyssa: *There is a bond there that should never be abused. It is the one constant in a vampire's life.* What would she be willing to do to stay at his side?

David and Mina had departed. As Alexis moved with Dante through the forest, following the jogging path she knew would come out behind her home, Dante remained silent, head down, gaze trained on the pathway. Alexis gave him privacy, involved in her own thoughts, though the odd absence of night sounds caught her attention. With a chill, she thought she knew why. *Predator*, as Mina had said. The creatures of the night stayed silent, motionless as he passed, instinctively hiding. But when she probed deeper than that, she stopped.

"What?" Dante's head came up. He stepped to her shoulder, a position allowing him to move forward or aft as needed, gratifying her with his willingness to protect her. It was falsely reassuring, she knew. His idea of protection might involve tearing some innocent apart before she could establish it was a power walker tuned into their iPod. Of course, it was the thought that counted, right?

"What do you feel?" he asked.

"Don't know," she responded truthfully. "It was different from the diner. Sometimes I catch a passing whiff of somebody else's house-cleaning issues, if that makes sense." She forced a lighter tone. "I'm starving. Want to watch me make a late dinner? You can taste things, right?"

He turned her to face him. Alexis tipped her head back, dreading that impassive look. Instead she was surprised by one that was . . . well, *tender* would be going overboard. *Concerned* seemed more accurate and sensible. "Alexis—"

"Let's not." She shook her head "I really think it would make sense for you to stay out of my head except when you need to talk without words. You can't worry about my moods, okay? You've got too many more important things to deal with right now. I'm kind of . . . I've got a crush on you, first-sex infatuation, whatever. You're not at a place that you can give back to that, and you shouldn't. I do understand that, really—"

Could she sound more idiotic? Maybe this was why girls had sex and first relationships early. She handled so many things well, with complete confidence, and yet the way he made her feel made her so . . . adolescent.

"Why are you helping me, Alexis?"

She frowned. "I wish you'd stop asking me that. I just want to, all right? I think you're worth helping. And you can read my mind. You know."

"No." He shook his head. "No more than you understand my emotions. You cannot read what I cannot read myself, and I think it is the same for you, what is going on inside of you."

"I'm not used to being confused," she said irritably. "You're inaccessible."

At his blank look, she made a face. "I can read emotions, meaning I can *read* them. Like a book, with words. You're a foreign language. I feel certain things from you, but I can't get into your head, really grasp the meaning. That shouldn't matter. I should know you're reflecting what you yourself are dealing with, but . . . *aargh*." She threw up her hands. "Fine, I'm sorry. It's selfish, but I want to know how you feel about me. And no, I don't want you to tell me. I want to know, to *feel* it. And I can't. It's frightening, because I told them you would be fine here, that it would all work out okay, and it turns out . . . I'm just guessing, really. I don't know. I just know I want you to be okay. I want you to be all right here. And that's different, you know?"

He blinked. "Females are confusing."

Alexis gave a half snort. "I guess we can be." Following his glance down, she saw she'd curled her fingers in several strands of hair lying against his chest. She was twisting it against his pectorals and the soft stuff of his shirt. She suspected it reflected the tangled state of her mind. She really needed food and sleep. She'd had the sandwich Mina had requested, but it had gone down like sawdust with her worry about other things. She'd only eaten half.

"Perhaps we can help each other," he said, drawing her attention. Taking her fingers in his, he splayed them out on his palm. "If I concentrate on one moment, very hard, maybe you can help me understand what it is I'm feeling. You are not alone in your confusion, Alexis," he said, so softly that the rumble of his deep voice was almost lost in the weighted silence of the forest. "I have felt only anger and hatred for so long. But it . . . pleases me, I think, that you want me to be here. Is that what you feel?"

She realized he wasn't asking about her feelings, but his own. His expression was concentrated, as if he were holding the emotion steady within himself with effort. Alexis closed her hand on his, listening with the sense she had. Slowly, as if his feelings were a nebula, slowly oscillating, drifting through her mind, one side turned up toward the light of her gift, reflecting the direction of his thoughts.

The smile bloomed first in her heart, her hand tightening on his. "Yes. You're pleased. That's what that feeling is. You're . . . glad."

His expression was somber. "Now, what do you sense?"

She closed her eyes. With his flame-colored eyes so intent on her face, it was easier to keep her own emotions disengaged that way. But the smoke sifted and what she felt now had a lighter feel to it, a tickle like feathers. It reminded her of her father tumbling her through the clouds when she was barely more than a toddler.

"Laughter," she breathed. "Amusement. We smile or laugh when we feel that way. What are you remembering?"

Opening up a window into her mind, he showed her the scene when she'd laughed at Clara's absorption with Marcellus. Her joy had planted and germinated within him, such that he'd had the unfamiliar urge to smile with her, even though he hadn't understood the humor.

"I know you've sent me a picture, but that's the first time you sent me a movie. Wow." She grinned. When his lips twitched then stilled, uncertain, she lifted onto her toes, teased the corners upward. "It's a smile," she said softly. "Don't be afraid of it. Imagine me laughing. Remember the mother and little boy at the craft room, when he asked you for a face painting."

"Will, and his mother." Another emotion came at her then, and this one was not laughter. Alexis stopped, her fingertips resting on his mouth. His eyes were only inches from hers as she let it flood her. "What is this one?" he asked.

"Sadness," she murmured. "Different from anger and hatred. Sadness is . . . a feeling of loss, like you lost something, and you won't get it back."

"Yes," he said slowly. "It feels that way."

"Oh, Dante." Squeezing his hand harder, she pushed away anything but the desire to help him understand his own emotions, as foreign to him as a new language in truth. "This is working wonderfully, but why don't we take a break for a little bit? I am *really* hungry and tired. It's hard to run around all day with a guy who doesn't eat. Well, not like the rest of us do."

Of course, the reminder of when he had last eaten and how

brought a flush to her face. Dante cocked his head at her, and a little tug happened at that right corner again, a very sexy almost-smile that caught her breath. "Is it my turn to read your emotions?"

"No," she said firmly. She angled her head down the path. "I'll race you there. No vampire cheating. You have to run like a human."

"As tired as you are, perhaps I should run on my knees? That should be slow enough."

"Okay, that was definitely a smart-ass thing to say." Stepping into him to put him off balance, she took off.

He caught her in seconds, of course. When he captured her about the waist, she ducked under his hold and managed to slip by him to take another few steps. Then he caught the hem of her shirt and swung her around into his arms, such that she was laughing breathlessly.

"You're cheating," she informed him. "Racing means whoever can run the fastest, not grabbing hold of the other person to slow them down."

"I was distracted," he said. When he lifted her under her arms, she settled her legs around his waist, her arms around his neck. "When you run, it's a challenge. I feel I must catch you."

He's a predator . . . The meaning didn't feel sinister now, though it wasn't safe, either. That pleasurable ripple low in her belly intensified as he gripped her buttocks in a firm, kneading hold. "If you don't let me eat, I'll be no good to you at all," she complained.

"A hungry servant is more motivated to please her Master."

Cold fear returned. Not because of his words and what Mina had told her about vampires. This *was* like what she'd felt behind the diner. Sharp and sudden, like a gunshot in the back.

She didn't have to tell Dante. Almost as soon as she registered it, he'd dropped her to her feet and thrust her behind him to face the threat.

The man watching them was crouched in a tree, comfortably as a bird, despite the fact he was at least Dante's size. He looked about forty years old, but Alexis assumed that was deceptive, since he was a vampire. Handsome, with styled blond hair and cold green eyes.

"You're new in this territory. I'm Terence." His eyes glinted. "Like your servant, I'm hungry. I expect you to share her with me."

It was like a scene from *National Geographic*, two males fighting for the same helpless gazelle. Jonah's words came back to her. *All you have to do is call . . .*

No. Dante's mental voice was a sharp, undeniable command. *I will handle this.*

"Your expectations mean nothing to me," Dante responded. Glancing at Alexis, he jerked his head toward a large tree behind him, wide enough to protect her back. *Go and stay there until I tell you to do otherwise.*

She wanted to argue, wanted to suggest something that might avoid a fight, but his glance and the commanding power behind the words forestalled any thought. If servants were what Lyssa and Mina had implied, her arguing with the vampire Terence considered her Master would be viewed as a sign of Dante's weakness. Thank goodness she'd learned a lot about animal behavior at the Conservancy, though the same behavior seemed far too often to apply to human males. She couldn't find humor in the thought, though, for Terence's eyes were following her movements closely. His hunger was palpable, and not just for blood. Mindful of Dante's earlier words, she didn't run, trying to avoid the appearance of frightened prey.

It didn't matter. As soon as the blond vampire's eyes left Dante to follow her, her vampire leaped. A cry escaped her lips when Terence launched himself from the branch—toward Alexis.

Dante intercepted him. She only knew that because Terence didn't reach her. She wasn't human, but she wasn't equipped with accelerated sight to track their movements. The evidence of their struggle was all around her though, the heat of it blasting her, the sound of snarls. Tree limbs, thick as her arm, snapped off when they hit. The earth plowed up in gouged furrows as they thudded into it and rolled, leaves and dirt spraying up and showering her. She yelped as she was slammed hard into her tree, so her breath left her and her teeth snapped down on her tongue. When she fell to the ground, dazed, she realized they'd run into her in their fight. They were a few feet down the trail, grappling. Terence had Dante down, his back to her.

Seizing a broken limb, she scrambled to wobbly legs and rushed forward, taking a swing at the blond vampire's head. The solid *thwack* was heartening, but Terence turned into the blow, knocking the weapon from her hand. She had a brief impression of Dante's crimson eyes before everything accelerated.

Stars exploded in her brain as Terence hit her. With her body hurtling through the air, she tried to shift, reach for her wings, but she was moving too fast and a tree met her too quickly. She slammed into it ten feet off the ground and landed hard, her ankle giving way beneath her.

There was a guttural bellow, like a creature chained in the bowels of Hell, raging for more souls to eat. A blast of energy caught her in its maelstrom, the turbulent nebula one pure illuminated killing rage, so devoted in its purpose she was overwhelmed by its weight, thrust to the ground by its intentions. Choking smoke, electrical energy and a roaring gripped her heart in terror. It was the Dark One world, all over again, come to reclaim her.

Dante. She hadn't realized how well she'd blocked the aftermath of her fear until the terrible winds of that place surrounded her again, intending to take her back. Only this time Dante wouldn't be there, and she'd be alone, subjected to the grasping talons and fetid bodies of the Dark Ones, pushing in on her, wanting to feed on her pain . . .

"Alexis." *Alexis.* The second command was sharp, resonating through her mind, but it was the worry behind it that made her turn her mind outward, summon the courage to focus on her surroundings.

"Oh, Goddess. Oh, thank the Lord and Lady." She was lying on the jogging path, earth and leaves clutched in shaking hands. There was dirt on her face where she'd pressed her cheek to the ground to stay beneath the wall of flame. Smoke assailed her nostrils, and when she lifted her head, she saw the nearest trees were charred, the branches gone, trunks blackened. A larger pile of ash was scattered across the pathway. Ash with bits of chalk in them. Not chalk. Bone, like a cremated body.

She jerked her attention from that to her companion. She couldn't look beyond his gaze, windows to a hellfire furnace, but he seemed fine, for he lifted her so she was cradled in his arms, held against his chest. His voice was gruff, tense. "I am going to spank you for not listening to me. I'll take you back to your home."

She nodded, keeping her arms folded against herself. Despite the overwhelming heat before, now she was shivering from a place so deep inside her there wasn't enough hot chocolate, warm robes or fuzzy slippers in the world to make her warm.

She must have passed out, for the next thing she knew, he was laying her on her bed. Glancing down, she saw her shirt looked like it had been scorched in the dryer. One section of skirt hem was blackened, crumbling at her touch, though the rest was intact.

"Should we call your mother . . . or father?"

Some part of her wanted to, the terrible fear of being sucked back into the Dark One world far too close, but another part of her warned against it.

"If that is what you need, you should call them," he said, and there was fury in his voice. She couldn't handle anger right now. She wasn't sure what she could handle. She was so cold.

"I am not angry with you." He was, of course, but he was struggling not to be.

"What was all that?" she rasped, and put her hand to her throat.

"I took care of him. He is gone."

"But . . . how?" She saw now he was also marked with ash. The poet's shirt she'd liked so much was done for. Slashes in the shirt and bloodstains suggested the skin beneath had suffered open wounds, though none were visible now.

"Later. What do you need? There is a bath. And clothes. Are you hurt?"

"I don't know, I'm just . . . I'm so cold." Her teeth were chattering and she still had her arms folded around herself.

Muttering a curse, he drew a blanket off the trunk she had at the foot of the bed and wrapped her in it, and then the coverlet around that, so she was cocooned in both. Then he went into the bathroom and started the water in the tub, running it so hot she could see the steam rising, billowing out toward her. But still she shook. There was no amount of fabric that would be warm enough.

Turning off the tub, he came back out. Stripping off the remains of his shirt, leaving on the jeans, he unrolled her. She thought he was going to take her to the tub, but then he slid onto the bed, bringing her up against his chest before he rewrapped her, throwing the blanket ends loosely over his own body as he folded his arms around her.

The warmth of a living body. *Yes.* That was what she needed. It permeated her flesh where the blanket had been unable to do so, and her shivering became a jerking that seemed worse but wasn't. The warmth stealing in seemed to activate nerves that had become numb.

"I don't think . . . I handled b-being in the Dark One world . . . as well as I thought. I was so . . . s-scared we were going b-back there. That we were b-back there."

"It was the magic." He had his jaw pressed against the side of her head. She realized he was rubbing her back with both hands, soothing and yet probing at once, and wondered if he was checking for broken bones. She thought she was fine. The slam against the tree and Terence's punch in the face had been the worst, but thank goodness she wasn't human, not beneath the skin. She was far more resilient. And now she was a human servant as well, and Dante had said they were hard to kill.

"More primate than human," she mumbled. "Did you know monkeys can fall out of trees thirty feet high and their skulls won't crack? Not usually."

"That explains why you are so hardheaded. I told you to stay by the tree."

"I didn't want him to hurt you."

"He was not going to hurt me." The derision in the tone, the arrogance, eased something in her chest further.

"Ten feet tall and bulletproof, *hmm*?" She felt logy all of a sudden, the warmth making her tongue thick, no energy left in her body. "Well, I didn't know. Didn't get the memo." She let out a little snort. "Bet you don't know what any of that means."

"No, I don't." His lips touched her temple and she jerked again. Her throat hurt, with smoke or unshed tears, she didn't know. *Oh, God, don't let me fly apart.*

His arms tightened, teetering her on the edge of hysteria. "You are safe." But there was something bubbling beneath the surface and it disturbed her, told her everything wasn't all right.

"*You* are all right." He tipped her chin so she would meet his eyes. But when she did, the emotion she was sensing erupted from him. "I am still . . . angry. I told you to stay *put*."

His snarl would have sent her skittering from the bed if she had the energy, but the expostulation knocked her receptors back into active mode. Of course, she didn't really need them. From a wealth of childhood mischief, she'd seen this reaction from her father plenty of times. Another kind of warmth stole into her chest, helping her even more than the blankets.

"I'm all right. Nothing a bath, a bottle of wine and a half gallon of ice cream won't fix. Really." She attempted a smile, but instead her eyes filled with tears and she started to shake again. "I'm sorry. Can you please just keep holding me?"

Putting her head down on his chest, she let herself cry. Though she wasn't sure what his reaction would be, he embraced her uncertainly, then with more confidence as she clung harder. He began to rub her back in circles again, slowly fondle her nape. Stroking the side of her wet face with his knuckles, he held her so close to his warm body she felt almost like he'd pull her inside of him if he could.

Her hands crept up his chest, her fingers whispering along the silver band around his throat. The way he'd accepted her putting that collar on him had felt like a declaration that he was hers. He would give her his trust. As misguided as she knew that belief was, she held on to it as a comfort for right now.

Time passed, for when her eyes opened next she saw it was just past midnight. He was still holding and stroking her, murmuring to her, fragments of sentences. Amazed, she realized he was trying to sing to her, broken pieces of a lullaby. Something revived from his memories of his mother?

Tilting back her head, she looked into his face. He'd loosed his hair from the braid she'd made, and it brushed her hand as she raised it to twine in the strands. He watched her, eyes like embers of starlight in the waning dark, his sensual lips firm. The light showed him

as beautiful, but it was in shadows that his face became too mesmerizing to look away, everything perfect about it etched by the myster-
ies of the darkness. It made her wonder if the truth of what Dante
truly wanted lay somewhere between Mina's cynicism and Alexis's
optimism.

"Everyone keeps asking me this question: 'What do I want to do
here?'" Dante took his gaze to the window. "I know the answer to
the question, but I will not give it to them."

"Will you give it to me?"

He looked down at her. "Perhaps. But for right now . . . I've never
had anything I wanted to take care of. I want to take care of you,
keep you safe. Touch your face, know you are well." When he furrowed his brow, examining his own thoughts, she closed her hand
over his, her throat thick from more than smoke. "I like that hum-
ming noise," he added.

"The refrigerator?"

He nodded. "It's . . ."

"Soothing?"

Dante's regard on her mouth and the line of her cheek was a
physical stroke. His hand tightened against her back. "Yes. Exactly."

"Will there be other vampires, do you think?"

"Lady Lyssa told Mina she would notify the territory overlord I
am here. He was to instruct the vampires in this territory that I am
to be left alone for the next thirty days. There was likely not time
to . . . send the memo?"

Her lips curved. "You learn fast."

"Your mind is a good teacher. If they obey her, I expect we should
have no further problem. Not that he was much of one. You worry
too much."

"Your confrontation management skills take some getting used
to," she said, holding the smile with effort. "I think you're right
though, that we won't have more trouble. After seeing her and Jacob,
I can't imagine anyone going out of their way to piss them off."

"You have your own confrontation management skills." He studied her. "You avoided one by bringing up their child, even though you
placed yourself at risk by drawing their attention."

"Sometimes people get caught up in defending their particular boundaries. Children don't care about boundaries." Her fingertips found his collarbone and caressed it, though she continued holding on to his hair, reluctant to let go. Her other hand gripped his waist.

Dante wondered if she realized how tightly she was holding him. Even after her sleep, he could feel the struggle within her to contain her nerves, the emotions disturbed by the vampire's attack. Sliding his fingers into her curls, he began to stroke through them, following the line of her skull. When he reached her throat under her ear, she tilted her head into his touch.

The lullaby *had* come from his mother. He hadn't remembered it for over two decades. It had not served him when he stopped being a scavenger and became the hunter, so he'd buried it. But wanting to ease Alexis's fears had unearthed the memory, a gentle, terrible gift waiting in his subconscious.

Though his mother's wrists had been manacled against rings embedded in the stone, they were placed low enough that when he pressed against her leg, her fingers could touch his head. Those few times he could be near her without Dark Ones, she'd stroked him, slow, unsteady. That song had caught in her throat, a rough music disrupted by her pain. The notes had come through, though. After she was gone, sometimes he'd curl up in whatever hole he'd found for the night, pretend the hand stroking his head was hers instead of his own, and hum that tune.

Adjusting his back against the headboard so Alexis lay against his chest, he let her doze again. She would still want a bath, though the water was cooling. He could heat it again, using a more low level version of what she'd call his confrontation management skills. As his fingers drifted over her body, his gaze traveled her room. The stuffed animals and sheer curtains, the gleam of a parking lot light giving the panels a silken moonlight look. The softness of the mattress under him, the ticking of a clock.

His mother had tried to offer him comfort in a world that mocked it. This world overflowed in comforts in comparison, but to him that made its dangers even more hazardous, because it was harder to see them coming.

Hatred and rage, pain and darkness. They had those things here, but in a random dispersal, like a handful of sand thrown into the wind. Whereas they'd *been* the air of his world. He'd been suckled on them for over sixty years. It wasn't a new thought, but for the first time, he did wonder if his soul was still trapped there, on the other side of the portal. Alexis had pulled his body across, but he wasn't all the way in. She seemed determined to hold on to him, though, no matter what it cost her.

That feels good.

Something low in his gut tightened at the sleepy thought. He'd ask her what emotion he was feeling later, maybe after they washed off the ash and blood, the smell of the magic he'd unleashed. Or perhaps he'd do it, take the washcloth and soap to make her skin slick and fragrant, turn lingering shadows of fear in her gaze to desire.

At least he understood that feeling. Or he thought he had. In the Dark One world it hadn't been a feeling but a physical compulsion, a need no different from eating or relieving oneself. With her, it was a way to go beyond confusion and decision, something clean, simple, right. But he was finding she gave him that even when he wasn't inside her body.

She projected peace, safety, warmth, things he'd never had but somehow understood when he felt them from her. She'd helped him from the beginning. Not just with the painting and sculpture, but how she'd stood up to her father's will.

He dwelled on that one. Her father was obviously stronger, more powerful. But he'd allowed it. He'd *respected* her decision. This was a world full of peculiarities. A powerful angel who let his daughter make a decision he did not believe was wise, rather than forcing her to obedience, was just one of them. Power was handled differently here, like the varying direction of the wind, rather than a mallet that kept others hammered into their place.

He looked at the woman sleeping in his arms. She'd ignored or disobeyed him several times now, and it wasn't because of the despised metal collar around his throat that he hadn't punished her as he would a Dark One who disregarded his commands. The Dark Ones were always seeking ways to take his power away, claim it for themselves. Their lives were a struggle for dominion. Alexis's motives were different. He remembered her hurt when he implied her fate was of no concern to him.

That was no longer true, if it had ever been true. He'd been prepared to battle the vampire, prove his strength was greater, and then allow the creature the opportunity to submit or die. But the way his gaze had crawled over Alexis's flesh, and then his fist striking her, sending her hurtling back into a tree, had sealed the vampire's fate. The red rage that had covered Dante's mind tolerated only one outcome. Death to the one who dared touch her, cause her pain.

But what did that make him? Who would punish him for harming her, for planting the fear that was still making her cry out in her sleep? Disturbed by his thoughts, he pushed them away as her fingers tightened on his thigh, her face pressing into his neck.

Resuming his stroking, he stumbled through the lullaby once more.

Twenty-three

MARCELLUS settled on the roof of Alexis's town house and folded his wings, glancing at Jonah and David as they came in next to him. "Cleanup wasn't too difficult," he reported. "They'll think it was a cigarette fire that burned itself out on the trail. I scattered the ashes so the bone shards wouldn't catch a park ranger's eye. Vampire and definitely Dark One energy readings. Dante was involved, whatever happened."

David looked toward Jonah. "Alexis?"

"Is fine, as far as I know," her father answered. "She sent me the message that a vampire attacked her and Dante. Dante handled it, which explains the Dark One fire."

"It took out a hundred-foot swath, very uniform," Marcellus supplied. "He had to have doused it himself, else it would have had a more erratic pattern. Did the vampire queen not honor her promise?"

"She confirmed Jacob talked to the territory overlord shortly after we left," David explained. "So this appears to be a matter of timing only. The attacking vampire hadn't been informed Dante wasn't an unprotected loner in the territory. There should be no other aggressive moves toward him, at least not during his thirty days. Hopefully he'll be intelligent enough to accept her offer for guidance after that," he added. "If nothing else, it will spread the word among the vampires here that he can hold his own."

"That won't matter," Jonah said flatly. "He'll be back in his own world then."

"It's not his world, Jonah," David responded. "It was where he was born when his abducted mother was raped there."

Jonah's mouth tightened. "You were there, David, when Lex came back through, bruised and covered with blood. You've seen the way he looks at all of us. He's more Dark One than anything else."

"Marcellus once said the same thing about Mina." A hardness entered David's voice. "You weren't so ready to agree with him then."

Marcellus shifted uncomfortably, readjusting his wings, but Jonah held his lieutenant's gaze. "I had some evidence that Mina's fate was undecided. I haven't seen that in Dante."

"Perhaps because you don't want to see it."

Jonah's dark eyes sparked. "You don't have a child. You don't understand."

"No, I don't have a child. Which is why I'm seeing this from a different perspective." David shook his head. "Jonah, every one of us wanted to take him apart limb from limb when they came back through that portal. But you can't miss how she looks at him. She sees something no one else sees. I do understand that, quite well."

"Which may mean both of your perspectives are distorted," Marcellus ventured, hoping to defuse the sizzling tension. Sometimes he thought the two were more like father and son than they realized. "One of you sees him as evil, the other as misunderstood good. Perhaps I should go check on her and report a balanced perspective?"

"I will look in on my own daughter," Jonah said. "But thank you, Marcellus, for offering."

"It's late." David's tone was now neutral, though Marcellus noted the tension hadn't left his shoulders. "Since she indicated she was all right, wouldn't tomorrow be soon enough?"

In answer, Jonah gave him another searing look. He left the town house roof in one easy leap, which they knew would land him on the ground before the front door. When Marcellus raised a brow, David shrugged. "Where do you think Dante is sleeping, if he sleeps? And do you think Lex is wearing flannel footie pajamas?"

"Goddess save us." Marcellus shuddered. "I don't have a child or a female, and I'm beginning to think an angel's mind stays clearer without either one."

"Perhaps." A smile crossed David's face, easing it. "But a smooth journey is rarely an exciting one, Marcellus."

"Yes, my life is full of boredom," he snorted. "Since I fight for . . ."

"You fight for the Goddess," David finished firmly when he stopped. "You protect her world, as all of us do."

"Just not on the front lines of the Legion any more." Marcellus gave his scar a disgusted look.

"Would you get over it? I swear, you're worse than an old woman."

"An old woman who can whip your subordinate lily-white buttocks halfway across the galaxy."

David's smile spread into a grin. "There's the captain I know. Sir."

Marcellus snorted and went to a squat, his wings holding him in that position. Though David said nothing, he did notice the strain to the effort in Marcellus's left wing. Thank the Goddess, when Mina shut down the rifts from the Dark One world, the need for large scale actions or fierce fighting had been curtailed for a while. But battle practice continued, and in competitions where Marcellus had excelled, he'd now fallen into the middle of the pack. Despite David's teasing, he knew it weighed on Marcellus's mind, as it would any of them. The angels of the Legion lived for their service to the Goddess.

David tactfully turned the topic in a different direction, looking down toward the parking lot. "I admit, I expected you to be more of Jonah's opinion on all this. Since it's Dark One blood that has kept you from fully healing."

Marcellus didn't immediately answer. Instead, he watched the cat crossing the quiet parking area. He'd returned Timeshare Cat, or T, to Lex, but while she was chaperoning Dante, she'd given his care over to Clara. The cat, despite Lex having responsibly neutered him, lived up to his name and tomcat nature. He seemed to have no problem sauntering up to Clara's town house instead of Lex's. Marcellus couldn't blame the cat.

Goddess, he was being an idiot. The girl was a child, and Lex's friend. Feeling David's regard, he switched his mind to the topic at hand. It was time to give the young angel the answer he deserved. Marcellus reflected that he'd probably withheld it for far too long.

"In centuries past, I watched angels fall in the face of greater numbers of Dark Ones. They could have retreated, perhaps, and fought another day, but they held the line so other angels could have that honor. They fought darkness despite the weakness of their bodies, and knowing the consequences of doing so. But they also knew they had the reward of serving the Goddess, and that their life energy would rejoin hers."

He met David's gaze. "Your witch fought the darkness inside of her for years, with no justification other than her own stubbornness. She stood strong, even when we reviled her. No one promised her any reward for her courage and endurance. No one championed her. Not until you. When she eventually did what she did, closing down the Dark One world, she did it believing she would lose you, the only thing she'd ever needed or valued, or that had needed or valued her. I was ashamed."

David's brow creased. "Marcellus."

"She didn't lose you, though it was a near thing." He cleared his throat, lifting a hand so David would let him finish. "And I realized then there can be a spark of light in the darkest night, but we can be too blind to see it if we cling to what we've always known and believed. On better, less selfish days"—his hand went to his chest, brushed the scar—"I think this is a reminder of that. Dante may be the evil he seems to be, a lost soul who cannot be saved. Or, like your witch, he may be something different. I will not make the same mistake again."

"You know, you guys keep coming around, they're going to cite you for loitering."

Glancing left, they found Clara leaning on the low wall running the roof perimeter of the adjacent town house. She cocked her head, her bright eyes focused on Marcellus. "Nice evening to take a girl out for a flight, don't you think?"

David coughed over a chuckle as Marcellus scowled. "Your ability to see us is irritating," he informed her.

"You're not really irritated. You're mad because you almost smiled when you saw me. I know these things. I'm clairvoyant. Hence the name *Clara*." At their expressions, she laughed. "You guys are too easy. My mom had no clue, she just liked the name. It's a little annoying though."

"You should be asleep," Marcellus grated.

"It's three a.m. It's hard for any clairvoyant to sleep during that time. Too many otherworldly things moving about." She lifted a Tupperware bowl. "I've got some great pound cake Mom made. If I eat it all I'll be far too heavy for you to fly around. It tastes like manna from Heaven, so honestly I think that's the recipe she uses. Want to share?"

"We don't really eat," David explained. "Not in this form. We can, but it all tastes like sawdust."

"This won't taste like sawdust, I promise. There's no way." When her gaze turned to him, Clara paused, studying him. Abruptly, she beamed at him. "Congratulations. You must be really excited. I didn't know angels . . . well, I guess they can, because Alexis has never said she couldn't have babies."

David's brow creased. "Excuse me?"

Clara blanched. "Oh, crap. She hasn't told you yet. Sometimes, when it's late or I'm flustered"—she shot a self-conscious look at Marcellus—"I get confused. I think she was getting ready to tell you pretty soon, else I wouldn't have confused it. If your wife or girlfriend is scary, don't tell her I was the one who told you."

"You have no idea," Marcellus said dryly.

David was staring off into space, his expression torn between shock and sudden light-headedness. "Excuse me," he said all of a sudden, and vanished.

"Wow," Clara blinked. "Did he just—"

"No. He flew, but faster than your eyes could follow."

"Oh. It was still freaking impressive. Damn it, I hope I haven't caused trouble."

"I expect you're quite practiced at that. But it will be joyous news to him." Though he privately wondered if Mina's reaction would be far different.

"Good." Taking a step onto the ledge, she cocked her head, her gaze passing over him with a blatant appreciation that would have amused him if she didn't inexplicably get under his skin. "Well, I didn't plot it or anything, but looks like we've got the rooftop all to ourselves." She glanced at the starry sky. "Romantic night, *hmm?*"

Marcellus gave her a narrow look. "I am four hundred years old."

"Cool. I'll keep that in mind when I bake you a birthday cake. Okay, in about three seconds, I'm going to jump over there. I assume you'll grab me out of the air if I fall short."

Marcellus straightened. "You will not. We are not circus animals, to perform for your—"

"Three." Clara leaped into open space, the cake holder hugged against her body.

———

FROM his enhanced hearing, Jonah knew both occupants of the room were sleeping. He knew David was right, that he should come back. But the explosion of energy so close to his daughter's home, the obvious use of Dark One power, had been unsettling, to say the least. He wanted to confirm she was all right, for Anna as well as himself.

The key she kept in the planter next to the door always irritated him, but she'd rightly explained that humans held no danger to her. The cloud of tranquil energy around her neutralized any random threat of theft, rape or murder. "It's a chicken and egg thing," she'd explained to him. "There has to be a reason to want to harm me, Pyel, and most people want to be near me so they can feel good. Wanting to harm me would be because I'd made them feel bad."

No, the type of enemy who would attack her would be otherworldly, one not deterred by locks on windows or doors. For instance, the kind who would pull her through a dream portal.

Jonah wasn't completely oblivious to David's point, or Marcellus's. He just wasn't ready for them to be right. His daughter's heart was like her mother's, pure feeling. She had the key not just for Clara, but for all manner of people she'd befriended and granted refuge. He knew about all of them. A young, single mother who occasionally needed someplace to nap on her lunch hour, close to her office. A teenage boy who lived in a bad neighborhood and came here to study after school. There'd been a plethora of stray dogs and cats she'd placed in homes, though she'd kept the big buff-colored tomcat, saying he was meant to be here.

Whereas Dante, her latest stray, shouldn't be in the same dimension.

Sliding into the town house, Jonah closed the door. His nostrils flared, scenting the blood drops on the floor, but it was only a small splattering. She was fine, she'd said so. Still, he moved through the living area with silent caution, taking in the usual comfortable arrangement of sofa, easy chairs, coffee table. She liked open spaces and simple decorating, for practical as well as aesthetic reasons. Bric-a-brac on tables could be swept off by a wing, the same way a golden retriever would do it with an enthusiastic plume of a tail. A faint smile touched his lips, recalling the saucy remark when she moved in, anticipating visits from him and other angels of the Legion. She was so different from him and Anna, and yet so alike as well. He marveled at the miracle of it every day.

A flash of movement at the window caught his startled gaze. Marcellus winged by in a sharp banking maneuver. He caught a glimpse of a woman's flailing arms, her body securely caught in his grasp, just before his captain's reassurance came into his mind, letting him know whatever the situation was, it was under control.

When he stepped to the bedroom door, Jonah braced for the likelihood she was sharing her bed with the Dark Spawn. If they were in a bare, postcoital state, he might put his eyes out with a hot poker.

His daughter was in her favorite oversized sleep shirt, her shoulders visible over the warm pile of blankets on top of her. She was curled on her side. Dante was with her, curved behind her body, his arm over her chest, large hand cupped under her upper arm as she held on to his forearm in her sleep. Fortunately, he appeared to be wearing jeans, and of course Mina's silver collar.

Clustered around Alexis's front was a plethora of the stuffed animals normally on the floor. Plush ponies, puppies, kittens, bears and Pooh characters were grouped at her abdomen, legs and around her head. Dante's other arm was under it and she clasped his hand on that side, closing the circle between them.

Jonah noted the split on her lip, and knew that was likely where the blood splatter had come from.

"I didn't do that."

He shifted his gaze to meet Dante's. The hellfire color glowed in the darkness like a demon's. He'd spoken low, so Alexis didn't stir.

"I know." Jonah forced out the words. "She told me she got in the way."

"Yes. And no. She was trying to help, and did not stay where I told her to."

Yes, that happened. He didn't have to look far to know exactly where his daughter had gotten *that* trait from.

Dante's watchfulness suggested he was ready to leap up if Jonah gave him cause. Lex stirred restlessly, making a questioning sound in her sleep. He murmured to her, one hand stroking her fingers, and hers tightened on him. She subsided.

Jonah studied her. "She's all right then? No injuries."

"Bruised only. She said nothing was broken, and that she would know if it was. She believes that, but I do not know if it is the truth."

A reminder that the bastard knew everything that went through Alexis's head, making her completely vulnerable to him. Jonah's jaw tightened. "She's likely right, but tell her I want her to see Raphael or one of his healers tomorrow, to be sure. I will be checking to see if she receives the message, and obeys it."

"I will make sure she does."

Jonah indulged the visual of twisting his perfect face into the shape of wet clay, snapping his spine like kindling. "You may have inadvertently marked her as your servant," he said, just as low, "and Lady Lyssa may have told you that meant certain things, but know this. She is not yours. She makes her own choices."

"I know." Dante brought his attention to her face, as if she was a puzzle to him. "You give her choices, though you could easily take them away. Because she is your daughter and you . . . love her." When he looked at Jonah, something equally menacing entered his gaze. "What if that gets her killed? Is that something your love allows?"

"Here to now, *you* have been the greatest threat that's ever been made against her life. You took her against her will, and out of hatred and cowardice, not love."

Jonah cursed himself as, picking up on the rising tensions, Lex stirred, her lids opening. She took in the arrangement of animals in front of her first. With some surprise, Jonah realized she hadn't done that, for she giggled, reaching out to touch several of them. "Were you keeping me barricaded?"

"They seem to comfort you, and make you laugh. So I put them around you, like a Protection Spell." Dante cleared his throat. "It is the same principle. Your father is here."

"I know." She smiled sleepily, stretching out her hand. "I knew you had to come by and check on me. Worried old bird."

"You and your mother have an equal lack of respect for my age." Jonah came to her then, taking her hand. She kept her other around Dante's forearm, holding them both connected to her.

"It's because you get to look like you're thirty your entire life, while she and I will eventually get wrinkled and saggy. Unless my angel side is stronger than the mermaid." She winked and pushed herself up. She was stiff, he could tell by the sudden flinch. When Dante helped lift her to an upright position, Jonah dropped to a knee by the bed to accept Lex's embrace. Her arms slid around Jonah's shoulders, Dante drawing back as Jonah returned the hug. She smelled of lavender and vanilla, only a faint trace of Dark One magic fire and sulfurous smoke remaining in her hair.

"I had a bath a little while ago," she said, as if reading his mind. "But it's probably going to take another to get it all out. I'm all right, Pyel. Dante was amazing. One minute there was a vampire, and the next, just a big pile of ash."

Jonah met Dante's gaze. "Fortunate that he was there, then. David confirmed Jacob spoke to the territory overlord. There should be no more attacks."

"Good." Conscious of the antipathetic feelings coming from them both, Lex suppressed a sigh. She understood why they felt as they did, but it was difficult to accept. It's only been a day, she reminded herself. So rarely in her life had there been discord with or between those she cared about. She knew all about dysfunctional families, though. Just like with those, she found her heart aching. Knowing there was nothing she could do for it without the passage of time only made it harder to accept.

"Pyel, is there any other threat out there right now?"

That brought their focus back to her, though that was the only benefit she could see for the new worry she'd be bringing to her father.

"None that I know of. The Goddess has no enemies actively moving against Her here at this point. Why?"

"I don't know. This is crazy, but earlier . . . I felt the vampire, right before he came upon us. But even before that, when we left the community center, I felt something different. I guess it could have been another vampire, but after feeling his energy, it wasn't the same. I really couldn't classify it. It was somewhat familiar, but in a twisted way, you know. Or not twisted." She frowned, thinking, "Different, and the same. Goddess, I'm not making any sense."

Dante inclined his head at Jonah's glance. "She is not. I am not seeing it any clearer in her mind."

"Thanks," she said dryly, and elbowed him in the stomach. His brows lifted.

"What is that for?"

"Patronizing a woman is never a good idea," David noted from the door. "If she has cosmic power, it can be even worse. Trust me."

Alexis smiled at them both, but felt David's distress. "Are you all right?"

"Fine," David said, giving her a nod that was courteous but warded off further questions. "Mina is having a more prickly day than usual. She suggested I make myself scarce for a few hours or she'd disintegrate the universe to be rid of me."

"Oh." Alexis hoped her godmother wasn't serious. "Well, since you're all here, and we're all up, I can make us some tea and an early breakfast."

"No, you need more rest." Jonah put a firm hand on her shoulder before she would have emerged from the bed. Dante's arm tightened on her waist, reinforcing the same message.

"But I want—"

"No, Seabird," Jonah said, in a tone that brooked no disobedience. "Can you tell me anything else about what you sensed?"

"No," she said, giving up and settling back. "But later today, I'm sure I'll figure out what it was. It may have just been something unrelated to us."

At least, that was what she hoped. With Dante pressed against her back, and her father in front, she'd never felt so safe.

She played with her father's fingers as Dante eased her back down on her side, drowsily pleased when he started stroking her hair. "Tomorrow I'm taking Dante to the Conservancy. We'll be there most of the day, okay? Give Myel a hug and tell her everything's going well."

"All right. Sleep deep, Seabird." Jonah ran his knuckles along her cheek, Dante pausing so their hands did not touch. As her eyes drooped, and she succumbed again, a light smile on her face, Jonah's dark eyes slid up to meet Dante's. The two males held that position for a weighted moment until Jonah rose and moved without another word toward the door.

"Angel?"

He paused, glanced over his shoulder. Dante stared at him through the darkness. "I have no interest in causing her harm."

"That's not the same as being willing to do anything to keep her safe," Jonah responded. His tone was dangerously quiet. "If we have to send you back, you'll fight to the death to prevent it. Which means you will sacrifice my daughter's life."

"I did not intend to bind her to me with the marks."

"Your intentions mean nothing to me, vampire. Every action has a consequence. Her mother risked her life to bear her." The power of Jonah's anger ratcheted up, so that the heat in the room increased exponentially. "There is nothing I would not do to keep her safe and happy, even if I had to spend an eternity in Hell to make it happen."

"You can only say that because you haven't spent an eternity in Hell," Dante spat back.

"Jonah, don't. Leave it be, for now." David brushed his arm as he felt his commander's fury rise. Jonah's sword was far too accessible in its back harness. The young angel wondered if Lex was still awake, and, like him, waiting tensely to see where this would go.

"Step carefully, vampire. And remember what I told you. You don't deserve her. She sure as Hades doesn't deserve you." Turning abruptly, Jonah strode out the bedroom door.

David waited until he heard Jonah leave the town house. Dante was watching him in the darkness, but David delayed several heartbeats before he spoke to the vampire himself, keeping his voice low.

"He cut his heart out of his chest, gave it to a Dark One army, and risked eternal slavery to them to keep his mate safe. Perhaps it isn't the same, but he's got a ballpark idea. Plus, he's right."

When the shadows of bad memories moved within him, David knew Dante saw it in his face, from the sharpening of the vampire's gaze. "When you love someone completely, you'll do anything to protect them, even if you sacrifice your soul. Because if you don't, you destroy your soul anyway."

Twenty-four

ALEXIS noticed Dante was quieter than usual when she rose. He indicated he had no need for blood, but he made her eat her normal breakfast. As he sampled her scrambled organic eggs and arranged her Cheerios in various patterns on the table, she watched him, hoping for a clue, but he fended off her tactful attempts to analyze his mood.

He told her David had returned with several sets of secondhand clothing in Dante's size while she slept. But when she caught him staring at the clothes laid on the sofa as if he was somewhere deep in his mind, not looking at the clothes at all, she chose the direct approach, closing her hand on his on the table. "What's the matter?"

"What does the word *deserve* mean? Can one word have two meanings?"

Lex considered that. "I guess it can. *Deserve* is a tricky one. It means what someone has earned. What they've worked for . . . Like being born in a Dark One world. You did nothing to deserve that, because you were an innocent baby. But because of the twenty years you spent planning your escape, you'd done enough to earn, or deserve, a chance to be here."

"*Hmm.*"

He turned his attention back to her, as if seeing her for the first time that morning. She'd pulled her hair back from her face with a barrette, and wore the Conservancy T-shirt over her swimsuit. It had a manatee on the front and *volunteer* embroidered on the pocket. She'd put dark jeans with it and white canvas sneakers with cartoon-style manatee sneaker locks on the laces. He stopped there, studying them. What went through his mind dispelled the shadows emanating from him, easing her concern.

"Before you make some remark about how cute I look and I have to deck you, we should go. We're supposed to look approachable," she added, "especially for the kids."

He chose a dark blue T-shirt to go with black jeans, and she found a navy blue Conservancy staff bill cap for him to wear. At first, she encouraged him to twist his hair under it, but it was far too thick. He fingered it. "I would blend more if I cut this."

"No," she said immediately. Biting her lip at his raised brow, she admitted, "Okay, you might. You're so striking, the hair just enhances the whole I-am-a-famous-rock-star thing." *But I really like your hair.* She gave herself a mental shake. She'd woken up this morning, determined to put aside the feelings, which could hamper him learning how to be a part of this world, and she was already falling down on the job.

He was looking at her closely. "Hair grows back. If I do cut it, it can be grown long again, to please you. As a vampire, it grows far faster to a certain length."

She nodded, but when she picked up her keys and billfold, he closed his hand over her wrist and tugged her to him. He bent his head so his lips were close to her mouth. When she looked up at him, several strands of that hair had fallen and curtained one side of her face, closing them in a quiet space together.

"Tonight, I will take my time and savor every inch of you. I wanted you to rest last night. But I will not wait much longer to have you under me again."

Then he slid his hand to her nape and brought her to her toes so he could tease her lips apart, score her tongue lightly with his teeth, holding her with one hand only as she clutched the front of his shirt for balance.

Even as she was swept away by it, there was a strange quality to that kiss, as if he was seeking to pull something from her, needing something she wasn't sure how to offer. He dissolved that worry into heat, though, when he found the line of her swimsuit bottoms through the thin denim and traced them. After that provocative caress, he delved into the depression where her bottom curved under and met the juncture of her thighs. When he cupped her over that sensitive area, she gasped into his mouth, leaned harder into his body. "Dante . . ."

Slipping to the front of her jeans, he opened them and found her sensitive sex. She had a brief flash that she was going to be really late, and then decided she was wrong, for he was stroking her clit with unerring accuracy and tempo. Because of the loosened waistband, he slid his other hand down the back of the jeans. She jerked as his fingers went between her buttocks and began to tease the rim there, working her between the two pressures so she was shamelessly stroking herself on his hands, leaning her forehead against his shoulder. The soft cries caught in her throat gained in strength.

"Come for me," he ordered. "Gush against my hand, Alexis. Let me feel your fluids."

She spasmed just at the words, and clutched his skin beneath the shirt. In a matter of seconds, he'd robbed her of thought, splitting her between mindless pleasure and on-the-edge-of-a-precipice terror. It was scary, to free-fall so quickly at his touch, as if she had no will of her own.

I am your will. He thrust three fingers inside of her, rubbing, and she cried out, biting the shirt and his flesh beneath. He growled his approval. Two of his fingers in the back slowly pushed into her virgin rear entry, slow, tickling, teasing. *I have not yet taken you here. I may do that tonight, after you make my cock slick with your warm, willing mouth.*

"Oh . . ." Her guttural response was mouthed against his shirt, heated and wet, for her body was shuddering. She couldn't have remained upright except he had her pressed against her kitchen table, which was braced against the nook wall. Her knee was on one of the chairs, and he brought a second one near with a quick hook and jerk of his foot. He lifted her other knee up on it so she was on her knees on the two chairs, spread for him over the open space. The jeans constricted, pressing the seams against his hand, which drove his fingers deeper into her.

With a cry, she shattered, her release flooding as he'd ordered, making his hand that much more slick as he pumped the fingers inside of her, continuing to tease her anal area as well. As she bucked, she followed the orgasm on a white-water rapids ride through her spiraling mind, a kaleidoscope of colors and images. Her other hand had fallen to the waistband of his jeans, the belt holding them. Un- bidden, she imagined him spanking her with that belt, for disobeying him yesterday. She'd be bent over his knees, her bottom pale and red both from the stripes, her cunt wet and pink for him, needing to be filled and claimed by his cock.

Those weren't her thoughts, she realized. They were his, planted in her mind. He was letting her see his desires, his demands, in the way he thought and spoke of them. Instead of being revolted, she was short of breath, her sex pulsing with another hard aftershock that had her pushing her head harder against his chest as she rode it out.

When she was at last done, her moans having left wet spots on his shirt, he slowly withdrew his hands, caressing her. He made her taste her fluids on the hand he'd had inside her sex, and she suckled his fingers shamelessly, earning a dangerous growl from his own chest that made her wonder if they were going to be even later.

But he drew back at last. Instead of letting her do it, he adjusted her swimsuit, tucked her shirt back in and zipped the jeans, slipping the button closed while his mouth rested on the crown of her head. His arm slid around her, holding her while she trembled and shud- dered. She realized she was not as steady on her feet this morning as she'd supposed.

"I think I need a muffin," she whispered. "One of those really gooey ones with chocolate chips and a million calories."

"A good idea."

"And I should probably change—"

"No." He lifted her chin then. The motion made her realize how hard he was, pressed against her belly. When she would have sought him, he shook his head, caught her hands. "I want you soaked. I want you to remember my hand there, for however many hours we are at this place, and think of no other male. They will smell your scent and know you have been pleasured by the one who has claimed you. Who will take you tonight as I wish to do now."

Primal words she should brush off as belonging to his frame of thinking, not her own. So why did she respond so passionately to them, as if they were a mirror of her deepest desires?

"Humans don't smell that well, really." She cleared her throat. "But don't worry, I'll remember. If that was a prelude, you might kill me before we get to tonight. Slow, you said?"

"Very slow," he confirmed.

Though Dante suspected it would take a great act of will to wait until then, let alone go slow. Each time he had the desire to touch her like this, the urgency was such he couldn't slow down. He knew he'd never had anything like her, but for that reason alone he wanted to find the discipline to slow down. He wanted to peel all of her clothes off, lay her out on her bed. Perhaps find some way to bind her wrists and ankles so that she had to surrender everything to him, and he could devote hours to tasting her skin, caressing it with his fingers, pleasuring her over and over. Giving her water and food from his mouth.

Had Lyssa been right about a vampire's nature, the way they felt toward their servants? It had been one of many things she'd discussed with him, alone in her study, but now the memory of that specific discussion sprang up into his mind, disturbing him with the truth laid out before him.

———

"YOU'VE never had a human servant, have you?" Lyssa crossed her legs in a whisper of movement, her long-nailed fingers resting with casual elegance on her knee. "Mina said that Alexis believed you marked her as an accident, that you didn't really know how a marking occurred."

He was not comfortable admitting error or weakness in front of anyone, particularly this mysterious stranger. He shrugged, a non-committal answer.

"You are protective of her, but there is a destructive streak to you as well. You need to guard against that, and not just for the obvious reason that the angel and the witch will destroy you if you harm that child."

"She is not a child. I have met children."

"She is very young, compared to my age. And a sexually mature woman, or male, for that matter"—she gave him a meaningful glance—"is quite often just a child in an adult body. Don't interrupt."

She leaned back in her chair. "Vampires have certain personality traits, Dante. They differ from humans, angels and mermaids in that respect, and it is one of the reasons none of them are entirely comfortable around us, except for the rare human who wishes to bond with one of us, who becomes a servant by choice." At his shift, she nodded. "Your servant did not choose, no more than you were aware you were making the choice for her. Fortunately, the girl seems devoted to your well-being. It may grow into a true master–servant relationship, or it may not. She may be merely a way station for you, though letting a marked servant go has its own problems. We'll cross that bridge if we get to it.

"However, in a true vampire–servant relationship, you will dominate her, sexually as well as many other ways." She gave him a quelling glance before he could speak again. "I am not suggesting a course of action, but a simple fact. It's innate to us, and therefore essential to how we order our world. I've already seen you demonstrate that irresistible compulsion to ensure she submits to you. The surrender of the servant's body and blood, heart and soul, is required by any vampire Master or Mistress. Unfortunately, as you've also already demonstrated, for a young vampire, it is a very dangerous compulsion, one that has often resulted in a dead servant."

Dante's gaze sharpened on her. "I have no reason to kill Alexis."

"But she may end up dead through your ignorance or actions, which is just as bad." Lyssa held his gaze, her own relentless. "It's another reason I strongly encourage you to come to me when these thirty days are over. I can help you learn to manage your compulsions, compulsions that may be exacerbated by your other blood, making them that more dangerous."

She rose, bringing their meeting to an end. "In the meantime, the best advice I can give you is to listen to what her soul tells you. With careful practice, you can delve that deeply into a third-marked servant. It will let you know if you are asking too much or pushing too hard. You cannot listen to her words or only her mind, because humans are often confused by their own feelings. But their souls will never lie to you."

IT was good advice, for Alexis was obviously confused and flustered. As she drove, talking in short, nervous bursts, she kept shifting. The wetness between her legs was uncomfortable to her, but titillating as well. She was already thinking of what the night would bring, keeping the tender flesh between her legs swollen, needy. He hadn't counted on the fact that making her wait would be an equal torment to him.

She had her hand on the console between them and he closed his over it, running his thumb back and forth over her palm. Twisting, turning, never a true pattern. Too much like his feelings about her, tangled with his thoughts about Lyssa's words, Jonah's disturbing observation and David's follow-up.

"Here we are," she said, pulling in front of the Conservancy and parking. "Before I start my shift, I'll show you around, let you know the types of things you can do. We're open, but it's a weekday, so it should be fairly quiet. You can feel free to wander around while I help Branson feed and clean everyone up. Is that okay?" She gave him a false, bright smile. "After we close and Bran leaves, you and I can have the place to ourselves for a couple hours. I'll show you some really amazing things."

"Yes," he agreed, then refused to release her hand. "Alexis, what is the matter?"

"Nothing."

But once he asked the direct question, he saw it in her mind as if his query had spotlighted the answer, hiding amid the jungle of her other thoughts. She continued to worry that if she kept giving in to her desires, she couldn't stay objective and truly help him.

"You cannot deny me, Alexis." He spoke softly, holding her gaze. "As I have said, I would not suggest you try."

Before she could marshal the irritable retort her mind was building to that, he caught the stubbornly tight chin. "You *are* helping me. Whatever happens in thirty days, it will not be your fault. Do you understand?"

"It's not that easy. I want you to be able to live here for hundreds of years to come."

"Yes, I know." And he wondered what the feeling swelling inside of him in reaction to her hope was called. He cradled her jaw. "But I must be able to kiss you whenever I wish."

"Really?" He was relieved to see worry replaced by that light he was beginning to recognize as humor. "Well, I can't think when you kiss me, so I'm no good to you then."

"I like you mindless. A few minutes ago, your mindlessness made me willing to do anything I had to do to stay with you."

She stilled, staring up at him. The shock in her mind was no less than what he felt inside himself. Where had that come from? He was here because he'd spent two decades trying to get free, that was all. She'd been the means to get him here. Since he'd bound her to him, he might possess a territorial need to keep her, but he wanted to stay *in this world*. He was willing to do anything in order to accomplish *that*.

A honking noise broke the moment. Alexis's attention went to a car driving by, and she waved to the driver. "That's Branson, my co-worker." As Dante's gaze followed the man as he got out of his car, Alexis's hand tightened on his arm, drawing his attention. "This is going to be like the craft room, only busier, a lot more people. I need you to trust me when I say this is a safe place. Anything you perceive as a threat is 99 percent likely not to be one. So before you decide to incinerate or maim, do you think you could run the situation by me first, so I can clear it up before you strike? I don't want you to hurt yourself. Or anyone else."

"I will try."

Reaching up, she passed a gentle finger over his mouth. "Thank you for saying that, a second ago. Even if it was just a heat of the moment thing."

Then she got out of the vehicle, calling out in a friendly voice to the man, Branson. A relaxed voice to the untrained ear, but Dante could hear the tension beneath it, see her thoughts. She wasn't sure how well this was going to go. She was afraid he might . . . torch the place?

I will endeavor not to do so, he reiterated with more firmness.

She stopped, looked back over her shoulder at him and attempted a smile. *Good. Because I suspect Pyel would be really miffed if you did.*

I do not fear your father.

I don't want you to fear him, she rejoined, sadness crossing her face. *I want you to know him, to respect him. And him to know and respect you. That is what I want.*

If I am deserving of respect. He kept that thought to himself, puzzling over the meaning of the word once again.

———————

SHE needn't have worried. After an hour or so, Dante came to the conclusion that most of the people in her world were engaged in entirely baffling but mostly non–threatening activities. He spent the first hour sitting on a bench within sight of the area where she and Branson were doing daily tasks related to the sea creatures. It did take some effort to remain still and relaxed while people sauntered, ambled and scurried from exhibit to exhibit. Big and small, young and old, even some elderly people in buzzing contraptions she called *scooters.* When he asked her, she explained that they couldn't walk due to health problems.

A couple of the wheeled contraptions didn't have a motor, and he preferred their quietness. He was surprised, though, when one came to rest next to his bench. Glancing left, he saw a young girl studying him. She was dressed differently than the others, whose wide variety of colors in T-shirts, shorts and jeans had a certain symmetry to them that blended. She, on the other hand, was all in black. She had silver rings in her nose and large, heavy boots and red and white striped stockings on her thin legs. Despite her age, she was dying. The scent of fatal sickness was undeniable. In the Dark One world, she would have been his next meal. From what he'd seen of the environment here, she perhaps had a year or two.

She met his gaze with frank interest. "Want to go get naked with a jailbait crip? Give her a lasting memory before she croaks?"

He blinked. "I am with a female." He nodded toward Alexis. "She told me that it would make her angry, and she would no longer want to . . . get naked with me. Though I think I could talk her out of that, I sense it would upset her."

The girl's heavily lined eyes widened. "And you don't want to upset her."

He shook his head. "I have done that too much already."

"You talk weird. That's cool, though. I like your collar. It's Goth chic. Not every guy can pull that off without looking like a poser." As Dante raised a brow, she looked toward the tank. "That's her? With the manatees? She's really pretty."

"She's beautiful." The words came to Dante before he realized he was going to say them. Her brown hair gleamed in this lighting, the tendrils wisping around her face from the way she had it pulled back. While her outfit was similar to those of the other staff, and not too different from the visitors', there was lithe grace to her movements that emphasized every curve the clothes modestly delineated. Her angel blood emitted those waves of warmth and reassurance, and when her blue eyes turned to someone asking a question, she offered a genuine smile and an interest that instilled confidence in whomever she was addressing, bringing balance and . . . peace. He thought of how she'd looked with her snowy wings and the sparkling jewel-like scales of her tail.

"Yeah." The girl was studying him. "You're gone over her all right. My name's Reba." She extended her hand. "You're the most interesting guy visiting this place today. All the rest are tourist cookie cutouts."

Dante studied her hand, then took it. When she shook, guiding

288 JOEY W. HILL

him through the unfamiliar greeting, there was a faint tremor in her hand and her grip was weak. "My name is Dante. You are pretty, too. You are dressed differently, though."

"Yeah. You dress the norm, like one of them"—she nodded to the brightly colored visitors—"and you're just another pathetic kid in a wheelchair. You dress like this, you're mysterious, intriguing. Bad attitude waiting to happen. You looked at me like you'd never seen anyone in a wheelchair."

"I hadn't, before today," he said honestly.

"There are no people who can't walk where you're from? What does someone do who breaks a leg or hurts themselves?"

"They die," Dante responded. "Only the strong survive, and only if they are clever. Strength is not enough."

"*Hmmm.* Yeah, you figure out quick in this thing that your brain has to be better than your motor control. So *woohoo* to survival of the fittest. Want to see what I can do?"

"As long as it doesn't involve taking off your clothes."

"Your loss." She shrugged. "Perv. But no. Watch this."

Fishing a rubber band out of her jacket pocket, she stretched it between her fingers. "I'll bet you a kiss—no tongue, out of respect for your girlfriend, and she'll give me that much, unless she's a heartless bitch—that I can hit that asshole over there."

She nodded across the carpeted area to where a boy about her age was hanging over the ledge of the stingray exhibit and using a pen to poke the creatures, despite signs noting the animals were not to be touched. "I'll hit him in the ass hard enough to make him jump and put his hand on his butt in front of everyone."

Dante gauged the distance, the number of people moving through the area, the velocity capability of the band. It would be near impossible. "All right."

She took aim and then went still. Utterly still, in a way Dante recognized from having waited in secret places for the right second to move, to attack, to maneuver. He'd focused so hard on everything, it was as if all things started moving in slow motion, until he knew precisely when to—

Snap.

The boy at the rail yelped and clapped his hand to the seat of his baggy jeans, looking around and glaring. When he spotted the rubber band, his attention went to a group of younger boys laughing at him. In two steps he'd reached the first one and grabbed his shirt front.

"Hey, pukeface," Reba called out, loudly enough to get his attention. When he looked toward her, she toggled another rubber band around her erect middle finger, which appeared to be some form of insult. He scowled, but when he noted the chair, whatever retaliation he'd had in mind apparently vanished. He settled for sneering "freak," before he disappeared down a corridor directing patrons to other attractions.

"So pay up, pretty boy," Reba said, giving him an expectant leer.

Dante settled against the wall, crossing his arms. "Why are you here? You are not looking at sea creatures and educational displays."

"I like it here, so Mom drops me off when she has errands to do. Gives her a break from looking at her dying daughter, and me a break from her looking at me like I'm already dead." Reba rolled her eyes. "God should plan better. If he's going to assign people to be parents, he needs to makes sure the ones who get terminal kids can hold it together until the funeral. Mom's shed enough tears for all the starving people in India. By the time I croak, she'll need drops to fake it for the funeral. The well's gotta be dry."

"That was a nice hit."

Dante glanced up to find Alexis had joined them. She was surveying Reba with her hands on her hips. "We could use you as a regular monitor on the tanks."

"Yeah, make the crippled kid feel useful. Gives me warm fuzzies, cue the sappy music. Piss off, no offense." Reba snorted and put her hands on the wheels of her chair. She couldn't make her exit though, because the odd stranger was holding one wheel fast. No matter how she tried to move it, it wasn't budging.

"She doesn't do that." Dante met her gaze squarely. "She does not lie to make you feel better. She means it."

"I've seen you here regularly of late," Alexis noted, as if Reba hadn't said anything offensive. "If you want a volunteer job, let me know. I think people would pay attention to you."

"Because I'm in a wheelchair."

"Because as long as you have rubber bands, they wouldn't like the consequences of ignoring you. I've watched you maneuver that thing. You'd probably do a better job at getting between a trouble-maker and the tank than someone on foot. After all, if you knock someone down, what are they going to do? Say a crippled girl whipped their ass?"

Reba stared up at her, and Alexis gave her a grin. Try as she might, she couldn't seem to hold on to sarcasm around the woman. She had a freakish urge to ask her for a hug. Unsettled, the teenager glanced at Dante. "I won a kiss off him, and he hasn't paid up. I think he's scared of *you* whipping his ass."

"With tongue or without?" Alexis didn't miss a beat.

"I let him off without. But if you're willing to negotiate that for my volunteer time . . ."

"Don't push your luck," Alexis chuckled, but she cocked her head at Dante. "The kiss is a fair request."

Reba had the odd feeling they were talking without words. Their eyes stayed locked as if they were the only ones in the room, and Alexis's lips parted as if he'd said something to her that any girl would like to hear. But then Reba got very distracted as Dante rose from the bench, laid his hands over hers on the wheelchair arms and leaned down. Hair as dark as a panther's coat spilled forward. He kept on his dark sunglasses, the ones that had made her think he was blind when she approached his bench. But blind people didn't look toward you, and he had. She sensed a peculiar heat from behind the lenses as he leaned in.

Now faced with the reality, Reba was gripped by a blink of abso-lute terror. She was going to mess this up, be a dork, oh-my-God he was really going to kiss her, and then he was. Lips firm and the right kind of hot and moist over hers, gentle pressure. No tongue, but definitely not some weak-assed kiss he'd give a kid. It shot heat to parts of her she'd been sure didn't have feeling.

It might have been over in three or four seconds, but when he straightened, her world was doing a slow spin. "Wow," she said, her throat thick.

"Yeah, I've had that reaction, too," Alexis smiled, but there was pain to it. God, Reba didn't want to make her jealous. Everybody should have a boyfriend like this. But Reba had a feeling it wasn't jealousy, particularly since Alexis said right after, "How would you feel about staying after hours and swimming with us and the manatees?"

Twenty-five

AFTER the Conservancy closed, Alexis apprised Bran of what they'd be doing with the girl in the wheelchair. It only took a little push to get him past worries about liability, and a call to Reba's mother reassured him that she was on board, thrilled her daughter had been offered the rare and usually prohibitively expensive chance to swim with manatees. That settled, Alexis locked up after Branson and then took Reba to a locker area to help her change into an extra swimsuit she had.

While Dante waited on them, he thought about his merangel. When he'd kissed the girl, he'd felt a wave of sadness from Alexis. He could read her thoughts. He just couldn't understand the emotions that went with them, damn it all.

When Reba returned in the swimsuit, a towel lying modestly over her thin legs, she rolled to the viewing tank and flattened her hand against the glass, watching the manatees swim past it. Dante slipped into the locker room, where Alexis was preparing the oxygen tank that Reba would wear so she could breathe underwater. He propped in the door silently, watching her. The brown tail of her hair curved over her shoulder, and her fingers moved competently, but those feelings had grown like the balloons he'd seen people purchase for their children, expanding in her mind, pushing out any other thought.

"Do you need a tank? You don't have to breathe, right? Not like us."

"No." He put his hands on her shoulders. "Alexis, what is it?"

"I feel her emotions, Dante. I always feel them. She wants to live so much. And she deserves to live. Look at her. What an amazing kid." She shook her head. "I have the filters, but for someone like that, I don't want to use them. I want to give them anything they want, because they're going to get so little, you know?"

Dante wrapped one of her curls around his hand, let it slide away and tumble down her back. "Her lips tasted like that fruit you were eating this morning."

"Orange. She probably has on an orange citrus lip gloss over that black lipstick she was wearing." With a rueful smile, Alexis straightened and stripped off her shirt. "Can you help me cross the straps?"

He wasn't sure what she meant until she'd unfastened the swimsuit straps and rethreaded them over her shoulders, crossing them and explaining where the hooks were. "I can't wear them straight for this. My wings will snag them."

"Aren't there rules about showing humans your true form?" He pulled his attention away from the pleasant display of her bosom she'd given him, suspecting now was not an appropriate time to let lust take the uppermost hand.

"Yeah. Pretty strict ones. But angels will appear to kids and pets, and despairing people, to give them comfort, though it's not really laid out in the rules. It's just known, like upping a dying person's morphine until they drift away in their sleep, rather than keeping them suffering."

As always, the images in her head helped fill in the gaps that his lack of experience with her world created. It captured him for several heartbeats, though. A place where, when the end came, there was an effort to make it as merciful and pain free as possible. *Astounding.* Threading the straps down her back, he let his knuckles slide over her soft skin, the delicate protrusion of shoulder blades, the tender nape.

"It's surreal, isn't it? Here you are in a locker room, hooking my swimsuit, when three days ago you were in such a different place, a different frame of mind." Her gaze drifted out to Reba, visible through a crack in the locker room door. "Like her. It's odd to do normal things, like getting up each day and brushing your teeth, combing your hair, watching a dumb commercial on television, when you know that your hourglass is tumbling faster than everyone else's . . . at least as far as they know. I guess I almost died a few days ago, so we never do know, do we?"

He stared down at her nape. "Why do you not hold that against me, Alexis, the way your father does?"

"Because I was in your world." She looked at him at last. "You're scary, Dante. I won't deny that. But two days were unbearable. I can't wrap my mind around being there for decades. What's remarkable to me is not the dark, scary side of you, but the fact you managed to keep that spark of light. That means something, something really important."

He wasn't sure how he felt about that, but if she knew what it meant, he wasn't ready to hear it. Realizing that, he changed the direction of their conversation onto surer ground. "On the other hand, I think my darkness explains many of the things I feel when I look at you."

Alexis couldn't help pressing her lips together, moistening when his gaze fell upon them. He'd hooked the sunglasses in his pocket while alone here with her, and her stomach contracted at the things she saw in his eyes. "There are dark, wicked things that I want to do with that mouth, with your body," he said. "I want to pull your soul inside of me, chain and hold you to me forever. A tether, like those birds I saw upstairs in this place."

"The raptors?"

He nodded. "I heard the woman caring for them say that, when certain ones are used as hunters, a tether is placed upon their leg. The master wraps it around his hand to hold the bird there. I have that desire with you, but . . ."

"Yes?" she breathed it, not sure how she got the word out.

"When I was watching you, before Reba came, I only wanted to sit and let that light of yours warm me. It makes me wonder which one of us is truly a tethered hawk."

Silence stretched between them. His hand remained in her hair, his fingers tangling, fondling. Alexis broke the contact reluctantly, picking up the swimming trunks she'd found for him. "Have you ever swum before?"

"No." He stepped back. "Lady Lyssa told me that vampires do not swim. That we sink and must use the strength of our arms to pull ourselves up. But that seems like it will help, since your manatees like the lower levels of the tank."

"That's mostly when visitors are here. They get more active when it's just us." She lifted the suit. "Anyhow, you might want to put this on so our young companion doesn't get any more outrageous ideas that could get you arrested."

While he stripped off his clothes and slid on the swim trunks, exposing the muscular body, she realized she felt the same as he did. She wanted to just sit, gaze at the marble perfection that looked so cold but she knew was so warm, so vibrant and strong, compared with the pale, thin and weak limbs of the girl she'd helped change. The blessing and cruelty of time displayed so obviously together made the sadness swell in her again.

"Alexis," he murmured. Now dressed, he nodded toward the cracked door. "Look."

Reba's hand was pressed to the tank and the two manatees were butting their noses against the glass, as if answering her. She looked over her shoulder with a wide smile as they left the locker room and came to join her. "It's like they're saying get your asses in here so we can play." She arched a brow. "I was beginning to think you two were going to fuck like rabbits before we went swimming. I'm not saying I blame you, but you wouldn't want my time to run out while waiting on you, right?"

"More language like that, and I'll jam your wheelchair brake," Alexis informed her archly, even as she felt a pang at the girl's joke, too close to her own thoughts. Pushing that away, she proceeded to tell the girl how to use the tank, giving her some basic instruction on it.

"How about you two?" Reba said when she was done. "Where are your tanks? And does he wax or what? He has no body hair."

Alexis glanced at Dante, then back at their guest. "We won't need tanks. Reba, we'd like to be ourselves while we're with you, all right? Can we trust you with that?"

The teenager studied them both, her cynical mask slipping and showing uncertain curiosity. "I don't exactly know what that means, but as long as you aren't serial killers who like to lure visitors to stay after hours with a promise to swim with the manatees, I'm cool with just about anything."

"On a normal day, that's exactly what we are, but for today we figure we'll indulge our alter egos." Lex pushed the wheelchair up the ramp to the door that led to the tank entry point. Dante took over for her as she swiped her card and took them inside.

Before she could ask Dante to help her get Reba out of the chair and into the water, he anticipated her thought. Bending, he slid his arms beneath the girl's body, and she calmly hooked an arm around his neck as he took her to the water's edge. Lex guided her to hold on to the ladder while she got in the water with her. Dante kept his hand on the girl's arm, even as she held on to the ladder tightly.

Reba let out a nervous laugh. "It's kind of ironic, but I'd rather not drown, okay?"

"We will not let any harm come to you," Dante said. His voice was firm, that commanding tone capable of sending shivers down Lex's spine. It was absolute reassurance he meant what he said. She thought of the hawk comparison again and warmth coiled in her belly.

Reba's gaze went to his sunglasses. "Why do you wear those?"

"Because of these," he said, and removed them.

Reba drew in a breath. "Those aren't contacts, are they?"

"No. No more than those are paste and glue." He nodded and Reba followed his glance. It was a good thing he still held her arm on the ladder, because she would have dropped like a stone at the sight of Lex treading water behind her, her wings now exposed. They were gliding across the water slowly like a butterfly's, keeping her aloft. Reba's gaze skittered down at the flash of color beneath the water's surface. "That's . . ."

"A tail. I'm a merangel. Don't be startled," Alexis said, then thought to add, "I don't mean about me. Leroy is coming up beneath you and is going to nose your legs."

"No freaking way." Reba looked between them, laughing unexpectedly and wiggling in the water as the manatee rose higher, brushed her lower back. "That tickles. He won't bite, will he?"

"Only once or twice." Alexis grinned. "I'm kidding. No, he won't bite."

Reba shifted her gaze back to Dante. "So what does that make you?"

"He's part vampire, part something else."

"I was kissed by a vampire. Wow. Okay, I am awake, right? Tell me I'm not hallucinating on my meds. Because if I am, I'm going to be so pissed."

THEY only half convinced her she wasn't, but she came to the conclusion that even if she was hallucinating, it was best to make the most of it before she detoxed. Alexis got the small tank strapped onto her, and then, when she was ready, she had her put on the mask, loosen her grip on the ladder and slowly descend into the large tank. Despite her bravado, initially Reba clung to her fingers. Alexis expected Dante to take some time to enter, but in short order, he passed them, headed to the bottom of the tank. He controlled the descent so he didn't move too fast, but it was obvious there was no buoyancy to his body. He simply sank, the strength of his arms alone capable of moving him. Reba pointed to him, her lips stretching into a grin around her mouthpiece, and then they were floating down to join him. The other manatee was there, sleeping, but Leroy rammed him, as if reminding Buick they had guests.

Alexis smiled and guided Reba's hand to the area behind Leroy's ear where they liked being scratched, and then behind the front flippers. Since she was down here, Lex did another quick examination of Buick's propeller wounds and confirmed they were healing well.

As she did, Reba's questing fingers slid over her wing, another hand finding her tail. When she shifted her attention, Reba froze, but Alexis smiled and nodded. The girl, relieved, continued to explore, touching the tail fins, their flowing texture. She bent to study the overlap of her scales, then gazed upward at the froth of feathers flowing through the water as Alexis used both tail and wings to balance herself. Reba's eyes shone when she looked back at Alexis. While Alexis had always loved being a merangel, seeing the pleasure such a thing brought to Reba made her even more fiercely glad of it. Speaking in the manatee language, she asked and the creatures accommodated, bringing their bodies close to the girl, delighting her with their proximity and letting her put a hand on each of them as they slowly swam to the other end of the tank, carrying her along.

When they returned, coming to rest on the bottom of the tank again, Dante moved closer, reaching out to touch as well. Buick floated, examining this new variable. While it appeared he had his doubts, Lex reassured him that Dante was a friend, even if he was somewhat scary. Buick made an accepting noise and returned his attention to Reba. After a brief investigation of the creatures, Dante moved off another few feet. He passed his hands back and forth through the water, turned, lifted his feet. Using his arms to move upward and then back down, he did a somersault, testing the properties of the water. Looking toward her, she saw some of the same shine of discovery in his eyes she had in Reba's. It made her want to never leave this moment.

But after no more than fifteen minutes, Alexis felt Reba fighting her exhaustion. Dante recognized it, too. When the girl shook her head, a stubborn set to her chin, he simply caught her around the waist and propelled her upward, even though she called him something around the mouthpiece Alexis knew wasn't complimentary.

When they surfaced, Dante lay her on the concrete apron next to the pool so she could get her breath. Alexis came to the ladder, holding the slick metal handrails as Dante squatted over the girl, his dark hair pasted in long wet strips down his broad back. His crimson eyes intent on the girl's face, he touched it with light, questing fingers, so that she opened her eyes and nodded in reassurance.

"I'm all right. Wow." She looked toward Alexis. "Was that one of those, 'I can't have what a lot of kids get, so I get something maybe they never will?' Like crazy Make-A-Wish Foundation shit?"

"Maybe. You're worth something like this. I like you."

"Oh. Well, it was great, probably the best thing ever. I'd still trade it for sixty years of normal boring life, you know? But don't tell anyone, because that sounds so uncool."

Dante drew back to the other side of the ladder, one foot in the water while he sat on his hip facing the two women. His toes grazed Lex's thigh and her glance strayed toward him. He was now studying her damp shoulders, the beads of water rolling down her neck onto the upper curves of her breasts.

"Why don't you guys go and swim for a while? It's going to take me about thirty minutes before I can even move from this spot, so you might as well go do what it's obvious you want to do." Reba closed her eyes, a wistful smile playing on her face. "The things I'm too young to know about. That I'll always be too young to know about, right?"

"I don't think it's wise to leave you here . . ." Alexis began.

Reba shook her head. "I'm going to lay here like a dead fish. I promise I won't move until you get back. Unless I get the sudden urge to run the New York Marathon. Then I'm history."

Lex smiled, stretched over the ladder and closed her hand on the girl's thin leg. "All right. We'll go check on the adjacent tanks, and be back soon. I can sense strong emotion, Reba, so if you need us to come back, concentrate really hard and I will return."

Dante put his hand on her other leg, drawing Reba's eyes to his. "And if you break your promise to her, and endanger yourself, I will not be happy with you."

Reba shut her mouth at his expression and looked toward Lex. "Something 'other,' *huh*? It's kind of creepy awesome. Sexy *and* scary."

Lex bit back a smile. "In so many ways, Reba. All right, we'll be back." She slid back into the water, the soles of her feet touching Leroy's back as he passed under them, making another loop in the tank. He did that often, reminding her how much happier he'd be once he was rehabilitated and in the open ocean again, where he belonged. Glancing at the vampire descending next to her, using his arms to keep an even pace at her side, she knew he was another creature like that. Right now, everything was new, and except for the collar at his throat, the limits of his world seemed suitable enough.

But by the time thirty days were done, he'd be itching to explore the full extent of this new world, far beyond the narrow scope of her own. A wild creature couldn't handle confinement.

That day is not today. Dante's voice resounded in her head. His hand enclosed hers, his features all the more clear and potent beneath the water. *Your own world is limitless in a far different way, Alexis.*

He didn't pursue that further because the manatees circled them, curious what they were doing. Alexis opened the narrow gate that led into the larger exhibition tank and gave them both a parting scratch, gesturing Dante in so she could close the gate behind them.

This tank has a lot more fish. There are also manta rays and a couple sharks. They're predators, but they won't hurt us. They've fed. Plus, no animal ever tried to hurt her. Bran found it remarkable but also useful. Whenever they had a difficult treatment to do on an animal with teeth or claws, she was the one called to hold and soothe the creature during the procedure.

Dante nodded, acknowledging her thought, and then she let them into the Conservancy's most popular exhibition tank. She'd told Bran she'd check the filters on the water processor, so there was a practical reason for being here, but part of it was wanting Dante to see another part of her world. As he gazed about, she thought of his words and wondered if he was right. How many creatures had access to the water, earth and sky the way she did? She could show Dante things he'd never seen before, in all of those places.

The fish ranged in size up to three feet long, their silver bodies a soft glow as they glided among schools of more colorful fish. The manta rays swept by in majestic flight. Everything was in motion in the water, though at night she'd seen them resting in groups on the ledges of the coral reef, moved only by the slight cavitation of the water. It was a quiet world like that. More than once she'd floated to the bottom and lay on the rocks with them as she did in the ocean, keeping them company, wishing they could all return to the sea. This was not a bad place, where manatees, sharks and dolphins were only kept if they couldn't be rehabilitated and returned to the sea, but she wished they all had that option, to swim as far and free as they wished.

The sharks made a curious pass around Dante, but veered off sharply and moved away, sensing a predator far more dangerous than themselves. A manta ray brushed her leg with the cat fur softness of his wing. The filter was in good shape, so she snapped the grid closed and moved back to Dante.

What do you think of it? You should see Neptune's kingdom. I'll take you there if you want. It would be a little tiring to pull yourself all the way up, but I could help with my tail and wings. The trip down would be easy, though.

He nodded absently, watching a group of fish turn in unison. Another fish dove down abruptly, chasing a school with a burst of speed. Both altered their course to narrowly miss the outcropping of rock that had been added to the area to simulate their natural environment. She could imagine him standing there for hours to do just this, while visitors walked past the viewing area and wondered if he was a life-sized form of one of those tiny figures often put in a home fish tank.

Did you ever think about it? Doing something that would end your pain?

He didn't look at her. *I did. I found you.*

Alexis touched his arm. *I mean like the morphine thing. Did you ever think of killing yourself so it would all be over?*

He kept his gaze on the fish. *No. I did not know what existed after death. Except for my mother, all those I have seen die, died fighting, as if they saw through the eyes of approaching death what lay after, and it was worse. Plus . . . it was never quiet enough to think about it.*

I'm not glad for that. But I am glad you never considered it. Never did it.

Dante did look at her then. He'd noted how nothing in the tank made aggressive movements toward her. Not sharks, or any other creature considered her food or enemy. Nothing attacked her or had the desire to do so, except a vampire more focused on himself than her well-being. But he knew how the creatures in this tank felt, because he was feeling it himself, right here and now. A simple desire to be near her.

She floated in the water without motion, her pale wings holding her, the red and gold jeweled tail balancing her, so the only sway to her sinuous body was from the water's movement. Her eyes were so vivid beneath the water, the blue capturing his attention, drawing it to her pink mouth. The delicate gill slits below her ears were only a flutter, giving her air. The feathers moved as if in a breeze. He'd not been told whether she was the only one of her kind, but it struck him now that was possible. Like him, she might be the only one.

But her uniqueness wasn't in her physical form. It was in the way she looked at life, at everything, at him. Her belief in his *spark*, as she called it, existed, no matter her species. No matter how he adapted to this world, it was likely he'd never find anyone else who saw him that way. He didn't even see himself that way. But he didn't doubt her belief. He was in her mind, knew she was pure light and truth. Though he was a vampire, that light could draw him out of any shadow, even if it meant burning in the sun.

She had her hand out to her side. Lifting his own so their finger-tips touched, he pulled her toward him. She drifted to him like a cloud moving across a blue sky on a sunny day, something he'd never seen until these past couple days. When she reached him he circled her waist, stroking his knuckles over the scales layered low on her hip, the bare hipbone above, then toying with the tiny jewel winking at her navel. Fish passed above, behind, around them, and there was a silence to the water that was a sound all its own.

Shift to your human form. I want to be inside you here, and I want to see your face.

I won't be able to breathe.

I'll give you air. Just because I don't have to breathe doesn't mean I can't provide you breath.

Her hands came to rest on his shoulders. With his feet braced apart on the tank floor, which was covered with sand and shells, pieces of shiny rock, her tail curved inward, the fins brushing his ankles, the muscular column of it sliding along the inside of his thigh. Her eyes were luminous, and though he felt the response of her body, something made him tighten his grip on her, commanding her attention before she shifted.

Alexis, do you want this? For me to be inside you now?

Her lashes were so long and thick, and the way they swept down, that sweet surrender, a sign of submission, tightened things inside of him. But for some reason he wanted the sweetness of hearing it was willing, that it reflected her desire as much as his. Not because he overwhelmed her, not because she thought he needed it. Not because it was a temporal experience only.

Leaning in, she pressed her mouth to his sternum, then stretched so she was at his throat, and her teeth marked him there, making blood surge into his cock and his hand tighten on her even further, desire starting to overtake thought. Her wings briefly closed on his shoulders, then slipped away, a silken touch.

I've wanted you inside me from the second I woke this morning. And even before that, in my dreams.

Her body moved against his, a sinuous ripple of movement, and the wings simply dissolved before his eyes, shimmering away out of existence with no evidence they'd ever been there. The scales became something smooth and different in texture, the soft skin and firm muscle of her calves and thighs. Lifting them to wrap around his hips, she used her hands to push the swimming trunks out of the way, working them over his arousal and then down, one agile foot taking them the rest of the way. Holding her with one arm, he guided her down on his length, and plunged into a body warm, slick and willing for him, causing him to groan.

She pressed against him, drawing his attention, and he remembered. Cupping her head and covering her mouth with his, he gave her breath from his body. She relaxed against him, though her little moans and whimpers as he brought her down further on his cock coiled things inside him tight. He wanted to drive deeper, so deep he'd never need to withdraw, never need more than this, because if he drove deep enough he would be complete, at peace.

He pushed the swimsuit top out of his way so he could arch her up against him. Leaving her mouth briefly to suckle a taut nipple, he drew in the cool wet water with it. While she had a greater lung capacity than a human, he sensed how the lack of air, the shortness of breath, ironically heightened her arousal. He couldn't indulge that for long, though, because he found it hard to resist her mouth, the pleasure of exploring it as he was giving her air. He teased her tongue and lips as he worked her body on his, moving slow, like the water environment itself, a still, drifting place where pleasure could build at its own pace.

He opened his eyes while kissing her. As if sensing his attention, she opened hers. He stopped, holding them both there, locked together, blood pounding, the pulse of his and her sex creating its own friction, her fingers tight on his arms, her body melded to his, trusting him to give her air, trusting him with her life.

She dwelled upon the spark she sensed in him, but he knew the concern he and her father shared was the vastness of his darkness. At times like this, when his passion was greatest, that rage rose up against her own overwhelming light. As if it were a threat and castigation both for which he should punish her, conquer her, make sure she knew his control was absolute. Yet amid all of that maelstrom, that spark of light still reached for her, knowing she was his only hope of salvation.

Which made no sense. He was here, he'd made it so. He didn't need any more saving. The Dark One world was behind him and he would not go back.

Like their coupling, his understanding of it eluded him. He couldn't bring himself to question, not right now. Her skin was so soft, her mouth, her cheeks, her breasts, the slope of her abdomen, the generous curve of her buttocks, the length of thigh, even the tender sole of her foot, pressed insistently against his own flexing buttocks, made him crave, need, hunger.

He thrust in harder, drew out slow and watched her mouth shape itself in a moan of reaction, her eyes closing again. He closed his own then, focusing on giving her air and pleasure both, one arm around her back, one between them to please himself with the nipple against his palm, the weight of the breast in his hand. She seemed to find pleasure in him as well, her hands sweeping his chest, the column of his throat, teasing the area that was so sensitive on a vampire. And then down, to the joining part of their bodies, wrapping her hand around him as he came partway out of her, her fingers caressing as he drove back in, going in to the hilt.

Please, Dante . . . I want to feel your seed inside of me.

Then come for me, merangel. Show me how much you want that. I want you to scream inside of my mouth, dig into my shoulders with your nails.

He pressed her against one of the rock ledges, taking her lower so he could lay his body down upon her. Her hands slipped down, fingers raking his back as he hitched her legs up higher, changed the angle and dove deeply into slick female flesh.

She cried out into his mouth, gasping as he kept the driving rhythm, pushing her up and over that precipice, feeling his own control trembling on it. White flashing light, spiraling fire, were all in her mind, all thought driven out before the power of that climax. Just rapid images, erotic, needy, the things she wanted him to do to her, needed him to do to her. It shoved him over that same cliff. He gripped the rock, crumbling it beneath his strength as he pounded his hips against her, pushing her legs out wide, ratchetting their clutch higher up his back. Her breasts quivered with the impact, brushing his chest in tiny, rhythmic feathers of motion that made him even harder. A manta ray swam over her head, dipping its wings as it turned, sliding along Dante's back. Life moved around them, accepting them, accepting what they were doing.

In the Dark One world copulation was always public and open, as he'd told her, no different from relieving oneself. But this . . . the plethora of life around them somehow felt like a confirmation of the act, an embellishment to it, something that gave it special meaning. Made the act itself special. He hadn't acknowledged it to himself, but he did now. Being inside of her body had a different meaning to him than any other sexual experience he'd endured or inflicted on another.

She made an approving murmur in his mouth as he climaxed, holding tightly to him. In her aftermath, he saw in her mind how she took pleasure in his body, the expressions on his face as he released, the way his hands held her. How he swept everything away, making her . . . his. *His*. That was the word in her mind, an answer to the earlier question of whether she wanted this. And not because he'd made it so, overpowered her. She felt like her heart and soul were his, that she'd given them to him. *Given*.

The idea was so stunning and disturbing at once, at first he didn't feel another disturbing current running through the water, but Alexis did. Her mind froze.

Reba. She's frightened of something.

He pushed himself off her, her slick muscles releasing him with a spasm that shuddered through them both. She was already in motion, though. Alexis swam for the grate, shifting as she swam, a blur of motion and distortion that left several feathers and scales behind, suggesting it was not the most graceful turning she'd ever done. She reopened the grate latch, got them through and then into the manatees' tank. They ascended together, her wings and his normal speed making it barely a blink of time before they were surfacing. Dante made sure he broke first, however, wanting to be between her and the lip of the tank, not knowing what might be waiting for them.

Reba yelped as he exploded from the water, using one hand to catapult himself out of the tank and onto the deck, crouched over her. He glanced around, nostrils flared.

"He's gone, whatever he was. God, you guys got here fast."

Alexis emerged only a blink later, using her wings to take her halfway out of the water as well, hovering above the surface, looking around. "That's that same feeling," she said to Dante. "Like the diner. The one I told Pyel about. Can you feel it? Track it?"

"I'm not leaving you here alone, both of you unprotected."

"We need to know what it is."

"He was like you," Reba said to her. Her voice trembled a little, though she looked like she was calming down. "And he actually didn't hurt me. He scared me mostly because he came up on me unexpectedly and I was on my back like a turtle. He had wings, sort of angel-like, but not what I think of as an angel."

"Leathery-like?"

"A little." When she nodded, Alexis blanched, looking toward Dante.

Dark One?

I don't see how. They couldn't use the rift I or the witch created, and there are no other openings. Dante frowned. *Also, Dark Ones carry the stench of fear and violence, despair. No matter its intentions, it would have killed her because it would not have been able to resist helpless prey.*

"You know, it's rude to talk when people can't hear what you're saying," Reba ventured, her hands closed in tight balls against her abdomen. "Of course, no more rude than it is to practically jump on someone dripping wet and naked." She attempted to give Dante a lecherous perusal, but ended up with a quick flick before she focused hard on his face, her skin pinkening. "Much as I thought I'd like seeing a guy naked, it's a little . . . overwhelming this close. God, I really want to be in my chair. Feeling a bit like a stranded fish here."

Alexis nodded to some towels and Reba's chair by the locker room door. Dante went to them, knotting a towel around his waist. Despite the lingering air of danger and worry, Alexis knew no female would have been able to keep herself from looking. Still she was somewhat mortified that she was no more capable of resisting than Reba, who tilted her head up to watch the view upside down. Then the girl gave her a sidelong glance and mouthed, *What a fucking incredible ass.*

Alexis tried for a stern look, but failed and sighed instead. Dante returned and lifted Reba back into her chair. "Reba, you said he didn't hurt you. Did you feel anything when you saw him? Did he say anything?"

"He asked, 'Where is the evil?' He looked me over, like he had radar to tell I wasn't a threat. I told him I didn't know about any evil. He said he could smell it, so I said the place had just closed for the night, and maybe evil had taken off with the visitors, but left some of its stench behind. So he left same way he arrived. Poof, he was gone."

Alexis moved to the deck, shifting back to her human form and knotting a towel around her bare body. "You're something else, Reba."

"Don't I know it." She managed a tired grin. "But 'Where is the evil'? Talk about melodrama. What do you think that's about?"

Alexis met Dante's eyes. He nodded. "I suspect whatever it is, it is looking for me."

Twenty-six

NOTHING in the parking lot indicated who their strange visitor might have been. All she knew was it wasn't the same energy as the vampire, so it wasn't likely another unsanctioned vampire attack. Still, Alexis sent a message to her father and David, so they could ask the Legion to scout the area. They waited until Reba's mother picked her up, then headed for Lex's home.

While she kept her senses tuned all the way there and found nothing, she was relieved when she shut the door of her town house and had them both safely ensconced inside. While Dante was showering off the tank's salt water at her suggestion, she pushed aside her weariness to practice some old hearth magic. Sprinkling salt at the window and doorjambs, she murmured a Protection Spell. It might not stop anything capable of attacking Dante, but it would serve as an additional security alarm, buying precious seconds. For the first time in a long time, she even removed the key from the outside pot.

Now that the incident was over, she found herself getting irritated about it. As if getting him used to his new environment wasn't challenging enough, every time she turned around they were being attacked by vampires or Goddess-knew-what. Still, it wasn't like she was used to life being predictable.

As she made herself a dinner with choice tidbits she knew Dante would like to sample, she listened to him in the shower with the hint of a smile. Earlier thumping had suggested he was investigating her cabinets, making her hope he wasn't dismantling all her toiletries. If he mashed her lipstick tubes putting the caps back on, she was going to consider child locks. Regardless, he was now in the water flow, if the sounds of bottles opening and closing were any indication. She had lavender- and jasmine-scented hair and body products in there, and it amused her to think of him emerging smelling like a combination of the two flowers.

Putting on some romantic piano music, she lit candles and resolved to shrug off her worries. A vampire didn't walk out of a hell dimension after sixty years, go to a couple scenic spots, learn how to use a shower and do hunky-dory, happily-ever-after. There was no manual for this. They had to keep going the direction they were going and see what happened. Taking a page out of Reba's book, she'd give herself permission to celebrate the small things, because there might not be as much to celebrate as they faced harder challenges.

Would he ever be able to share tenderness with her? Laughter? Those were things she'd always expected to find with the male to whom she gave her heart, but he had little of those things to offer himself, let alone anyone else.

When she looked up to see Dante standing in the doorway, watching her set the table, she gave a half laugh. "You're too good at that."

He didn't smile. "This male you wanted. What other traits did you want him to have?"

"I don't think it really works that way with love. You can imagine, but where you end up may be somewhere different. It doesn't mean anything."

He shook his head. "That is not the question I asked. I can reach for it in your mind, but I'd rather you tell me. I am not the person you would have picked for yourself, Alexis, or that your family or your friends would have picked for you. They want you to have . . . *love*. I've heard this word in your mind, theirs . . . I saw your father display it toward you when he held you and your mother, when we returned. Love. You love him, your mother . . . many others. It is an easy thing for you, like sunshine."

She gripped the fork instead of putting it on the napkin, needing the illusion of employment. "You'll learn about it in time. You've only been here a few days."

"Alexis," he said softly.

She shook her head, closing her eyes. "Please don't say it."

"Not saying it does not change the truth. If I can ever understand this feeling, it is likely to be years before I learn enough of it to love another the way you do, or those around you. From what I see, trust is a large part of this feeling. Understanding. Regard. I have fought for my life, for everything that I am, every day of my life. And I have lost, often. These kind and soft things you experience every day are as foreign and suspicious to me as my world was to you."

Alexis looked up then, for she felt a sharp and piercing emotion from him, like a fatal stake through the chest. The comparison chilled her. He met her gaze. "It is possible that Mina and your father are right. After all these years, it may have taken too long to get here. The only place I truly belong may be the place I most abhor."

Distractedly, she realized he did smell faintly of the jasmine shampoo she had, but she was more concerned about the aching reaction she'd now identified. *Resignation.* Goddess, was he really thinking he should go *back*? What the hell had happened in that shower?

"*No.*" She slapped down the fork and faced him, her hands clenching into fists. "That isn't true. This is your world. I wish . . . Damn it, Mina, my father . . . all of you. You just need to give it time. When people get out of prison, they talk about how freedom is scary at first. Sometimes they want to run back to their jail cell, to the familiar. You are not a coward," she said fiercely. "You can do this. I will help."

"At what cost to yourself?" He straightened from the doorway and came to her. "I've seen enough of this world already to know you shouldn't give up all you are to someone who can promise you nothing."

"That's my choice."

"No. It's my choice. That, out of everything else, is the most clear. In thirty days, I could destroy all that you are and leave you a shell."

"I'm not that fragile."

"I think you are far more fragile than you are willing to accept, when it comes to your heart."

It might be a moot point, if I've already given my heart to you. And angels only give their hearts once.

"You are only half angel." He turned away from her, glanced at the table. "What are you having for dinner?"

She stared at him. To her ears, he'd just proven his point, that it might take decades for him to love someone, or at the very least, not slice her heart to ribbons when she offered it to him on a platter. But she couldn't be struck down by his words, not when they were merely a weapon guarding his real feelings on the matter. Just as she sometimes forgot he could hear her thoughts, he'd apparently forgotten that, while his emotions were hard for her to decipher, some things were as clear as lighthouse beacons.

On top of the vampire attack and the mystery of what else was hounding his heels, she wouldn't tolerate him turning on himself. He damn sure wasn't going to go back to that Dark One world. Her father, Mina, even Dante himself, would have to walk over her feathered, finned, pink skinned, multispecies dead body to do it.

When his head swung around to give her a sharp look, she pivoted on her heel, marching out of the kitchen to the living area. "Let's try some dancing before dinner. I've lost my appetite."

"You are angry."

"What gave it away?" She went to the music player, punched in a playlist of ballads at the tempo she wanted and turned to face him. He was wearing jeans and a white dress shirt that he'd not yet buttoned. His chest still had a bead of water here and there. Every girl's idea of a poster pinup, no denying it, but it was more than that.

She'd let herself get distracted by Mina's talk of sexual dominants. While there was no doubt he was one of those, what if the compulsion that made him claim her was simply a different version of what she felt toward him? It was a physical deception, the way a woman's anatomy yielded, men's equipped to invade. The truth of it was a stronger magic, such that when the two were locked together, she was just as capable of holding him in her body as he was of taking hers.

"You're absolutely right," she said, as his eyes narrowed. Lifting her chin, she stripped off her overshirt, revealing the thin tank she wore under it, no bra, so her breasts moved generously under the thin fabric, the nipples prominent, dark smudges. She moved toward him. "You don't match my catalog list of what I wanted in a guy, not in the slightest. Steady, gentle, loving. Tender and playful, with an easy laugh and a love of animals, children, anything weaker than him that might need his help. He'd have a kiss that makes my knees weak, just a little, and I'd look forward to his touch."

Stopping in front of him, she met his gaze in bold challenge. "I wouldn't crave it like water, and his kiss wouldn't drown me. He wouldn't be immersed in violence and death, pain and loneliness. I wouldn't be absolutely certain there's an unbreakable line connecting us, and that's all that's keeping him from disappearing forever into desolation. You don't choose who you love, Dante. Love chooses you."

"So should I be grateful for your pity?" His lip curled.

"There's a difference between compassion and pity." She gripped his hand, guided it around her waist, and laid her other one on his shoulder with firm intent, a determined dancing posture. "What about you? You'd let me go, just like that? It would be okay with you if I found another guy, one who'd touch my breasts"—she brushed them over his bare chest with deliberate provocation—"fuck me, make me scream out with pleasure when he put his tongue—"

Dante let out a warning growl, fire growing in his eyes, and she slid her thigh across his groin. "In my cunt," she said precisely, "so wet for him that I'd beg for his cock, hold his hair and tug him closer, grind myself against his face."

"You don't talk like this, think like this."

"I don't belong to you, you just implied it. So you don't tell me what to do, how to think. Who to love or fuck."

"Stop it." But he didn't move. If anything, his hands tightened on her waist, pulling her closer. "Or I'll—"

"What? Spank me?" She turned lithely in his arms, rubbed her backside in one provocative stroke against his cock, which she found was getting satisfyingly hard. She pushed all thoughts out of her mind except one. She imagined a man that wasn't Dante. Instead it was a man with golden hair and seafoam eyes pushing her back on her bed, taking her clothes off, murmuring to her in a sexy accent as she trembled in his arms, wanting to be his forever, surrounded by his love and care. Dante's snarl cut through the thought, his hand clamping on her throat hard enough to constrict air, his hand at her waist stilling her so she was held tightly against his pelvis. In one move, he swept the table free of her settings, all of it hitting the floor with a hard clatter, a shattering of glass. Pushing her face down on the surface, he curved his lean, powerful body over hers. She'd been wearing a loose, faded pair of jeans, and he did not undo them. He simply ripped them down the back so they fell limply to the floor, and he dispatched the panties the same way, a rough tear that jerked against her skin, leaving her exposed to the air. The tank became tatters next, making her gasp as he left her completely naked and exposed, vulnerable as he held her to the table with one hand on the back of the neck. She could feel his fury, his possessive rage provoked, and it made her tremble, but that wasn't her only reaction.

"You think you can give me up and I won't be with someone else?" she pushed harder. "You'll be some generous martyr and do without me, or pretend I don't matter? I can feel your feelings before you even know you have them. You don't share, Dante, and you don't give things up. You're a selfish bastard who will keep what's his, because you can't bear to lose another single fucking thing in a life that's been full of losing."

One more word, and you will be very sorry you pushed me this way.

Closing her eyes, she imagined her blond lover in vivid detail. The curve of his jaw, a little unshaven, because she did like that stubble, something Dante didn't have. Strong hands, cupping her breasts, making her hum with pleasure as his thumbs teased the nipples, making her arch up toward his mouth . . .

She was ready for physical retaliation, but she hadn't expected a mental invasion. Dark fire swirled into her thoughts, and her golden-haired lover burned up in ash, replaced by a different lover who stepped out of that fire, gazed down upon her with flame eyes, dark hair and a mouth meant for carnal sins. She wanted to reach up to him, and realized she couldn't, for her bed had been replaced by a metal frame onto which she'd been stretched and bound, unable to move, though she could feel the trickle of response between her legs as his gaze covered every inch of her with intense heat. *You will have nowhere to run from me, not in your mind or heart, or soul. I am there, because it is all mine.*

She swallowed, feeling an unexpected frisson of fear, for as certain parts of her automatically tried to shut down, he was there, deep inside, where every trace of disappointment, betrayal or loss were kept, some in various stages of healing or transforming from active thought into a softer remembrance. Every insecurity she had about him or herself, it was all there, and he was turning those stones over, examining each one. Then he went even deeper, to childhood nightmares. Now she *was* frightened. There was no sense of the world she'd been in. There was just this, a place of her and him, and fire. It was not the Dark One world or her own. It was a place of Dante's making, a prison to which he could take her anytime he chose, using the strong binding of that third mark.

While he was plundering her soul, he started on the outside as well. He began on her feet first, licking, biting, nuzzling, working with excruciating slowness up her ankles, her calves. Sweat beaded on her body as the flames closed in. The only thing keeping her from being burned alive was his command that kept those dancing tongues of fire just outside the frame. But he took one in his hand, passed it close to her body, dropped it on her flesh for a bare second of searing heat before he swallowed it with his mouth, then brought the heat and wetness of his tongue to her flesh.

She writhed and moaned. She called out his name and begged. He was ruthless with the pain and pleasure both, alternating them. He bit her, taking samples of her blood high on her thigh, at her ankle, then licked and suckled and kissed her flesh, sometimes so hard that left marks as well.

Spread open the way she was with no friction, the arousal built to unbearable heights, but he had no mercy for her now. He stayed away from her throbbing, soaked sex, the jutting points of her nipples, but gave in-depth attention to every other part of her, until she was crying out the way she would in orgasm, without the orgasm. He didn't respond to her pleas, using her as he desired, as if she was a slave in truth to whom he owed nothing, and she owed him total obedience. She fought the restraints when it became unbearable, but he continued teasing her with his mouth.

"Please, Dante . . ." Opening her eyes at a touch of coolness, the powder-fresh smell of her own room, she realized she *was* on her own bed now, but tied down like the vision into which he'd propelled her. He'd used belts and scarves from her closets. Looking down her body, she saw him back at her inner thigh, licking away drops of blood from the area he'd just bitten. Not even a hair on his perfect head touched her needy, pulsing sex. And he was still fully clothed, except for the open shirt.

He rose as her eyes opened, and left her in the room alone. She barely had time to wonder where he'd gone when he was back, bearing the casserole she'd left on the stove. Coming to the head of the bed, he sat on the edge of it and used two fingers to dig into the tightly packed vegetables and pasta. "You will eat your dinner now," he said.

She figured he'd lost his mind, because her body could care less about food. It wanted him. But at his searing expression, she parted her lips, and he fed her from his fingers. Her body was trembling, sweating, and she was making little whimpers in her throat. What had just happened? Somehow, he'd used that third mark in a way she hadn't expected, and there'd been nowhere for her to hide from him. It had been terrifying, yet at the same time, at some level, she knew it wouldn't have been possible to go that deep that fast, without her willingness to take him into all those dark rooms. Whether he wanted to deny it or not, she *had* given him her heart, everything she was.

He met her gaze, but continued to make her eat. The act of giving it to her from his fingers, making her submit to his will, made her even wetter and needier. Her sex was contracting so much on its own she wondered that she didn't come, just from that motion.

"You will not come until I say you can."

"But I'm not yours. You implied as much. You'd give me away, so that means I can choose anyone to replace you."

Perhaps it was the frustration of her body that made her crazy enough to keep taunting him. She might not hold the reins on the third mark, but with her gift, she knew that she could reach him at the most visceral level, the place he didn't even understand himself.

In answer, he made her eat ten more bites, and each one was harder to swallow than the last. Because between those bites, he reached down and fondled her breast, or teased her clit. Oh-so-briefly, but each time it sent a spasm of reaction through her, such that she bucked and cried out. When she subsided with tiny jerks, he'd feed her another mouthful, until she couldn't handle it anymore. On bite eleven, after he pushed the casserole into her mouth and withdrew, so much like the provocative sexual slide of his digit into another kind of wetness, she snarled and spat the mouthful of food at him. It hit his chest and face.

He tossed the plate aside. Before it hit the floor and shattered, he'd opened the jeans and straddled her face, feeding his cock between her lips. She took him willingly, but he pushed hard and deep, and there was a lot of him. She gagged.

Relax your throat, Alexis. I do not intend to show you any mercy.

She forced herself to focus on that, to get past the initial panic, and yet he was still a great deal to take, particularly as he was ramming himself into her wet mouth, holding on to the headboard, his hips pumping swiftly so she felt the rhythm of his denim-clad taut buttocks against her chest, her arms caged by the columns of his thighs.

He took a long while, so that she assumed his intention was more punishment than his own pleasure. Her jaw ached and tears of stress ran down her cheeks, and her cunt continued to weep and throb in the open air. She was making pure animal sounds in her throat, vibrating against him. Her mind shut down, so she stopped thinking about the why or how anymore. She was just obeying, seeking to serve his pleasure until he'd grant her own.

There was a hard pulse against her tongue and she redoubled her suckling efforts, determined to have him come in her mouth, to feel him release, but he had other plans. On that precipice, so close she felt his seed leak out on her tongue, he pulled free, showing her glazed, tear-filled eyes he was even more enormous than when he'd gone in.

He released her ankles and one of her wrists, but before she could think about how to take advantage of her freedom, he'd flipped her over, brought her up on her knees, her forehead pressed to the bed. He used his knee to knock hers further apart, and then he was fingering her sex, collecting fluids on his fingers so she shuddered even more. Then he was at the rim of her backside, probing there, using that fluid to slip into the opening she'd never thought of for sex. A cold apprehension knotted in her stomach, but he gave her no time for that.

He sank a finger in deep, and she made a noise at the unfamiliar sensation, her thighs quivering. Earlier today, in a far different mood, he'd told her he was going to go slow tonight, savor everything. While she hadn't pictured exactly this, there was no doubt savoring had occurred. She was afraid she might die if she couldn't come soon.

"When will you come, Alexis?" His voice was harsh, guttural.

She strained to pull her ragged thoughts together. "When you say I can."

"Good." The broad head of that enormous cock was at her rear opening, so she braced herself, but he wouldn't give her that opportunity. His fingers went below, took hold of her clit and began to massage. She was so close, and yet he'd said she had to hold back. She screamed in frustration, trying not to move against him, and in one smooth stroke, he'd broken through her anal muscles and sunk himself deep.

Holy Goddess, he'd split her in two. She wondered if the collar was activating, burning his flesh, because the pain was incredible.

However, mixed as it was with the arousal of her body, she suspected the protection spell wouldn't interpret his action as an attack. She was crying out, her body shuddering at this invasion, when he began to move, taking away his fingers so there was no possibility of her coming, just him slapping against her backside, bringing pain as she continued to burn inside. Tiny, bleating pleas came from her lips, but he was having none of it.

Mine. You obey me, submit to my pleasure. You will never taunt me like this again.

I will if you decide I'm better off without you. I'll . . . fuck everything that moves, complete strangers. I'll give my heart to someone who's the total opposite of you, who will treat me so much better, I'll never even think about you.

He snarled again, renewed his assault, so she yelped. Oh, God, this hurt. *Please, Dante, it hurts so badly, please stop . . . please.*

Abruptly he did, pulling out slow, but every movement of his body hurt the tissues, so tears were running down her face, making her sniffle and try to hide it by burying her face in the covers. Then his hands were on her, turning her, leaving the one arm tethered. He retied the other and her ankles again as that raw channel throbbed and her heart ached. She curled her fingers, needing to touch, but she made herself look into his face, show him he hadn't broken her resolve, even as she'd surrendered to his will.

As he stood at the footboard looking at her spread that way for him, she couldn't help but tremble more. All she wanted to do was love him, heal him. Be his. She didn't care how long it took for him to feel the same way. And she wouldn't consider it might not ever happen. The Goddess she knew had never been that cruel.

His mouth tightened, his eyes darkening further. At length, he moved back onto the bed, lying down upon her. Just that intimate contact made her cry out. He brushed her lips with his and, with a sinuous move of his hips, he slid his cock slowly, slowly, into her sex.

Though she wasn't sexually experienced, she'd been exposed enough to those who were to know that it might not be hygienic for him to go from that intimate rear opening to this needy one. But she'd always been immune to most infections, and she doubted Dante had ever had to consider the matter. And to hell with it, she didn't want to break this moment, no matter the consequences.

He stopped when he was in to the hilt, holding fast against her, his hands cradling her face so they were staring at one another.

"I don't deserve you, Alexis," he murmured. "You proving I'm a savage beast does nothing."

"I want you," she said, voice shaking. "I don't care what or who you are. I know you're mine. I knew it in that first dream." The pain in her backside was not the true pain, but what he had roiling in her gut. "You hurt me, you hurt yourself."

His thumb brushed her mouth, catching her tears on his fingers. "I'm sorry."

"I am, too. But you made me mad."

"And who is this blond lover of yours, this one you knew intimately enough to picture him in such detail in your mind?" There was violence simmering in Dante's eyes again, and Alexis managed to feel a tired flicker of amusement.

"An actor named Leonardo DiCaprio. He's a movie star. I don't know him personally, but I loved the character he played in this one movie, when he was a diamond smuggler in Africa. He had this really sexy accent. I've watched it a lot." She shuddered once again, and her muscles contracted on him. "I'd really like to come for you," she whispered. "I'm dying here."

"Then come for me, sweet Alexis." He began to move, slow, sure strokes that caught her on fire and turned her into a conflagration in a matter of seconds. When Alexis arched against him, the orgasm was as hard and ruthless as he was, wringing her out, making her buck for long seconds against his body, screaming. The sensation continued as he wrapped her hair in his fists, holding his jaw against her temple as he thrust into her with determination, releasing at last as well.

It made her take even longer to come down, the merciless aftershocks working her against him in spasms. He stroked her throughout all of them. Not until she was completely drained did he free her arms. When he lay down upon her, she buried her face in his neck, holding him tightly.

Don't leave me.

Dante closed his eyes against her hair. He didn't answer, but he did slide his arms under her and hold her tighter. He wondered if the feeling he was feeling now would split him in half, without him ever knowing what to call it. Or why her words sent shooting pain through every level of his soul.

Twenty-seven

THEY watched a couple movies that night, though he had an amusing aversion to seeing the movie she'd referenced with Leonardo DiCaprio. She flipped channels, showing him a range of offerings, comedy, drama, horror and sci-fi fantasy. Fortunately there were no vampire flicks, since she suspected the way the human world perceived vampires might need to wait for another day. After showing him how to use the remote, she fell asleep with her head on his thigh, her body and mind exhausted by their day together. As she drifted toward sleep, her lips curved when he began to stroke her hair.

Her dreams were not so pleasant, however. An apprehensive feeling took root, attended by a shadowy creature with leathery wings that might be a Dark One but wasn't. What made her most afraid was knowing that it wasn't evil, that its purpose was something undeniable . . . inevitable. She couldn't find Dante, but she knew he was there. No one would help her find him, though. Her father, Marcellus, David, even Mina and Anna, were all statues in a barren garden, a lonely wind whistling between them, coming from a landscape of fire and ice. Her pleas to them were met with dead stares, a lack of movement or reaction. There were no feelings. She was in a place where she could feel . . . nothing.

When she tried to leave, they closed ranks and boxed her in. Desperation rose, for Dante needed her now. She could sense his pain, but worse than the pain was the resignation. He had no fear. While he would not be caged, he was close to accepting an end, believing he didn't deserve anything more.

No, no, no . . .

Her eyes sprang open and she bolted upright on an empty couch. Sometime during the night, she'd pulled a blanket over her, or maybe Dante had done that, in an unexpected gesture of tenderness. But where was he? When she scrambled up, a quick search showed she was alone. No note. She'd not yet seen his handwriting. Would it be neat, or a broken scrawl? She had so many discoveries ahead of her with him, but where the hell was he?

Throwing a sweatshirt over a pretty demi-bra she knew he'd like, she wriggled into jeans and a pair of canvas sneakers and left the town house. As she closed the door and headed down the steps, she came to a full stop, smacking her temple with a hand. *Idiot.* She'd completely forgotten she had another way to find him.

Dante, where are you? She attempted to keep the panic out of her thought, but quickly realized it was a moot point when one was thinking rather than speaking.

I am here. In the park across from your home.

Still caught in the disturbance of her dream, she almost gasped in relief. Heading for the park at a trot, a few moments later she came upon him.

He had his back against a tree, and was sitting on the ground. Turned toward a grove of trees, he appeared to be watching the birds peck the ground for the remains of bread crumbs that had been left by someone sitting on the nearby park bench in the early morning hours.

An old woman. She left. I think I frightened her, sitting here in the darkness.

Alexis approached him. He was wearing the jeans and open shirt, the band at his throat a silver glint in the early morning light. His feet were bare. In some odd way, he appeared young, sitting there, staring at those birds. Alexis sank down next to him, laying a hand on his knee.

"Are you okay?"

His gaze roved over her face, her mouth, as if he was learning her all over again. She realized he wasn't wearing his sunglasses, and wondered what the old lady feeding the birds had thought.

"I don't think she could see very well. It does not matter, anyhow. As you said, humans will explain away anything they don't understand. Since most of them forgot the Mountain Battle, my eyes are a small thing."

She shifted to her hip and he surprised her when he lifted an arm and laid it around her shoulders, scooting her in closer against the morning chill.

"I don't want to go back," he said at last. "But that place they kept me while you were unconscious, it was like the Dark One world, but different. I fit there."

Hell. Lex wanted to deny it, insist he belonged in a world of light with her, but she remained silent, let him speak his peace.

"In the shower, I was thinking of everything that has happened. Not just the dangerous things, like the woods or the being that Reba saw while we were in the tank. I have been thinking of the things you have tried to show me, teach me. I thought as you did, that it was only a matter of time, but this is not the world I knew, where adaptation is about surviving, fighting. Here it is about living. Trusting." He met her eyes. "You have said that to me, several times. There are many things that I don't understand, that I'm not ready to accept. I was in an entirely different world for decades, as you said."

He gave her a bleak look, for him an almost vulnerable expression, one that shocked her. "In Hell, I will pose less of a danger. Make a more gradual introduction to your world. This will be less difficult for you."

"You aren't difficult," she said immediately, but he shook his head, squeezed her hands to bid her silent again.

"I have no wish to be your burden, Alexis. You say you are mine, my mate, my lover. To be that, I need to become something in this world. I have asked you several times why you helped me, do you remember?"

When she nodded, he glanced back at the birds. "Even at the beginning, when it was clear I was the one who'd kidnapped you, the first thing you did in the Dark One world was beg me for help. You see a part of me that is closed to my own eyes. This morning, watching you sleep, I finally realized that you have been telling me the truth about why you helped me. I just don't know enough to understand that part of you, and I could hurt you very badly in the process of trying to understand."

"You won't."

"Yes, Alexis, I would." He gave her a level glance. "For so many years, I just wanted away from one place, more than I cared about belonging anywhere else. And now I find that this is supposed to be my home, my mother's world, and it is a home that may not want me. I could carve myself a place here with blood and fear, but that is what I left. I want to know something different, but I do not yet know how to be different. You've shown me what is possible, but I must learn that road. What I want seems to be within my grasp, but it's a puzzle I cannot comprehend. So though I hold it in my hand"—his fingers tightened on hers—"I'm not sure I will obtain it."

She studied him, sitting so still, his back against a tree. He was a shadow in the night, something that most would miss, or when discovered, would strike terror into the heart of an unwitting pedestrian or early jogger. "Dante," she said quietly. "I've asked you before. We all have, but I'm asking you to tell me. What do *you* want?"

She wasn't sure if he'd answer, but then she was stunned to feel a door opening inside him that wasn't anger, but something far stronger. Something even her empathic senses hadn't felt because of how tightly it had been locked within him. It could implode if not handled gingerly, a nuclear bomb that would cause his cells to devour one another rather than reveal the secret they kept.

"Just this," he said at last. His tortured voice brought tears to her eyes. "I want this, Alexis. The ability to sit beneath a tree, smell grass, hear birds. Go to sleep and not have to stay on the edge of waking, prepared to fight for my life. I want to see and do the things you've done all your life and taken for granted because they were always there. Gifts you never think of as gifts because you've always had them, like the ability to breathe.

"I have done everything your father accused me of. And I would do it all again, just to have this," he gestured. "The ability to sit under a tree without fear. Without the stench of sulfur and blood in my nose." He stared back out at the night. "If they weren't going to let me have that, I was prepared to fight them, destroy whoever I had to destroy, but I'd turn this world into the one I left." His gaze shifted to hers. "I don't want your world to become that, even if I'm not allowed to be a part of it. The angel and witch want to send me back to the Dark One world. Before I found out about our marks, I would have preferred death to that."

"No." She gripped his arm. "You can't—"

"Would you want to live in that world, Lex? Would you want anyone you care about to be imprisoned in that world?"

"I wouldn't want an enemy in that world," she admitted. He nodded.

"I should go back to Hell, stay there for a while. If I cannot prove myself, then they can imprison me there if they feel they must. Because of our bond, I think they will agree to that. Then I will be in your world, the world of my mother, even if they never trust me enough to release me."

"Dante." Alexis firmed her chin. "It's way too early for this talk, you know? You really—"

A shadow crossed his face, a real one, at the same moment that odd feeling returned, strong enough to make her gasp. "Dante—"

Jerking her to her feet, he shoved her away from him, making her stumble over the tree's roots and fall to her knees. Before she could cry out in surprise, a net had fallen over him. Silver and gold strands, an enchantment. Alexis scrambled up and lunged forward, trying to yank it off him. As Dante fought it, she smelled singed skin, saw his fingers burn from the contact.

It didn't cause her harm, though. She threw herself at it, frantically seeking a way to lift it. *Pyel, help! Marcellus, David, please help us.*

She was grabbed from behind and flung back. Dante roared as she hit the ground hard. As she rolled, she came back to her feet and caught a glimpse of three creatures. Leather wings, long golden white hair, sharp eyes, long noses and a flash of pale skin were brief impressions as she launched herself at them, snatching up a rock. "Let him go."

Alexis, don't.

But she didn't heed Dante. The nearest creature turned, catching her wrist and snapping the rock out of her hand with one effortless move. "You are not part of the evil," it said in a voice like the music of wind and stream, of deep earth. She felt only calm impassivity, nothing else. "You are unwise to help him."

"Let him go." Struggling, she settled for a sharp kick that earned a grunt. A backhand sent her spinning through the air. Landing hard on the ground, she skidded several feet. She had time to think that she'd been sent flying through the air way too many times this week before the second creature was upon her. While he held her down, the net tightened into a ball, drawing Dante into a painful fetal position, rendering him even more helpless.

He'd been in this place before. His mind was shredding itself, trying to get around it, and she screamed at the torment of it. It shattered her filters, took her down into the madness of his mind. *I'd rather die than go back to that.*

"Who are you?" she wailed.

"We are the protectors of the Fen," the winged creature holding her said, studying her with ruthless detachment. "You are not part of this. Evil will answer for murder."

"Wait. You can't. He's—"

"It's irrelevant," the being said. "Good-bye."

A flash of light flooded the glade. Straining through that conflagration of Dante's rage and emotions and her own aching body, Alexis saw a silver-white portal open, felt the wild spiraling wind of it lash out and drive her back to her knees, even as she struggled to go forward. Dante's gaze met hers. The look in his eyes tore her heart from her. His fear and rage were soul deep. He couldn't be bound and made helpless again. He couldn't. He'd destroy everything around him if he had to. The collar would burn through his throat, taking his head long before he would ever stop fighting.

I'll find you. I promise, I'll find you.

Gripped by the sheer chaos of his mind, she was frozen by the sound of his voice, calm and dangerously impassive, devoid of emotion. *Let me go, Alexis. You have done enough. Thank you. If they kill me . . . I'm sorry for binding you to me.*

"I'm not," she shouted over that wind. But she wasn't sure if he'd heard her, because he was gone. She stumbled forward into the energy chasm left behind, a dead space that spread through the glade and dropped her to her knees.

She propped herself on one hand, but before she could attempt to scramble to her feet, a different energy invaded the glade, fierce, familiar and warm at once, accompanied by the rushing sound of multiple wings. Jonah's hands were on her shoulders. As she spun around to stare up into his stern warrior's face, she couldn't stop the tears. Dante was gone, but his emotions were still with her, tearing her apart inside.

She had no idea where he was, only the lingering certainty that the odd winged creatures meant to kill him . . . or worse.

Twenty-eight

"**P**ROTECTORS *of the Fen.* You're sure that's what they said?"
 Lex nodded mutely. They'd brought her to the Citadel in Machanon, the third level of the Heavens. From the parapets, she could see Eden in the distance, and focused on the rainbow that was always there, though sometimes its position shifted or the colors sparkled at different intensities.

Using the mark, her empathy, the crushing emptiness inside of her that gnawed, a terrible emotional hunger, she kept reaching out as far as she could for any sense of him. Once, a long time ago, she'd had a brief crush on one of her father's Legion captains. She'd been eleven, but she remembered how it had felt, realizing he would only ever see her as a child. While she could look on it now with the indulgence of an adult, she remembered the relentless agony of unrequited love to a girl just discovering adult feelings. This was that, multiplied by a thousand. She wondered that she could even breathe.

Her father caught her shoulders, turned her away from the view. "Alexis," he snapped in a voice that should have made anything tremble, even herself. From a far distance, she noted how tight with worry his face was.

You kill him, she dies. Mina's words.

Evil will answer for murder. The Fen protectors.

Her life might be about to be cut short, but that was hardly important. What was important was for the pain to end. She couldn't bear his pain. If he was destined to die, she hoped they did it quickly, and did not torture or restrain him. She couldn't even think of that. Her body jerked, a near convulsion that was somehow comforting.

"Alexis," Jonah repeated. This time the thunderous tone sent a tremor through the Citadel walls. Clouds began to darken above them. Several of the Legion glanced up and Alexis vaguely noted Raphael murmuring to Marcellus. The captain nodded, glanced at David, who stood at Raphael's shoulder, and was gone. The healer drew closer.

Jonah's grip was painful, bruising. So powerful. She'd thought he could protect her from anything. She'd therefore longed for adventures, the occasional thrilling brush with danger. This was the reality of it. Blood, violence, the fear in her father's gaze that he might lose her. The same fear she nursed about Dante. This was the type of violence and fear her father had faced for well over a thousand years.

She wanted to tell him she understood, but even now, she probably didn't. How could she understand the vast nature of his losses, what he'd seen, when just a brief exposure to the Dark One world and the idea of losing Dante, someone she'd barely met but had bonded with so quickly, made her feel like curling up and dying?

Marcellus had returned, and suddenly there was a very different presence amid all the angelic auras around her. Her mother, accepting a cloak to wrap around her now human form. Alexis was aware of her speaking to her father, and then she stepped in front of him to face her daughter.

"Alexis," she said sharply. "If you want to save him, you have to help us."

Help Dante. Save him. She could save him. Anna had saved Jonah. The daughters of Arianne . . . they were always called to do extraordinary things. They *could* do extraordinary things.

Alexis blinked, and her hands shot up, clutching Anna's forearms. She struggled through that bereft feeling. "Help him? We can help him?"

"Yes." Anna's brow furrowed, and she touched her daughter's

face. "I know it hurts, dearest, but you are very strong. Push aside the emotions, whatever it is that is interfering with your ability to think. Stop thinking about what might happen, and focus on what *can* happen. We need your help. Pay attention to your father. Use your filters. Get them back."

Alexis remembered other times when, learning to control her gift, she'd gotten lost just like this, overwhelmed by everything around her, her filters cast aside, like tools she didn't know how to use. But she *did* know how to use them, even with the new factor of the vampire's mark. Though it was like tearing dried cloth off a bloody wound, such that she let out a desolate cry that startled the angels, she lunged for that self-control inside of herself, pulled the filters back to her as if through quicksand, an effort that brought tears rolling down her cheeks, but she did it. They snapped in place, though she panted at the effort.

Straightening, Anna turned back to Jonah, nodded. Drawing a deep breath, he knelt by his daughter, the difference in height enough he was almost even with her gaze. "Alexis, the Fen are a simple people, in a world far from this one. They don't even have writing or reading skills in their societies yet. In fact, they would remind you of our Neanderthals. What is Dante's connection to them?"

Oh, Goddess. "He sacrificed one. He used her blood so you couldn't retrieve me until he released me. But I just saw the one . . ."

Lex faltered, remembering all that blood in the circle, blood that had been there *before* she arrived, before she saw the first sacrifice.

In contrast to her earlier catatonia, now she couldn't bear to be frozen in one place. Pushing off from the wall, she walked rapidly along the parapets, needing air, needing open space. Alexis rubbed her brow. Dante had been planning his escape for twenty years. At what point had he discovered he could make a dream portal work with humanoid blood? How many failures had he had, seeking the right combination of magic and sacrifice? And then there was the rift through which he sent his Dark Ones to retrieve them. Perhaps he'd further strengthened that opening the same way.

"He may have sacrificed dozens of them," she said dully, staring out at the blue sky. Her mother was beside her again, her father a silent presence a few feet away. "They'll hurt him, then they'll kill him."

"Not if they know an innocent's life is bound to his. Not if these protectors are like us." Marcellus spoke now, moving to join them. "We can promise them that he will be imprisoned here, subjected to the punishments of Hell for however long is necessary."

Alexis closed her eyes. "He was willing to go back and stay in Hell until he learned how to be safe, how to get along in our world. So he wouldn't hurt me or anyone else by accident. We talked about it, just before he was taken."

But you can't imprison or torment him. You just can't.

"If these protectors are like us"—Marcellus turned his attention to Jonah—"can you petition them for an audience on his behalf?"

David, leaning against the turret, straightened then, eyes thoughtful. "There's wisdom in that, Jonah. They are kin, in a sense, though we don't know much about them beyond their function to protect the Fen. I can see if Mina can figure out where they are and communicate with them, find a way to their world."

The pavilion shuddered, a breeze gusting across the battlement, rippling feathers and lashing Alexis's hair across her face. She pulled it back in time to see the angels scatter with the ease of long practice, making a space for Mina to arrive in a flash of fire. Unlike the other angels, David had not moved. She materialized so close to him, several of his feathers ignited. He gave her a deprecating look, dousing them with a pinch of his fingers. She responded with a saccharine baring of her teeth, then turned to Jonah. "Already done. The one who fulfills your role in the Fen world is named Seneth. I've explained there's an innocent's life at stake, her life bound to Dante's, and he's agreed to hear your petition. If you wish to offer one."

Alexis stared at Mina. "There's more. You have more, but you don't want to say it in front of me."

"I'm sorry," the witch said briefly, then she looked back toward Jonah. "Dante's sentence has already been declared, though it will not be executed until after our petition. They had a word for it I can't pronounce, but apparently it's a ritual death, accomplished by incremental dismemberment. Portions of his limbs will be cut off each day, one portion for each life he's taken, until even the stumps were gone, and then his head will be taken and his body burned." Mina paused. "A method that can kill a vampire or a Dark One."

Alexis knew her mother's steadying presence was behind her, but she couldn't feel the hands touching her shoulders, or register what lay behind the expression Jonah sent her way.

"If your petition is not successful, there is a way to save her life."

That brought everyone's attention back to the witch. "I've figured out how to cast a lock around Dante's life essence. For time's sake, understand it this way. I'd be enclosing him in a bubble, but a very powerful, eternal bubble. If his life is extinguished inside of it, I would basically strap down the binding, lock his remains in a be-spelled container. The energy outside that containment would be un-affected. In essence, the binding he put on Alexis would not realize he's dead. Ever. As long as it held, and I am certain I can spell it to hold for her normal life span, even if it matches Jonah's."

Mina looked at Alexis then. "It's still important to make a peti-tion. If they will not release Dante into our care, we can at least ask for the opportunity to impose this spell upon him, so that he will not take your life when they take his."

"No." Alexis spoke through stiff lips. "I won't allow it."

Mina arched a brow. "I wasn't asking your permission."

One way or another, they all wanted to imprison or hurt him. Even if he died, he'd still be trapped, a soul unable to free itself, unable to become anything else. The fragile leash on rationality broke, knocking down her filters. Dismemberment, death, isolation. She couldn't bear it. She wouldn't. "Then I will finish it here. I won't be the reason he's forced to suffer."

Her emotions, all the feelings around her, whirled inside her mind and heart, but at the center of that hurricane was an eye of deadly calm. Beyond thought, lost in feeling alone, Alexis picked up the dag-ger some obliging angel had left next to one of the whetting stones, focusing every corner of her mind, heart and soul on what she was going to do.

Alexis. No.

She froze. It was faint, so faint. But it was *him*.

Then it was gone as her father knocked the weapon from her hands, and yanked her attention from anything else as he lifted her up against the turret, slamming her against stone hard enough her head bumped. His thunderous visage was inches away from hers, and she'd never seen anything so frightening, not even in the Dark One world.

"Don't you *ever* consider doing something like that to your mother," he grated out. "Not ever."

In his gaze she glimpsed a pit of darkness as vast as Dante's. The darkness her mother's love kept in check. But her own darkness rose, an abyss she hadn't even known dwelled within her. As she gripped his shoulders and met him fury for fury, it welled out of her in a terrible voice, raw and enraged. "He is mine. I won't give him up. I won't let you sacrifice him for me. I won't let him be tortured or imprisoned. He is *mine*."

It went far beyond romantic possession. He was a part of her, something vital she had to protect and safeguard to keep her own soul intact. A part she might conversely destroy her own soul to keep safe.

Recognition flickered in Jonah's gaze, as if he'd just caught a startled glimpse of himself in a mirror.

"Jonah." Anna was at his side, her gentle hand on his silver wrist guard, her face stark with pain. "Stop this." Looking around at the assembled, she met Mina's eyes briefly. "You will go and tell this Seneth our position. Jonah will do everything possible to gain Dante's release. But if he is unsuccessful, Mina must be able to cast her spell."

Reaching over Jonah's arm, Anna drew her daughter's reluctant eyes to her. "Dante would not wish you to die with him. You've already told me he risked himself to keep you safe. Control your feelings, Alexis. You must continue to *think*, no matter how much you fear for him. We love you. We're your family. We will get through this together, whatever happens. All right? Can you believe in us that much? We are not your enemy in this."

Alexis swallowed, closed her eyes, feeling her father's grip ease. For once, though, their love didn't bring her the comfort she wished it would, and she couldn't bring herself to fully trust her mother's words. Because she always knew their feelings.

"All right," she whispered, though the mistrust in her heart was as painful as knowing her life would likely end, one way or another, in the next few hours.

Twenty-nine

S<small>ENETH</small> had mandated that only three angels, the witch and the affected innocent could come. Mina went very few places without David, though it was always unclear whose stipulation that was. Jonah, of course, would come to speak on their behalf, and Marcellus was chosen to accompany him as the third angel.

As Mina prepared the circle for the dizzying transport to the Fen world, Alexis stood apart, trying to do as her mother had said and which she knew was wisdom—steady her mind for what lay ahead. But when Anna came to her, took her hands, she found it hard to meet her mother's eyes and not draw away from her touch. Anna tightened her grip on her forearms, however. "I need you to listen to me, Alexis. I know it's difficult for you right now. Can you listen to me? Don't just say yes. Let me see you focus."

Dutifully, Alexis struggled, bringing her mind out of her worries and fears to center on her mother's blue eyes. "I'm here, Myel."

Anna gave her a searching look. "All right. No matter what terrible thing happens over there, above everything else, I need you to remember one thing. Trust your father."

The angel who, more than any other, wanted Dante dead. But Anna's nails dug into Lex's flesh. Her blue eyes were sharp, the core of steel showing itself.

"Do you understand me, Lex? *Trust your father.*"

All she could manage was a nod of acknowledgment, no more. Mina had begun to speak the words to open the rift and she gave Anna an impatient glance, warning her that her time to step back was drawing close. With one last look, Anna turned from her daughter to Jonah. Lex didn't hear what her mother said, but she saw Jonah's glance flicker toward her, then back to his mate. His gaze softened, though the hard set of his mouth didn't ease. He nodded, and her fingertips brushed his lips before Anna stepped out of the circle casting.

"This is going to be bumpy," the seawitch said. "It will work, but there was no time to make it pretty. Clasp hands."

Jonah closed his fingers over Alexis's, meeting her look briefly. Mina took her other hand, then David and Marcellus finished the circle. Lex had one more quick glimpse of her mother's face before Heaven disappeared, and she was in a whirlwind.

Mina was right. It was like being caught in a tornado with flying debris. But the unexpected made it even worse. *Hellfire.* Even as she was spinning out of it, she heard startled cries, because of her forced transition.

Just like the Dark One world, this world only accepted her mer-angel form, so she landed on a grassy knoll off balance, her clothes ripped and torn by the emergence of her tail, her wings flapping madly, a cross between a wounded bird and flopping fish.

She swore in a way that would have made Clara proud, but got herself aloft, hovering off the ground so her tail didn't drag. The only garment the transition had left her was the bra whose straps she wore crisscrossed all the time for just that reason. It was a little provocative for mixed company, particularly company that included people whose modesty requirements she didn't know, but it was better than nothing.

Forcing herself to get oriented, she took in her surroundings. The knoll overlooked a valley, dotted with trees and large, shaggy animals that were a cross between cows and buffalo. The sky was blue, vibrantly clear. In the distance, she saw small structures that might be huts, or tepees such as nomadic peoples used, but other than that, it was all nature. Grass, flowers, trees, sky and wind, bringing the smell of water, perhaps a nearby river or wide stream. It was like looking at preindustrial Earth.

The three angels had automatically moved into a circular flanking position facing outward as they came through, their feet barely touching as they used their wings as well, spreading them out to make it more difficult to make the two women a target. But after gauging their surroundings, the three settled back to the ground, folding their wings to allow her to see the delegation awaiting them.

She recognized the winged creature in the front, the one who'd told her she was unwise to help Dante. Since his stance was practically a mirror of Jonah's, she surmised he must be Seneth. His cheekbones were so sharp he looked almost foxlike. His dark, upwardly tilted eyes didn't have whites as well, another indication he and his kind were cousins to the angels.

Two more of his fellows flanked his right and left sides, but a whole group of them waited twenty feet or so behind these three. Then she realized they weren't there to overwhelm their own delegation. They were guarding Dante.

She bit back her cry only because Mina's hand closed on her wrist, nails digging in like Anna's, only Mina's nails were more like talons in their sharpness. "Be still and say nothing yet," Mina murmured.

They had him bound to a pair of timbers that had been lashed in an X form so his arms and legs could be stretched out upon them. What held him looked like irradiated barbed wire, cinched in tight and spiraling across his limbs, all the way from the joining corner of his thumb and forefinger, down his forearm and to his shoulder. His legs were the same, from foot to thigh. He'd been stripped, so she saw how the wire's razor points dug into his flesh. Fresh rivulets ran over the tracks that had dried on his limbs, chest and abdomen, giving him a macabre appearance. The X was propped up in a vertical position by scaffolding.

Because he'd been hooded with a thick hide covering, she couldn't see his eyes, though a hole had been cut for his mouth. A hard fruit had been thrust into it, his fangs embedded in the orb. Strings of beads, locks of hair, bracelets and scraps of brightly dyed cloth and ribbon had been hooked on the barbs over his suffering flesh. More were threaded through the silver collar.

Dante, we're here. I'm here.

His head tilted, and she saw a frisson of tension run through his muscles. As he moved, every weapon of the dozen guards was drawn. They faced the X as if they expected Dante to snap his bonds and split into an army.

Her reaction didn't help ease their watchfulness. As she opened the door to his mind, intending to use that connection to steady herself, she found a chamber engulfed in flames. The blast knocked her mind over, scattering her thoughts. Mina's hands closed over her arms, steadying her, but there was no escape from the raging, murderous fury Lex experienced. It was a bestial hatred, mindless destruction like the Christian version of end of days, Armageddon, the coming of the Beast.

She knew there was no devil, at least not that kind. However, the soul could accept evil and become what others feared, the stuff of nightmares. She fought to lock down her filters against it, even suspecting that his third mark made her far more vulnerable to his emotions than anyone else's.

"Let him go," she gasped. "Release him, please. You're making it worse."

Instead, Seneth turned his sharp gaze to Jonah. "He can torment the innocent with his mind?"

"He's not . . . tormenting me." She snarled through the maelstrom, though she could hardly blame them since it looked exactly like what they thought. Even the angels, knowing, looked unsettled. "I'm . . . an empath. I can feel what . . . he's feeling."

She'd inherited the ability of angels to understand and speak in any language, but did Dante know what they were saying? Or had lack of comprehension only added to his mindless rage? As she struggled for control, a movement to the right took her attention from the terrible display. Unlike humans, who lived in doubt of angel existence, the Fen apparently knew their protectors. A small group of them watched impassively from a grove of trees. All males, they carried spears, and had their hair adorned with more beads and long leaves twisted into ornamentation. They looked like wood spirits. Long blue and red streaks marked their faces and bare chests. From their ordered phalanx, it was obviously a tribal council of some kind.

Closing her eyes, she used force of will alone to slam down her filters. Getting torn open from the inside wasn't going to help Dante. With tremendous effort, she managed the magic and gradually the filters shut out the worst of it. Not wanting to do so, but testing herself, she looked toward him again. This time she noticed the beads embellishing Dante's torment were more delicately carved. Her gaze roved over the items, compared them to what was on the Fen males, and the terrible significance came to her. What hung on Dante belonged to females. Or had belonged to them. He'd said female blood was best for his magic. The Fen had turned him into a shrine to their murdered wives, sisters, daughters and mothers. *Oh, Goddess. How many?* And did she want to know?

Getting a nod from Mina, indicating Alexis was back in control, Jonah stepped forward. "Thank you for hearing our petition. We are angels," he said formally. "We protect the Earth, and other parts of our Lady's universe."

"We are the Bentigo. We protect the Fen." Seneth pulled his attention from Lex, nodded. "We know you as beings of worth and truth. Your presence is welcome here." His gaze shifted to Mina. "The witch's power is not as clear, but as she is your ally, we accept her presence."

On a normal day, Alexis knew Mina would have a retort to that, but underscoring the seriousness of the situation, she remained still and silent. Seneth looked at Alexis again, more closely.

"The innocent is your daughter."

"She is." Jonah inclined his head, acknowledging the Bentigo's intuition.

"She is lucky to be alive after exposure to this creature. He has taken sixty-two females of the Fen tribe over the past ten years."

Holy Goddess. Alexis fought to keep her face impassive, but her hands closed into tight balls at her side. A muscle flexed in Jonah's jaw, but he said nothing as Seneth continued.

"After we caught one of his foul minions, we determined it was this creature"—Seneth jerked his head toward Dante—"sending his slaves here to take the females. We could not find the rift in order to guard it, for it seemed to move each time it was opened. We also do not know what he was doing with them. But when their life essences disappeared, we knew they were dead to us."

"Did you ask him what became of them?"

Seneth looked over his shoulder briefly, his lip curling back in distaste. "We cast a Translation Spell that forces him to hear the accusations of the Fen and ourselves in language he understands. But he has not been conscious until now. When we brought him to this world, he escaped our netting. He killed several of us, and there would have been more if we'd not caught him from behind, flown him off a cliff. The drop knocked him insensible, and the deep waters below held him. He could not float, so we kept him there, below the water, bound until now. But he is a magical, dangerous creature, and we do not know his weaknesses. He is bound physically and by what magic we know. So we have not yet asked him anything."

So the collar was inert. Despite her chagrin at their losses, Alexis realized that fact with some sense of relief. Mina had said she'd only set up the protection for humans and one merangel, so the Fen and Bentigo were not included in its scope. And perhaps it only worked on Earth. The magic must have been complex for it to have such a narrow scope. Or, as Mina had implied, her intent was not to make him defenseless, but to give innocents protection.

Seneth returned his attention to Jonah. "The population on the Fen world is small. The attacks were concentrated on this particular tribe. Its female population has been depleted significantly."

The Dark Ones had likely focused on this area because the rift he'd created was here, and they would not want to linger long. Forcing herself to think it through, Lex realized the Bentigo must have the same challenge the angels did. Because of their abundance of Light energy, they couldn't enter the Dark One world in pure angel form. An angel like her father would be consumed within minutes, like a person in a vat of acid. She had survived only because of the protections Dante had put upon her. Using the blood of these females.

Her heart sank further, but she refused to accept defeat. Managing Dante's internal inferno, she opened up another thread toward the Fen, and found a different form of burning hell in the chief who headed up the council. He'd lost two daughters and their mother to Dante. The rage and grief boiling inside of him made her falter, drop closer to the ground. She realized David had moved in to support her on her opposite side, since her flagging energy was making her more difficult for Mina to hold up.

It wasn't just her energy weighing her down, though. She was going to lose here.

"My daughter saw what happened to one of the Fen." Jonah turned, then met her gaze. "Alexis."

Oh, Goddess. Don't do this, Pyel. But his gaze was relentless, demanding she speak. He loved her, yes. But he would never hide truth, or let her do it, either.

The Fen's fury and despair, Dante's barely leashed madness and the Bentigo's piercing regard and heavy weight of expectations nearly overwhelmed her anew. Goddess, this was why her gift could be difficult. To outward appearances she often looked like a drooling, weak idiot, because the battle she fought was in her head. She couldn't afford to be drowned like a tree standing before a cracked dam.

It is your gift. Your weapon. Yours to wield, given to you by those who understand you were the proper one to have it. It is yours.

Startled, she glanced into the unusual bicolored eyes of the witch. She'd not realized the witch could speak directly to her mind. Mina made an impatient face. *If you love him, prove to us why he is worth saving. Or have you changed your mind? Do you think it might be best to let him go, seeing all of these arrayed against him, including those you love? He killed sixty-two females. Do they not deserve justice?*

Lex looked at David and Marcellus, as well as Jonah, then came back to Mina. The witch cocked her head. *They are who they are for a reason. They know the difference between good and evil, and they are not often wrong, because the understanding of it is part of their blood. But it is also part of yours.*

She knew Mina was right. Her angel blood had supported and

strengthened her gift, eventually helped her learn which souls were beyond her gift, condemned to the consequences of their actions, nothing else capable of changing their dark course. Her gaze turned unwillingly to Dante.

He wasn't speaking. While he knew she was there, he'd immolated himself in his rage. Feeling its breadth and scope, she now feared she'd only seen it on a small scale.

She'd never had to stretch her gift as she had with Dante, reach past his actions and thought to find what was redeemable in his soul. But justice and redemption were closely linked, she knew. Her father's closest friend was the Lord of Hell, after all.

Dante had walked his dark path in isolation for decades, and he'd gone farther down it than anyone she'd ever encountered. Her father and the others wanted her to believe the spark she sensed in him was the effect of her own light wrapping around the weak flicker of his. But in the Dark One world, surrounded by hopeless desolation, violence and fear, he'd protected her in the end.

Not just because she was his key to escape. Not just because she considered her a possession, and in his world every possession required violence to keep, though in his mind he would likely think of it that way. He didn't yet have the internal lens to see anything different about himself. That was why he had her. She had seen and felt something different from him, in the very first dream they'd shared.

No, the angels were not often wrong. Looking at Mina, she remembered many of the angels had once felt she should be destroyed for her Dark One blood. Later, Mina herself had said they weren't entirely wrong, for the Dark One blood had been very strong in her, and all that held her from a decision to embrace it was her own will. A choice, made against all other forces in the world, and there'd been a point where it could easily have gone the other way. If it hadn't been for David's belief in her.

She didn't know that part because Mina had told her. She knew it because she felt it, in the binding that was so strong its unbreakable energy coursed through her now, a conduit, as David and Mina stood on either side of her.

Alexis lifted her head, let the power of that thought ripple through

344 JOEY W. HILL

her wings, giving her an additional lift from the ground so she stood taller before them, on an even level with the angels around her. She met Seneth's gaze and said the terrible words.

"He sacrificed most of them to build power for a blood ritual," she said quietly. "It was to escape his world and gain entry into ours. He also used some of them to bind me in his world and slow the fatal effects on my body there."

"And how were they killed? What did they suffer?"

Alexis met the Bentigo's eyes after flicking her gaze over the Fen. "It serves no purpose to hurt them this way."

"This hearing is to determine if his crime matches his punishment. You will answer."

Swallowing, refusing to look toward Jonah, she briefly sketched the details of how the one Fen she'd seen had been treated, the efficient sacrifice after the Dark Ones were allowed to torment her for what she estimated was a couple hours.

"Why did he not just come into our world, if he sought escape from his own?" Seneth's voice remained even, though she rocked at the wave of emotional response from the Fen. Thankfully, Mina answered, giving her a pause to sort through it.

"He couldn't come to your world. That's why the Dark Ones who served him came in his stead. He was bound into his world by a magic that said he couldn't leave until someone spoke his true name outside of it. But he was never named."

Never named. Alexis looked toward Dante again. His body was quivering, from rage or pain, or some combination of both, she didn't know. He was all reaction now, every sense honed for an opportunity. If she was the one to loosen his bindings, he would as likely kill her to get free as anyone else. Or would he?

"Circumstances do not excuse a crime of this magnitude," Seneth returned.

"No, they don't. But they do help to determine what the proper consequences are." Straightening her spine, Alexis moved forward until she stood beside her father, facing Seneth. Jonah tensed, yet allowed it, perhaps because he trusted Seneth. It still surprised her though, because she knew he wouldn't like her in this less defensible position, even with an honorable adversary.

Pivoting now, she looked toward the Fen. "I can feel your grief and pain. Your anger." She addressed the leader directly, meeting his eyes. She'd never been more glad for the angel-inherited boon of not only being able to understand all languages, but of being understood in them. "I have a mother. A best friend I consider a sister in all ways. If anything happened to them . . . If someone took my mother against her will, frightened her, tormented her, killed her, I would have the same grief and rage in my heart as you have in yours." The words were difficult to push out, because they weren't empty. She felt every one of them, as well as the reaction around her to the place her thoughts were taking all of them, including her father. "But I have a magic. My gift is to feel what another feels, understand the root of all of his emotions. I know your feelings and his both. They are two points on a web, a connection where destroying the one doesn't bring balance to the other. A life for a life doesn't change anything. It does not mend the broken strands. In some cases, it breaks more."

She paused, because her courage tried to fail her. Turning her gaze to Dante, she focused on the man behind the creature of hatred and flame, whose fury was hammering against her filters, wanting to douse her in the same killing fire. Alexis firmed her chin, turned her attention to Seneth. "Mina, the seawitch, has a way to kill him without killing me. If you permit her to perform the magic, then our fates are no longer linked. I am no longer a consideration."

Shock hit her from all sides, particularly from Jonah. There was sharpened curiosity from the Bentigo, vague comprehension from the Fen. Their heightened anticipation was a taste like bitter blood on her tongue.

"Yes. If she performs the magic, I won't die. Not physically. But I have a hope inside of me, a belief that it's possible to save the darkest soul. Destroy him, and I lose that hope. Hope is what fuels the gift given to me by the Goddess. Destroying the gift of a Goddess has far greater consequences than this moment."

She turned back to Jonah then. Though Dante's pain was tangible, tearing at her heart, she said the words, knowing that, like the web she'd just referenced, her words were a tapestry. One dropped thread would make it all unravel. She could feel the power of it spinning out with every word, a spell without manipulative intent, a spell with truth as its magic. She just had to hope they were receptive to it.

Jonah's dark gaze was riveted on her face, ancient wisdom reflected in the lines of his handsome countenance. He understood truth above all things, even when it was difficult to face. She prayed he had that courage now, though she'd never known him to lack it.

"Pyel, when I was little, you were right to try and protect me from those who carried evil in their hearts. I was a child, and I had no way of protecting myself, no awareness of how they could hurt me. But it's not right any longer. Dante is the gateway to the destiny I was meant to serve."

So many things those filters had blocked when she was growing up, things that had been too difficult for a child to process. His desire to protect her, the depth of his love, so deep, vast, incomprehensible. Unconditional. Even as those memories overwhelmed her heart, Alexis knew she had to speak not as his daughter, but as a woman who knew her path. He stood unmoving, his wings and the hem of his tunic ruffling a little in a breeze coming up the knoll. A late afternoon sun gleamed on the pommel of the short sword handle visible over his left shoulder.

"Everyone had a vision of what my gift would become, how much it would expand, how powerful it would be. But I don't think any of you realized that what I kept trying to do as a child was fulfill its purpose before I was mature enough to handle it. This gift isn't meant to shine light on those who have a moment's pain, those who aren't lost. Things that anyone with exceptional intuition could figure out. It was meant to take me as deep into the darkness of a terribly lost soul as I need to go and give him a way out, a hand to hold. One of the first things you taught me, Pyel, was that I didn't need to be afraid of the dark."

She steadied the tremor that had gripped her voice, because she couldn't block the reaction from his heart. Without thought, she reached out, placed her palm on his chest, felt it beat there and raised her gaze back to his face. "Dante is one of those. His potential is limitless, I can *feel* that. You've already seen his capabilities. What he will become if he can find that path will far eclipse whatever I do to help him find it."

"And yet," Mina murmured, "without her guidance, none of that is possible."

Alexis glanced at the witch, but Mina wasn't looking at her. She was looking at David.

"This is who I am," Alexis continued, putting her resolve in her voice. "What I'm meant to be. I know it every time I look at him."

Turning back to Seneth, she looked into the inscrutable face. "I would like to show you what I mean. Will you release him for one moment, if I promise he will not cause you or the Fen harm? I've no intention of taking him without your permission."

Seneth met her father's gaze over her head. Whatever he received there caused a flex to his jaw, a rustle of his leathery wings. "One violent move, and we will take him down," he said. "If you are caught in the middle, that will not be our concern."

"Allow me to cast a protective circle, then," Mina spoke.

"We already have a magical binding in place," one of Seneth's males responded.

"I'm certain you do," David said smoothly, before Mina's caustic look and tongue could slice out whatever remark her expression indicated she intended. "But Mina shares the same blood as your captive. The casting will therefore be that much more impenetrable. No chance of harm to the Fen outside of it."

No. As she met Mina's look, Lex knew what kind of circle Mina was casting. It would have two purposes, and one of them was unthinkable. Before she could protest, the witch's mind cut into hers like a knife blade in truth, causing her to wince. *I understand what you are trying to accomplish, but if he does not have a few minutes to orient himself, your chance of success goes from slim to none. This gives him time to calm down, unless he kills you.*

Alexis pressed her lips together hard. He would not hurt her. She knew it. Somewhere in the storm of his mind, Dante was there.

Seneth nodded. "We will permit the witch to do this."

As Mina moved forward, Jonah touched Alexis's arm. She looked up into his face. "I need to do this, Pyel."

Jonah's mouth tightened. "It is my hope that one day your children will teach you how it feels to *allow* them to place themselves in harm's way."

"I don't need to be taught, Pyel. I feel it." Alexis lifted her hands, tangling her fingers in his feathers as she had when he'd whirled her through the sky, only a few short days ago.

———

JONAH closed his hands over her wrists. As he held her, he saw the brief flash of anguish in her eyes. She did understand the pain she caused him. She always had. Children had to be immune to their parents' feelings in certain areas to become self-reliant. He knew that, as well as he knew that Alexis had never been anything other than a loving, devoted daughter. She'd known how difficult it was for him and Anna to let her have more freedom, find her own way, particularly when the battle to have their only child had been so hard. There was no way they could have felt or done anything differently, because they never could have stopped loving her. He loved her now.

"You did good, Pyel," she whispered, a smile curving that beautiful mouth. It looked the same as it had to him the first time she'd smiled as an infant. "I love you. Don't worry. He won't hurt me. But the next few minutes may be a little scary. You might not want to look."

Thirty

WHEN Jonah at last withdrew, Alexis noted David shifted to the left of his commander's shoulder, Marcellus to the right. Mina stood off to the side, her focus on the circle she'd cast. The aura of power emitting from it with the smell of sulfur and burning flesh caused an uneasy ripple from the Fen, a narrowing of Seneth's gaze. "How do I release him?" Alexis asked, fighting to keep her voice steady.

Instead, Seneth nodded to two of his men and they approached the X. Seneth began to chant, an Undoing Spell, as they loosened the wires and then swiftly removed themselves from the circle's enclosure. Alexis gave a brief beat of her wings, taking her into its perimeter as the green light of the Bentigo's binding power on the X shimmered and then died. Closing her eyes, she shut herself off from everything but Dante, and reached out to his mind.

This time she moved fully into it, no hesitation. There was a sense of darkness, a brief stillness as she transitioned through her reality into the core of his emotions, then all Hell broke loose. Literally.

It was the Dark One world again, but worse, for there was no sense of up and down. She was in a sphere of pain and burning that rolled over and over, no ability to orient herself inside of it, or escape the lick of that torment. Helpless. She was helpless again, and she couldn't stop whatever they might do to her. She would become beaten down again, mindless, scurrying across the ground like the lowest scavenger. Mocked, beaten, sodomized. She'd be the sole toy of cruel children with no other diversions.

With no point of reference, she grasped at the first thing that came to her mind that belonged to her alone. The rapid rolling, the fiery descent. Minus blue sky, white clouds and pulsing waves of rage, it was the first time her father had dropped her out of the sky.

You have to find yourself, your center, to right yourself.

These feelings of helplessness and pain were not her thoughts, they were Dante's. He was here. No. This was his soul, eaten up by hellfire and rage. That was why she couldn't find his physical manifestation. She was *inside* of him.

Dante, I'm here. It's all right. They've released you from your bonds. You need to come to me. Don't fight.

Fire roared over her, disrupting her mind again, spinning it loose into terror and fear. Mental agony now had a physical component. Something had struck her, sent her spinning and slamming to the ground, trampled her. She used her wings to twist back up into the air, though her tail didn't quite clear the ground, the fronds scraping the grass. She sought him again, using her voice as well this time.

"Dante, please stop. Come to me. Calm, be calm. I'm here."

Come to you? His voice was savage, the hiss of a serpent, raking across her nerves. *I come to no one. I will destroy all of them.*

No, you won't. You don't want that. That's not what you want, remember? You want to sit in a park, under a tree. Watch birds fly, the wind move through the trees.

She cried out as fire slashed over her back, and she rolled again, this time to put out the flames in her wings. Opening her conscious mind briefly, she saw her father pressing forward with Seneth. They would have charged the boundary, but they ran into a wall that knocked them both back. The power at the circle's edge shuddered. Mina, her blue and red eye gleaming, focused on balancing it. She wasn't going to permit anyone through, even as Jonah turned on her. David assumed a protective stance in front of her and unsheathed two daggers. His face was resolute, dangerous, though the conflict was tearing inside him, trying to serve his commander and protect his mate at once.

That was not her fight. This was. And it couldn't be a fight. She returned her full focus to her goal. *Dante.*

This is another prison. I am trapped here.

No. It's just to protect them until you calm down. You aren't yourself.

"I am Dante." The ground below her shuddered. The smell of burning flesh increased. The thunder of his words tore out of his throat, reverberating through the circle and beyond, a howl that echoed throughout the Fen world. "This is what I am. Utter destruction to those who would try and stop me."

The energy blast bent the circle outward, she was sure of it, like an explosion inside of a metal box. She hit the ground again, instinctively covering her head as the earth erupted around her. Trees with limbs overhanging the circle snapped and speared the ground. Lightning forked, but all of it from the sky above the circle, so the shards of it struck near her, the electrical force blasting her upward so she slammed against the circle's edge.

Holy Goddess, this was raw Dark One power, pulled together with his vampire immortality to underscore his point. He would obliterate them. They would never get that wire on him again. Except Mina knew how to draw this circle around him, isolate and then incinerate him. Though she was inside of it now, Alexis had no doubt the witch could simply lift the sphere above her when it was needed, leaving her bereft on the ground like this. She'd have failed him. And herself.

Alexis tightened her chin and rolled back up onto her hip. Getting back into the air took some awkward movements, thanks to the shudder of electric current still sloshing back and forth in the circle like water in a jostled fish tank. She did it, though, her feathers standing on end from the static.

She focused her physical vision, keeping her psychic senses wide open, despite the strain of doing both. Perching on the top of that wooden X like a vulture, he gripped the wood with his bare toes.

352 JOEY W. HILL

He'd shed the hood and gag, of course, but he was still stained with black blood and sweat, his hair hanging in his face so all she saw were the glowing eyes. Likely because of the adrenaline coursing through him, he was also fully, impressively erect, his cock brushing his bloody abdomen. He looked like a virile demon from a sensual nightmare, where mayhem and utter surrender were a double-edged sword.

A *double-edged sword*. Focusing on that, shoving away the weariness trying to close over her, she moved forward, forcing her wings to engage and pull her to the center of the circle. When this was over, she was giving herself the mother of all naps. Telling herself she might not move out of a bed for a month, she stilled the quivering that was threatening to take over her whole body.

He was watching her approach with that eerie, unapproachable stillness, but she could feel all the things pouring from him. Most were frightening, dark, an impenetrable tunnel surrounded by that fire, but she stepped into that tunnel again, reached out a hand.

Please, Dante. Come to me. Come kneel here at my feet so they understand what you wish to be. What you want.

Like a starving, groveling beast. His lip curled back. His claws scraped the wood. *Surrender like a slave.*

"No," she said quietly. As she moved forward, she realized one of her wings was no longer working properly. Swiping at hair in her face, she realized it wasn't hair at all, but blood trickling from her brow. "That's the surrender you've always known. This is different from submitting to hatred and fear. This is surrendering to love."

A sharp pain dropped her to the ground, telling her the wing she'd broken in his world had snapped again. She didn't have the resilience a full angel had, her hollow bones far more like a bird's brittle extremities. But she managed to pull herself up on her arms, move a few more feet, though the grass slicing under scales was painful. She met his gaze and despaired at the loathing she saw there, the need for violence.

Please, Dante. Please. Surrender to me. To who you really want to be. So you can be under that tree again. Think of everything we've shared together. Every thought you've had while you were with me.

How much time passed? She wasn't sure. The heat inside the circle was stifling, and flames continued to crackle on the edges, shooting high along the wall of the binding and curving inward, telling her the circle of power Mina had cast was a sphere for Dante's death, just as she'd suspected.

His gaze met hers and coldness grabbed her vitals as she remembered his ability to read her mind, not just hear the thoughts she directed to him. *No, Dante. It doesn't have to be your death. Not if you come to me. Please. Mina and Pyel wanted to protect me, that's all. My fate matters to you, too. Remember?*

The fire spread, eating away the interior of the circle, boxing her in. She pushed that awareness away and centered on him alone. His malevolence and darkness seemed absolute, but she kept her focus on that spark, fanning it with every thought and feeling she could. It was a spark far different from all the flames leaping around her and starting to scorch her flesh. Exhaustion closed in with the fire and smoke. That fatigue she'd been unable to shake ever since she'd returned from the Dark One world was dogging her again, because there hadn't been enough time for long naps and proper meals. Hadn't been enough time for anything.

Desperate, she gave him her images of what they'd shared to help him remember his own. If she'd had more time, she could have made more of a difference. Oh, Goddess, if she lost him, she would lose everything, and not just because her words to Seneth and the Fen about her destiny had been truth. It was more personal than that.

Dante would tear her soul in half if he was lost to her. He'd come to her in his dreams, and yet she thought maybe he'd always been there, the shadowy form of what she knew was hers. Nothing easy or the answer to a girl's romantic dreams, but a real, overwhelming devotion and love, something that would consume and elevate at once, always be a roller-coaster ride of challenge.

Dante, don't let me lose you. I believe in you.

She couldn't breathe anymore. Her vision was getting gray because of the effort, or perhaps because Dante's power had been an explosion of Dark One poison so much like what was in his world. She hadn't really gotten over her last bout with it.

But if this was the cost, she'd take it. Distantly aware of angry discord going on outside the circle, she hoped Mina understood and didn't take the choice away from her.

Dante, I love you. I would die for you, but I'd really rather not. And I don't want you to die. Please trust me. Come to me. Surrender to me.

Her arms were trembling. In another moment her cheek would be pressed to the hot ground, the ground that was even now burning her scales as if she were lying on heated tin. She'd give anything for that terrible stench to go away, the smell of death and hopelessness, decay and things best forgotten. As her arms gave out, she let out a cry.

She stopped just short of that heated surface. Dante's hands were on her upper arms, bringing her upright again. Her tail curved in a shimmering red and gold arc between his feet. Though his palms were almost as hot as the ground, and slick with sweat and blood, they could have been engulfed in flames and she would have welcomed the brand of their touch. Lifting her weary head to look at him, she gave him a tear-streaked smile. He stared at her, so many things struggling in his confused, tormented soul, more than she could understand, as always. She'd always had trouble reading him, because so much was there. But she would decipher every feeling, offer something to each one. Comfort to his sadness, companionship to his loneliness, love to a heart that had received so little of it. *Please, Goddess, give us the time. We both surrender to Your Will. Please help us.*

She held her breath. As his head slowly bowed, tears spilled out of her eyes. Since she couldn't stand, and he was already kneeling, he had to go lower. Curling up on his side, his wary gaze never losing its intent lock on her face, he laid his head on her lap.

Her hand fell to his shoulder, then over his bare hip, stroking him, soothing him. It took a while, long enough that she was shivering with pain, but then the flames withdrew, retreating to the outer edge of the circle, dying away until it was just her curved over Dante on a tiny, circular patch of hot but unscorched earth.

Taking a deep breath, she laid her hand on the silver band at his throat. On an impulse, she fingered the latch, and it sprang free at her touch. She'd collared him, she could release him. High emotions run-

A Mermaid's Ransom   355

ning through her, she slid the band out from under his throat. He remained motionless, though she felt a quiver run through him. Laying it aside, she put her hands on him again.

Blinking, she looked up and met Seneth's gaze. Surprise, speculation, but nothing else. Of course, the Bentigo were the judge, not the jury. Changing her probe, she directed it toward the Fen.

Her heart fell, stabbed by cold fear.

They were afraid of the magic they'd just seen, overwhelmed by it. But there was no alteration in their feelings. The anger was still there, the grief. Over it all was resentment at what she'd shown them. They weren't interested in healing his soul, or her destiny. What they wanted was blood and vengeance.

No, that was surface. Pushing aside her despair and pulling on a deeper well, she found the under layer. What they wanted was an easing of their pain and loss, and only time could bring them that. After Dante's execution.

Like the angels of her world, the Bentigo apparently knew the minds and desires of those they protected. Seneth spoke. "It appears you stand alone, angel's daughter."

She swallowed over a throat aching with tears and smoke. Dante's fingers tightened on her thighs. The bestial rage of the violent sorcerer had receded, leaving something far more heartbreaking. He was glad to be free of the bindings. They had hurt. He was glad for the softness of her thighs, her touch, however brief it might be. He was weary, so weary he wasn't sure any of it mattered anymore.

No, she demanded, as more of her tears spilled. Dropping onto his face and shoulder, they left a trail in the ash and soot.

"Alexis." It was her father speaking. She raised her face toward him, even though she didn't want to do so. Her feelings, her sense of failure, overwhelmed everything else, so she couldn't interpret his state of mind, but she knew his impassive expression. It was the way he looked when he was facing the most difficult of choices, or when he was concealing great emotion. "Come here, Alexis. Come stand beside me."

Go to him. I surrendered to you, but you must obey me. I will not have you in the middle of whatever is about to happen.

I won't leave you.

You must. Do this one last thing for me, and know that you have done far more than I ever deserved.

"Alexis." Jonah's voice was sharp now, sharp enough to cut through her emotions. She choked on a sob and looked back at him. He extended a hand, his voice gentling. "Come here, Seabird."

Trust your father. Unbidden, her mother's words came to her. But how could she trust him to do what she wanted him to do, when she knew it would be against everything he knew was right? Even what she knew was right. But the right thing wasn't always the *right* thing.

Go to him, Alexis. This time, it was Dante's voice in her head. *I will allow your witch to kill me. I sense what she has done in her spell. Though she will not override their death sentence, she doesn't intend to give me back to them. She will make it quick, and I will not be bound or made a slave. They are right, Alexis. No matter why I did it, I took from them. And you have shown me . . . made me understand something of what it would be to lose someone like that. Give me the gift I cannot give them. Let me know the one I came closest to loving is safe.*

She wouldn't do this, wouldn't just step aside and let them or Mina kill him. It was wrong, but she didn't know how to make them understand that, any more than she'd already tried.

"No," she repeated, and levitated off the ground. Though it was agonizing, she forced her damaged wing to help her move. Her fingers slipped off of Dante reluctantly, but she moved and hovered at the edge of the circle, placing herself between him and Seneth. "I will not let you harm him."

At his implacable look, she reached out through the circle's barrier, closed her hand on his crossed forearms in desperation. "There is a reason there are gods wiser than us, who understand what we don't. He's in our world now, learning to be different."

When his expression didn't change, she looked toward the Fen. "You may not be in a place where you can forgive him enough to let him go. But justice is as deep as a river, and as unfathomable. Let his justice be meted out during his life."

"Alexis." Jonah's voice was low. "I am only going to say it once more. *Come here and stand beside me.*"

If he had to do so, he would snatch her back next to him before anyone here was even aware movement had occurred. A lump grew in her throat. *No . . .*

Alexis. Dante's soft voice in her head broke her heart, as he repeated his words. *Obey him. I will accept this punishment.*

They were all united. She'd lost. *The witch will make it quick . . .* That was the best outcome now. She turned and faced Dante. He'd risen to his feet, but the eyes on her face were no longer enraged. They held tenderness, something she'd taught him. Their touch was a caress. Her heart clogged her throat. Protection or no, her soul would be incinerated with him.

She wanted to go to him one last time, but he gave a faint shake of his head, jerked his head toward her father. Stifling a sob she thought might choke her, she turned and moved out of the circle, relying on the one wing and the base of her tail to move her along at a crippled shuffle that reflected how she felt inside. Scraped raw, burned to ash, aching from a beating that would never heal. Numb, she kept her head down, wondering if she could just close her eyes and imagine this wasn't happening. Her father's hand touched her arm, guided her until she stood at his side. David, Mina and Marcellus stood shoulder to shoulder with them, Marcellus's arm going around her waist to take her weight.

"Now," Jonah said mildly, adjusting to face Seneth. "It appears she does not stand alone."

———

AT first she wasn't sure she'd heard him right. Apparently, Seneth felt the same way. He blinked. "You would reject what is clearly the course of justice here?"

Jonah lifted a shoulder. "There are times justice must take a different path. What guides us is balance. As she said, until the past several days, he's never known anything else but evil and death. Now, thanks to my daughter, he has. He is not pure evil, with no interest in being more than that. I think you and I both sense that." Jonah held the gaze of the Bentigo commander. "I believe that he could be and do something different with his life, if he had the chance. We can't get back the harm he's done, but if he's willing to change who he is, help and save others, then by killing him, we lose his attempt to balance the scales. One life cannot pay back sixty-two lives, not unless he has the chance to save the lives of three times sixty-two souls. And my daughter's gift is not a light matter to be dismissed, either. I do not exonerate him from his crimes. He will pay for them. But let him pay a different way."

As Seneth shifted, Jonah did as well. In a blink Alexis felt the energy alter between the two groups. Marcellus and David became far more alert, and Jonah's hand was now resting with deceptive casualness on his sword hilt. "I advise you to give us this opportunity," her father continued in the same reasonable tone. "You know we are honorable. I do not believe the lives lost to the Fen should go unanswered. Trust us to make sure that amends are made. But give us his life."

Seneth looked toward the Fen chief. The tribal leader seemed to have a dialogue of body language with the others, a rapid communication Alexis couldn't follow, since her own tensions had drawn up in a knot, blocking all others. At length, the leader surprised her by walking forward and looking directly at her. "Give us her life instead."

The slide of steel from three scabbards was swift, but not as swift as the response within the circle. Naked and bloody, Dante hit the circle's edge closest to the Fen so hard the binding flashed in reverberation. Seneth's angels moved to block him, though the circle held. Barely. Lex noted a strain to Mina's expression that suggested his impact had taken its toll on even the witch's strength. But Dante's gaze never left the Fen chief, even as the electrical current of the circle's edge sparked in front of him.

"You touch her, you scratch her, you make one move toward her, and nothing will hold me away from you. You will join your wives, sisters and mothers."

The escalation to combat was something she'd never experienced, but in that heartbeat, she felt Seneth's protectors preparing for full engagement, as well as her father. The only ones who weren't were the Fen.

The Fen leader held Dante's gaze. After a weighted pause, he nodded, as if he'd received an answer. He raised his hands, apparently a gesture indicating his next words would be of import. The Fen behind him stilled, as did the Bentigo, the only movement the rustle of the leathery wings as the wind strengthened. The myriad emotions sweeping Alexis came from all directions. Violence, sadness, fear, anger, hatred. The hushed moment was so significant, she could almost feel the universe holding its breath, waiting for the decision.

When the Fen leader spoke, his face might have been carved from stone. His voice was wooden. "When evil becomes something good, the weapon has two edges." He lifted his spear, gestured to the bladed end. "One day, you will know what you took from us. Not in your mind. In your soul, your heart. When that day comes, you will prefer to die a thousand deaths than face what you are."

His gaze turned from Dante, toward Alexis. "Because all worlds are just, it is when you love her the most that Fate will take her from you, as payment for what you have done to us. And that loss will have the power of sixty-two broken hearts, to shatter your soul three times sixty-two times."

The words died away on the knoll, echoing among the silent audience. The chief nodded to Jonah. "Take him from our world and never let him return. We will mourn our dead."

Thirty-one

WHEN Mina brought them back to their world, she transported them to Machanon. Though Lex was worried about Dante's injuries, she noted his wounds were healing already, most of what the Bentigo had inflicted upon him tender red lines only, not open wounds. Even so, she noted he held himself stiffly, and suspected he needed blood.

It made her wonder about the wounds that couldn't be seen, the ones that were usually more severe than anything that could be done to the flesh. Was it possible to heal such wounds, when the salt of slain innocents had been rubbed into them sixty-two times?

She was sure that thought was uppermost in more minds than hers. The mood was somber. Though she'd succeeded in bringing Dante back, this couldn't feel like a victory to any of them. The angels spent their entire existence protecting the innocent, not those who harmed them. Yet they had stood with her, been willing to fight the Bentigo, who were creatures of the Light as well.

The angels are rarely wrong . . .

When they arrived on the outer bailey of the Citadel and oriented themselves to their return, she saw Dante's gaze alight on the Garden of Eden. It was a distant roll of green, the silver blue of the river winding through it, the rainbow a ribbon stretched over it that never faded. She'd wanted to take him there. Had her own yearning toward it tugged his subconscious in that direction now, or was he just focusing on something lovely and clean, trying to manage what had happened?

He took a seat on the parapet, his back to them all, and a stillness settled over his shoulders. Visibly, it was as if he'd turned to stone, a permanent gargoyle seeking the horizon for answers, but Lex could feel the powder keg of his emotions. She wanted to go to him, but instead, Raphael's hand fell upon her, and it was backed up by Jonah shifting in between them.

"Let him heal you first," Jonah said quietly, brushing a knuckle against her cheek to temper his words. "You're about to fall down, Seabird."

She just wanted to touch Dante, see his eyes for one second, but then he spoke in her head. *Go with them, Lex. I will wait here. He's right.*

As she hesitated, torn, Raphael touched her arm. "We can go inside the turret right here. You'll be less than twenty feet from him."

She wondered, because looking at that wide back, she suspected Dante was much further away, perhaps as far away as the Dark One world.

RAPHAEL healed the break and strengthened her with an infusion of light energy that cleaned out the damaging effects of the smoke and fire. However, as he pressed his palms on her chest and back, his attention focused on whatever he sensed going on inside of her, she felt his concern, the dissipation of his usual cheerful aura.

Lex glanced up at him. "It's permanent, isn't it?"

Raphael pressed his lips together. "It's difficult to have a patient that can read her healer's emotions."

"I've been tired since I came back." Lex raised a shoulder. "The Dark One atmosphere would have destroyed any of you. Dante's protection helped me survive, but it didn't make me entirely immune to it, did it?"

"No." He held her gaze. "The damage is irreversible. I wasn't certain when you returned from the Dark One world. I needed time to see the rate of recuperation of your body's systems. There was some marginal improvement, but it's not enough. You'll be more susceptible to injury. That's why your wing broke again so easily. Your lung capacity has been reduced by a third. And your muscle weakness . . . if you rest, convalesce properly, receive regular treatments from me, as well as blood from your vampire, it won't degrade rapidly, but it will continue. Your life span . . ." He stopped.

Closing her hand on his wrist, Alexis managed a weary smile. "Might as well just say it."

"Your life span has likely been cut in half." He grimaced. "However, I cannot say how dour a prediction that is. Unlike your mother, who we know will live until three hundred unless she's injured, or your father, who would have to be struck out of the sky, we don't know how long you'll live, because your blood falls somewhere in between them. I just know it will be less than any of us want."

Alexis swallowed. "Well, isn't that the way it always is? I can still have children, right?"

"Childbearing is an enormous strain that may exacerbate your symptoms. It's—"

"Raphael." Her grip tightened. "Can I still have them?" Her gaze flicked toward the outer bailey, where her father was standing, speaking to several of his captains. Raphael followed her look. He sighed.

"Yes. You can still have them."

"Okay." Lex took a deep breath, wrapping her mind around it. A glance toward the wall showed Dante still in statue-mode, thank Goddess, because that meant he likely wasn't listening in. "You're a Full Submission angel, right?"

Raphael nodded.

"Can you block everyone out there, including my father and Dante, from hearing what we're doing or saying in here?"

Raphael studied her, then closed his eyes. As the door slowly swung shut, a cocoon of energy settled over them, as strong as the heat that had surrounded her in the circle, only this was pure comfort, the warmest, safest times of childhood wrapping around her.

Raphael, being the healer he was, knew what was needed. He opened his arms and she went into them, letting the sobs take her.

———————

WHEN she emerged into the bailey, her wings were working properly again, so she stayed in that form, stretching them out to feel the afternoon sunshine. Someone had brought Dante new sunglasses and a belted half-tunic, and he'd moved to a portion of the parapet shaded by the turret. He didn't look toward her, and though she ached to feel his arms around her, hear his voice, she was glad to have this steadying moment to just look at him. Raphael skirted around her, pressing her shoulder briefly before he approached the vampire, likely to check on his physical status.

She felt her father at her shoulder and looked up at him, giving him a smile. "It turned out to be a beautiful day, didn't it?"

Jonah nodded, looked out at it with her. "You're all right?" he asked.

"Yes." She leaned against his side, putting her temple on his shoulder, letting his arm hold her up. White clouds floated past. "The beauty helps, doesn't it? Helps you remember that light and dark are a balance."

He put his fingers beneath her chin. "Yes. And when a male is blessed with a daughter and mate like I have, the light is strong enough to blind him."

She held on to this second, feeling the beauty of the day, his love, Dante's existence and the potential for all of it wrap around her, bolstering her. "I'd like to take him to Eden," she said at last. "May I, for just a little while? He can bathe there and recuperate. I'd intended to ask your permission to take him there earlier, but things got a little derailed." She attempted a smile and failed. "The whole abduction and fight for his life thing."

Jonah's dark eyes roved over her face. Unlike him or even Dante, she'd never be able to hide her feelings behind an impassive mask. She needed to touch Dante, feel that he was alive, back here with her. She needed to be with him without others.

Some of the happiest days of her childhood had been in Eden, playing with the animals and on the grass with her parents. There'd been long afternoons with the three of them napping there, her sandwiched between them, her father's wing stretched over them both, curved around Anna's back like a blanket. Their soft even breath, the rush of the water. It was Paradise. Deep in their ancestral subconscious, all humans remembered it, a dream they all hoped hadn't been one.

Though she could tell Jonah understood, he wasn't entirely placid. There were things they needed to resolve between them. He was probably going to take her to task for taking the lead the way she had, admonish her for risking herself as always . . .

Instead, he turned and placed his hands on her shoulders as she hovered before him, her wings holding her aloft. "You are an angel of these Heavens, just as I am. You need no one's permission to go to Eden. You did what every parent hopes and fears today, Seabird. You surpassed me."

Unbidden, tears returned. As he had when she was little and had scrapes, he plucked a feather, dabbed it like a handkerchief at the corners of her eyes. "Now, enough of that," he said gruffly. "I need to let your mother know you're all right."

"That *we're* all right." She sniffled and caught his wrist brace, the heel of her palm resting on his. "She worries more about you than she does me. She knows you're far more likely to get into trouble."

His arms and wings closed around her, flooding her with reassurance. Things had changed between them in the past several days, and they could never go back. They would both mourn that, but at the same time, she knew it was all right. Everything would be as it should be.

Pulling away at last, she held on to his hand an extra moment then turned, moving to the parapets where Dante stood facing Raphael. The healer sat upon the parapet with his amused expression back in place.

"He's not letting me touch him," he explained, "But he's moving well enough. His vampire constitution will heal him. He just needs a bath, desperately. After that, I'd recommend a muscle-deep attitude massage."

"Thank you, Raphael." She wanted to smile, but now that she was close to Dante, she couldn't. She could barely breathe. As she turned to face her vampire, the restraint on her frayed emotions nearly crumbled. She'd almost lost him. More than that, she knew how his soul-deep rage at being imprisoned and helpless had nearly consumed what was left of his tattered soul. But it hadn't.

He was strangely blank to her right now, but she was certain her belief in that wasn't resting on hope alone. Not trusting herself to say or do anything else, or think about the possibility of rebuff, she glided forward. Sliding her arms around his waist, palms traveling up his back, she hooked his shoulders. She could fly weights greater than her own with her wings for a short distance, but her arm strength needed help.

I'm taking you somewhere to clean up. Can you put your arms around me?

She closed her eyes as his arms slid over her shoulders, hands under her wings, mostly bare legs and feet capturing her tail to steady their passage as she went aloft. Even though he was covered with blood and filth, there was the flutter of dark hair against her lips, the muscles in his body shifting against hers. It was him, and he was alive.

The trip to Eden was a short one, and they didn't speak, though she sensed him gazing around, taking in the magnificent silver spires of the Citadel they'd just left, the sight of other angels in the sky going about their daily business.

Unlike earthly rainbows, Eden's had a glittering substance to it that coated her skin as she passed through it. She remembered times she'd played in the rainbow, positioning herself so those five colors striped one of her wings. She'd giggled, asking Jonah to make it permanent. Those colors passed over Dante's face, highlighting the harsh planes, the set of his mouth.

She landed them near the river. If they'd come a day or so ago, she might have dropped him in for fun. Right now, her emotions had built to the point she could barely speak. It was hard enough to let him go, move back and transform to her human form so her bare toes could grip the soft grass. She discarded the bra, leaving her skin free to feel the soft touch of Eden's breeze and gentle sun.

All she wanted to do was run to him, embrace him, but she couldn't tell by sorting his emotions what he wanted. He moved away from her after they landed, walked to the water's edge to stand under the canopy of a shade tree and stared all around him. She couldn't blame him. She'd grown up an angel, used to seeing marvelous sights, but there was still something about Eden. It contained peace, a quietness of the soul that was contagious while that soul rested within its embrace.

Eden's many magics included this blissful isolation. There might be others here now, but they would not be seen unless the powers that drifted through here knew a soul needed someone else's presence. Now Dante watched a pair of deer move to the water's edge and drink, gazing at him curiously before drifting on. They passed so close he could touch the deer's flank. He lifted a hand as if he intended to do just that, but then his gaze lighted on the blood staining him, and he closed it into a fist.

She couldn't bear it. She knew she should give him a few seconds, but instead she walked down to the water's edge where he stood. Under his silent gaze, she unbelted the tunic around his waist. There was a small pouch hanging from the belt, and when she removed it, the contents were lumpy, hard. When she glanced up at his face, he shook his head, apparently not interested in explaining, so she set it aside with the clothing.

Interlacing her fingers with his, she caressed his knuckles, absorbed the warmth of his palm. She'd intended to lead him to the water, but instead, she just stood there, holding that one hand, staring at it as the tears ran down her face.

His arm slid around her shoulders slowly. As it tightened, she took one hesitant step in, then another, her movements jerky from the emotions gripping her. Then she was against his chest, her face pressed into his throat, and his hand spread out on her back, a cautious stroke. Reassurance, affection, it was all so new to him, but she didn't care. If anything, it made his stilted attempts all the more precious to her, because she knew he did nothing except that he wanted to do it.

Why are you crying, merangel? I am free.

Because I was afraid I was going to lose you. And I've only had you a few days.

That should have made me much easier to forget if the Fen had killed me.

He handled terrible things so matter-of-factly. She squeezed her eyes shut, let the horror of his words pass. Then she spoke into his skin, because she liked how she could move her lips against him that way. "So I'd be easy for you to forget, too. There are many females in the world, Dante. A lot of them will be prettier, or more like you." She thought of Lady Lyssa's beauty, and a legion of other faceless vampire women, just as breathtaking. "I'm only going to have you a short time."

His crimson gaze was intent on her face as he took her shoulders and held her away from him. Sitting down on the bank, he drew her down beside him, his brow creased in thought. "You are not as clever as I thought you were, Alexis."

Stung, she pulled back, but he wouldn't let her go. "The Fen, though they are not as simple as I thought, are still simple. And yet they saw what you do not."

"What's that?"

He sighed. "I have already seen women in your world. At the park, on your television. Your mother, the seawitch. Many are beautiful, and they all interest me. As everything about this world interests me."

She bit her lip. "See—"

"Hush," he said absently, watching squirrels play in a spiral around the trunk of a tree covered with flowers the color of sapphires. "But from the first dream, you were different. There is something . . . different that happens with you. A lightness inside my chest, when I am with you. Nothing is right, but everything may be, eventually, as long as I have you near me."

Cupping her face, he caressed her worried brow. Alexis savored the contact, pressing into his touch. "There is a connection between us," he murmured, watching her reaction. "I am no longer certain it was only my magic that brought you through to my world. The strength of the bond between us may have been the essential ingredient the magic needed to succeed. And your witch was right. When you pulled me through to your world, I should have been obliterated. Magic does not forgive the breaking of its rules. The only way it was possible had to be because you and I are a part of one another. Which may be the only evidence there are some merciful powers in the world," he added flatly.

When Alexis tilted her face into his palm, pressing her lips to it, he drew away. "I'm filthy with blood. You will not suffer me like this."

She didn't care. She just wanted him. She wanted to have a short hour where she didn't have to weigh her feelings against what he had or hadn't done and decide what to do. All of those things mattered, would have to be dealt with, but this moment was the most important one now. Her emotions were going to overcome her, because everything she'd seen and heard, it still meant nothing against how much she wanted and needed him. And the conflict of that was going to tear her apart if she couldn't lose herself in him for this small bit of time. Eden didn't judge. Eden just was, bringing out the best in every soul. Maybe that was why she'd wanted so desperately to bring him here. To confirm what she'd assured everyone else she knew.

My crimes are not your burden, Alexis. I will deal with them. But—

He shook his head, the set to his face telling her to leave it alone. Swallowing, she managed to speak, though there was jagged glass in her throat. "Then let me help wash off the blood."

"All right." He rose, taking her hand to pull her to her feet, and when he did, the gravity of the slope took her a step or two into him, bare body against bare body. Despite his intentions to be clean before he touched her, Dante didn't push her away this time. Despite her intention to hold herself in check, Lex had her arms around his neck, body pressed tight against him and face in his neck without any careful deliberation at all. She felt his sigh, and knew it was relief, an easing of pain, for both of them. Bending to put an arm under her thighs, he lifted and took her to the water.

It was shallow, and the water was of course the temperature most conducive to her desires. Cool, but not cold, and balanced by the warmth of the breeze that continued to play along their bare skin. He waded in, stopping at his waist, and let her legs down. Alexis stayed as close as possible, holding him, and he kept a tight grip on her as well, apparently reluctant to part, which reassured her beyond measure. Using her hands to wet his arms and chest, she began to wash the blood away. But he stopped her to take them both under, make them completely wet. When they came up, he was deeper, up to the chest, which put her in to her neck. Twining around him, she used the grip of her legs to hold on to him as she explored his skin, caressing the blood away.

The physical wounds were nearly gone now. Starting at his skull, she stroked his wet long hair, following it down to the water's edge, where the strands floated in the water like a sea fern, only much softer. What was going on in his head? Oh, Goddess, she was a love-struck, besotted idiot. He was alive. *Hers.* Every wounded, fascinating, tormented inch of him.

Putting his hand behind her neck, he brought her to his mouth, driving every thought from her head as her body surged to life beneath his touch. She cried out in relief against his lips. His other hand spread out further, fingers teasing the top of her buttocks, nudging her against the broad head of a hard shaft that told her where his mind was now, regardless of what troubled waters it had been visiting.

But then he drew back. Despite the obvious urgent demand of his body, he traced her lips, her cheekbones, absorbed in looking at her. Her legs trembled in their grip upon him as his words resounded in her mind.

Know this. If there had been nothing in this world but you, it would have been worth everything to get here. Do not ever be ashamed of your ability to love, Alexis. Even if I do not understand it yet, I am not such a fool that I don't see it for the treasure it is.

From the first time she'd met him, he'd never said anything carelessly, or without intent, careful consideration. She promised herself to remember that in the future, whenever his lack of spontaneity drove her crazy.

The tears fell again despite the wry thought, and fell even faster when he leaned forward and placed his lips on them, kissing each one away, a strand of emotion that twisted into the physical. He adjusted his position, stretching her ready opening as he began to take her down on his cock. It was passion, but with this emotional connection, it was affirmation, a way to split her heart in two even as she rejoiced at the pain.

The distance between them disappeared, and he was kissing her mouth again. Her arms slid around his shoulders, nails digging in as he seated her fully, and her body rippled in erotic response. Closing his hands on her shoulders, he arched her backward so he could put his mouth on her breast, sucking the water off the nipple and then drawing it deep into heat and a different kind of wetness. Her hips moved of their own accord, but his voice came into her head.

Be still upon me, Alexis. Do not move until I tell you that you can.

That powerful command could be a mere whisper in her mind and still hold her immobile, though a mewl of frustration came from her lips, her body quivering with the desire.

The more you obey me, the wetter you get. I want you that way for me.

Never had she imagined being taken like this in her childhood paradise, but now it became the perfect setting, all the colors, vivid and yet soft, like the enchantment of an Impressionist painting, a soft, dreamlike haze, the most brilliant colors coming from inside her head, spots in her vision as her desire rose.

He was taking his time, nursing her breast as if he planned to do that for eternity, and the longer he did it, the more out of control she felt. Her body stayed still, but she was moaning, pleading, gasping his name, becoming so mindless she was soon going to be saying words that she was sure the blessed environment of Eden had never heard among its hallowed trees.

Her muscles spasmed along his length involuntarily and he slid halfway out, then back in. It was enough. With a surprised gasp, she started to come. Realizing her dilemma, he shoved back in, but then held her still on him, letting her muscles milk him and the release come from deep inside of her instead of from her clit, a powerful, stunning reaction that had her shuddering, moaning in deep, guttural sounds.

Holding her close to him, he began to move through the water, the impact of each step an aftershock that had her whimpering. When he reached the bank, he laid her down, holding her with the strength of one arm, keeping them joined. As his palm shifted, he caressed that flame on her lower back, the sign of his third mark upon her.

"Come for me, too," she whispered, reaching up to his face, tracing the pale brow. "Let me give you blood."

He thrust deep into her again, wrenching a raw cry from her throat for he became rougher, finding his own release. Their hands met and he held them out to either side of her, demanding a full surrender. She tilted her head away, knowing everything he wanted and needed from her, and she moaned as he bit into the artery, taking her blood in a shuddering finale that seemed to float on and on, the two of them adrift on a sea of their own desires and deepest wishes.

When he finally let go of her hands, she slid her fingers down his broad back, reveling in his weight upon her, face pressed into her neck, the strands of his hair across her lips. He kept up his movements for a while even after his release, and she moved with him, a soothing, sensual rock that had no beginning or end, the rhythm itself a circular language that could answer every fear and question she had.

Pressing a finger to his mouth, she collected a tiny smear of blood there. He licked it from her skin, causing a shudder to go through her still aroused body, and then met her gaze.

"The beads and ribbons."

"What?" she asked.

"The pouch. Your father gave it to me to hold them. I brought back the beads and ribbons, the things they put on my body from the females I killed." He traced the curve of her face, her lips. "I'm not sure why, but it was important. I thought I should keep them with me."

There were storms behind his gaze, clouds gathering in his consciousness she knew had been only temporarily held at bay by the beauty of Eden. And those clouds were dark, fearsome.

"I love you," she said, wanting him to hear it, to see it in her face. "No matter what happens. I belong at your side."

Curling her hands in his hair as an anchor, she lifted up enough to press her lips to his. She wanted him to take her again, until she had no energy left. She wanted him to know it was going to be all right. There was nothing in the Goddess's world that wasn't possible, no matter how dark the depths of his soul. Lex would never fear his darkness.

————

HE took her twice more, until she could only hold on to him, reveling in his pleasure, letting her own steal over her like a languid tropical sea. They slept, but eventually, she knew it was time to leave. Fortunately, her wings had enough strength to get her back to the Citadel, but she knew they'd need a lift to get back home.

Despite the ethereal nature of their afternoon, as they landed Alexis had the sudden, horrifying worry that her cries had resounded through Heaven, but none of the angels looked abashed or embarrassed in any way. Her father was reading. One of his favorite pastimes in Machanon was studying lore and history on the parapets while overlooking the Heaven he was sworn to protect. Rising at her return, he gave Dante an expressionless nod, but took her hand in his, telling her Anna sent her well wishes and the hope her daughter would come to her soon.

"I will, Pyel. For tonight, though, I'd really love to get a good night's sleep," she admitted. "Can someone help us get there?"

Mina had already departed with David, so Marcellus and Jonah agreed to get them home. In order that they could move more swiftly, Jonah had Lex change to human form and don a borrowed tunic. They all recognized that Dante didn't relish being carried by either angel. So Marcellus had Dante thread a hand through his weapons' harness, and the angels went at a swifter speed than Alexis could manage. Otherwise, the flight back to her town house was uneventful. It was night there now, which made it easier to land on the roof unnoticed. Stars were out, and music was playing in one of the units.

Dante moved to the edge to gaze down over the area, obviously scoping it for anything threatening. Jonah and Marcellus began to discuss the safety of the town house, alarming Alexis. She wondered if they intended to stay the night in her small place. All she wanted was to get to bed, with Dante curved around her, and let the tranquility of the night temporarily heal all things, in that magical way the late hours of the night could.

But before she could tactfully try to steer them toward that end, the roof maintenance door opened. The three males glanced that direction, but it was Clara.

"I knew you were coming," she whispered.

The way she looked Lex over, lingering worry in her gaze, suggested she knew more about what had happened to them in the past few hours than Lex would have liked her to experience. Then Clara sighted the others. "Oh. Okay, I didn't sense everyone else. Is this a meeting? Do I need to—"

"No, you're fine." Alexis couldn't quite suppress a smile when her friend's gaze latched onto Marcellus. The angel was quite aware of her attention as well, his response an amusing mixture of lust and exasperation, and something else . . .

"Oh my God. That's your father?"

When Alexis nodded, Clara's eyes got rounder. "How . . . how old is he?"

"Over a thousand years. He doesn't remember exactly."

"And your mom is immortal, too?"

"No, not exactly. She'll live until she's three hundred. But she won't age the way humans do, not until she gets close to that age."

"So your dad looks like a fireman's calendar pinup after a thousand years, and your mom pretty much gets to always be drop-dead gorgeous. God, remind me that we can only be friends until I start getting wrinkles and my boobs droop. Then I'm cutting you out of my life entirely. It would be too depressing to see you wearing minis when I'd be looking for control top panty hose."

Alexis's brow rose, but then Dante spoke, returning her attention to him. Only he wasn't speaking to her.

"You stood with me." He had turned to face Jonah.

Jonah glanced at Marcellus, then squared off with the vampire. "I stood with my daughter."

374   JOEY W. HILL

Dante shook his head. "The tide had turned. You could have taken her out of there and left me to my fate."

"Yes." Jonah's gaze flickered to Alexis, then came back to the vampire. "But she was right, as much as I didn't want her to be. However, like the Fen, I have far to go before I feel your life might be worth the suffering my daughter and so many others have endured to preserve it."

His aversion to the conversation obvious, Jonah turned toward Alexis, but Dante wasn't done.

"No. That's not all of the truth."

Alexis stepped forward, but Marcellus drew her back, shaking his head in warning.

"You are pushing your luck, vampire," Jonah said, low.

Dante cocked his head. "You could have killed me, when I first arrived in your world, before you knew about the third mark. You wanted to. Even the witch's barrier wouldn't have stood in your way."

Jonah inclined his head. "Yes, I could have. If you had not done what you did during those first few moments, I would have."

Alexis drew in a breath, but neither male looked her way. "And what did I do?" Dante said, when Jonah didn't volunteer further information.

Jonah gave him an even, measured glance. "You took one vital second to move my daughter behind you, so she would not be between you and danger. In battle, a second is the difference between life and death. You protected her on instinct."

He stepped forward then, bumping toes with the vampire. Dante's fangs bared, but the light in Jonah's gaze was no less aggressive. "Bear in mind, vampire, it was the *only* thing that saved your life. I trust from this second forward you will always put her well-being first. Reconsidering my decision, and acting on it, would take far less than one vital second. Count on it."

"God, every male's nightmare of a father-in-law," Clara murmured.

The humor eluded Alexis, for she felt something else from Dante then, something that had her moving forward in protest even as Marcellus tried to stop her again.

"Alexis is now home safely," the vampire said. "If you will take me there, I intend to stay in Hell."

———————

DANTE saw the stark shock in her face, the painful betrayal. He had surprised all of them, but she was the one who closed her hand on his forearm, tugging him around to face her alone. "What? You're leaving?"

"It is better for me to be there for now." Dante didn't know if she understood how hungry he felt looking upon her gentle face, but his hands had a mind of their own, sweeping hers aside to draw him to her, his grip possessive on her hips. He wanted her, needed her, and yet he had to leave. Her body leaned into his, wanting to change his mind. He wanted to share his thoughts with her, but he hadn't sorted them out for himself yet, and she couldn't make this decision for him. In her mind, she was pleading. She could take care of him, help him . . .

"You have. But there are things . . ." He switched to her mind, because it was easier. *It is not because I don't want you. But I need to go there. I need to think.*

"You won't come back." Her hands curled into his bare chest. "You'll get all stupid, the way males do, and think I'm better off without you."

"I can't think around you," he said. "I won't destroy you through ignorance or blind need."

"But I—"

"No," he snapped. "You will stay here, and I am going. That is all. This is my decision, not yours."

She whitened at the anger in his voice. Yes, he was not used to someone disobeying his will, actually arguing with him, but it wasn't that which made him curt with her. The last thing he wanted to do was leave, which was exactly why he needed to do so. Jonah had stepped back, giving them some space, but his expression for once wasn't condemning. Though Dante was doing what Jonah had warned him not to do, hurt his daughter, Jonah understood.

Despite that, he saw the father's eyes dwell on her with a trace of the same regret he had aching in his chest. An unfamiliar emotion, and one he didn't like at all. There was nothing more he could do or say to change what must be done. As he'd done all his life, he made his decision and acted upon it.

"Let's go," he said brusquely, and turned his back on her.

Thirty-two

WHEN evil becomes something good, the weapon has two edges . . . One day, you will know what you took from us.

He hadn't understood their language in his own world. To him, they'd been no more than rough, primitive tools for his needs. Yet that judgment haunted him with its ominous, profound clarity.

Because all worlds are just, it is when you love her the most that Fate will take her from you . . .

He'd gone back to that stone platform in Hell, to stare down into fire. To listen to the distant weeping of those facing judgment, striving for redemption to start again.

He was alone for a while, but in time he felt the presence of the dark-winged angel. Dante kept staring downward. "Could I be one of those?"

"No. Your path to redemption doesn't lie in Hell's chambers. I told you this."

Dante turned. Lucifer squatted on the point of rock above him like a magnificent sculpture, his muscular body marked with those finely lined symbols that emanated power. The dark wings swept low along his back, trailing down the side of the rock. His black eyes rested on Dante, red flame flickering in their depths.

"Then what is my path to redemption?"

"You will find it, if you truly desire it. But I fear the Fen are right.

The price you pay is commensurate with the crime you committed. You are likely to lose her at the moment you learn how to love her with your entire soul."

"Then I will have nothing more to do with her. I will stay here, or go somewhere else." He swallowed. "I will go back to the Dark One world, where I cannot hear her, see her . . ."

But he *could* hear her. He could hear her thoughts, touch her soul whenever he wished, because he'd third-marked her. Beyond that, he'd created a connection that would reach through worlds, over any distance. He wouldn't be able to resist it.

"There is such a thing called a gift, Dante," Lucifer said. His deep timbre resonated against the rocks, vibrated in Dante's bones. "It is something given freely, with no expectations. It is rare, because what people often call a gift comes with conditions, whether conscious or unconscious. She has given you a true gift, and wishes to keep offering it to you. She has accepted the risks. Do not make the mistake of thinking she doesn't understand."

Lucifer cocked his head as if listening to something, then turned his gaze to Dante again. "Her father made that mistake with her mother as well. Purity of heart is not innocence or gullibility. There are exceptional souls who understand every life stands at the fulcrum of a scale, between living in that moment, cherishing it for everything it is, and realizing that life is a journey. Sacrifices and pain have a purpose, as much as laughter and joy do. That kind of soul has a faith that eclipses all else, and it is so rare, it might break the universe itself if it was darkened."

"Which is why I should—"

"You don't darken it with death. You darken it by not accepting the gift. That's the only thing that could truly destroy Alexis."

He rose to his full, intimidating height, and jerked his head toward the other side of the rock. "You have a visitor."

Dante spun, surprised, for he'd heard and sensed nothing. Surprise was quickly replaced by wariness and more than a little hostility when he saw it was the seawitch.

"One of your quieter arrivals," Lucifer noted to her. "Jonah would be less than amused to know you can do that."

"He knows I arrive in his precious Citadel precisely the way I do to annoy him," she responded, her one blue and one crimson eye glinting up at the Lord of the Underworld.

Lucifer made a noncommittal grunt and departed with a nod to Dante. His outcropping of rock was only briefly vacant, however. David landed there, taking a silent perch in the same watchful posture.

They still didn't trust him. He didn't blame them for that, particularly when it came to the seawitch. Facing her in this place of solitude with no other distractions was dangerous. It made his violence boil forth anew. He'd imagined ending her a hundred times, a hundred ways. The vulnerable neck beneath his hands, breaking it, twisting it, ripping into heated flesh, hearing her strangled cry.

He told himself he remained where he was because he'd seen the witch's power. A fool would think her vulnerable. If she had any weaknesses, her sharp-eyed angel mate covered them. But it wasn't that which stayed his hand. He couldn't say what it was yet, but something had changed within him since he'd been around Alexis.

Unfortunately, while it harnessed his hatred, it didn't abate it. Logically, he knew there was no reason to hate her more than any other. Since his mother and until Alexis, no one had done anything for him. Why should the witch incur his special wrath?

"I've given it a great deal of thought," she said, jerking his attention to her. "I think your mother did name you."

When he said nothing, she paced the stone, glancing over the edge. "She never told you, because your true name holds power. She never wanted that power to leave you. It became another reservoir under which to put the core of yourself, hold it inviolate. You sought that reservoir in yourself unconsciously. She would have whispered the name to you as a baby, marked you with her blood to set it."

"I will never know what that name is."

"One day you may remember it, but it doesn't matter. It added to the power you have now." Fishing about inside her cloak, she took out a slim volume, placed it on another protrusion of rock. "Since you seem determined to sit down here and brood, I brought you a way to pass the time. Dante's *Divine Comedy*. It's about a man who travels through Hell to get home, because he is denied the usual road. You chose an apt name."

"What do you want?" he asked, his brow furrowing.

"I shouldn't have left you there," Mina said. "I'm sorry."

Dante wasn't entirely sure he'd heard her right. He barely restrained himself from asking her to repeat herself. In a blink, her usual sarcasm had vanished like a Fading Spell. Her steady look showed compassion, an emotion he could identify, thanks to Alexis.

"I was new to hope then," she continued quietly. "My own soul has struggled between good and evil all my life, even being here. I had no room to believe that someone who'd been trapped in a Dark One world would have the strength to keep up that battle for as long as you had. I should have realized that there was still hope for you, and sixty-two lives might have been spared. What remains to be seen is if there will be a sixty-third casualty, or if my lack of judgment is irreversible."

"My decisions were my own, witch. I know what I am."

"Do you?" She cocked her head. "I'm not so sure of that."

"I know what Alexis is. And I know what I am not. That tells me who I am."

"*Hmm.*" Crossing the distance between them, she sat down on the edge of the rock several paces away and dangled her feet over the side as if she was dipping them in a pond. She leaned back on her arms, studying the view in front of her. "If you push me, I'll take you with me. And it's a long fall."

He set his jaw. "I don't need you in my head."

"I wasn't. I share your blood. It's what I'd think of doing." Cocking her head, she glanced up at him. "Why are you hiding here, away from her? The battle for good and evil is comprised of choices, but for those like us, we have to have someone to help us. We can't do it alone. Not indefinitely."

"She loves me."

"Believe me, greater miracles have rarely happened." Mina turned her gaze to her mate. "Maybe once or twice."

"I do not know what love is. There is no way I can ever deserve her."

"Probably not. But that's irrelevant." Mina pinned him with her bicolored eyes. "You did what you had to do to survive. There was nothing in your life to tell you what you were doing was wrong, until she came. Since you can live for a few thousand years if you manage not to piss someone bigger off—another major miracle, I might add—you can spend a lot of that time making up for what you've done. You do have a debt to pay, but denying yourself the thing that inspired you to be better, particularly when she wants you as well, isn't the right thing to do."

"Why do you argue this with me? You, of all people, should know." He pointed at David. "He is strong. An angel. A male. He can handle what is inside of you. She can't."

"Really?" She arched a brow. "Chivalrous chauvinism exists even in the Dark One world. How reassuring. You're probably right. She's a merangel who survived two days in your world, who backed you down when your temper was fully unleashed, who convinced a group of males who had every reason to kill you in a hundred different ways to let you go. She's obviously not strong enough to handle anything."

"I have shortened her life," he snarled. "She thinks I do not know this, but I do. I've already killed her."

Mina didn't blink. "We all die, vampire. It isn't how long we have that matters."

When he set his jaw, she shook her head. "You're not even willing to try. The same being who spent decades working on one weak dream portal is averse to working his ass off to deserve her."

"Witch." He set his teeth. "You are goading me."

"What gave it away?" She sprang to her feet and stabbed his chest with a finger as sharp as a talon. "You've been brave enough to survive that world. Be brave enough to learn how to live in this one. Which means loving as well."

"None of you want me around her." He wrenched away from her. "Why do you come now to argue with me about it? My soul is stained. How do you remove or change or alter a permanent stain? There's too much darkness in me. *I'll infect her.*"

Moving away, he circled the perimeter of his temporary home, trying to escape the rush of emotion, but it became too much. He fell to his knees and roared, the echo of it coming back upon him, a wild beast, untamed, unwanted, unsure of its place or its prey. He wanted the witch gone, all of them gone, so that he could stay here in this stasis where the aching emptiness in his chest at least was soothed by the sounds of fire and torment, a mirror image of his own substance. He'd come here thinking to find answers and he'd found only silence, something important missing. Something he couldn't have.

But when he rose at last, his fists clenched and eyes blazing, Mina was still there, regarding him impassively.

"You're surrounded by those who know there is often a wide chasm between what we want and what is right, Dante." She stepped forward. "But you can straddle both, if you know the way."

Before he could jerk back, she'd grasped his hand and put it on her chest, over her heart. A tremor of energy coursed beneath his feet, then shot upward through his body. He was flailing, dropping through darkness, into an abyss of pain and fear, desolation. It was Dark One energy, only instead of being in that world, he was merely inside the head of the seawitch. A light pierced the fog, reaching for him. Panicked, he clawed toward it, but he was not in charge of anything. Instead, he was being pulled, as if held backward and forward by tethers that moved him at a controlled pace toward it. As it drew closer, it grew too bright. It was going to illuminate the darkness of his soul, destroy that nocturnal, damned creature and leave nothing of him, because that was all there was. He cried out and bucked as his body began to glide into that light.

Then it stopped. He hovered there, his body bisected between his familiar darkness and the light that created such yearning and fear both. But as he drew deep breaths, struggling for control, he began to feel something different. Tendrils of . . . tranquility. It was how he'd briefly felt, sitting under the park tree in Alexis's arms, puzzled and yet warmed by her every action, her smile and love.

He broke out of the vision. Mina stood before him, still holding his hand to her heart, her eyes swirling with the darkness he knew far too well. It had taken over her features, turned both eyes red, elongated her fangs and turned her fingers into talons in truth. Her Dark One side. But he still felt that tranquility emanating from her. As he focused, he realized why. David stood next to her, his hand resting on her shoulder, his one black and one white wing spread, the feathers fluttering in the breeze created by her magic. His gaze was intent on the seawitch.

As Dante struggled to absorb what he was seeing, Mina spoke in a sibilant whisper, the Dark One language. "Balance implies more than one side, Dante. Do not deny yourself that."

With another blink, she was herself again, her eyes bicolored once more. David was back on the perch above him as if he'd never left.

Dante stared at her. She was beautiful now, but he remembered, back when he'd first seen Mina, she'd been scarred. Something mesmerizing about her had existed even then, powerful and frightening. She was the clean breath of another world, another way of living. He'd told himself he never believed her promise to release him if he proved himself. And yet, during the Mountain Battle when the curtain had drawn back fully, he'd been inundated by those many images of earth. Green, blue and colors of all kinds. He'd been close enough to see blades of grass, the stalks of flowers and trees . . . He'd wanted to be a part of it, burned to be a part of it, and then she'd slammed the door in his face.

Wanting wasn't an affordable luxury in the Dark One world, but when his anger had ignited, sweeping away fear, he'd realized desire—true, gut-level desire, a desire that gripped the soul—could not be denied.

Mina was watching him. As if she could hear his every thought, the realization that swept through him, she inclined her head. "Your intent is noble," she observed. "But noble idiocy serves no one."

With that acerbic comment, she left, David casting him a wry and almost sympathetic glance before he launched himself to follow in her wake.

HE wanted to see her, but he expected her to come to him, in Hell. As if he was Lord of the Underworld himself. Alexis was sure he expected her to come eagerly, because she couldn't bear to be away from him. Because she'd been aching with need for him ever since he left, not just due to the third mark, but because of what he'd said, that they were somehow part of one another.

Damn it all. The fact all of that was true made it all the more inexcusable. Would it have killed him to occasionally send her a thought, something simple? "Hi, how are you? Doing fine down here in Hell. Wish you were here." When she'd lost her pride and called out to him, more than once, he'd been radio silence. Even for this, he'd sent Marcellus with his message.

No, she wasn't that easy. No way, no how. She made him wait a day, had a gripe session with Clara that involved tears, chocolate and Clara playing the loyal friend by telling her he was a jerk and she deserved better. Then in the morning her friend kissed her and said, "Go get him, honey."

Jonah came to the town house to take her. Her mother was with him, and gave her a brief hug. They'd seen one another many times since that terrible night, so there was little to say. But as Jonah exchanged information with Marcellus, she had a few minutes to curl up on the couch, settle her nerves and watch her mother arrange fresh flowers in a vase.

Lex had picked them just this morning. Ever since he'd left almost a month before, she'd been collecting things she thought he'd like to see, like a widow who wouldn't believe her husband was dead. Okay, terrible analogy, but until his request had come, she'd been moving perilously close to those waters. He hadn't even come into her dreams. Though she'd dreamed of him, her imagination and desires had always been the conjurer, not him.

It had been hard to order her thoughts when he was in there picking things apart before she made her own decision on things. But now she didn't care if he did that. Maybe it only annoyed her because he anticipated her needs before she had them herself.

He hadn't asked, but she'd sent him her blood. She'd convinced Raphael to take it at regular intervals when she came for his treatments, and send it to Dante via David. She might have lost all pride, but she knew the intimacy of a vampire blood taking and she couldn't bear the idea of someone else doing that for him. She was his servant. Just her.

She wouldn't ask for his blood in return, not yet, but before long she knew Raphael would press the issue. She was hoping for a response from Dante before then. However, there'd been no thank you, no message, though David said he did take it for his nourishment. At first that had given her hope, but as the silence stretched out, she wondered if he was going to relegate her to an anonymous blood donor, rather than the fully bonded vampire–servant relationship she'd seen in Jacob and Lyssa. Something she was willing to embrace, if only he'd come out of his hole and let her. *Idiot male.*

"I can hear your thoughts as if you're shouting." When Anna turned to her, Alexis was struck by the disarming blue eyes which, coupled with her gentleness, gave so many the mistaken idea of fragility. Maybe she'd proven a few people wrong on that score herself. It made her proud to be her mother's daughter, enough that she'd tried not to sob in her arms from loneliness more than once or twice. Tigger, on the other hand, was in danger of water rot.

Her mother stroked her hair back from her temple. Sighing, Alexis leaned her head into her hand. Anna and Jonah knew about her physical condition now. It would have been impossible for Raphael to see her every few days without Jonah's knowledge, anyway. Plus, despite her desire not to hurt them, Alexis knew they deserved to know.

Fortunately, Raphael's healings were going well. She was following his rest and diet instructions to the letter, so some of her energy had returned. That helped, but she'd still feared a delayed reaction from Jonah to the initial news. However, aside from visiting and checking on her more often, he'd said nothing, not even a tirade against the vampire he'd view as responsible for it.

"Myel?"

"*Hmm?*"

"What did you say to Pyel, before we left for the Fen world?"

Anna's brow furrowed. "I told him to be safe and take care of you, of course."

"But there was something else, wasn't there? You told me to trust him, and there was a particular intensity when you did it. It was the same when you were speaking to him, before we took off. And the way he looked at you, and then me . . ."

"Oh, that." Anna shrugged, her lips curving. "I told him the same thing. I told him to trust his daughter."

Lex swallowed, shifted her attention to Jonah. As if feeling her regard, he glanced over his shoulder and gave her a smile, his gaze caressing her face.

"Thanks," Alexis managed with a thick throat, glancing up at her mother. "And thanks for saying the same to me. I forgot how much I can depend on him. He's forgiven me, but I still feel so awful . . ." *About that. About Dante. About everything.* "I didn't trust him, because I knew how he felt about Dante. And what was weird were his feelings didn't change. He still didn't like Dante, but I trusted him anyway."

"You're so close to emotions, Lex. It's your great gift and your curse. Actions are not always based on our feelings. Sometimes they are counter to them, when we love someone enough to act on *their* feelings, not our own." At Alexis's expression, Anna sat down on the couch and slid an arm around her. "Trust is always the most difficult between people who love one another. Particularly in dangerous situations. Because we love one another so much, we're afraid the decisions you make will take you from us."

"Like Dante, deciding to go back to Hell. He may decide to stay there always." Alexis got it out, though her voice quavered.

"He might," Anna responded, and cupped Lex's cheek. "But if you love him, you'll figure out how to deal with that. That's how love works. It can bring Heaven and Hell together if it needs to do so."

"You think so?"

"I have faith." Anna smiled then. "After all, your own birth was proof that miracles exist."

———

So here she was. Lucifer had met them in the upper chambers, and they'd been winding their way through tunnels for a while, long enough for her nerves to be jangling. Any other time, she would have been soaking up everything around her, because she'd always had avid curiosity about Hell, and about the angel who ran it. But now her mind was completely on Dante, and what he would say to her. Or she to him.

Lucifer stopped at last, and Jonah with him. "Go to the end of this tunnel," the dark-winged angel told her, his deep voice a sensual, soothing slide along her nerves, though his dark, flickering eyes were unsettling. "It will open up to a narrow bridge. The bridge takes you out to the platform. That is where he prefers to stay, though he has handled tasks I've given him well."

"Sounds like a great new hire. Make sure he gets a good dental plan."

Lucifer raised a brow. Alexis bit her lip. "My apologies, my lord."

"Female temper is not unknown to me. Or its causes." Lucifer nodded to the tunnel. "Go to him. He missed you very much, Alexis. Remember that."

Lucifer was not given to sentiment, so she wanted desperately to believe him. Jonah gave her an encouraging nod, though his mouth was tense. She touched his arm, then started down the tunnel.

Once she disappeared from their view, she stopped, drew a steadying breath and closed her eyes. Her woman's heart had been hurt, her pride abused, but even swamped by loneliness, she couldn't deny one thing. She'd understood why he'd done it. That was what had made her angriest of all.

For the first time in her life, she'd discovered love, and her angel blood held the upper hand, telling her he was the one. The only one. For as many years as she had.

She had to trust, like Anna had said. But she couldn't bear losing him.

Gathering her courage in both hands, she stepped out of the tunnel, onto the narrow bridge Lucifer had indicated.

Dante stood at the other end, waiting for her on the platform. It was a little scary, the chasm flickering with the lights of hellfire from down below, but it was comfortably warm, and he was here. He was paler, making her think she hadn't sent blood often enough. Otherwise, he looked so fine, standing straight and tall, his face impassive, beautiful as ever. He wore a black half-tunic, like the angels' battle skirts, and the pouch strung on the belt, but that was all. His feet were bare, just as they had been in the Dark One world.

She could tell nothing from his eyes, but they were riveted on her face. If she could fight back the tangled coil of emotions rising in her chest, she might be able to feel what he was feeling. But if he stayed remote from her here, as he had in her mind, she might lose it. She'd kick his perfect ass off the edge of the precipice.

"I'd rather avoid that."

She closed her eyes. She'd longed for his touch so much that even his voice, that mesmerizing roughness mixed with velvet undertones, was a stroke on her skin. Embarrassingly, she couldn't move. She'd had the courage to come here, but now she couldn't find it in her to cross the bridge to him. But when she opened her eyes, he was on the narrow passage, right in front of her, within touching distance.

The dim flickering light of this chamber of Hell made his crimson eyes dark, a rich Burgundy wine. He reached out, his hand closing on her cold one at her side, tugging her forward. She resisted, but of course he was stronger, so she took two steps forward and he closed the distance, bringing her against him.

"I missed you," he murmured into her hair. "I'm sorry."

She drew in a deep, shaky breath, letting out a little sob as his emotions flooded over her. He *had* missed her. Ached for her. Wanted her every second, as much as she'd wanted him. She wanted to scream. "Why didn't you talk to me?" she managed.

"Because of the Fen. Because of Eden."

"What?" She didn't lift her head to look at him. She was too overwhelmed. It was so good to be in the circle of his arms. She felt safe there, she realized. She could do and be anything as long as he surrounded her like that. She didn't dare move, not wanting to do anything that might make him move away. "I don't understand."

"Mina was right from the beginning. I need to deserve the world you're offering me."

"You're not evil."

"I've done evil things. No matter the reason," he interjected before she could protest. "I still took lives that were not mine to take.

You are the greatest gift any male could wish, but I obtained you through evil means."

He was going to reject her. Push her out of his life. She could feel it coming, and the reaction in her breast was helpless anger, a despicable desire to plead. Before she could, he tilted her chin up to him.

Those eyes had the power to destroy her, she knew it. She looked upon his face and knew she couldn't survive without him. Her fingers crept up, clutched his waist as if she could hold him to her. He was inside of her in all ways, and if he left her again, it would be unbearable.

"I thought about that, Alexis," he said quietly, his mouth tightening. "I thought about putting distance between us so Fate might overlook the debt due, what the Fen chief said might happen. Then I realized our connection already exists. There is no way to hide it, to starve it. You are my greatest weakness, Alexis."

It startled her, but his gaze held hers without wavering. "You are also my greatest strength. You knew that, when you told me to come to you. By surrendering my heart to you, I was stronger in that moment than I'd ever been. And I know now I have to have enough ease in my soul to love you the way you deserve."

She let out a little sob, and his voice grew husky. "I've heard every thought you've had. Felt every tear you shed into your pillow. Seen Clara's attempts to cheer you, and the times you swam with your manatees, and then in the ocean alone, trying to come to grips with your fears and sorrows. I have been with you every second. I've known a lot of torments, but feeling your loneliness and pain and denying myself the right to reach out to you . . . I'd prefer to endure all the punishments here before feeling that again."

She sucked in a shaky breath, taking her hands to his face. "Then don't leave me."

He closed his eyes. "I have to be sure what I can offer to you first."

"You offer me everything, just by existing."

"No. That is your love talking." He closed his hands on her wrists. "It is beautiful, and true, and you mean it with all your heart, I can feel it. But just because you feel it is true doesn't make it true, Alexis. Everyone knows I'm not good enough for you. And they're right."

Her heart sank into her knees. It would break, as soon as he said the words she knew were coming.

"However, I have a dilemma. I can't become good enough without you."

She halted in midstruggle, biting off the battery of responses she'd intended to fling at him when he made his inevitable, ridiculous declaration that she was better off without him.

"No doubt you would be," he said gravely. He turned his head, brushed his lips over her palm so that heat tingled across it. "But you were right about that, too. I'm selfish. Giving you up is one thing I am not prepared to do. Not now, not ever."

"I'm really confused," she admitted.

In response, a smile spread across his face.

It stopped her breath. Her heart skipped a beat. It was spontaneous, yet learned, and seeing her reaction, he was just as amazed by it. Letting her go, he reached toward his mouth, but she beat him to it, taking her fingers to his lips. Never had she felt such a surge of hope from such a simple thing. A vampire Dark Spawn's ability to smile.

His gaze became jeweled, a sparkle of ruby fire. Tightening his hands on her again, he spoke against her touch. "I will need your help to become a person deserving of your love, or the Fen's forgiveness . . . or the Goddess's mercy. I expect all of that to take a very, very long time." A shadow moved over his expression. "If you die before then, I shall be very angry at you."

Alexis pressed her lips together. "You know."

"I knew when Raphael told you. It was part of why I stayed in your mind, making sure you were doing what he suggested for you. You are doing better. I'm glad. I will not love you if you insist on dying."

She wanted to smile now, but she couldn't. She stretched her fingertips up to brush his lips again. "You love me?"

"I want to do so, even more than I think I wanted to escape the

Dark One world. Perhaps they are one and the same thing. All I know is that these many days without being close to you were as lonely to me as all the years I spent there. I need you, Alexis."

Swallowing over a treasure chest full of emotions, she lifted to her toes, but he was already bending to meet her, his hands sweeping down to pull her hard against his body, enough that she gave a little gasp into his mouth. The kiss was so hungry on both sides it was awkward, rough, but in a way she didn't mind. Locking his arm around her waist, he lifted her, taking her off the narrow bridge and onto the platform. He brought them both down to the ground, and though the rock wasn't comfortable, she didn't care. She needed a different hardness right now, one that made all the rest irrelevant. She'd been empty and desolate for weeks.

He already had his hands under her skirt, finding the thin panties. He didn't rip them, merely drew the panel aside as she found him under the half-tunic. Closing her hands on the steel of his shaft, she guided him to her.

He was letting her lead, something he'd never done before. She didn't want that, didn't want him to restrain the innate urge of a vampire to claim and take. Perhaps he was denying his own nature as part of his penance, but he didn't understand it was a pleasure she *needed* to feel, as much as he needed to unleash it.

That is, he didn't understand it until she had the thought, and then his eyes blazed. She matched him with all her blatant hunger in her heart and mind. *I'm yours, my lord. Remember? Take me as you want me. I love you, and I belong to you. Willingly.*

His gaze locked with hers. *I think you need to understand that I belong to you, merangel. Just as much. Perhaps more.*

He turned them then, using his preternatural strength to bring her over him into a straddle, unlatching the belt so he could take the tunic off and leave himself open to her pleasure. His cock pressed between her legs, along the channel but not yet penetrating her, and she moved against him instinctively, earning a hiss and growl of approval. Her hands roamed over his chest, then down the flat plane of his stomach as his fists clenched, muscles tensing there.

Alexis pulled off her thin knit shirt, unlatched her bra and let it fall to the side, baring herself to his hungry gaze. When she cupped her breasts, feeling bold, he contracted beneath her, almost violently, as she flicked the nipples with her fingertips, making them even harder. Tightening her stomach, she leaned forward, still holding them until her nipples pressed high on his chest, her throat hovering above his mouth.

"If you belong to me, my lord, then I command you to drink. Feed yourself from me."

The hesitation was brief, as she felt the ripple in her own mind that suggested he was delving into it, finding out if this was what she wanted most. *Yes. Goddess, yes.*

With another growl, he scraped her, once, twice, an erotic tease that had her hands tightening on her breasts, her sex rubbing against his involuntarily. Reaching down, she grasped him so that as his fangs sank in and she arched her neck back with a cry, she pushed herself down onto his full length, letting him stretch her wide and impale deep.

Holy Mother, yes. This was what she'd needed so badly. Not just the sex . . . that was amazing, but it was merely the conduit to that sense of renewed connection. She didn't want it to break, not ever again. His hands gripped her biceps, hard. She laughed, a throaty, sultry sound as his instincts overwhelmed him and he turned them. Now she was on the bottom, spread for him, him drinking from her neck and moving rhythmically against her, taking her even higher.

I missed you. Please don't leave me alone like that, ever again.

I'll try. I missed you, too.

Simple words. When it came to love, he wasn't a poet, but since it was all new to him, she thought he was Shakespeare. That was another thing to add to her growing list of things to show him. Shakespeare plays in the park in the spring, softball with the Conservancy staff in the spring. Evenings with Clara trying to get everyone to do karaoke.

He halted on that pinnacle and she shuddered. "Don't stop."

His face was strained as well, telling her that stopping hadn't been an easy decision. But he gazed at her now, the two of them teetering on that brink.

"I need to stay down here for . . . a while longer. While I learn . . . more control." He flashed his fangs at the double entendre, a feral smile, and tightened his hands to ensure she stayed still. "And understanding. But would you consider . . . staying here"—his gaze quickly traversed the chamber, then came back to her face, seeing every quiver, the quick lick of her lips, her hammering pulse—"now and then? If I could provide you a better place to stay? With a library and books, and places to swim?"

He shifted and she cried out. "Persephone," she gasped. "Like Persephone. Down in Hell three months, then above for the rest, because her lover was the king of Hades."

She didn't know if he knew who Persephone was, but she didn't want to explain now. She wanted to say yes and go over that precipice with him. His eyes flamed with the pleasures of desire as she had the thought, and she increased her legs' grip on him.

Please, Dante. I will be with you wherever you are. You'll never get me to leave your side again, I don't care what ridiculous excuse you use. I want you, no matter what. I know what you deserve, who you are. Please . . . I'm dying here.

That look came into his gaze, the one that made her even hotter and crazier at once. He liked her begging, and she loved the way he looked at her when she did. So she did it again, and he began to move slowly, even as she felt his own restraint faltering. She felt so many things from him, and overriding it all was the need to claim her, bring her back fully inside his heart and soul through the physical act they were doing now.

Please come inside me. I need to be reminded I'm yours in all ways.

That shattered him, as she hoped and thought it would. It wasn't a trick, though. Just simple truth. She was his. As he was hers. Neither Heaven nor Hell, Fate nor the decisions either one of them made, could change that. She knew that now. There were some things that didn't stop being truth because the world fell off its axis.

She held on as he surged into her. His hand caressed her jaw to hold her steady as his fangs sank in again. When he groaned against her skin, she tumbled over herself, crying out her release.

Their affirmation rebounded against the stone walls of Hell. Echoing throughout all its chambers, it offered a slim but fierce sparkle of hope to all those seeking redemption.

The reminder that the only true path to it was through love.